WAR TRASH

This Large Print Book carries the
Seal of Approval of N.A.V.H.

WAR TRASH

HA JIN

Thorndike Press • Waterville, Maine

Published in 2005 by arrangement with
Pantheon Books, a division of Random House, Inc.

Thorndike Press® Large Print Basic.

The tree indicium is a trademark of Thorndike Press.

The text of this Large Print edition is unabridged.
Other aspects of the book may vary from the original edition.

Set in 16 pt. Plantin by Ramona Watson.

Printed in the United States on permanent paper.

Library of Congress Cataloging-in-Publication Data

Jin, Ha, 1956–
    War trash / Ha Jin.
      p. cm.
    ISBN 0-7862-7188-4 (lg. print : hc : alk. paper)
    1. Korean War, 1950–1953 — Prisoners and prisons —
Fiction.   2. Korean War, 1950–1953 — Fiction.
3. Chinese — Korea — Fiction.   4. Prisoners of war —
Fiction.   5. Translators — Fiction.   6. Large type books.
I. Title.
PS3560.I6W37 2005
  813′.54—dc22   2004062048

TO MY FATHER,
A VETERAN OF THE KOREAN WAR

As the Founder/CEO of NAVH, the only national health agency solely devoted to those who, although not totally blind, have an eye disease which could lead to serious visual impairment, I am pleased to recognize Thorndike Press★ as one of the leading publishers in the large print field.

Founded in 1954 in San Francisco to prepare large print textbooks for partially seeing children, NAVH became the pioneer and standard setting agency in the preparation of large type.

Today, those publishers who meet our standards carry the prestigious "Seal of Approval" indicating high quality large print. We are delighted that Thorndike Press is one of the publishers whose titles meet these standards. We are also pleased to recognize the significant contribution Thorndike Press is making in this important and growing field.

Lorraine H. Marchi, L.H.D.
Founder/CEO
NAVH

★ Thorndike Press encompasses the following imprints: Thorndike, Wheeler, Walker and Large Print Press.

CONTENTS

Prologue 9
1. Crossing the Yalu 14
2. Our Collapse South of the
Thirty-eighth Parallel 37
3. Three Months of Guerrilla Life 61
4. Dr. Greene 83
5. Compound 72 on Koje Island 120
6. Father Woodworth 144
7. Betrayal 160
8. A Dinner 175
9. Before the Screening 189
10. The Screening 216
11. Compound 602 221
12. Staging a Play 246
13. An Unusual Request 254
14. A Test 268
15. Meeting with Mr. Park 281
16. Meeting with General Bell 289
17. The Abduction of General Bell 301
18. After the Victory 351
19. The Apprehension of
Commissar Pei 366
20. Arrival at Cheju Island 383

21. Communication and Study   395
22. The Pei Code   411
23. The Visit of a Young Woman   432
24. Raising the National Flag   440
25. Another Sacrificed Life   461
26. Kill!   473
27. A Talk with Captain Larsen   485
28. Entertainment and Work   501
29. A Surprise   516
30. The Final Order   522
31. At the Reregistration   532
32. Back to Cheju   549
33. Confusion   579
34. A Good Companion   599
35. In the Demilitarized Zone   606
36. A Different Fate   632
    Author's Note   660
    Acknowledgments   663

PROLOGUE

Below my navel stretches a long tattoo that says "FUCK . . . U . . . S . . ." The skin above those dots has shriveled as though scarred by burns. Like a talisman, the tattoo has protected me in China for almost five decades. Before coming to the States, I wondered whether I should have it removed. I decided not to, not because I cherished it or was nervous about the surgery, but because if I had done that, word would have spread and the authorities, suspecting I wouldn't return, might have revoked my passport. In addition, I was planning to bring with me all the material I had collected for this memoir, and couldn't afford to attract the attention of the police, who might have confiscated my notes and files. Now I am here, and my tattoo has lost its charm; instead, it has become a constant concern. When I was clearing customs in Atlanta two weeks ago, my heart fluttered like a trapped pigeon, afraid that the husky, cheerful-voiced officer might suspect something — that he might

9

lead me into a room and order me to undress. The tattoo could have caused me to be refused entry to the States.

Sometimes when I walk along the streets here, a sudden consternation will overtake me, as though an invisible hand might grip the front of my shirt and pull it out of my belt to reveal my secret to passersby. However sultry a summer day it is, I won't unbutton my shirt all the way down. When I run a hot bath in the evenings, which I'm very fond of doing and which I think is the best of American amenities, I carefully lock the bathroom, for fear that Karie, my Cambodian-born daughter-in-law, might by chance catch a glimpse of the words on my belly. She knows I fought in Korea and want to write a memoir of that war while I am here. Yet at this stage I don't want to reveal any of its contents to others or I might lose my wind when I take up the pen.

Last Friday as I was napping, Candie, my three-year-old granddaughter, poked at my exposed belly and traced the contour of the words with her finger. She understood the meaning of "U . . . S . . ." but not the verb before it. Feeling itchy, I woke up, only to find her tadpole-shaped eyes flickering. She grinned, then pursed her lips, her apple face tightening. Before I could say a word, she spun around and cried, "Mommy, Grandpa has a tattoo on his tummy!"

I jumped out of bed and caught her before she could reach the door. Luckily her mother was not in. "Shh, Candie," I said, putting my finger to my lips. "Don't tell anybody. It's our secret."

"Okay." She smiled as if she had suspected this all along.

That afternoon I took her to Asian Square on Buford Highway and bought her a chunk of hawthorn jelly and a box of taro crackers, for which she gleefully smacked me twice on the cheek. She promised not to breathe a word about my tattoo, not even to her brother, Bobby. But I doubt if she can keep her promise for long. Certainly she will remember seeing it and will rack her little brain trying to unravel the mystery.

My grandson Bobby, a bright boy, is almost seven years old, and I often ask him what he will do when he grows up. Shaking his chubby face, he answers, "Don't know."

"How about being a doctor?" I suggest.

"No, I want to be a scientist or an astronomer."

"An astronomer must spend a lot of time at an observatory, so it's hard for him to keep a family."

His mother's fruity voice breaks in: "Dad, don't press him again."

"I'm not trying to make him do anything. It's just a suggestion."

"He should follow his own interests," my son calls out.

So I shut up. They probably think I'm greedy, eager to see my grandson wallow in wealth. But my wish has nothing to do with money. From the depths of my heart I believe medicine is a noble, humane profession. If I were born again, I would study medical science devotedly. This thought has been rooted in my mind for five decades. I cannot explain in detail to my son and daughter-in-law why I often urge Bobby to think of becoming a doctor, because the story would involve too much horror and pain. In brief, this desire of mine has been bred by my memories of the wasted lives I saw in Korea and China. Doctors and nurses follow a different set of ethics, which enables them to transcend political nonsense and man-made enmity and to act with compassion and human decency.

In eight or nine months I will go back to

China, the land that has raised and nourished me and will retain my bones. Already seventy-three years old, with my wife and daughter and another grandson back home, I won't be coming to the States again. Before I go, I must complete this memoir I have planned to write for more than half of my life. I'm going to do it in English, a language I started learning at the age of fourteen, and I'm going to tell my story in a documentary manner so as to preserve historical accuracy. I hope that someday Candie and Bobby and their parents will read these pages so that they can feel the full weight of the tattoo on my belly. I regard this memoir as the only gift a poor man like me can bequeath his American grandchildren.

1. CROSSING THE YALU

Before the Communists came to power in 1949, I was a sophomore at the Huangpu Military Academy, majoring in political education. The school, at that time based in Chengdu, the capital of Szechuan Province, had played a vital part in the Nationalist regime. Chiang Kai-shek had once been its principal, and many of his generals had graduated from it. In some ways, the role of the Huangpu in the Nationalist army was like that of West Point in the American military.

The cadets at the Huangpu had been disgusted with the corruption of the Nationalists, so they readily surrendered to the People's Liberation Army when the Communists arrived. The new government disbanded our academy and turned it into a part of the Southwestern University of Military and Political Sciences. We were encouraged to continue our studies and prepare ourselves to serve the new China. The Communists promised to treat us fairly, without any discrimination. Unlike most of my fellow students who specialized in military science, however, I dared not raise my hopes very high, because the political courses I had taken in the old academy were of no use to the People's Liberation Army. I was more likely to be viewed as a backward case, if not a reactionary. At the university, established mainly for reindoctrinating the former Nationalist officers and cadets, we were taught the basic ideas of Marx, Lenin, Stalin, and Mao Zedong, and we had to write out our personal histories, confess our wrongdoings, and engage in self- and mutual criticism. A few stubborn officers from the old army wouldn't relinquish their former outlook and were punished in the reeducation program — they were imprisoned in a small house at the northeastern corner of our campus. But since I had never resisted the Communists, I felt relatively safe. I didn't learn much in the new school except for some principles of the proletarian revolution.

At graduation the next fall, I was assigned to the 180th Division of the People's Liberation Army, a unit noted for its battle achievements in the war against the Japanese invaders and in the civil war. I was happy because I started as a junior officer at its headquarters garrisoned in Chengdu City, where my mother was living. My father had passed away three years before, and my assignment would enable me to take care of my mother. Besides, I had just become engaged to a girl, a student of fine arts at Szechuan Teachers College, majoring in choreography. Her name was Tao Julan, and she lived in the same city. We planned to get married the next year, preferably in the fall after she graduated. In every direction I turned, life seemed to smile upon me. It was as if all the shadows were lifting. The Communists had brought order to our country and hope to the common people. I had never been so cheerful.

Three times a week I had to attend political study sessions. We read and discussed documents issued by the Central Committee and writings by Stalin and Chairman Mao, such as *The History of the Communist Party of the Soviet Union*, *On the People's Democratic Dictatorship*, and *On the Protracted War*. Because about half of our division was composed of men from the Nationalist army, including hundreds of officers, the study sessions felt like a formality and didn't bother me much. The commissar of the Eighteenth Army Group, Hu Yaobang, who thirty years later became the Secretary of the Chinese Communist Party, even declared at a meeting that our division would never leave Szechuan and that from now on we must devote ourselves to rebuilding our country. I felt grateful to the Communists, who seemed finally to have brought peace to our war-battered land.

Then the situation changed. Three weeks before the Spring Festival of 1951, we received orders to move to Hebei, a barren province adjacent to Manchuria, where we would prepare to enter Korea. This came as a surprise, because we were a poorly equipped division and the Korean War had been so far away that we hadn't expected to participate. I wanted to have a photograph taken with my fiancée before I departed, but I couldn't find the time, so we just exchanged snapshots. She promised to care for my mother while I was gone. My mother wept, telling me to obey orders and fight bravely, and saying, "I won't close my eyes without seeing you back, my son." I promised her that I would return, although in the back of my mind lingered the fear that I might fall on a battlefield.

Julan wasn't a pretty girl, but she was even-tempered and had a fine figure, a born dancer with long, supple limbs. She wore a pair of thick braids, and her clear eyes were innocently vivid. When she smiled, her straight teeth would flash. It was her radiant smile that had caught my heart. She was terribly upset by my imminent departure, but accepted our separation as a necessary sacrifice for our motherland. To most Chinese, it was obvious that MacArthur's army intended to cross the Yalu River and seize Manchuria, the Northeast of China. As a serviceman I was obligated to go to the front and defend our country. Julan understood this, and in public she even took pride in me, though in private she often shed tears. I tried to comfort her, saying, "Don't worry. I'll be back in a year or two." We promised to wait for each other. She broke her jade barrette and gave me a half as a pledge of her love.

After a four-day train ride, our division arrived at a villagelike town named Potou, in Cang County, Hebei Province. There we shed our assorted old weapons and were armed with burp guns and artillery pieces made in Russia. From now on all our equipment had to be standardized.

Without delay we began to learn how to use the new weapons. The instructions were only in Russian, but nobody in our division understood the Cyrillic alphabet. Some units complained that they couldn't figure out how to operate the antiaircraft machine guns effectively. Who could help them? They asked around but didn't find any guidance. As a last resort, the commissar of our division, Pei Shan, consulted a Russian military attaché who could speak Chinese and who happened to share a table with Pei at a state dinner held in Tianjin City, but the Russian officer couldn't help us either. So the soldiers were ordered: "Learn to master your weapons through using them."

As a clerical officer, I was given a brand-new Russian pistol to replace my German Mauser. This change didn't bother me. Unlike the enlisted men, I didn't have to go to the drill with my new handgun. By now I had realized that my appointment at the headquarters of the 180th Division might be a part of a large plan — I knew some English and could be useful in fighting the Americans. Probably our division had been under consideration for being sent into battle for quite a while. Before we left Szechuan, Commissar Pei had told me to bring along an English-Chinese dictionary. He said amiably, "Keep it handy, Comrade Yu Yuan. It will serve as a unique weapon." He was a tall man of thirty-two, with a bronzed face and a receding hairline. Whenever I was with him, I could feel the inner strength of this man, who had been a dedicated revolutionary since his early teens.

Before we moved northeast, all the officers who had originally served in the Nationalist army and now held positions at the regimental level and above were ordered to stay behind. More than a dozen of them surrendered their posts and were immediately replaced by Communist officers transferred from other units. This personnel shuffle indicated that men recruited from the old army were not trusted. Though the Communists may have had their reasons for dismissing those officers, replacing them right before battle later caused disasters in the chain of command when we were in Korea, because there wasn't enough time for the new officers and their men to get to know one another.

A week after the Spring Festival we entrained for Dandong, the frontier city on the Yalu River. The freight train carrying us departed early in the afternoon so that we could reach the border around midnight. Our division would rest and drill there for half a month before entering Korea.

We stayed at a cotton mill in a northern suburb of Dandong. Inside the city, military offices and supply stations were everywhere, the streets crowded with trucks and animal-drawn vehicles. Some residential houses near the riverbank had collapsed, apparently knocked down by American bombs. The Yalu had thawed, though there were still gray patches of ice and snow along the shore. I had once seen the river in a documentary film, but now, viewed up close, it looked different from what I had expected. It was much narrower but more turbulent, frothy in places and full of small eddies. The water was slightly green — "Yalu" means "duck green" in Chinese. A beardless old man selling spiced pumpkin seeds on the street told me that in summertime the river often overflowed and washed away crops, apple trees, houses. Sometimes the flood drowned livestock and people.

One morning I went downtown to an army hotel to fetch some slides that showed the current situation in Korea. On my way there, I saw a squadron of Mustangs coming to strafe the people working on the twin bridges over the Yalu. As the sirens shrilled, dozens of antiaircraft guns fired at the planes, around which flak explosions clustered like black blossoms. One of the Mustangs was hit the moment it dropped its bombs, drawing a long tail of smoke and darting toward the Yellow Sea. As they watched the falling plane and the hovering parachute, some civilians applauded and shouted, "Good shot!"

We drilled with our new weapons and learned about the other units' experiences in fighting the American and the South Korean armies. We all knew the enemy was better equipped and highly mechanized with air support, which we didn't have. But our superiors told us not to be afraid of the American troops, who had been spoiled and softened by comforts. GIs couldn't walk and were road-bound, depending completely on automobiles; if no vehicles were available, they'd hire Korean porters to carry their bedrolls and food. Even their enlisted men didn't do KP and had their shoes shined by civilians. Worst of all, having no moral justification for the war, they lacked the determination to fight. They were all anxious to have a vacation, which they would be given monthly. Even if we were inferior in equipment, we could make full use of our tactics of night fighting and close combat. At the mere sight of us, the Americans would go to their knees and surrender — they were just pussycats. To arouse the soldiers' hatred for the enemy, a group of men, led by a political instructor, pulled around a hand truck loaded with a huge bomb casing which was said to be evidence that the U.S. was carrying on bacteriological warfare. They displayed the thing at every battalion, together with photographs of infected creatures, such as giant flies, rats, mosquitoes, clams, cockroaches, earthworms. The germ bomb, which was said to have landed near the train station, was almost five feet long and two feet across, with four sections inside. This kind of bomb, we were told, would not explode; it would just open up when it hit the ground to release the germ carriers. To be honest, some of us had rubbed shoulders with Americans when we were in the Nationalist army, and we were unnerved, because we knew the enemy was not only superior in equipment but also better trained.

Throughout this period we attended regular meetings at which both civilians and soldiers would condemn American imperialism. An old peasant said his only farm cattle, a team of two, had been shot dead by a U.S. plane while he was harvesting sweet potatoes in his field near the border. A woman soldier walked around among the audience, holding up large photographs of Korean women and children killed by the South Korean army. A reporter spoke about many atrocities committed by the American invaders. Sometimes the speakers seized the occasion to vent their own grievances. They often identified the United States as the source of their personal troubles. A college graduate of dark complexion even claimed to an audience of eight hundred that his health had been ruined by the American film industry, because he had watched too many pornographic movies from which he had learned how to masturbate. Now he couldn't control himself anymore, he confessed publicly. These kinds of condemnations, high and low, boosted the morale of the soldiers, who grew restless, eager to wipe out the enemy of the common people.

On the night of March 17 we crossed the Yalu. Every infantryman carried a submachine gun, two hundred rounds of ammunition, four grenades, a canteen of water, a pair of rubber sneakers and a short shovel on the back of his bedroll, and a tubed sack of parched wheat flour weighing thirteen pounds. We walked gingerly on the eastern bridge, because the western one was partly damaged. Each man kept ten feet from the one in front of him. The water below was dark, hissing and plunging. Now and then someone would cry out, his foot having fallen through a hole. A tall mule, drawing a cart, got its hind leg stuck in a rift and couldn't dislodge it no matter how madly the driver thrashed its hindquarters. The moment I passed the tilted cart, it shook, then keeled over and fell into the river together with the helpless animal. There was a great splash, followed by an elongated whirlpool in the shimmering current, and then the entire load of medical supplies vanished.

Having left behind our insignias and IDs, from now on we called ourselves the Chinese People's Volunteers. This was to differentiate us from the army back home, so that China, nominally having not sent its regular troops to Korea, might avoid a full-blown war with the United States. We were ordered to reach, within fourteen days, a town called Yichun, very close to the Thirty-eighth Parallel. The distance was about four hundred miles, and we would have to walk all the way. It was early spring, the air still chilly; the roads were muddy, soaked by thawing ice and snow, hard for us to trudge through. The divisional headquarters had two jeeps that transported the leaders and their staff. Sometimes the jeeps would drop off the officers and turn back to collect some limping men and those who could no longer march thanks to blisters on their feet. I walked the whole time except for once, when Commissar Pei wanted me to get on his jeep so that I could figure out the meaning of the English words on a folded handbill someone had picked up on the way. It turned out to be the menu of a restaurant in Seoul, which must have served Americans mainly, because the menu was only in English. I couldn't understand all the words, but could roughly describe the dishes and soups to Pei Shan. The entrées included broiled flounder filet, beef steak, fried chicken, meat loaf.

Besides the commissar's orderly, a clerical officer named Chang Ming, who edited our division's bulletin, often boarded the jeep. I envied him for that. Whenever we stopped somewhere for the night,

Chang Ming would be busy interviewing people and writing articles.

Commissar Pei seemed a born optimist. He often laughed heartily, jutting his chin and showing his buckteeth. He looked more like a warrior than a political officer. By contrast, our division commander, Niu Jinping, was a wisp of a man, who had once been the vice director of the Political Department of the Sixty-second Army. I often saw a cunning light in Niu's round eyes; in his presence I was always cautious about what I said. When he smiled he seldom opened his lips, chuckling through his nose as if his mouth were stuffed with food. He was a chain-smoker, and his orderly carried a whole bag of brand-name cigarettes for him. Both the commander and the commissar were in their early thirties, and neither was experienced in directing battle operations.

Back in Dandong City, I hadn't been able to imagine the magnitude of the war's destruction. Now, to my horror, I saw that most villages east of the Yalu lay in ruins. The land looked empty, with at least four-fifths of the houses leveled to the ground. The standing ones were mostly deserted. Most of the Korean houses were shabby, with thatched hip roofs and walls made of mud plastered to bundles of cornstalks. Many of them were mere huts that had gaping holes as windows. It must have been hard to farm this rugged land, where boulders and rocks stuck out of the ground everywhere; yet it seemed every scrap of tillable soil was used, and even low hills were terraced with small patches of cropland. We came across Korean civilians from time to time. Most of them were in rags, women in white dresses that had faded into yellow, and old men wearing black top hats with chin straps, reminding me of Chinese men of ancient times. Here and there roads had been cratered, and teams of Chinese laborers were busy filling the holes, carrying earth and stones with wicker baskets affixed to A-frames. The farther south we went, the fewer houses remained intact, and as a result most of us had to sleep in the open air.

Generally, during the day it wasn't safe for us to march, because American planes would come in droves to attack us. So only after nightfall could we move forward. After Shandeng, a rural town, the air raids were constant and sometimes even took place at night. Every infantryman carried at least sixty pounds while each horse was loaded with five times more. Without enough sleep and rest, the troops were soon footsore and exhausted. On the fifth day heavy rain set in and made it impossible for us to lie on the ground to sleep. Some officers in our Political Department clustered together with a piece of tarpaulin over their heads. Many men, too tired to care about the downpour, simply put their bedrolls on the ground, sat on them, and tried to doze that way. Some, staying in a chestnut grove, tied themselves to the trees with ropes so that they could catnap while remaining on their feet. The rain continued in the afternoon, and because we couldn't sleep and the enemy bombers were unlikely to come in such weather, we ate our lunch — which was parched flour mixed with water, as sticky as batter — and went on our way.

The following night, as the divisional staff was about to enter a canyon, suddenly three green signal flares whooshed up ahead of us. At first I thought they must have been fired by our vanguard, but then some officers began to whisper that someone on the mountain was signaling our whereabouts to the enemy. I had heard that a good number of Korean agents worked for the Americans on the sly, but I hadn't expected to encounter something like this in the wilderness. As we were talking about the possible meanings of those signals, four planes appeared in the southeast, roaring toward us.

"Take cover!" a voice ordered.

Some of us rushed into the nearby bushes and some lay down in the roadside ditches. The planes dropped a few flash bombs, a shower of light illuminating the entire area; our troops and vehicles at once became visible. Then bombs rained down and machine guns began raking us. Some horses and mules were startled and vaulted over the prostrate men, dashing away into the darkness. A bomb exploded in front of me and tossed half a pine sapling into the sky. I lay facedown on the slope of a gully, not daring to lift my head to the scorching air, and keeping my mouth open so that the explosions wouldn't pop my eardrums. Around me, men hollered and moaned, and some were twisting on the ground screaming for help. Some, though dead or unconscious, were still clutching their submachine guns.

The bombardment lasted only five minutes but killed about a hundred men and wounded many more. Along the road, flames and smoke were rising from shattered carts and disabled mountain guns.

As I looked for Chang Ming, I saw two orderlies coming my way, supporting an officer. I recognized the officer, Tang Jing, the quartermaster of our divisional staff. He looked all right, though one of the orderlies kept shouting, "Doctor, doctor! We need a doctor here!" But all the medical personnel were busy helping the seriously wounded, assembling them for shipment back to our rear base. Division commander Niu ordered an engineering company to dig a large grave at the edge of a birch wood to bury the dead.

Finally Dr. Wang turned up with a flashlight and asked Tang Jing, "Where were you hit?"

The quartermaster didn't register the question, his fleshy face vacant while his eyes glittered without a blink.

"Are you injured?" the doctor asked again.

Tang Jing opened his mouth but no sound came out. He was trembling all over, unable to speak a word. Dr. Wang felt his forehead and then his pulse. Everything seemed normal, so he didn't know what to do. We had to reassemble and continue to march, but we were unsure whether we should take the quartermaster along. Another doctor, Li Wen, arrived, and together

31

the two doctors checked him again, but they found nothing unusual except that his temperature was slightly above normal.

"Shell shock. He lost his mind," said Dr. Li.

"Can he hear?" an orderly asked.

"I'm not sure."

"What should we do about him?"

"We'd better send him back. It'll take a long time for him to recover."

"I can't believe this," said Chang Ming, who had joined us for a while. "He's such a strapping man, yet he lost his mind so easily."

The two orderlies helped the quartermaster to his feet and walked him toward a team of stretcher bearers who were going to carry the wounded back to our base. I had been struck by the vast number of Chinese laborers in Korea. Most of them came from Manchuria, and some were over forty years old. They were able to mix with the Koreans because they could speak Japanese, which had been taught in both Manchurian and Korean schools during the Japanese occupation; yet their lives here were as precarious as the soldiers'. Although constantly under air and artillery attacks, they had to repair roads, build bridges, unload supplies, and ship the casualties back from the front. A lot of them had been killed or wounded. Right in front of me walked a reedy boy, about fifteen years old, carrying one end of a stretcher, on which lay a man with his face bandaged. The wounded man kept wailing, "They lied to us! They lied to us!"

Our divisional leaders were unsettled by the loss of lives, equipment, animals, and supplies, but I was more shaken by Tang Jing's case. For a whole week his expressionless face went on haunting me. Never had I thought a man's mind was so easy to destroy.

The next morning, on a roadway leading to Seoul, we ran into a group of U.N. prisoners, about seventy men, marching past us from the opposite direction. The majority of them were Turks, some tall, some quite short, with haggard faces. At the end of the procession were about a dozen Americans, mostly large men wearing parkas. One of them wore steel-rimmed glasses and a tufty red beard. The POWs couldn't walk fast on account of injury and fatigue, and some hobbled along, one using a shovel handle as a crutch. The Chinese guards, toting rifles with fixed bayonets, were rough with them. One officer yelled in a strident voice, "Faster, don't drop behind! You need a ride, eh? I tell you, we have no vehicles to relieve your pampered feet." Although the prisoners couldn't understand him, they looked frightened and hung their heads low.

The encounter cheered us up a little. Our political officers began working to convince the rank and file of the enemy's weakness despite their airpower. Likewise, the U.N. side had never slackened its psychological work either. The roads we trod were strewn with leaflets, dropped by American planes and printed in both Chinese and Korean, urging us to capitulate. One had an ancient couplet on it: "How piteously the skeletons lie on the riverside / Still dreaming of a pretty bride!" Another showed a woodcut in which a young woman stood on the shoulder of a mountain, gazing into the distance, longing for her man's return. We had been ordered to ignore the leaflets. Many men pocketed them to roll cigarettes with or to use as toilet paper, but once you glanced through these sheets, a heavy sadness would stir in your chest, sinking your heart.

Our food supplies, carried by the horse carts, had been used up by the end of the first week, so now the only thing we had to eat was the parched flour in the tubed sacks draped across our chests. Some men found and picked wild herbs — dandelions, purslanes, wild chives, and onions. There was a kind of wild garlic in Korea, whose heads were still tiny but good-tasting, pungent and crispy, not as spicy as the regular garlic. You could eat both their heads and their green tops, but they were scarce in the early spring when most herbs were just beginning to sprout. Some trees were sending out yellowish leaves, which many men plucked and ate. I didn't eat many wild herbs or tree leaves, because I couldn't tell poisonous ones from good ones. Quite a few men were not as cautious and suffered food poisoning.

There were so many troops moving toward and back from the front that as soon as it was dark, the roads turned chaotic, noisy, and jammed with traffic — trucks, artillery pieces, carts drawn by animals, teams of Chinese porters carrying supplies and ammunition, and lines of stretchers loaded with the wounded. Once I saw a camel laden with mortar shells. Every night each regiment of our division had about a hundred stragglers, incapacitated by exhaustion and sore feet. A movement was started among the ranks, called "Leave No Comrade Behind." Officers and Party members were supposed to help carry bedrolls, guns, and bandoliers for those who had difficulty keeping up. I was moved when I saw squad and platoon leaders fetch hot water for their men to bathe their feet. This marked a difference between the Communist army and the Nationalist army, in which even some junior officers had eaten better food than their men and had often abused their inferiors.

We arrived at the Thirty-eighth Parallel on time, but a third of our division could no longer stand on their feet. My legs were swollen and one of my shoes had lost its sole. Our divisional leaders pleaded with the Headquarters of the Chinese People's Volunteer Army for a week's rest, but the superiors allowed us only one day off. We ate a hearty meal — rice and pork stewed with turnip and broad potato noodles. After the meal, like sick animals, we slept in the mountain woods for the rest of the day.

2. OUR COLLAPSE SOUTH OF THE THIRTY-EIGHTH PARALLEL

The fourth-phase offensive had just ended two months ago in February; I wondered why we were starting the fifth one so soon. Common sense dictates that the success of a large battle depends on the buildup of supplies and munitions and on the thorough preparation of troops. Although several field armies had just arrived from interior China, most of the men were bone-weary from the arduous trek and unfamiliar with the foreign climate and terrain, let alone the nature of the enemy we faced. We were told that this offensive would wipe out ten American and Korean divisions and drive all the hostile forces to the south of the Thirty-seventh Parallel. In our superiors' words, "We're going to eliminate some of their unit designations." I had misgivings about that because our equipment was far too inferior, but I didn't reveal my thoughts to anyone. For the time being my job was to help

Chang Ming edit the bulletin. Ming had graduated from Beijing University and majored in classics, for which he was well respected, even by higher-ranking officers. He also knew English but couldn't speak it fluently. I spoke the language better than most college graduates because in my teens I had attended classes taught by an American missionary in my hometown.

On the evening of April 22, 1951, suddenly thousands of our cannons, howitzers, mortars, and Katyusha rocket launchers began bombarding the enemy's positions; thus started the fifth-phase offensive. As usual when the Chinese forces unleashed a major attack, a full moon hung in the sky, ready to facilitate our men's night fighting. Our Sixtieth Field Army, composed of the 179th, 180th, and 181st Divisions, was assigned to attack the Turkish Brigade and the U.S. Third Division, both positioned in front of us. The battle proceeded so smoothly that our divisional leaders were bewildered — in just one day we advanced more than ten miles without encountering any serious resistance. Why didn't the enemy engage us? Had they been overwhelmed by our bombardment? Or were they just eluding us? Or was this a ruse to lure us farther south? Our superiors had their doubts, but neither Commander Niu nor Commissar Pei, who lacked the requisite training and experience of senior officers, could guess what was happening. They just executed the orders issued by headquarters. As a rule, without approval from higher up, they were not allowed to order troop movements. This restriction, leaving no room for the officers' own initiative, directly contributed to our later defeat.

We stayed put for several days and didn't go farther into enemy-occupied territory. A week later when the second stage of the offensive started, most of the Chinese and the North Korean troops swerved east to attack the South Korean army. Our division's task was to wedge ourselves between the American and the South Korean forces, specifically to prevent the U.S. First Marine and Seventh Divisions from moving east to reinforce the South Koreans. We occupied the hills south of the Han River, whose water wasn't deep in spite of its swift current, and thanks to the favorable terrain we held our position for five days. The two American divisions didn't break our defense line, though they were superior in both firepower and number.

By now, most of the Chinese and North Korean field armies were thrust deep inside enemy-occupied territory; some had pushed forward seventy miles south of the Thirty-eighth Parallel. Then the order came for all units to stop attacking. Obviously the operation had gone awry. The truth was that our field armies had advanced so fast and so deep that our supply lines had crumbled. Apart from the logistical disaster, our men on the front had suffered heavy casualties. The enemy had adopted "magnet tactics" — whether we attacked or retreated, they would always remain close enough to inflict casualties on our forces. This time they dragged our troops deep into South Korea, cut their connections with the echelons, isolated and encircled them, and tried to annihilate them. Apparently the enemy had gained the upper hand, so the Headquarters of the Chinese People's Volunteer Army had to call off the offensive. Most of the line officers had no idea of the situation, and some even assumed we had won a victory. I came to know of the truth because I often served as a secretary at the meetings at which our divisional leaders discussed plans of action.

A few days later the Americans launched

an all-out counterattack. Their artillery shells and aerial bombs landed on the hills defended by our division, loosening the dirt and cutting down trees, some of which burst into flames. Despite not knowing what to do or where to go, we held our line and fought back the enemy's advances again and again. Not until the afternoon of May 22 did we receive orders to move north, cross the Han River, and build a defense along its north bank. Immediately we began to retreat. But that same evening another telegram came, ordering us not to cross the river, and instead to set up a defense line on the south shore and hold it for four days to cover thousands of wounded men being shipped back from the front. This was easier said than done. We had no food left, and our right flank would be exposed — the Sixty-third Army, which was supposed to cover it, had already retreated to the north of the river. How on earth could we fight in such disarray? The enemy saw our predicament, so they assembled more men, tanks, and artillery, and kept pursuing us.

Under cover of darkness we managed to reach the designated position and established a defense south of the Han River. By now the enemy was closing in from three sides; in fact, we were the only division left on this side of the water. During the day we had fought back the enemy's attacks, but we suffered staggering casualties. The report came that the First Battalion of the 538th Regiment had been wiped out by bombing raids, and that every one of the remaining units had been reduced to half its original size or even smaller. At the divisional headquarters the leaders argued whether we should retreat farther, crossing the river, or hold our current position. The latter course meant we would have to face annihilation the next day. But without orders from higher up, all the leaders could do was talk. They dared not make any decision on their own; as a result, the whole division was bogged down, giving the enemy time to seize a ford downstream.

We managed to hold our line the following day. At night the order finally came to cross the Han River immediately and reorganize our defense on its northern side. Without access to any ford, the heads of our division just picked a crossing spot randomly. A platoon of sappers stretched three iron wires across the river. Gripping the wires, the troops entered the rushing current. Thanks to the recent rain, the water was swelling, much deeper than a month ago when we had crossed it charging south. At some places it reached our necks. Starved and exhausted by a whole day's fighting, few of us could walk steadily, and some were washed away and drowned. Before half of our division reached the north bank, the enemy started shelling us. Then two planes appeared, dropping bombs and strafing the troops in the river. The explosions roiled the water, which was turning reddish with blood while people were screaming and scrambling. Many were tossed off the wires, drifting away, their arms thrashing the water until they were submerged. The crossing cost us more than six hundred casualties, among whom were the few girls in the Medical Battalion. Gone were the stretchers, together with the wounded. Gone was the cart loaded with food supplies for the divisional leaders — a gunnysack of rice, dozens of cans of meat and fish, two barrels of hardtack, a bag of spiced pork jerky, some twenty packs of cured tofu, a box of cigarettes. The newly appointed quartermaster got so furious that he threatened to shoot the cart driver, flashing his pistol at the poor man's face.

By the time we reached the north shore, the enemy had already occupied the high hills in that area. They came to attack us right away. We were still dripping wet, but without delay we began to build our defensive position along some ridges. The fighting that followed was fierce and more men were killed. Fortunately the hilly terrain prevented the enemy's tanks from operating efficiently; otherwise they could have wiped us out right there, since we had left our artillery pieces on the south of the river and had no way to stop the tanks except by pitching the few Russian-made grenades still in our hands. Before abandoning their cannons, the soldiers had pulled the breechblocks and dropped the sights into the river so that nobody could use the guns again. Some men would not shoot their draft animals, but afraid others might kill them for meat, they set them free. Some of the horses and mules wouldn't go away and followed their former keepers to this shore.

It was hot the next day. Hungry and thirsty, even many officers at the divisional headquarters collapsed. It was harder to endure thirst than hunger. The enemy saw this and blocked all the trails leading to streams. Commander Niu sent one of his bodyguards to fetch some water with a gas can and a bunch of canteens from a creek at the foot of a hill, but the man was shot dead before he could get there. So we gave up trying to obtain water. Tormented by hunger, some soldiers devoured whatever they could lay their hands on. Men from southern China even ate toads and snakes. Many died because they had eaten poisonous mushrooms or a kind of wild onion that had forked leaves and that would blacken your lips a few moments after you swallowed it. Moans and curses rose from every direction. Dead men were scattered here and there like bundles of rags, some still holding a grass root or a tree leaf or a sprouting twig between their lips.

Toward evening we received two orders within the space of half an hour. The first one, as though our division were still intact, instructed our divisional staff together with two regiments to move west and occupy the mountain behind Maping Village; the other regiment was to go along a trail to Jiader Hill, which was opposite the mountain, facing the village, so that we could hit the enemy from both sides and cover the retreating field hospital charged with caring for thousands of wounded men. As soon as we received the order, our headquarters sent the 538th and 540th Regiments on their way to the village. But before the divisional staff could set out, another order arrived, calling for two of our regiments to march to Jiader Hill while the other one transported our division's hundreds of wounded men to Maping Village, then proceeded to occupy the mountain behind it. The higher-ups emphasized that our task was to cover the field hospital until they had brought back all the wounded, and that the 179th Division would cover our rear once we got there. By now one South Korean and two American divisions had caught up with us, and some of their units were encircling us from our right flank. Perplexed, Commissar Pei argued with Commander Niu over which order to follow. They both sat on boulders behind a huge rock, smoking Great Production cigarettes with dazed faces.

Pei stressed that from now on we should take into account the actual situation when we executed orders from above. There were new developments every hour, and our superiors were too far away to see what we were facing. The commissar said, pointing northwest, "The truth is that if we don't take that hill first, it'll be difficult for us to retreat."

"You should trust the leaders and our brother division," said Commander Niu.

"This is more than a matter of trust," Pei replied. "Our men's lives are at stake now."

"The telegram says clearly that the 179th Division is on the mountain and will cover our line of retreat."

"Well, we can't be sure of that."

"Rest assured, all right? We must follow the second order, which was meant to countermand the first one."

"But our division is already terribly understrength, down to a third of our normal capacity, no artillery, and almost out of ammunition. How can we possibly stop the enemy?"

"I'm aware of that, Old Pei, but as officers we have to obey orders."

That silenced the commissar. So without further delay messengers were sent out to catch up with the troops already on their way west and to deliver the new order which demanded that the 538th and 540th Regiments turn southwest and set up a defense line on Jiader Hill and that the 539th Regiment carry the wounded to Maping Village and then proceed to occupy the mountain behind it. Strange to say, a part of the order was altered in the process of delivery, and the whole 539th Regiment was dispatched to Eagle Peak, a hill almost eight miles to the northeast! They were ambushed by the Americans and got smashed.

Thus we lost the opportunity to seize the mountain behind Maping Village, which could have enabled us to retreat and save the remaining units. We had to trudge five extra miles of precipitous road to reach Jiader Hill, and this depleted our strength and delayed us in fighting our way out.

At daybreak, when we had arrived at Jiader Hill, gunshots burst out on the slope beyond Maping Village. Bewildered, Commissar Pei and Commander Niu again had an exchange of words. Pei said, "The enemy is probably already on that mountain."

"Why can't you trust our brother division?" Niu retorted. He looked like a withered old man now, his puckered face covered with dust, and his left arm hung in a bloody sling.

I happened to be present, so Pei turned to me with a smile. "What do you think we should do, Comrade Yu Yuan?"

I was taken aback because I was merely a clerical officer. I ventured, "Maybe we should send some men to reconnoiter."

So they dispatched a squad led by the commander of the reconnaissance company to the mountain. Hardly five minutes after the men had left, artillery shells thundered and threw up dust clouds in Maping Village. Now, obviously the brother division wasn't there; the mountain was already in the enemy's hands! (Later we learned that the 179th Division had sent a regiment to our rescue, but they were blocked and reduced to four platoons by the Americans.) We were entirely isolated now, forty miles away from the nearest brother unit. Within an hour the enemy took Maping and the nearby villages; in addition, they had already occupied all the hills in that area. With little ammunition and only three thousand men left, we were totally trapped. The South Korean Second Division was approaching us from the front.

More devastating was that since the previous evening we had lost radio contact with both the headquarters of our Sixtieth Field Army and that of the Chinese People's Volunteer Army. Commander Niu held an emergency meeting, which most of the regimental leaders attended. After briefing them about the situation, he said, "We must decide what to do now — fight our way out or hold our line to wait for reinforcements."

While the meeting was going on, artillery

shells exploded around the headquarters, which was just a shallow pit behind a low wall built of brownish rocks and mud, probably for shepherds to shelter themselves from wind. Pebbles, clods, and rock chippings, tossed up by the explosions, pelted down. Projectiles were zinging all about, followed by shock waves. The enemy was visible in both the south and the east, while some American troops were reported to be closing in from the north. A guard at the site of the meeting was even killed by sniper fire. Slapping his knee, Commissar Pei said hoarsely, "One lesson we've learned these days is that we didn't lose that many men in actual fighting, most of the casualties were inflicted by artillery. If we stay here, we'll be pounded to powder. Besides, we're out of ammunition. How can we defend our position? Who knows if there're any reinforcements coming to us at all? We must fight our way out!"

Following him, the other officers argued that in addition to artillery, the enemy had air support and always fought a battle on two dimensions — on the ground and from the air. If we stuck to one spot, we'd play right into their hands. We had no alternative but to break out of the encirclement.

Hao Chaolin, the division's artillery director, who was without a single gun under his command now, said, "Commander Niu, please give orders! We can't let the enemy continue wasting our men like this. These troops are the last ones our division has!" A large mole kept moving near the edge of Chaolin's left eye as he spoke.

Niu declared, "Get ready to fight our way out! The operational staff will request approval from our army's headquarters immediately. We'll set out the minute we get permission."

Fortunately radio contact was reestablished, but we waited three hours for a response from above, which didn't come until after five p.m. Permission was granted. The telegram ordered us to reach Eagle Peak, in the northeast, and stated that our army was regrouping beyond Maping Village. The higher-ups seemed in confusion too — the message didn't make sense, the two places were in opposite directions. Nevertheless, we started out northeast at six o'clock.

To reach Eagle Peak we had to pass a deep valley, about two miles long. The 538th Regiment marched at the front; behind them was the divisional staff, followed by the 540th Regiment. More than

51

two thousand men crowded into this valley; it was difficult to maneuver, and we could only go forward. In no time the troops were in disorder. Some men straggled behind and slipped away into the woods and bushes. Who could blame them? The whole division hadn't eaten a single meal for four days, so whenever possible, the men would step aside to look for things to eat. Sometimes they picked up a bag of roasted soybeans dropped by a kitchen cart, or took handfuls of parched flour from a tubed sack still strapped across a dead man's chest. Occasionally they chanced on a bag of rice left behind by the South Korean army. Having no time to cook, they just munched the grains raw. We were all like hungry ghosts, fearful but unable to stop wandering around. During the forced march, many men couldn't keep pace and dropped behind. Some new soldiers would fall to their knees or lie down whenever shells exploded nearby. A large number of the recruits from the former Nationalist army deserted. One of them not only defied orders but also fired at the deputy commander of the 540th Regiment, who was seriously wounded in the head and later died in the POW hospital.

Several times the troops at the front were

hit by enemy artillery, and again we suffered heavy casualties. At sunrise, when we finally reached the west side of Eagle Peak, there were only thirteen hundred men left, and the enemy had already occupied all the heights in that area. The leaders of the 538th Regiment organized an assault unit, composed of about fifty Party members, many of whom were junior officers. They set out in the triangular formation — "three as a group like an arrowhead" — and took the main hilltop from the enemy, so we had a foothold for the time being. But they were overwhelmed by the enemy's counterattack in the afternoon and lost the position. This meant that our attempt to break out of the encirclement had failed.

At dusk we heard by radio from our Sixtieth Army's headquarters again. Commander Hong ordered us to head northwest for Shichang, a village, to meet with some brother units already on the move to our rescue. For hours our men had been searching for things to eat on the mountain. When the officers finally assembled them, there were about four hundred men left. They were organized into three companies, and together we started out for Shichang. The divisional leaders were so exhausted, so weakened, that their bodyguards had to support them on the way. I limped behind them; my heart was filled with fear, so heavy, as if jammed with lead. Never had I thought that the war could be so chaotic and so bloody.

In fact, we were now walking back the way we had come. According to the map Shichang was about fifteen miles away, but because of fatigue and artillery attacks we covered only ten miles over the course of a whole night, during which the earth seemed to shake under my feet. At some spots, the soil had been loosened so much by heavy bombardment that the dirt reached our ankles when we walked through it. The next morning, as we were about to enter the valley we had passed the night before, suddenly a voice came from down the slope to the right. "Commissar Pei, Commissar Pei, take me with you please!"

"It's Doctor Wang," said Tiger, Pei's bodyguard.

Pei told Commander Niu, "I'm going down to have a look. I'll be back in a minute."

"Don't stay too long, Old Pei," Niu said.

"I won't."

The commissar could no longer walk steadily, so Tiger and I supported him down the slope to see the doctor. Chang Ming offered to come with us, but Pei said we'd be back shortly. Ming had sprained his neck and marched with his head tilted at an angle of forty-five degrees, so the commissar refused to let him accompany us.

Dr. Wang's right knee was injured and he had lost consciousness the night before. At the sight of us he wailed, "Please take me along, Commissar Pei! I'm still useful." His pockmarked cheeks were bathed in tears. Beside him lay a leather medical box, which I picked up and strapped across my shoulder. I helped him to his feet and together we climbed the incline to catch up with the retreating troops, gripping the branches of osier shrubs all the way.

When we got back to the trail, there was no trace of our men. My heart lurched; scared and outraged, I was reduced to tears.

"Don't cry, Yuan," Pei said to me.

"I never thought they'd abandon us like this! We're their comrades," I said.

"I screw their mothers!" cursed Tiger, his baby face streaked with tears.

Together we entered the valley. After a few minutes' walk, when we had just passed a stretch of marshy land, a voice

55

shouted from the edge of a larch wood, "Commissar Pei's coming!"

"Take us with you, Commissar Pei!"

Voices followed one another. Then from the grass some men rose to their feet, waving and shouting. A few staggered toward us. We went down the slope to see them. Thirty yards later I felt dozens of eyes staring at us from three directions.

"Have pity!" a man moaned.

"Please, I'm my parents' only son."

"Send us back to China!"

"Oh, don't leave us behind!"

"I'll recover soon. Commissar, please assign a stretcher to me."

"Don't dump us in Korea!"

There were about three hundred men in the valley, mostly wounded by artillery, some burned by napalm, and many poisoned by mushrooms and herbs, their lips purple and their faces swollen. A few weeks ago they had all been strong men in the pride of their youth and vitality, but now they were more piteous than a swarm of lepers. For a moment I was so horrified that words failed me.

To my surprise, Pei Shan announced loudly, "Comrades, I won't abandon any of you. We shall fight our way out and get back to our base."

Some men began sobbing and cursing the American imperialists and their own superiors who had deserted them. After they had assembled around Commissar Pei, we divided them into three teams. Now I had to assume some kind of leadership because I was an officer. We covered the dead with sheets and thin quilts, roughly dressed the wounded, and assigned the men to help each other in pairs. Before we set off, the commissar gave a short speech. "Comrades and brothers," he said, "it's obvious we're surrounded. Now in front of us are two enemies: one is the American invader and the other is hunger. We must grit our teeth to endure hunger. For the time being this is all we can do. We're going to set out now. On the way every Party member must help others and must be a model of bravery and loyalty. We're going to use the cover of darkness to slip through the gaps in the enemy's lines —"

He was interrupted by an American plane flying slowly overhead, which was broadcasting a message urging us to capitulate, promising to treat us humanely. An endearing female voice said in standard Mandarin: "Chinese soldiers, your national leaders say you volunteered to come to Korea, but in your hearts you all know you didn't come here of your own free will. Your leaders stuck the name of the People's Volunteers on you and sent you here as cannon fodder for Stalin and Kim Il Sung. Now, you have no food or warm clothes, you dare not speak your minds, and you cannot write home. Think about it, brothers, are you really volunteers?"

Hearing those words, a few men broke into sobs. As the plane was banking away temporarily, Pei said, "Don't be taken in by the enemy. Remember we're Chinese and must never betray our motherland. If I find anyone who wants to surrender, I'll shoot him on the spot." He slapped his pistol.

At this point Tiger appeared. From somewhere he'd gotten hold of a mule with a lopped tail, which must once have belonged to a mortar battery. He patted the half-filled sack of grass that had been placed on the mule's back as a saddle, and said to Commissar Pei rather proudly, "Sir, you can ride on this from now on."

"No, I won't!" Pei's eyes shone with determination. To our astonishment, he pulled out his pistol and shot the mule in the forehead. The animal dropped to the ground, gasping noisily while blood flowed out of its mouth and its legs stretched as if pulled by invisible ropes. With his left hand on Tiger's shoulder, Commissar Pei raised his voice and announced, "Comrades, we must live or die together! I shall *walk* with you all the way back to our lines. Don't lose heart. We must help each other and find our way out."

Why did he shoot the mule? Just to show his resolve to these men? Or to assure them that he wouldn't run away? Or to frighten them into obedience? I was confounded, and so was Tiger, who looked upset and hurt, but we didn't dare say a word. If only we could have stayed a little longer and cooked some mule meat before we had to leave.

We set off for Shichang Village. Dead tired, we couldn't walk fast. The enemy didn't shell us at this time; probably they saw that we were just a bunch of wounded men and could hardly get anywhere, no immediate threat to them. When darkness deepened, we began moving faster in the direction of Shichang, at the pace of about one mile an hour. Without a map or a compass or stars in the sky, we just followed our instinct for direction. The commissar, Tiger, Dr. Wang, and I walked at the head of the first team while the other two groups marched behind us.

Originally I had thought I would be assigned to lead a team of the wounded men, but Pei had ordered both Tiger and me to stay close to him. Perhaps he was scared too. Tiger carried on his back a leather bag containing Pei's personal belongings. The commissar, suffering from a stomachache caused by an ulcer, pressed his fist against his belly from time to time. He told us that if we couldn't break out of the trap, we would go to the mountains and wage guerrilla war, waiting for an opportunity to return to North Korea.

To our horror, at daybreak the two teams behind us had vanished. We couldn't see whether they had purposely quit following us, or had been captured by the enemy, or were simply too exhausted to march anymore. I guessed they might have disbanded of their own accord. Now we had about eighty men with us, most of whom had belonged to the Guards Company and the Mountain Gun Battalion. Many officers were also in this group.

3. THREE MONTHS OF GUERRILLA LIFE

After a month of hiding in the daytime and trying in vain to find a rift in the enemy's encirclement, our team was reduced to thirty-four men. Whenever someone was killed or disappeared, I couldn't help but think about my promises to my mother and Julan. It seemed unlikely I would be able to make it home. But in spite of my fear and sadness, I forced myself to appear cheerful, especially in the presence of Commissar Pei, who always insisted that at all costs we must survive. Some of the remaining officers were familiar with guerrilla tactics. Our team leader, Yan Wenjin, the director of the divisional security section, had led dozens of guerrillas in both the war against the Japanese and the civil war. But we were in a foreign country now. Without the knowledge of its language, its terrain, and its people, how could we get the civilians' support that was the basis of guerrilla warfare?

Hunger was our most pressing problem. During the day we picked wild grapes and berries on the mountain, though we dared not move about conspicuously. The wild fruits, tiny and bitter, numbed our tongues and made a greenish saliva dribble out from the corners of our mouths. Commissar Pei couldn't eat what we gathered because of his ulcer, but he encouraged us to search for fruits and herbs for ourselves.

One morning Yan Wenjin ran over and beamed, "There's a dead horse in the woods!"

We all went over to take a look. The horse, a Mongolian sorrel, had been dead for some days. Its hair had begun to fall off, and the gun wound in its chest festered with rings of maggots like a large white chrysanthemum. Flies droned over it madly even though a man wielded a leafy branch to drive them away. Yet we were elated to find the carcass and immediately set about looking for bayonets, wooden shell boxes, and steel helmets. I went up a slope with two men to search the area beyond a patch of dwarf fir trees. As we walked, flocks of crows took off, cawing fitfully. Behind a low rise we came across four dead South Korean soldiers. In the middle of them lay a Chinese soldier, whose head was smashed and whose face was gone, eaten up by birds. Around him were scattered splinters of wooden grenade handles. Clearly he had detonated the grenades and died together with the enemy. We carried his body into a cavity under a juniper and covered him with stones and green branches. After saluting him, we went back with two bayonets and an empty box that had contained mortar shells. We had also found a brass lighter in a Korean man's pocket. The other groups brought back a bayonet, three helmets, and some wooden cartridge boxes too. From God knows where one man returned with a dented field cauldron.

Immediately they started butchering the horse. The air turned putrid as dark sticky blood dripped onto the ground. Soon, large chunks of the meat were being boiled in the cauldron, which had been propped on a horseshoe of rocks. Dr. Wang limped over. Frowning, he had a look at the carcass and then with a pair of tweezers poked the horsemeat in the pot. He said in a thin voice, "The meat is rotten. You'll get poisoned if you eat it."

Disappointed, we walked away to wash our bloody hands in a puddle of rainwater. Some men couldn't stop swearing.

To solve the problem of hunger, Yan Wenjin offered to go down the mountain with five men to search for grain. Commissar Pei let them go. They left after sunset, and we waited for them anxiously. But for five days we heard nothing from them. Later in the prison camp I learned that they had ambushed an American truck transporting a squad of GIs and some supplies. Three of them had been killed by a machine gun, and Yan Wenjin had been hit in the stomach and died on the way to the hospital. After that failed attempt, smaller groups were sent down the mountain to search for food, but none of them ever came back. By chance, I had seen through binoculars how three of our men fell into the enemy's hands. It was overcast that morning, but the air was clear. As our comrades were approaching the foot of the southern hill, suddenly about twenty GIs with two wolf dogs appeared in front of them. Our men swung aside, dashing away in different directions, but the Americans caught up with them and brought them down, some kicking them furiously and some stomping on their chests. For a moment a cloud of dust obscured the human figures. When I could see again, the dogs were springing at our men and tearing at their limbs. Viewed from the distance of one and a half miles, the whole scene was eerily quiet, without a single shot fired. Horrified, I reported the loss to Commissar Pei. His face fell, and for hours he didn't speak a word.

During this period of hiding, several men starved to death. However hard we tried, we simply couldn't get any grain and had to live on wild herbs and fruits, which day by day were becoming scarcer.

One afternoon a band of bareheaded soldiers emerged in the southeast, moving toward us. They looked like a platoon. After observing them through binoculars, Commissar Pei decided they were our men. Indeed as they were coming closer, we recognized their leader, Wan Shumin, who had been the deputy commander of an engineering company. Before we withdrew from Jiader Hill, he had led two squads to demolish a bridge on a roadway. They carried out the mission but were cut off from us and trapped in that area. Since then, they had roamed around to elude the enemy and look for a way to return north, to no avail. Two days before, near Maping Village, they had picked up a large sack of sorghum that smelled of gasoline. They hated to use up all the grain themselves, so now they offered some to us. We were all delighted, not just about the food, but more importantly, that these men were un-wounded and less combat-fatigued. Their arrival increased our fighting capacity and made us feel like a functional unit again.

Commissar Pei's mood often affected us. He was our mainstay, as though he had always known what to do and where to go. In fact he was just ten years older than most of us. When he was happy, we tended to be in good spirits too. Unfortunately, thanks to his ulcer, he was gloomy and miserable most of the time. But he could eat sorghum porridge now, so we saved half a bag of the grain for him, about thirty pounds. Luckily Tiger found a bottle of multiple vitamins and a pack of Fortress cigarettes in a secret pocket of the leather bag he had carried for the commissar. Pei offered a cigarette to everyone who was present. I didn't smoke at that time, so I declined.

From that day on Pei took three vitamin pills a day, which helped him a good deal. In addition, the cook boiled sorghum porridge so well for him that it looked almost like paste, and soon Pei stopped regurgitating food. Miraculously his ulcer began to heal.

Once again we attempted to find our way out of the hostile territory. A group of three men, all officers, was sent out to probe the enemy's positions, but they didn't come back. They were all Party members, unlikely to have deserted. Actually desertion made no sense if they wanted to go back to China alive, because they couldn't mix with Korean civilians and would be easily identified. Logically speaking, the only way to survive was to surrender to the enemy. But most of us, terrified by the propaganda that described in grisly detail how the Americans had tortured Chinese POWs, dared not think of capitulation. We had been told that the enemy would turn most captives into guinea pigs for testing biochemical weapons. As a result, many of us thought we would prefer death to captivity.

Having waited four days without hearing from the three men, we decided to seek a way out by ourselves. It was dangerous to remain in the same area for too long. We set off north, without any specific goal in mind. After about three miles we spotted the enemy on a hilltop. They saw us too and opened fire; we scrambled into the larch woods nearby. As we ran away, bullets swished past, clipping branches and

twigs. It was clear now that the three officers must have fallen into the enemy's
hands.

We climbed a foothill and went down
into a small valley. From there we saw a
puff of wood smoke rising from a hill
slope. Some civilians must have been over
there, so we headed stealthily toward the
fire. Coming closer, I smelled something
like cooked rice and my heart leaped.
Then a clearing emerged, in which a
middle-aged Korean woman in a long
white dress was chopping brushwood with
a hatchet to feed the fire under a dark pot.
At the sight of us, she yelled and dropped
the ax and ran back into a shed built of
wattles and bundles of cornstalks.

We loudly ordered her to come out, but
she didn't stir. We waited a few minutes,
then entered the doorless shed. Inside
crouched four women. One of them was
quite young, under twenty, her middle
finger wearing an aluminum thimble. They
looked clean and all wore the same kind of
shoes that resembled miniature boats, made
completely of gray rubber. The folded blankets and the indented straw on the ground
indicated that they lived here, hiding from
soldiers. They cowered together, shivering,
and one broke out sobbing. We couldn't

understand their language, so it was impossible to get anything from them. We brought them out of the shed; they were still trembling in the sun. When I removed the lid from the pot, a wave of steam rushed up with a sizzle. The rice looked glutinous and smelled overwhelmingly fragrant. I was amazed that under such circumstances they still had fresh rice. I had seen Korean families eat watery soup with only a few rice grains in it. Now all eyes turned my way, fixed on the cast-iron pot. I was sure that if the commissar had not been around, we would have wolfed down the food without hesitation. Pei took out his notebook and wrote "Chinese men," then stepped closer to the women and showed them the characters. He told them we wouldn't harm civilians and they mustn't be afraid. The oldest of them raised her thumb to acknowledge that we were a good army, though apparently they couldn't make out what Pei was saying. Then he wrote "Rice" on the paper and flashed it at them again.

"Opsumnida!" said the same woman, shaking her face, which was as furrowed as a walnut. Perhaps she meant "We don't have any."

I asked the youngest of them in English,

"Where is your home?" She couldn't understand me and kept shaking her head. If only one of us had been able to speak Korean. Or if only we'd had a few bottles of penicillin powder or atabrine pills, which I was sure we could exchange with them for food. Korean women were very fond of medicines and cosmetics, even soap and toothpaste. We kept glancing at their pot, but dared not touch the rice.

The encounter with the civilians convinced us that there must be grain hidden somewhere. We stayed up on the opposite hill and kept a close watch on the women, but they never came out of the clearing in the daytime. They seemed aware they were under surveillance. We figured they must have lived in the village at the southern end of the valley. So at night we went there to dig around among the razed houses in hope of finding some edibles. We found nothing.

Then one day we happened on another burned village, which we watched from a distance but dared not approach while it was still light. Though there seemed to be nothing left there, a wisp of smoke rose from the ruins. As we wondered if someone was cooking over there, a stocky woman came out of the village, heading toward the hill slope in the east. We followed her through binoculars and saw her enter the bushes. Five or six minutes later she reappeared with a bulging sack that must have held grain. So after dark, we went over to dig in the bushes and found a sack of rice too, about fifty pounds. Regulations said that we must never take anything from civilians, but we were hungry and some of us were dying. Commissar Pei took out his notebook and wrote an IOU, saying that we had borrowed the grain and would compensate its owner when our army came again to liberate South Korea. He placed the piece of paper into the empty pit and held it down with a cobblestone. The words were in a running script; I suspected that the owner would never figure out the meaning and would curse us like mad.

If only we'd had money to pay them. In contrast to us, the North Korean army was loaded with cash; every man had bales of it, because they had seized the South Korean government's currency plates in Seoul. Their soldiers always paid for everything they took from civilians, who were pleased but didn't know the banknotes were losing value. I often wondered why the North Koreans wouldn't share some of the money with us. I guessed our top generals must have been too proud to ask them such a favor.

To avoid being pursued by the enemy, we moved farther south, deeper into hostile territory. Since most fields had not been sown, we didn't expect to have ripe crops to eat in the fall, but there were orchards and groves of chestnut trees on some hills. We all hoped that our army would launch the sixth-phase offensive soon so that we could rejoin them. We didn't know that from now on there would be no offensives anymore — the war had reached a stalemate.

We settled in a wooded valley where a brook flowed. In the evening frogs croaked in the water. The next day we began to catch frogs, which were a delicacy to us. We would skewer about a dozen of them on a whittled branch and roast them over a fire. But within three days all the frogs had been eaten up, and no croaking rose up at night anymore. Once in a while we heard a wild animal howling, a wolf or a leopard, but we couldn't go hunting them because we dared not fire our guns.

Time and again we sent out men to search for grain. With few exceptions they would run into the enemy, and some of them would get killed. On average every twenty pounds of rice cost one man, so we mainly ate herbs, grass, and mushrooms, waiting for the fall when the wild chestnuts would ripen. Once about two dozen men were poisoned by a whitish fungus, which looked like tree ears and was juicy and crunchy, quite tasty. Half of us ate some, myself included. Afterward we collapsed, and a few men began groaning and rolling around with cramps in their stomachs. Fortunately Dr. Wang didn't eat any. He boiled several cauldrons of water and made us drink our fill so that we could excrete the poison. I was sweating so much that my vision was blurred. It took two days for us to mend, though nobody died this time.

To shelter ourselves from the elements, we fetched crates left by the Americans along the road and used them to prop up sheets of corrugated iron we had dislodged from a dilapidated shack abandoned by charcoal burners. We also spread pieces of cardboard on the ground so that we could sleep on them. I hated to go to the road north of the mountain, because it smelled awful there, the air rife with decomposing bodies, Chinese and Koreans and Americans, all left behind, unburied. Back in China, at the Huangpu Military Academy, we had been instructed that in a battle the dead must be buried quietly, as soon as possible, so that the troops couldn't see them; otherwise the sight of the corpses would weaken their morale. But here, in a real war, nobody cared.

The woods were deep here, providing good cover. During the day we would move about as little as possible; most of the time I just lay in the shade resting. Some calmness settled over me. I had with me a paperback of *Uncle Tom's Cabin* in the English original, which I often read with the help of the dictionary. Commissar Pei regretted not having brought along a full-length book; in his bag he had only a few booklets that were mere propaganda material. He mixed well with the soldiers, who could endure anything but the silence in the mountains. Yet they knew how to enjoy themselves. They made playing cards with paperboard and chess pieces with wood chips. During the day they often played for hours on end. I knew the chess moves well but preferred to remain a kibitzer. In addition to the games, every day Pei would tell them a story. A high school graduate, he was quite knowledgeable about ancient legends, and the stories he told fascinated the men. Hao Chaolin, a small sharp-witted man, also offered them stories, mainly those from revolutionary novels. I shared with them some episodes from *Uncle Tom's Cabin*. Some of the men were touched by the character Cassy, who poisons her baby son with laudanum to prevent him from being sold as a slave. They said that the American slave owners must have been crueler than most of the landowners in the old China, but they were amazed that even the slaves could eat pork belly, beans, biscuits, chicken. I translated the passages in which Aunt Chloe serves the slave Sam a big meal after he tells her the good news that Eliza and her son Harry have fled to the other side of the Ohio River so that the slave trader can't catch them anymore. In the scene Sam eats so many toothsome things — chicken wings and drumsticks, ham, corn cake, turkey legs. Granted that they were leftovers from the master's table, they seemed sumptuous to these starving men.

"What does turkey taste like?" Tiger asked me with his large eyes batting.

"I don't know," I confessed.

"It must be real good," another man put in.

I told them, "Turkeys are very big, almost like a small ostrich."

"My, a lot of meat the bird must have," Tiger said.

"It seems to me that the American slaves ate better than most of the rich families in my home village, tut-tut-tut," said a short fellow with a wide face.

Actually a similar notion had crossed my mind too when I read those pages for the first time. I had thought America must be a bountiful land where nutritious food was available for everybody, even slaves.

The soldiers chatted a great deal among themselves, bragging about their hometowns and their deeds in the battles they had fought in China. They also talked at length about the dishes they had tasted or heard of: Nanking cured duck, Jinhua ham, stewed lamb sold at street food stands in the Northwest, whole fried carp and roast pigs served at dinner parties in the North-east. A man from the South even boasted how delicious fried rats were. I said he was disgusting and no matter how hungry I was, I wouldn't touch such a thing, though I knew the dish was a delicacy in some coastal areas.

Some of us had picked up American cans left at their deserted campsites, and we couldn't help but wonder what kind of food GIs ate. We were impressed by their abundant resources. Tiger often said he wished that when the war was over, he could bring home just one pile of the shell casings the Americans had discarded, so he could sell the brass — which would be enough for him to live on for the rest of his life.

Gradually I developed a kind of attachment to the commissar, who seemed more and more amiable to me. One day when we two were alone, he confessed that he'd once had his doubts about intellectuals in the army, but that I had made him think differently. To the servicemen, most of whom were illiterate, every college graduate was an intellectual. Apart from my loyalty to our comrades, Pei must have been amazed to see that I could read alone for hours without respite and immerse myself in a novel written in English, of which he had read an ornate translation long ago. He was especially pleased that at night I would do guard duty for an hour, just like the enlisted men among us. He told me that if he got killed, I should help Chaolin lead them. I said I couldn't accept such a responsibility; I wasn't a Party member and was unsuitable for leadership. Besides, Chaolin was very capable and might not need my help at all. But the commissar insisted, "Your deeds are your qualification. You should lead our men if worst comes to worst."

What he implied was that I should succeed Hao Chaolin if they were both lost. In truth, although I was calm in appearance, I was apprehensive at heart. What would happen to my mother if I perished in this foreign land? I missed my fiancée terribly. At night I often dreamed of her and my mother and woke up tearful. I wondered if my comrades had heard me babble in my sleep. Could Julan and I communicate through dreams, telepathically? Or were the dreams nothing but the vagaries of my mind? One night I saw her face shine with a mysterious smile, as if she had some secret but meant to keep me in suspense. As I stretched my hand to touch her tilted eyebrows, she faded away and I woke up with a numbing ache in my chest.

When the other men laughed heartily listening to Pei, I often remained pensive. One day the commissar said to me, "Why don't you teach us some English?"

"What for?"

"It will be useful. We'll fight the enemy again. Teach us some words we can use on the battlefield."

So I began to teach them English, just

some phrases and short sentences, such as "Hands up!," "Drop your weapon, we spare you!," "We don't kill prisoners," "Don't move!," "Surrender, you are safe!," "Don't die for American imperialism!"

There was no paper to write on, so I used a stick to inscribe on the ground the written characters representing the English sounds so that the literate ones among them could have some phonetic guidance. I couldn't possibly make them pronounce the words accurately, since half of them didn't even speak Mandarin well. But they were eager to learn, even if they did complain about the pain inflicted by the English pronunciation on their tongues and jaws. A few claimed they had sore throats. I was amazed that in just a few days they could rap out to one another what they had learned. Most of them were smart men who would have gone far in their lives had they had the opportunity and the education. I wondered why they would concentrate so much on learning a few foreign words that they might never use at all. Heaven knew what would happen to us tomorrow; we might get captured or killed anytime. The enemy was just two miles to the north.

I suspected that to them the act of

learning must represent some kind of hope. At least this meant there was still a future, on which they could fix their minds. Their limited awareness of the larger world and their inert response to the menace of death endowed them with the strength needed for survival. I was moved by the tenacity of life shown in their desire to learn.

One afternoon, as we sat near a cliff learning how to sing a folk song, a man rushed back from the bushes where we would go and relieve ourselves. He shouted at us between gasps, "Enemy! They're coming from both sides!"

Immediately Tiger began pushing Commissar Pei toward the edge of the cliff, which wasn't very steep, overhung with tussocky grass and jujube shrubs. "You must go down now, sir!" he urged. As Pei was hesitating, Tiger shoved his shoulder forcefully. The commissar tumbled down and disappeared; then four or five men jumped down too. Tiger raised his pistol to fire at the enemy coming out of the woods. As he was about to retreat, a bullet hit his arm. "Oh!" he yelled. Then another bullet struck his neck and he died instantly, his blood flowing down the granite rock he fell on. The rest of us were pinned down by machine guns and couldn't move. While I was wondering what to do, a grenade landed near us. Our cook picked it up, but before he could throw it away, it went off. A burst of light opened in front of me and a wave of heat swept me up. Then everything turned black.

When I came to, I realized I was in a vehicle, probably a jeep. The cool air was brushing my face, which must have been swollen. The sky seemed quite low, with the tattered clouds jittering violently. Someone said in English, "Damn, we let some of the gooks get away."

A breezy voice answered, "Relax, man. We got eight of them, not bad."

"Are they Koreans or Chinese?"

"Must be Chinks."

"How can you tell?"

"They don't wear no uniform."

The jeep horn tooted, then some passing vehicle beeped back. The man in the passenger seat called out, "Hey, how's it going?"

"Swell," someone cried back from a distance.

They caught me! This realization shot a sharp pang to my heart, which seemed to jump up and block my throat. Two other Chinese men, whose faces I couldn't see, were also lying in the jeep. I couldn't tell if they were dead or alive. I could still move both arms, but my legs were numb. I tried to wriggle my toes to make sure they were still there; to my horror, I couldn't feel anything in my left foot. I touched my left thigh, which felt wooden. Hard as I tried, I couldn't move the leg; it must have been fractured. I touched my crotch — we had been told that some Americans would castrate Chinese POWs — but everything was all right there except that my thigh was bandaged. It seemed my captors meant to keep me alive. Why didn't they kill me? It would've been better that way. At least people back home would treat Mother as a Revolutionary Martyr's parent and the government would take care of her.

Where were they taking me? To a prison? To a hospital? I was overwhelmed by fear and shame. What should I do? We had never been instructed how to act honorably if we were taken prisoner, except to kill ourselves. Only Commissar Pei had once said that if we fell into the enemy's hands, we must never tell them the truth: always lie to them. That was all the preparation I had received for this situation. I was confused. Why hadn't the Americans finished me off? That would have made their job much simpler.

4. DR. GREENE

I was shipped to the First Closure of the POW Collection Center in Pusan. The city, then the provisional capital of South Korea, had so many American military offices and supply stations that the bustling streets reminded me of the Chinese city Dandong on the Yalu River, though more automobiles rolled around here and ships in the foggy harbor loomed like small buildings. Besides, this was a much bigger city with an airport. The closure I was put in comprised a hospital and several large compounds, each of which held over a thousand prisoners. The Collection Center was a transit point, where wounded POWs received medical treatment. But most prisoners stayed here just a few days; after being processed — registered and interrogated — they would be sent to different camps in other places.

My left thigh was fractured. A piece of shrapnel had hit the area near my groin and shattered the femur. Because of my injury I didn't go to registration, which I heard was a tedious process — the waiting lines were long there, though the clerks, mostly North Korean prisoners, were sympathetic to Chinese captives. Nor was I interrogated like other POWs, some of whom collapsed under the torment.

Nonetheless, I was ordered to have my fingerprints taken and to provide the information needed for registration. A stout American officer and a Chinese interpreter came to our ward, in which over seventy patients, wounded and diseased, were lying on canvas cots. The ward was in a large iron-framed tent with a plywood floor and two entrances. The air was foul in here. The officer asked me my name, rank, education, my unit's serial number, and questioned me about my immediate superiors. I told him that my name was Feng Yan and that I was a new recruit, serving as a secretary in an infantry company in the 539th Regiment. The Americans must have known that regiment's serial number, so I told him the truth: 3692. He showed me a bunch of snapshots of Chinese soldiers who all looked like officers, and asked me whether I knew any of them. I didn't recognize a single one. I was still weak, having been operated on just three days before, so after a few more questions the officer and the interpreter left, saying they'd come again. Throughout the questioning, I didn't speak English, fearful that I might reveal my true identity.

Outside the compound fenced with barbed wire, forty yards away from the gate, stood a white-stuccoed building, two stories high, with a red-tiled roof and dormer windows. Before the war it had been a schoolhouse, and now it was occupied by the Operating Section, which the patients called the Butchery. Almost every day dead bodies were carried out of it and then stacked in front of the closure's admission center, to join those who had died en route to the hospital. I had spent four hours in that building three days before. After I was placed on a table, two doctors had talked in whispers about my leg. I couldn't understand their words completely, because I was still delirious and unfamiliar with their medical vocabulary. They sounded unsure about the procedure to come. An anesthetist injected some drug into my lower abdomen and the small of my back, and then they tied down my arms and calves. When a nurse had spread a white sheet over my belly, one of the doctors smirked, saying, "I never thought there'd be so many patients to cut when I was drafted. This definitely beats any residency."

"I guess I'll be qualified for chief surgeon after the war is over," said a tall doctor with blond eyebrows. Apparently he was in charge of the operation.

My heart shuddered as I realized they were two medical school students who probably hadn't completed their course work yet. I closed my eyes tight wondering if I should beg them to save my leg, but I decided not to talk and just endure it. Outside, a downpour lashed and blurred the windowpanes.

"Ow!" I yelled as one of them poked my wound.

"It hurts?" asked a concerned voice.

Before I could answer, the tall doctor said, "We should start."

The anesthesia hadn't taken full effect yet when they began cutting me. Bouts of pain radiated to my insides and to my neck and head. Despite gritting my teeth, I couldn't stop groaning and twisting while their instruments explored my wound.

The room turned foggy. All the objects — the intense lights, the bottles hung on a steel stand, the bluish caps on the human heads — all seemed to be floating and bobbing around. A moment later I blacked out.

When I came to, my left thigh was dressed with a wooden board tied alongside my leg and hip. "You're all set for the time being," the tall doctor said to me with a grin. "You'll keep your leg."

"Thank you," I sighed.

"You speak English?"

I shook my head and regretted having blurted that out.

"Do you understand what I'm saying?" he asked again.

I didn't respond, just stared at him. With a wave of his hand he summoned two orderlies to take me away on a stretcher.

Besides the American medical staff, there were more than three dozen orderlies working in the hospital. Most of them were Chinese who had cooperated with our captors and had been assigned to work in the building, carrying patients and cleaning. As "collaborators," they probably wouldn't be going back to mainland China, where they would be held accountable for their behavior here, so they treated us according to their own moods and whims. Sometimes they even beat patients. The two orderlies who carried me back to the ward made fun of me all the way, saying I was lucky the doctors hadn't sawed off my leg.

The minute I was returned to the tent I

began shivering. The doctor hadn't pre-scribed any painkiller for me, so I sweated and moaned throughout the night and the next morning. Thanks to the fellow in-mates who gave me water to drink and even fed me some rice porridge, I survived that night. Among the ward mates there was a man from the Guards Company of our division, Ding Wanlin by name, who had suffered a bullet wound in his left side, which had almost healed. His bed was next to mine. He had recognized me, having seen me with Commissar Pei a few times, but I didn't remember him. He was con-siderate to me and sat at my bedside for several hours that night, wiping the sweat and tears off my face now and then. Mean-time, a Korean man, wounded in the chest, raved continually and flung his hands as though quarreling with someone.

Later Ding Wanlin told me that our divi-sional staff had been captured by the enemy two days after they had abandoned us in the valley strewn with the stragglers, but Commander Niu had managed to flee back to North Korea with his orderly and a few officers, because a squad of guards had run in the opposite direction and drawn the enemy away.

In spite of my weak condition, I could

eat. My appetite was remarkably good, perhaps kindled by the hunger I had suffered in the wilderness. At long last there was food, though we couldn't eat our fill. I was given a bowl of dry milk every morning and sometimes a can of beef or tuna for dinner. Once we were each issued a fruit compote, which I enjoyed very much. At a regular meal each patient could have one bowl of steamed rice, usually with a ladle of vegetables, salty turnip or carrots or cabbage. Sometimes a half mug of soup was added as a side dish. The standard enamel bowl the prisoners used was not small, four inches tall, six inches in diameter at its top and four inches across at its bottom. To be honest, the food was better than I had expected. I told myself I must eat to get well so that I could return home in one piece.

Wanlin and I promised each other never to disclose our true names and identities to the enemy. He was twenty-one, two years younger than me, tall and bony, with a straight nose and thin eyes. When he spoke he often burbled a little, as if he were still an adolescent whose careless innocence hindered the clarity of his speech. His smile displayed his yellow, lopsided teeth (most of us hadn't been able to brush our teeth for months, so although we had tooth powder now, our teeth still looked awful). I was grateful to him, because he often helped me relieve myself and fetched meals and water for me.

In our tent there was an emaciated man with a fractured thigh, whose name was Zhou Gushu. He was from a different division and had been captured near Wonju the previous winter. His leg was encased in plaster and had been operated on several times. He hurt terribly and was bedridden. He often cursed Dr. Thomas, the tall, blond one in charge of my case as well, and said that man meant to experiment with his leg. Gushu wept a lot, at times tearlessly. I thought that he was too much of a crybaby and that he had better have more self-control, because the tent housed more than forty Koreans who might laugh at us Chinese and view us as weaklings.

Then one day his pain was so overpowering he couldn't eat his midday meal. Wanlin went over, moved the bowl of cabbage soup closer to him, and tried to persuade him to have some. As he spoke, Wanlin caught sight of a maggot wiggling on Gushu's bed. He opened Gushu's blanket and found more maggots. He put away the bowl and went out. In no time he returned with an empty vial and two thin sticks and told Gushu to turn on his side. After collecting the maggots into the bottle, he raised the tail of Gushu's shirt and saw a swarm of the grubs gathering on his lower back, at least fifty strong. Another two patients also lent a hand in rounding up the larvae. Though they had wiped the small of Gushu's back clean, more maggots were creeping out from the top end of the plaster cast. We were all horrified — there must have been an army of them deep in there eating away at his leg.

At the demand of the other patients, two medical personnel arrived with pliers the next morning. When the cast was pried off, balls and balls of maggots appeared wriggling and crawling about. The flesh around the wound was whitish and decayed, messy with pus and blood; the maggots had even bored into the adjacent areas too, where the skin had been intact originally. I turned my head away, my guts twinging.

For the rest of the day Gushu groaned without stopping; his breathing was labored, and from time to time he would tear at his chest. He cursed Dr. Thomas relentlessly, believing the surgeon had intended to mangle his leg. Most of the patients in the tent shared his belief that he had become a guinea pig for germ experimentation.

He was taken to the Operating Section the following day. A patch of skin was peeled off from his other thigh and grafted onto the wounded one. I wondered if the young doctors here were capable of skin grafting. Maybe this was the first time they had even attempted such a job.

Gushu was carried back in the afternoon. He was given a soporific for the night, so he slept soundly. But from the next day on he couldn't stop moaning with pain. He said, "Why didn't they just finish me off? They can use my body parts any way they like once I'm dead." In fact, as I learned later on, the next year when he went through his seventh operation and his leg became numb, another American doctor insisted on amputation, but Gushu refused, saying he'd die rather than lose his leg. Eventually they did manage to save it, though he had to use crutches when walking.

His condition frightened me, because day by day my thigh was getting hotter and more painful. On the morning the bandage was removed, I saw that my wound hadn't healed at all. Actually it had festered some, though it began scabbing around the dark fringes. There must have been a lot of pus in it. Seeing the mess, I almost broke into tears. Wanlin lifted a mug of cold water to my lips. That kept me from losing my mind. Though I tried, I still couldn't move my bad leg, which felt disconnected from my body and kept shooting jolts of pain to my spine.

That afternoon I was given an x-ray. The film indicated there was another piece of shrapnel in my thigh, causing the infection. I would have to undergo another operation. On his visit the next day, Dr. Thomas told me with a boyish smirk, "If you want to save your leg, you'll have to get another cut. This shouldn't be a big job, though. The bone was set all right. I'm pleased with that."

I glared at him the whole time. Before the Chinese interpreter could translate his words, I yelled in English at the top of my lungs, "I don't want you to operate on me!"

Dr. Thomas was taken aback. "He speaks English," he said to the interpreter.

The patients in the tent were surprised too. I shouted at him again, "You're just a clumsy butcher who didn't even finish medical school."

He paused. "How can you be sure of that? Do I need to show you my diploma?" He looked quite innocent and screwed up his left eye, grinning.

"You said that last time when you were cutting me. You're just a pseudo-doctor in job training."

"Well, I'm impressed by your memory. You know what? I don't enjoy working here. I'm sick of cutting people day in and day out. These endless surgeries have ruined my spirit, not to mention my appetite. These days I hardly eat lunch. You're right — treating you guys makes me feel like a butcher."

"I don't want you to treat me."

"I'll see what I can do about that. Wait till tomorrow. You're not the one who calls the shots, you know."

I didn't say another word. He turned to the door, followed by the spindly interpreter.

The moment Dr. Thomas disappeared, the other inmates began gathering around me. "You speak English good," said a long-faced Korean man, who called himself Captain Yoon. He looked urbane and expansive; I had often seen him sitting by himself near the side entrance of the ward, thumbing through a thick book.

I was disconcerted. Now they thought of me as an officer. This might expose me to danger, and the enemy might interrogate me thoroughly. What should I do? Admit to these fellows that I studied in college? No, somebody would betray me if I told them the truth.

I managed to say in English to Captain Yoon, "I've almost forgotten my English. Just now I was angry, so some words came back to me."

"Did you go to college? Me went Seoul University, major in economics, but I joined the North Korean People's Army. I want liberate and unite my country."

"I didn't go to college," I said. "I learned some English from a missionary in my hometown."

"Good, me impressed." He gave a loud bray of laughter.

Six or seven Korean men cackled too. I wasn't sure if they understood our exchange. They must all have been loyal to the Communist army, otherwise Captain Yoon wouldn't have talked about himself so offhandedly. I had heard that the North Korean POWs were well organized in the prison camps. Some doctors and nurses at the hospital were Koreans too, captured by the U.N. forces, and the Korean Communists had penetrated many parts of the prison system. It was whispered that there was even a Kim Il Sung University established secretly in a camp.

The next day, when I was placed on the table for the second operation, I was terrified to see Dr. Thomas in the high-ceilinged room. He came over and patted me on the upper arm, smiling. "Look, Comrade Feng Yan, I may have to do the job today."

"I don't want you to touch me!" I said. "Send me back."

"Wait a minute. Let's be clear about this." The smile vanished from his face. "The other doctors have their patients to take care of, so I have to do the job."

"I don't want to be operated on today."

"Can't you see that I'm helping you, to save your leg?"

"I don't need any help from a pseudo-doctor like you."

"You Reds are hard to please."

"Send me back!" I shouted.

"Stop yelling!" jumped in a male nurse.

Another one added, "You shouldn't be insulting Dr. Thomas this way. He's doing his best for you."

I caught sight of two orderlies passing the door, so I cried at them in Chinese,

"Come and help me, brothers! Rescue your compatriot!"

The American medical personnel seemed puzzled, looking at one another without a word. I saw hesitation and worry in Dr. Thomas's eyes. I yelled in Chinese again, "Help me! Take me back to my tent! Brothers, we're still comrades-in-arms! Save me please!"

But neither of the orderlies came in. Eyes closed, I went on shouting for all I was worth. By now the doctor and nurses had stepped aside. They gathered by a window and whispered something I couldn't quite hear. Then a nurse left the room.

I continued yelling and kicking my right leg, sickened by the smell of putrefaction and rubbing alcohol. Two or three minutes later the nurse returned with a doctor I hadn't met before. The new arrival came up to me and patted my forehead. I opened my eyes fully and was amazed to see a female face. She was in her late twenties, slender with gaunt features, and the insignia on her cap indicated the rank of major. Her auburn hair, short but neat, stuck out from beneath the brim of her cap. Her clear hazel eyes gazed at me kindly as a smile displayed her uneven teeth. To my astonishment, she said in excellent Mandarin, "I'm Dr. Greene. Can I take a look at your wound?" She had a slight Shanghai accent, but she spoke so spontaneously that I wondered if I had heard her right. Dumbfounded, I just stared at her. She smiled again, this time coaxingly. "Can I look at your wound?" she repeated.

I nodded yes. As she bent down to examine my thigh, the other doctor and nurses also gathered around to observe. My wound was very close to my groin, so my sex was fully exposed, which made my cheeks burn with embarrassment. Wordlessly I shut my eyes tight. Her fingers were sensitive, touching and pressing my wound gently. I felt as if something cool and soothing were being applied to it, easing the pain somewhat.

After examining me, she drew herself up and said, "Your wound is very deep and was already festering when you arrived. We had to get rid of the gangrenous tissue first and wait for the inflammation to subside a little before we could take out the bone fragments and the shrapnel. I can assure you that Dr. Thomas did a good job in setting the femur last time, so today we can open the wound to remove the shrapnel and the bone fragments."

"Thank you. I was so worried," I sighed and turned to look at Dr. Thomas, who was a first lieutenant. He grinned at me like a big boy.

"I understand," she said.

After talking with Dr. Thomas briefly, she asked me with a smile, "Can I operate on you today?"

Eagerly I nodded my agreement. She ordered the nurses to give me an IV and put the ether mask on me. I felt calm in her presence, as if she had been sent over to save me. At the same time I heard some metallic clanks that were disquieting, and something warm was placed on my right leg.

Soon I lost consciousness.

I don't know how long I was out. It must have been three or four hours, because when I woke up I heard a male voice shout in the corridor, "Chow time." Then I saw beads of perspiration on the woman doctor's smooth forehead. Her large eyes observed me intently as she said, "Do you want to see what I got out of your leg?"

I nodded, so parched I couldn't utter a word. With forceps she lifted from a white enamel dish a splinter of shrapnel, black and bloody like a twisted button. She said,

"It was this sucker that shattered your femur. We took out all the bone fragments too."

"Do you think I can walk again?"

"Of course, I'll make you walk. But for the time being you'll have to stay in bed. Then we'll have another operation to fix everything once and for all."

Another operation! Tears welled up to my eyes. Ashamed, I averted my face.

She patted me on the shoulder and said, "Don't worry. I'll put you back on your feet."

When I turned to look at her, she was heading for the door. Her white back was straight, her shoulders thin and delicate.

This operation alleviated my pain and I began to mend both physically and mentally, though I had grown more homesick, often fingering my half of the jade barrette at night. My captors had stripped me of everything except for this token of Julan's love and her snapshot, both concealed in my undershirt pocket. The smoothness of the jade reminded me of my fiancée's skin and often set me daydreaming.

Sometimes I also thought of other women — some Korean women who, from somewhere close by, would sing in chorus for an hour or two every evening. Their songs would drift in the dusk, sad and soulful. Sometimes the tunes were wistful as though complaining about a betrayal or a missed opportunity that wouldn't be offered again. Whenever they started their chorus, I would listen to them. As they sang, the air would seem galvanized and the men in the ward would stop chatting, their eyes turning more distant, brighter, and sometimes watery. How I wished I could have made out the women's words. Their fearless voices brought to mind the girls in the countryside of my home province, who often vied with one another in singing love songs when they were working in the rice paddies or picking tea leaves on the hills. If only I could have walked out of the tent and looked at those women across the barbed wire!

Wanlin and I talked about them, but he couldn't figure out who they were either. In the evening he often went out; once he saw a few Korean women who were all civilians, though they seemed to be detainees too. Our Korean ward mates certainly knew more about the singers, but there was no way for us to communicate with them on such a subject. I felt too awkward to ask Captain Yoon about them.

In the meantime, Gushu's leg, unlike

mine, was deteriorating. Seeing that I was recovering rapidly, he pleaded with the hospital to let Dr. Greene treat him too, or to give him Colonel Osman, who was an experienced surgeon from Florida, known to the prisoners as a kindhearted man.

Two weeks after my operation, Dr. Greene and Dr. Thomas came to our tent, both wearing white coats. At the sight of them I tried to sit up, but she stopped me and said in English, "Lie down. We just came to see how you've been doing."

She and Dr. Thomas must have been making their ward rounds. She checked my wound. "Excellent, it's healing very well," she said, her eyes lighting up. "Tomorrow we can operate on you to repair the bone once and for all."

"Thank you, Dr. Greene," I said.

I was still excited after they left. At last I believed I would walk on both legs again.

The following day I was taken to the Operating Section for the third time. Again Dr. Thomas was present in the room. After I was laid on the table, Dr. Greene bent forward a little, putting on gloves. She asked me, "You very much want to walk without a crutch, don't you?"

I nodded.

"After this operation," she said, "you

should be able to walk soon."

My eyes misted, so I shut them immediately. She didn't see my face, since the chubby anesthetist was putting the ether mask on me. Soon I was unconscious.

When I woke up, I saw Dr. Greene leaning against the wall with her eyes closed. She looked pale and exhausted. I wasn't sure whether she was taking a breather or was already done with the operation. The front of her white gown was stained with my blood, but she didn't wear gloves. Seeing that I had come to, she gave me a half-smile and said, "Everything went well." Her words set my mind at rest.

Every three days after the operation, she came to check on me and the other orthopedic patients. It was getting cold: cicadas had stopped chirring in the willow crowns and all the bumblebees had vanished. In the early morning I often saw little frost clouds hanging above my ward mates' faces. We had been issued more used clothing. Each man now had a felt coat, another blanket, and a set of olive fatigues. On each jacket were painted two white letters, *P* on the right sleeve and *W* on the left one. A few men had the *P* and *W* on the breast pockets of their jackets instead. As for the overcoats, the two letters were stenciled on the backs. I couldn't put on my pants yet and had to cover my legs with two blankets all the time. During the day, when Wanlin had no need for his bedding, I used his blankets too.

I remember vividly the day when Dr. Greene came to take out my stitches. It was on October 31, 1951, six days after the first anniversary of China's entering the Korean War. Having removed the twelve stitches with scissors and tweezers, she helped me get out of bed, then said, "See if you can stand on your feet now."

I began trembling, both hands gripping a tent pole, a piece of rough-hewn timber. I dared not let go of it at first. Then slowly I shifted all my weight to my legs and released my grip. She came around and stood in front of me, saying, "Ah, you can stand by yourself now, very good. I'm impressed. Come on, a step toward me."

Several inmates were watching us. Although I pulled myself together, I couldn't move. It was as if my feet had rooted into the floor. She urged me, "Come on, take a step. Be brave, soldier."

Too ashamed to disappoint her, I clenched my teeth and slowly stretched forward my left foot. But after having lain in bed for more than three months, I couldn't keep my balance. As my body lurched forward, she reached out and held me by both shoulders. She said, "Come, try again. Don't be afraid. You can do it."

Her face was so close to mine that I smelled her sweetish perfume and I felt myself blushing. I made my utmost effort to straighten up my back and then advanced a step. Miraculously, I didn't fall!

"Good, try another step," she said.

So I did one more, which marked a new beginning in my life. Clapping, she smiled like a child. If she had not been in uniform, nobody would have taken her for a soldier, let alone one on the enemy's side. When she had helped me come back to my bed, I was sweating all over. She sat down too.

"What's your name?" she asked.

"Feng Yan." I was surprised by her question.

"I know. I mean what two characters do you go by?"

I had no pen, so she pulled out her ballpoint and handed it to me, together with a prescription pad.

I wrote out the words "Feng Yan" in a cursive script. I had practiced calligraphy for years, so the characters came out handsomely.

She looked at the two words for a moment, then said, "You're an excellent calligrapher and a good-tempered man, I can tell. Can you teach me how to write the characters?"

Unsure whether she asked that as a lark or in earnest, I answered, "You speak Chinese very well, so you must write it well too."

"Not at all," she said. "Although I grew up in China and graduated from Tongji Medical School, I've never been able to write the characters well. When I was a child, I didn't spend time doing calligraphy. Later in college when I took notes in class, I just scribbled everything down and didn't pay attention to my handwriting."

Now I understood why she spoke Chinese so fluently and treated us so kindly. I didn't ask about her parents, who must have been missionaries. The medical school she'd attended in Shanghai had been well known for its Western-style education, where most courses had been taught in English and some by foreign professors. After the Communists took over the country, that school had been closed down. I couldn't contain my curiosity and said to her, "May I ask you a question?"

"Of course you may."

"How come you've become an army doctor here?"

"It's a long story."

"Did you volunteer?"

"Yes and no. Last year, after graduation I went back to the States to see my biological mother. On my way back I stopped in Japan. The Korean War had just broken out and army doctors were in short supply, so I was recruited by the Far Eastern Headquarters. Then I came to Korea."

"Don't you hate China because we came to fight the U.S. Army?"

"When I joined up, I'd never thought China would take part in this war. Later China rushed in, but I still can't hate China, to be honest. I was raised in China, which is my second country." She turned thoughtful, then continued, "I have a question for you too. You have no airplanes, no warships, and no tanks; how can you possibly win this war?"

I said sincerely, "MacArthur's army would have crossed our border and seized Manchuria if we hadn't come to Korea. We had no choice but to fight the better-equipped aggressors. But with justice on our side we will win this war."

"You're very idealistic," she said. I

could tell she was dubious.

By now several inmates had moved closer to listen to our conversation, so I switched the subject. "Do you really want me to teach you calligraphy?" I asked.

"Of course."

"But how can I do it?"

"That's easy. Tomorrow I'll bring you some paper and a pen. You write a sheet of characters as models, like in a copybook. I'll take it back with me and copy the words. This will be a good way to spend my off-hours."

I agreed readily, determined to do what I could to repay her.

Toward the next evening, she came with a shiny black fountain pen and a sheaf of white paper. On the top page were three big characters, Ge Su-Shan, which looked stiff and slanted toward the right. Obviously her handwriting had been affected by her sloping English hand. She said, "Here's my Chinese name. You see, this is the best I can do. Can you teach me how to write my name well first?"

I began to explain to her how to inscribe the individual strokes, the horizontal one and the vertical one. Then with the pen I illustrated the left-falling stroke, the hook, the dot, and the right-falling stroke. She tried to write a few, but couldn't do them well. I was surprised that this was difficult for her, but I also could see that she had attempted calligraphy before, just as every pupil had to practice it in a Chinese elementary school. Frustrated, she asked me to hold her hand to inscribe the strokes so that she could feel how the pen was supposed to move. This was a common method in teaching calligraphy, we both knew. Yet I hesitated, reluctant to touch her hand, in part because I was a prisoner but mainly because of the inmates gathering around to observe. Their eyes unsettled me.

"Come on," she said. "Don't you Communists believe in equality between men and women? At this moment I'm your student."

Her words embarrassed me, so I held her hand. Together we began writing the strokes. Her hair and her clothes exuded a whiff of tobacco; she must have been quite a smoker. I had noticed that the tips of her index and middle fingers were slightly yellow. Although her hand had silky skin and slim fingers, it was quite strong, its muscles tight and its bones sturdy. I was surprised to find her fingernails rather stubby. Her hand felt more like a male laborer's. This put me somewhat at ease, and we concentrated on the hook and the right-falling stroke. In a way I was moved by her letting me hold her hand to practice. I smelled of DDT, which had just been sprayed on me for delousing.

After half an hour's practice, she could do most of the strokes decently. She was happy about the progress.

When we stopped for the day, she asked me to write some words she could take back and copy in her spare time, since she couldn't come every day. I thought for a few seconds, then carefully wrote down this ancient poem:

> *Sand dunes are glimmering like snow*
> *Beyond our camping ground.*
> *Behind us, moonlight*
> *Is frosting a frontier town.*
>
> *Whence comes the tootling pipe?*
> *For a whole night*
> *The soldiers think alike*
> *Of the distant fireside.*

She read the lines silently, her lips opening and closing, revealing her strong teeth. Then she told me, "Actually I studied this poem in middle school. But it means more to me now."

Lifting her head, she said to the patients around, "You should all take good care of yourselves. When the Panmunjom negotiations are over, you can all go back to rejoin your families." A few men sighed. She glanced at a man's handless arm and added, "I hope this is the last war of mankind."

I wanted to say something, but words deserted me.

From that day on Dr. Greene came to see me once a week, handed in her homework for me to correct, and took back a page of sample characters I had inscribed for her. When she was here, she also checked my wound, which was healing fast. The inmates would gather around to see her homework and often praised her progress. Gushu was quite attached to her, saying she was a saint, because she had managed to stop his wound from suppurating.

Although our ward accommodated over seventy patients, most beds were unoccupied during the day. I found that a good number of the men were ambulatory and were actually fairly healthy; they were probably remaining here because the hospital offered better board and lodging than the regular prison camps. I wondered why the doctors didn't discharge them. There was so much deliberate confusion of identities among the POWs, who often destroyed their ID tags and changed their names randomly, that the doctors could hardly keep track of all the patients. Beyond question, some of these men were malingerers, good at faking illness. The hospital seemed to have become a vacation place for many POWs.

Now that I was able to move around with the aid of crutches, I often left the tent. It was already early winter and most trees had shed their leaves. Naked branches made the yellowish land appear more drab; even the sea to the south had turned gray. But in the north the hills were still green, scattered with patches of junipers and cypresses. I often watched seagulls flying in the sky draped with ragged clouds. The birds had no walls or fences to confine them. How precious the idea of freedom was to a prisoner! I couldn't help but compare myself with almost every creature my eyes fell upon. Even my worm's-eye view of American airplanes often set me imagining how free the pilots must feel up in the air.

One day I heard some women singing a Russian song, "The Evening of Moscow

Suburbs," which had also been popular in China; afterward Captain Yoon told me that that compound, number 12, contained only female prisoners. I could see a corner of their barracks, which must have held hundreds of Korean women. The reason we had mistaken them for civilians was that some of them had been guerrillas and still wore long-sleeved white dresses, black skirts, or baggy slacks. Later I heard that there was only one Chinese woman in that compound. I had known her, Zheng Dongmei. She had served in our division's song-and-dance ensemble and worn a pair of short braids. She was full of life and so cheerful that wherever she was, you could hear her singing and laughing. But she wasn't a good soldier and could pitch a grenade only fourteen yards; in a live throw she got one of her front teeth cut in half by a splinter of shrapnel from a grenade she herself had flung.

From where we were, I could see only a small portion of the women's quarters across a broad dirt road. Beyond their compound was the TB ward, which housed hundreds of consumptives. Somehow tuberculosis was still endemic to Koreans. In the evenings I would stand by the barbed wire and listen to the women singing. Though far away, I could hear their songs clearly because they always sang in chorus. Their voices transported me into reveries. They chanted all kinds of songs, sometimes passionately and sometimes lightheartedly, such as "Spring Is Coming," "Marshal Kim Il Sung," "The Anthem of the Korean People's Army," and "The Anthem of the Chinese People's Volunteers." Later I heard them sing "Defending the Yellow River!," "Solidarity Is Power," "The East Is Red," and some other Chinese revolutionary songs, which Dongmei must have taught them. They also chorused Korean folk songs, whose names and words I couldn't know. I liked those songs best. Contrary to the strident fighting airs, the folk songs sounded gentle and nostalgic, at times almost angelic. One morning I caught sight of two toddlers, a boy and a girl, playing with tin cans and wooden sticks in the women's compound. They looked dirty and wore rags, but they laughed and ran about nimbly. With their mothers jailed here, they too had become POWs.

Not far away from our compound was the First Closure's admission center, where the prisoners were registered and processed. In front of that hut there were dozens of corpses stacked together like firewood. I wondered why the Americans didn't immediately get rid of those nameless bodies, which gave out a fetid odor — made even worse as it combined with the smell of the open-air public latrine. The latrine was fenced with a tarpaulin wall and had four hundred pits in it.

One afternoon as I was limping along the fence, I saw a tall man in the adjacent compound whose large, bony body and shoulders, viewed from the side, looked familiar. He was smoking beyond the four rows of barbed wire. I walked over. His hair was disheveled and his face emaciated, marred by a curved scar; his right forearm was bandaged. My heart began kicking as I recognized him — Commissar Pei!

He turned to face me. His eyes brightened, but he didn't say a word, just smiled. Quietly I stopped before him and said, "How are you, Commi—"

"Shh, I'm Wei Hailong now and used to be a cook. Call me Old Wei."

"Sure, I'll do that in front of others." I had to raise my voice a little because we were about fifteen feet apart.

"Always say you didn't know me until we met here," he said.

"I'll remember that. My name is Feng

Yan now. I told them I was a secretary in an infantry company."

"Good."

While we were talking, we both kept glancing right and left to make sure we were alone. He had been captured a month ago, together with the only three men left with him. To date his identity hadn't been disclosed, though he jokingly said this was just temporary. He was certain somebody would betray him soon, because there were so many prisoners who had seen him as their commissar. I reported to him on my situation. To my surprise, he had heard of my association with Dr. Greene and encouraged me to get along with her so as to obtain information on the outside world. I told him about the Panmunjom talks, of which he had also learned. Though in disguise, he was apparently still a leader here, well informed and full of plans. He wanted me to remain loyal to our country and to pass on to him any news I heard.

To me his words were orders, so I became more at ease during my later meetings with Dr. Greene. I gave some of the paper she had left with me to Commissar Pei, which he needed badly.

About half a month later, Dr. Greene found a lump in my thigh. She felt it with her fingertips for a long while, then told me, "It looks like I should give you another operation."

My heart trembled. "Do you have to?"

"Yes. But it'll be a small procedure."

She let me feel the lump in the back of my left thigh. True enough, it was hard and as large as an egg. She said, "I was worried that the muscle damage was so massive that some extravasated blood might form a lump. At the last operation I cleaned everything, but even so, a lump has now grown inside. If we don't get rid of it in time, it may develop into a tumor. I don't want to leave it to chance."

Knowing that another doctor might not be so willing to help me, I said, "I'll follow your decision."

The morning after the next I had the surgery. And because I lay prone on the table this time, Dr. Greene assigned a male nurse to hold my chin so that I wouldn't suffocate. This time Dr. Thomas again assisted her. He seemed more skilled than before; perhaps I had that impression because I no longer hated him. I didn't wear an ether mask, so I remained conscious the whole time. While Dr. Thomas was giving me stitches, Dr. Greene replaced the nurse and held my chin until the entire procedure was over.

The operation was a complete success. From then on I could walk steadily, though I still needed a crutch for the time being. Whenever Dr. Greene came to check my condition and hand in her homework, I would ask her whether there was new progress in the Panmunjom negotiations, which we knew had run into difficulties. Then I would pass any new information on to Commissar Pei the following afternoon.

Three days after the Spring Festival of 1952, Dr. Greene came into our tent and said gloomily that there would be a group of patients going to Koje Island soon, and that I was on the list. So was my friend Wanlin. She took out a sheet of paper and told me, "I wrote a doctor's note for you. It says you shouldn't do any heavy work at least for half a year. If they want you to work, you can show them this."

I took the note but was nonplussed. All I could bring out was "Dr. Greene, I will remember you for the rest of my life. Thank you for saving my leg!"

"That's a doctor's job." She smiled and went on, "You can keep the pen as a souvenir. Maybe someday I'll go to China to take calligraphy lessons from you again."

I must have looked teary, because she said with genuine feeling, "Don't be upset.

118

We'll meet again. All my friends and former classmates are still in China. They're waiting for me to go back."

She pulled out a large manila envelope and handed it to me. She said, "Remember to give this to the doctor in the camp."

The envelope contained my medical records and x-rays. In a way I wanted to leave the hospital, because I could move around quite well now. Also, our ward had grown spooky lately. A week ago a legless man, a Korean officer, had hanged himself on a tent pole. I couldn't imagine that he could have done that alone — some of his comrades must have given him a hand.

Dr. Greene stood up to leave. As she walked out, both Wanlin and I went to the door and watched her moving away with slightly lurching steps. We shouted, "Thank you, Dr. Greene! We'll remember you. Good-bye."

She turned around and waved at us, then proceeded with her ward rounds. In no time she disappeared beyond the gate guarded by two South Koreans. It was snowing, the wind whistling and howling by turns. Fat snowflakes were fluttering down like swarms of moths.

"I'll miss her," Wanlin said to me and grimaced in an effort to smile.

5. COMPOUND 72 ON KOJE ISLAND

Koje Island lies southwest of Pusan, about twenty-five miles across the sea. In ancient times, it was a place to which criminals and exiles were banished. During the Second World War the Japanese had incarcerated American POWs there. Now the expanded prison site had become the central camp that held the majority of Korean and Chinese captives. On our way to the Pusan dock, I grew more anxious about the trip. Although I was going to join thousands of my countrymen, among whom I might feel less vulnerable, life in that camp would undoubtedly be much harsher than that in the hospital. I was agitated by the thought that the prison officers might ignore Dr. Greene's letter and subject me to hard labor that could reinjure my femur.

Together with over two hundred prisoners, I was herded into a U.S. landing ship, whose coverless interior reminded me of a railroad cargo wagon. Above our heads stretched many horizontal steel bars that would support canvas if it rained. The ship, designed for transporting vehicles and tanks, was too lightly loaded, and as it plowed through the ocean it shuddered without stopping. Some prisoners unbuttoned their jackets and even took off their shoes to sun themselves. The guards didn't bother to interfere. I dozed all the way, leaning against a hot, sweating wall.

We arrived at the island in less than three hours. With a clank the front gate of the ship was let down, and an officer ordered us to disembark. Outside, the sun was glowing on the muddy shore fringed with a white ribbon of salt. A few black fishing boats, their masts tilted and their gray sails half folded, were moored in the silty shallows, and whorls of cooking smoke were rising from them. Under my feet the dark beach was studded with countless tiny holes. As I wondered what they were, a field of crabs, each just the size of a thumb, suddenly appeared at the mouths of the holes. But a moment later they all vanished from sight, retreating into their caves. I couldn't help but marvel at the uniformity of their movement and involuntarily stopped in my tracks. "Get moving!" a tall GI shouted at me.

We started out for the camp in the east. I was tense, unsure how long the march would be. But luckily among us there were several men with injured legs, so we didn't walk fast. Despite limping along, I soon forgot my anxiety, fascinated by the clear streams and the dwarf trees on both sides of the road. The distant hills looked lovely, with pines and cypresses crowded together like clusters of spires. Above a rocky summit a pair of white herons soared beneath the flossy clouds. All the way I said to myself, What a secluded place, ideal for a hermit.

The march took half an hour. On arrival, the Chinese and Korean prisoners were separated and then led toward the sprawling stockade that was the prison camp. There were approximately thirty compounds here. The Chinese went to Compounds 72 and 86 while the Koreans headed for other barracks.

The camp looked immense, divided into rectangular prison yards of various sizes, each surrounded by two rows of barbed wire supported by wooden posts. At every corner of the stockade stood a guard tower, over thirty feet tall. The big compounds were the size of a city block, whereas the small ones were as large as a soccer field. In between the enclosures stood many guard towers too. Wanlin and I were assigned to different compounds. Before we parted, I patted his shoulder and whispered, "Take care of yourself and make it home."

He looked upset and mumbled, "I'll often think of you."

"We'll remain friends."

"Yes, always."

He was led away in a group of more than twenty POWs. His head, half a foot taller than the others, was bobbing a little as he walked away with a swinging gait.

Three GIs frisked my group at the entrance to Compound 72. I had slipped the jade barrette half into my shoe and Julan's snapshot into the envelope containing my medical records, mixing it with the x-rays. A wiry guard, a Hispanic man with a wispy mustache, found the black fountain pen in the envelope. "You don't need this," he said and stuck it into his own breast pocket.

"Please, it's a present from a doctor," I said.

"How can I believe you?" He took the pen out of his pocket and pointed at the tip of its cap. "See this? 'Made in U.S.A.' "

"Give it back to me, please!"

"Why should I? You snatched it off of an American, didn't you?"

"Come on, it's a keepsake from Dr. Greene at Pusan. You can call the hospital and ask her."

"Stop wasting my time. Move on!"

"This is robbery."

"What did you say?" He punched me in the face and blood instantly filled my mouth; one of my front teeth had been knocked loose.

"I'm going to complain to your superiors."

"Oh yeah? Tell them to jail me or shoot me, you Red gook. You stole stuff from our dead."

Some POWs were gathering to watch from inside the compound, amazed that a prisoner dared to argue with a GI. I realized the pen was gone, so I walked away without another word. I wasn't certain whether the guard really believed I had robbed an American soldier of the fountain pen. He might have. I had heard that a Chinese captive was once beaten half to death by some GIs who had found in his cap a wedding band with an American name engraved on it.

Once I was inside the compound, my first impression was that I had returned to the Chinese Nationalist army: everywhere I turned, I saw people wearing the sun emblem of the Nationalist Party. My heart sagged. The Americans were only guarding the entrance and wouldn't set foot in the compound. Everything in here was left in the hands of the prisoners, many of whom had served in Chiang Kai-shek's army. With the help of the men still loyal to the old regime, the pro-Nationalist force had gained complete control. The elected officers among the POWs resembled those in the Nationalist army too, though they wore the same kind of fatigues as the other prisoners, with the same letters *PW* on their sleeves or breast pockets.

The eight thousand inmates had been organized into a regiment that consisted of four battalions, within each of which there were companies, then platoons, and then squads. In theory the leaders at all levels except the chief of the compound had been elected by the prisoners, but in reality most of them had been handpicked by Han Shu, the regimental chief, who had gone through an American training program in Tokyo and had been appointed the head of the compound by our captors. As was the practice elsewhere in the prison system, those who could speak some English usually served as interpreters and spokesmen for their units here.

I was assigned to the Third Company of the First Battalion. The company had about five hundred men and was led by Wang Yong, a former Nationalist army corporal. The First Battalion had a police force, composed of more than two hundred men, who were all POWs themselves. They were directly under the command of Liu Tai-an, the battalion chief. These policemen toted clubs wherever they went. I even saw some of them nap with the weapons held in the crooks of their arms. Whenever I ran into this mob of enforcers, my stomach would lurch.

Though crowded, Compound 72 on the whole was well equipped. It had three pools of water in the front area, a bathhouse, an education center, a large yard for laundry, a giant warehouse, a number of cottages serving as churches, a Buddhist temple, and a mosque. Most inmates were free to go anywhere within the compound, but someone like me who hadn't become a pro-Nationalist yet wasn't allowed to move around freely.

On my first evening in the camp, I ate my dinner, which was a bowl of barley mixed with pinto beans, and then lay down on a straw mat and covered myself with a blanket I'd just been issued. As I was dozing away, Wang Yong came into the tent, roused me, and ordered me to follow the others to the company's office and sign up for going to Taiwan. This meant I must refuse to go home to mainland China. I was shocked, but dared not protest. On the way there, I sidled off to the privy and didn't rejoin the others at the company headquarters afterward, so I avoided putting in my name for refusing repatriation.

At daybreak the next morning, Wang Yong came again and told me to pick up my bowl and belongings and follow him. Together he and I went out into the chilly air. My injured leg was still weak, and I couldn't walk as fast as he did. He slackened his pace a little. He was a thick-boned man, of medium height with bulging eyes. He reminded me of a butcher. He said to me, smiling tightly, "Feng Yan, you look like a well-educated man. To be honest, I like learned fellows. I won't force you to do anything against your heart. But if you're determined to follow the Commies back to the mainland, I must let you suffer some."

I remained silent. True, I had sided with the Communists, but this was only because I wanted to go home. Wang led me to the back of the compound and into the small tent that housed the Fifth Platoon. "All right, from now on you stay with them," he said, then left without giving me another look.

I realized that all the small shabby tents held only the inmates who wanted repatriation. We were obviously in the minority here. The pro-Nationalists, who were determined to go to Taiwan, believed that whoever intended to return to mainland China must be a Communist or a pro-Communist. In fact, most of us wanted to go home not for political reasons at all; our decision was personal. In the front part of the compound stood many rows of large tents with iron structures, all inhabited by the pro-Nationalists, each of whom had a mat for himself. By contrast, over seventy men lived in our small tent, crowded into a space of about nine hundred square feet. In the middle of the room a shallow ditch stretched across the dirt floor to drain out rainwater, and on both sides of the ditch every bit of space was occupied. Worse yet, every two men here had to share a mat made of cornstalk skins.

At night we lined up on the ground like packed fish — every pair of mat mates slept with their heads at opposite ends of their mat so that they wouldn't breathe in each other's faces. Even so, you had to place one of your legs on your mat mate's belly or shoulder; otherwise it would have been impossible for both of you to lie on the mat. During the night the air was so putrid and dense that the door had to remain ajar. As for food, we also got less. At every meal the officers at company headquarters would eat their fill, and the prisoners living in the larger tents could have a full bowl of boiled barley, whereas we each got only half a bowl. At first, although forbidden to get close to the front part of the compound, we could move around our tent. We could chat when basking in the sun; we could visit the other small tents, where we could play cards and chess with the men who wanted to return home. But soon Wang Yong revoked this limited freedom. We were not allowed to visit the other small tents anymore and were even prohibited from leaving our own area. When you wanted to relieve yourself, you had to report to your squad leader first, and sometimes you had to wait until you could go with a group. This kind of maltreatment gradually made some men change their minds and sign up as nonrepatriates so that they could move to the larger, more comfortable tents.

I always slept with my left knee raised at night. My leg hadn't fully healed yet and I was afraid someone might step on it in the dark. On the opposite side of the ditch, there was one man who was a pinwheel sleeper, often pushing and kicking others, who would then shout curses at him. Before I went to sleep I would massage my injured leg and caress the scar.

Once in a while I could still feel the touch of Dr. Greene's fingers on my thigh, the cool, soothing touch that had left a kind of sensation on my skin and muscles. I even fantasized that I would become a doctor someday so that I could operate on patients too. If only I had gone to a medical school instead of a military academy. But that was pure fantasy, just as I used to dream of being an architect who would put up grand buildings in our hometown. My parents hadn't been able to afford to send me to a regular college, so I had attended the military school for free. What made Dr. Greene different from others was that she had treated me with genuine kindness, which must have stemmed not just from her professional training but from real humanity. Whenever I was with her, I had felt her goodness flowing out like water from a fountain, constant and effortless.

In contrast, most of the time when I was with others, including my comrades, I couldn't help but grow vigilant, because there was always some ulterior motive behind every activity and every statement, and I had to take care not to be victimized. Here among my fellow countrymen I felt lonesome and often sat outside the tent alone. If only I could have had a book to read. With nothing to do and without friends, I had become more gloomy. Soon the inmates nicknamed me Stargazer, because I watched the sky a lot and could identify some stars by name.

Depressed and bored, many men in our tent gambled every day. They had no money, so they used cheap cigarettes as stakes. The Americans issued each of us one pack a week, at times two packs a week, which was generous. By comparison, on average an enlisted man in the People's Volunteer Army had barely gotten one pack of cigarettes a month. It was during the first days in Compound 72 that I started to smoke. Initially, after a few puffs I felt woozy, but two packs later I began to enjoy smoking, though it aggravated my coughing. In the daytime our small tent was full of hubbub, so I sat outside whenever it was possible. These men unnerved

131

me and I grew more withdrawn. How I wished Wanlin were here.

The men in the large tents were no better. They too gambled, with even more clamor and fierce squabbles. Some of them had lost everything they had, even their caps, shoes, and underwear. I wasn't sure who had provided them with mah-jongg, perhaps the prison authorities, or perhaps Father Hu, who preached here on Sundays. The gamblers had made card tables themselves, which were just slapdash pieces of carpentry. Without work and with too much free time, the prisoners simply had no other outlet for their energy and distress. The gambling had reduced some of them to insolent louts. Fights broke out time and again. How idleness could foster vices and bring out the worst in a man! If only they had been put to hard labor. Then at least they would have been too tired to behave aggressively.

Another thing upset me: the prisoners often fought over food in the mess lines. The men living in the large tents would eat before those of us from the small tents. The rule was that the daily ration for every prisoner should be 1.15 pounds of grain, but the leaders at all levels in the compound would take the lion's share first. For example, the regimental chief, Han Shu, a fluent English speaker who had been a platoon leader in the Communist army and had capitulated to the Americans without firing a single shot, would eat four dishes and soup at every meal, prepared by his personal cook, who had been seized from a fishing boat on the Yellow Sea. All the company and battalion leaders enjoyed special mess too. As a result, the prisoners who wanted to be repatriated to China could have, at most, half rations. Many men would hurl abuse randomly at the mess lines and wouldn't think twice about using brute force on others. I noticed that the illiterate ones among us were particularly quick-tempered at mealtimes. For a bowl of boiled barley, some of them wouldn't hesitate to knock a tooth out of another man's mouth or to give him a bloody nose. Every day there were at least two fights; sometimes half a dozen. Once the North Korean prisoners in the compound across the front road went on a hunger strike; the Americans left barrels of food at their front gate, but nobody would come out to pick up the rice and stewed radish. Then the camp's executive officer, Captain Lennon, came to ask us to show the Koreans how good this meal tasted.

Shamelessly, two hundred Chinese POWs flocked there, gorging themselves on the lunch, grinning and grunting like animals. I often wondered if some of these men would kill their siblings just for a ladle of boiled soybeans.

I still remember a fight I witnessed one day. At dinner, two men before me in the waiting line suddenly started yelling at each other. "You're behind me!" said a squat man with a Cantonese accent, baring his broad teeth.

"No, I'm in front of you," countered a tall fellow.

"Don't butt in again!"

"Damn it, when did I do that?"

"Right now!"

"Fuck off, okay?" The tall man poked the other in the chest with his fist.

"If you touch me again I'll kill you!"

"So." He poked him once more.

The short fellow lunged forward with his bowl raised in the air to hit the other man's skull. A few men stepped out of the line, restrained him, and pulled him away.

The scene saddened me. Why had they been so pugnacious? There was enough barley for everyone to have half a bowl, and they were not busy and had time to wait. Why did they act like such hoodlums? In private I shared my dismay with a fellow in my platoon, Bai Dajian, and he explained that they had feared the battalion chief, Liu Tai-an, would show up and ruin the meal, so they had wanted to reach the food barrels as quickly as possible.

Bai Dajian told me more about Liu Tai-an. Liu had once been a sergeant in the Nationalist army, but the Communists had captured him in a battle and put him into a logistic unit after a month's reindoctrination. Because he could drive, they gave him a truck. After his division crossed the Yalu River, at the first opportunity he drove three tons of salt fish to the American position and surrendered. Rumor had it that he was sent to Guam for two months' training and then returned to Korea. That was why he was appointed a battalion commander as well as the vice chief of the regiment — to help Han Shu keep order in the compound, since Han was a man of mild disposition and seemed indecisive. Liu Tai-an hated the Communists so much that he often publicly flogged men who wanted to return to Red China. The Americans had adopted a let-alone policy and didn't care what happened in the compounds as long as the POWs remained behind the barbed wire, so Liu ruled this regiment like a police state. Even some GIs called him Little Caesar. Sometimes he would show up at the kitchen at mealtimes with a batch of bodyguards and throw a fistful of sand into a barrel of boiled barley, then snarl at the men in the waiting line, "You're not even worth the food you eat!" Once he even peed into a cauldron of turnip soup in front of everybody. With Liu Tai-an looming in their minds, the inmates here would struggle to get their meals as soon as possible.

Whatever their reasons, the men's fighting upset me. They had once been comrades-in-arms, and many of them would again be comrades after they returned to our homeland. Why should they behave like brutes? When led by the Communists, they had been good soldiers and seemed high-minded and their lives had possessed a purpose, but now they were on the verge of becoming animals. How easily could humanity deteriorate in wretched conditions? How low could an ordinary man fall when he didn't serve a goal larger than himself? Unorganized for honest work or for a meaningful cause, these men were just a mob ruled by the instinct for survival. Sometimes I wondered if there was a

Communist cell among us, because I was positive that some of the prisoners were Party members and supposed to lead these desperate men. Yet all the Communists here kept a low profile, hardly distinguishable from others.

One morning, about three weeks after my arrival at Koje Island, I ran into Chang Ming, the editor of our division's bulletin. At first I wasn't sure if it was he, but then, spotting his bushy eyebrows and catfish mouth, I almost cried out with joy. He saw me too, but we pretended we didn't know each other because there were people around. He was on the other side of the barbed-wire fences, in Compound 71. I squatted down to retie my shoelaces while he stopped to do calisthenics. When everyone had gone out of earshot, we rushed to the fences and started talking excitedly. The first thing he asked me was whether I had signed up to go to Taiwan. "Of course not," I said proudly. He looked four or five years older now, though still robust. His thick lips were cracked. Miraculously, he hadn't been wounded.

Through four rows of barbed wire, he told me that having seen the chaotic state the POWs were in, he and Hao Chaolin had both admitted to the prison authorities that they were officers, so that they could be transferred to Compound 71, a small place holding only about two hundred Chinese officers and staunch Communists. I was surprised to hear that Chaolin had also ended up here. I guessed both of them must have been scared by the unorganized men and the pro-Nationalist force in their former compound.

"But we didn't tell them our true names," he said. "I'm Feng Wen now."

"What a coincidence — my name is Feng Yan!"

"So we sound like siblings now." He laughed — the same carefree laugh of a confident man.

"Did you meet Commissar Pei in Pusan?" I asked.

"He's here too, in Compound 86."

"Really? When did he come?"

"A week ago. He hasn't been exposed yet. We must figure out a way to protect him."

"Do you have regular contact with him?"

"We get instructions from him once in a while."

"What should I do? The men here are like hoodlums, although some of them want to return to China."

"Try to get along with them, I mean

with those who want to go home. Don't remain isolated. We made a terrible mistake last fall. We didn't think much of the leadership in the prison camp. Assuming we'd be returned to China soon, we didn't put a lot of effort into the elections. That's why most positions in the camp are held by the reactionaries."

"All right, I'll try to blend in with them. What else should I do?"

"We'll talk about it later. Our immediate goal is to get the leadership into our hands."

He also told me that there was another compound, Number 70, which held Chinese POWs. All the prisoners in it went out to work at the wharf and construction sites, and there were five hundred of them, all able-bodied. How I envied them! If only I hadn't been wounded. I would love to get out of the camp every day, even if it meant sweating like a coolie.

From that day on Ming and I met regularly, almost every morning. Following his advice, I began to mix with the men in my platoon. From the moment I joined them a month earlier, Bai Dajian had caught my attention. He looked familiar to me, though I wasn't sure if I had met him before. He was twenty-one years old, rather timid, but seemed trustworthy. Unlike others, he wouldn't gamble, never quarreled with anybody, and often sat alone absent-mindedly. As we got to know each other better, I found out that he had actually been my schoolmate at the Huangpu Military Academy, though one year after me. This discovery brought us closer. He had specialized in cavalry but studied at the academy only for a year. When the Communists disbanded our alma mater, he was still a freshman and was later assigned to the Fortieth Army. It turned out that both of us were engaged, so we showed each other photographs of our fiancées. His sweetheart, a nurse in Shenyang City, was an extraordinary beauty with large vivid eyes, a sharp nose, and clear skin, somewhat like a movie starlet. We both admitted that we missed our brides-to-be terribly and once even wept over their pictures.

Dajian had lost two fingers to frostbite. The story of his capture was so horrific that he couldn't tell it without gnashing his teeth. One morning in January 1951, his cavalry company had followed their division commander's Russian jeep to the front. The north wind was screaming, raising snowdrifts on the slopes and across the road, which was slippery and bumpy, rutted by American vehicles the previous fall. Coming out of a mountain pass, the commander spotted some snowmen to his left, about two hundred yards away in the woods. He told the driver to stop, wondering who on earth had found leisure to build snowmen in such a desolate place. He trudged over to the site with his orderly, escorted by a squad of cavalry. To their horror, they found that the figures were actual human beings, frozen to death, some standing, some lying on their backs, and some embracing each other, hardened into statues. They scraped the snow off one man and saw the Chinese Volunteer's uniform; the commander realized these were actually his own soldiers.

A whole battalion, over four hundred men, had perished without being noticed by their higher-ups. The commander began cursing the regimental staff, saying he'd have some of the officers court-martialed. The truth was that these men had been under his command as well, so he ought to have been held responsible too. His orderly identified the body of the battalion commissar, who had been known as an eloquent speaker. The division commander took off his own overcoat and covered the dead officer.

Then he ordered the cavalry company to ship the bodies back to a service center. Dajian and his comrades loaded the corpses on their horses, each pair tied together with a rope and placed over the flanks of a horse. But they could carry only 230 of the dead and would have to return to pick up the rest. They walked the horses back the way they had come, while the division commander continued toward the front.

In the evening the cavalry approached a frozen lake, ready to take a rest. Suddenly a contingent of Australians under the U.N. flag appeared and surrounded them, firing mortars and machine guns and ordering them to surrender. The horsemen, exhausted and having left their Bren guns and 60-millimeter mortars back where they had found the dead, couldn't repel the enemy. They didn't even have their bugle with them. So in just one charge the Australians subdued them and rounded them up. They made the cavalrymen unload the corpses and give all the Mongolian ponies to a South Korean mule train that transported ammunition and medical supplies for the U.N. troops. Then they marched the captives eastward through a chain of mountains for a whole night. The next morning they handed them to the Americans, who herded them onto three trucks, which shipped them to the POW Collection Center in Pusan. It was during the night march that Dajian's left hand had frozen. Later in the camp his index and ring fingers were amputated. A third of his comrades hadn't survived the march, left behind on the mountains and buried by snowdrifts.

"The Communist leaders sent troops to the front without enough winter clothes," Dajian said to me, shaking his round chin and breathing hard. "It's a crime. They used men like beasts of burden, like burning firewood."

Although there was truth in his remark, I dared not say anything about the Communists so openly in our tent. I whispered to him, "Shh, don't talk so loud. Some of them are here."

He was so angry at his former superiors that he often called them miscreants. I was worried about his outspokenness.

6. FATHER WOODWORTH

Sunday mornings provided an opportunity for all the men in the different tents to meet, because Father Hu would preach in Liberty Hall at the Civil Information and Education Center. The hall was a large tent that could seat fifteen hundred people. Over a thousand prisoners would go to Father Hu's sermons, which he delivered in Chinese, though he was from the United States. On the face of it this pudgy man was neutral, kind to everyone; but in reality he hated the Communists and served as a liaison between the pro-Nationalist POWs and the camp authorities. So the Communists were boycotting his Methodist church.

There were other religious groups in the compound too. I chose to go to the Catholic church in a small stone house with a Calvary cross atop it. Father Woodworth preached there on Sundays. I attended his service mainly because I wanted to learn English and also because my mother had been a Catholic when she was a young girl.

Besides, I couldn't afford to offend the Communists by going to Father Hu's service. There were only about forty attendees at Woodworth's sermons, but he didn't look discouraged and spoke just as passionately as if he were addressing a large congregation. For that I admired him more. Woodworth was a lanky man in his mid-forties, with greenish eyes and a wrinkled but intelligent face. His legs were so long that some prisoners called him the Drawing Compasses. He was a chaplain, in uniform like an officer.

He had noticed me from my first appearance at the church, probably because I was attentive when he was speaking. Most of the audience, not knowing English, couldn't make out what he said, and my facial expressions must have shown that I followed him. One day after the sermon, as he was taking off his surplice, I went up to him and said, "Father Woodworth, may I ask you a favor?"

"How can I help you?" he said.

"Can I have a copy of the Bible? I want to study it on weekdays."

"You can understand it in English?"

"Yes."

His eyes gleamed. "All right, I will have it delivered to you. Put down your name and unit number here."

He opened his spiral-bound notebook, in which I wrote down the information. Although I had said I could understand the Bible, I wasn't very sure of my English. Ideally I should have had a dictionary. I had lost everything when I was taken captive, including my dictionary and the dog-eared *Uncle Tom's Cabin*. Whatever kind of book the Bible was, it was at least something I could read.

Among Father Woodworth's forty attendees, a number of them seemed attached to him, probably because they intended to seek his protection, though some might truly have been drawn by his eloquent manner and his deep, resonant voice. These men were better educated than most prisoners, and the majority of them were pro-Nationalists. However, none of them knew English well enough to read the Bible or talk with Woodworth, so I must have been a rarity to him.

On Thursday afternoon the company's orderly came to our tent and summoned me to headquarters. Off I set for the office, which was just a two-room hut, with the Nationalist flag and the Star-Spangled Banner flying above its door. The company leader, Wang Yong, was sitting at his desk when I stepped in. He motioned for me to take a seat in front of him and then patted an opened parcel on the desktop. Without any preliminaries he said, "So, you're a well-learned man, Feng Yan. You know foreign words, eh?"

"Yes, I can read English."

He poured a splash of saki into a coffee mug and handed it to me. "Have some," he said.

"I don't drink, thanks."

"Wow, a clean man," he sneered.

He then offered me a cigarette, which I accepted. I wondered what he had up his sleeve. He said with narrowed eyes, "I tell you what, the minute you walked into this company, I could see that you're not an ordinary fish."

"Thank you for your attention." I pretended to take his words as a compliment.

"What I mean is you were an officer, not an enlisted man like you claimed."

"I was just a secretary, in the Third Company of the 539th Regiment."

"Come on, stop trying to hoodwink this old man. I served in both the White Army and the Red Army. I met hundreds of men and know you must've been somebody. I strongly urge you to go to Taiwan with us and not to follow the Commies. One of these days Generalissimo Chiang's forces will sweep away all the Reds and recapture the mainland. It's time for you to decide which side to take, and you better decide wisely."

"Chief Wang," I said in earnest, "to be honest, I'm not a Communist. The reason I cannot sign up for Taiwan is that I have an old mother at home. She's alone and I'm her only child. My father died long ago."

"You see, the Commies would even recruit an only son like yourself. They use men like ammo. Damn them, in just one battle with a British battalion last spring, our division lost over a thousand men. So much blood flowed on a hill slope that the next morning hundreds of rooks flew around with blood-stained wings. Still, the higher-ups called it a victory, because we had overrun the enemy's position in the end."

"That's true," I agreed. "I never thought so many Chinese would be buried in Korea." His words conjured up the horrible image I hadn't been able to shake off — that the war was an enormous furnace fed by the bodies of soldiers.

"Think about what I just said, Feng Yan. I won't force you, brother, but honest and true, you don't have a lot of time to shilly-shally anymore — everybody will have to decide soon."

"I'll think it over."

"Okay, let me know once you're done thinking. Now you can go and take this with you." He pointed at the parcel wrapped in kraft paper.

I dared not offend him. If he took a dislike to me, he could easily destroy me. Already he'd had a number of men taken to company headquarters and forced them to sign an anti-Communist vow, which he then posted publicly. By so doing, he had cut off those men's route of retreat to China, where punishment from now on would await them; thus he coerced them into becoming nonrepatriates. These days Wang was busy promoting a tattoo movement among the pro-Nationalist prisoners, who volunteered to have words and drawings marked on their arms, chests, bellies, and even foreheads. Technically this primitive procedure wasn't painful — with a writing brush they inscribed words or a picture on a man and then used a needle to puncture the skin stained with black ink. The words were mainly slogans, such as "Fight Red Bandits to Death!," "Oppose Russia and Marx!," "Capture Mao Zedong Alive!," "Loyal to Nationalism!," "Root

Out Communism!" The drawings included a radiant sun representing the Nationalist emblem, a knife plunged into a hairy pig that symbolized Mao, a boat bound for the Treasure Island — Taiwan. The tattooed men often walked around with their upper bodies naked to show off the words and drawings, which did intimidate many of us.

On the way back to my tent, I was delighted to see a brand-new copy of the Holy Bible in the parcel. It was the American Standard Version, leather-bound, with Jesus' words in red and a concise concordance at its back. Since it was too noisy inside the tent, I sat outside and began reading Genesis. The words made me slightly giddy, not because of the meaning of the Scripture but simply because I was reading something that wasn't just propaganda. I hadn't come across a real book for half a year; the deprivation had whetted my appetite. The English of the Bible was not difficult and I seldom came across a new word. This meant that from now on I could read some pages every day!

The next morning I met Ming again. I told him that I had been pressed to go to Taiwan and that soon everybody would have to make up his mind once and for all.

He said he had also heard this. In fact, in Compound 76, which held Korean prisoners, an operation was already in the works. It was called "the screening," at which every POW had to declare formally where he would like to go, the Koreans to North Korea or South Korea and the Chinese to mainland China or Taiwan. Ming also said that a few of our former comrades had been transferred to the company where Commissar Pei was now, because the Communists had regained power in the Third Battalion of Compound 86. Ming might go there soon, and the Communist leaders had offered the First Battalion of my regiment to exchange a pro-Nationalist for me so that I could join my comrades in Compound 86, but Wang Yong wouldn't let me go. This last piece of information unnerved me. Why would Wang keep me in his clutches? How could I be useful to him? Then it flashed through my mind that both the Communists and the pro-Nationalists were interested in me because I knew English.

In addition to preaching, Father Woodworth also taught the prisoners hymns at the education center on Wednesday afternoons. A burly Korean man played the accordion to provide music for him. More people attended the singing sessions than the sermons, perhaps just for the fun of it. Few of them, however, understood the contents of the songs; it was the music that attracted them. I liked the hymns very much. Whenever I heard the joyous, melodious tunes, my heart would leap. Regardless of the uncanny words about God and Christ, the music was the only beautiful thing in this hellish place. So more and more people went to learn to sing hymns.

On the last Wednesday in March, when the singing session was over, Father Woodworth called to me. Agitated, I walked up to him. He said in a sonorous voice, "I also want to ask you a favor, Mr. Feng."

A few inmates turned around to look at me while trooping out of the classroom, because usually a prisoner wasn't addressed as "Mister" by our captors. "Sure, what is it you want me to do?" I asked.

Fingering the lanyard of his pince-nez, Father Woodworth said, "Do you think you can put some of the hymns into Chinese?"

"I don't feel I can translate them well because I really don't know much about music. Even though I put the words into Chinese, they may be hard to sing."

"I don't mean to ask you to translate them into verse like the original. Just do a rough translation so that we can read it to the others before they learn how to sing them. I reckon that if they know the general meaning of a hymn, they can sing it better, don't you think?"

"That's true."

He unzipped his scuffed leather briefcase and took out a new notebook, a pencil, and some loose pages from a hymnal. "You can use these," he said.

I was moved and promised, "I'll do my best."

For a whole week I worked on the hymns, which were not difficult to translate — I was supposed to provide merely the gist of each song. From the next Wednesday on, I would sit in the front row when Father Woodworth taught us the hymns. Before we started singing he'd call to me, saying, "Number seven, 'There's a Wideness in God's Mercy,' " or "Number nine, 'Rock of Ages, Cleft for Me.' " I would stand up, turn to the audience, and read out my Chinese translation. My assistance to the chaplain drew people's attention in the compound. In the prison camp every company had at least one interpreter, who in most cases just knew a few words of English. So it was said that I

spoke English better than any of those interpreters, perhaps because I had talked with
Father Woodworth in front of hundreds of
men without being outwardly nervous.

I broke the pencil in half and gave the
part without the eraser to Ming when we
met the next Tuesday. He was excited to
have it and said, "I'll pass this on to Commissar Pei. We do need stationery badly.
He'll be delighted to see this."

"How's he doing?"

"So far he's okay."

"Give him my greetings."

"I will. By the way, I've heard you're
busy helping Woodworth, right?"

"Yes, it was he who gave me the pencil.
He wanted me to translate some hymns for
him."

Ming knitted his thick eyebrows. "You
did that, didn't you?"

"Yes."

"You're too naive, Yuan. According to
our information, Woodworth is also involved in persecuting our comrades, just
like Priest Hu. You must be careful."

"Really? He seems kindhearted."

"Only in appearance. He's behind many
things. In fact, Commissar Pei wasn't very
happy when he heard you were helping
Woodworth."

"I don't see why he should be unhappy." I was surprised that Pei knew so much about my activities.

"Religion is just spiritual opium. Woodworth means to weaken our men's resolve to fight."

"Perhaps he can help us."

"No. Never reveal anything to him. Be careful. He's not our friend."

"Okay."

"I want you to promise me not to tell him anything. This is a matter of principle."

"All right, I promise."

Some inmates were strolling nearby and we dared not remain together too long, so we parted company.

Ming's words made me think a good deal, though I wasn't convinced that Father Woodworth had been involved in persecuting the prisoners who wanted to repatriate. On Wednesday afternoon, after the singing session, while the audience was filing out of the hall, I went up to Woodworth and asked him about the meaning of "communion" in the line "the new community of love in Christ's communion." He explained to me the sacrament at which people drink wine and eat bread. He said he would have included that part in the service on Sundays, but most of us were not Christians, so it was unnecessary. I couldn't understand the Eucharist fully, never having attended one. Seeing that I was still bemused, he added, "Communion also means fraternity. Put it like that."

As we walked toward the door, I said again, "Father Woodworth, I have had a question on my mind for a long time."

"You can let me know it if you wish."

"You see, according to the teaching of the Bible, all the prisoners here are sinners, so we should be equal. Why are some inmates more privileged than others?"

We were now in the open air, which was warm with the feel of spring. He stopped short and said, "What do you mean exactly? Be more specific. There's something behind your question."

I pointed at the large tents and then at the small ones. "People are not treated equally here. The men living at the back are not even given their share of food."

"And you're one of them?"

"Yes."

"I'm sorry, but this is the way things should be done."

"Why?"

"Because most of you are Communists.

To me and to my God, Communism is evil."

"But most of us are not Communists at all. We stay with them mainly because we want to go home. As sons, we have our duty to our parents. Some men are husbands and fathers and ought to return to their families."

"I can understand it's a tough choice, but life is full of choices."

"For most of us there's no choice."

"Mr. Feng, you should know there are different kinds of duties. The highest kind is your duty to God and to your own soul."

"But we haven't been converted yet. Do you think those who are going to Taiwan are Christians?" There was an angry edge in my voice now.

"Listen, I'm not just a clergyman but also a soldier. I came with both the book and the sword."

Realizing the argument was getting nowhere, I muttered, "I thought you might help us because we're all fellow sufferers."

"Every man here can choose his own way of suffering."

He straightened his back and walked away. I had thought of asking him, "Then why do you teach us the hymns that praise the wideness of God's mercy?" But I didn't bring that out. Probably he taught us just to earn his salary and to convert a few pagans. My conversation with him upset me profoundly and shattered my illusion that there might be shelter in God's bosom for every person. Now I was inclined to believe what Ming had told me.

I mentioned to Bai Dajian my exchange of words with Father Woodworth. He and I were very close now, friends. I treated him like a younger brother, because he respected me and was two years my junior. "Woodworth isn't a kind man," he assured me, and his large eyes flashed.

"How do you know?" I was surprised by the certainty in his voice.

"The other day when they flogged a man with water-whips in the front yard, Woodworth happened to be passing by. The man cried, 'Father, Father, help me! Save me!' But Woodworth gave him a look, then walked away without a word. One of the hooligans told the man, 'Call him God, then he'll sure come back and save your hide.' They all cracked up."

The water-whip was a punishment invented by the pro-Nationalists here. They would tie a man to a stake and flog him with bands of canvas soaked in a bucket of water. The flogging would continue until the whole bucketful was used up.

Although Woodworth had never punished any inmate publicly, Dajian's account of his indifference disappointed me. It was rumored that he had even presented a dagger to Liu Tai-an, the chief of our battalion. I had seen the knife with a white jade handle, which Liu often put against an inmate's throat.

Soon Dajian and I both stopped attending the sermons and the singing sessions, though I still read the Bible every day as a way to improve my English.

7. BETRAYAL

At our next meeting Ming told me that someone had betrayed Commissar Pei. Surprised, I refrained from asking him to inform Pei that I had quit Woodworth's sermons and singing sessions. "There must be a traitor," Ming said. "Have you heard of Ding Wanlin, who was the bugler in our division's Guards Company?"

"Yes. He's a friend of mine, a good, humble man. He nursed me in the hospital. Why do you ask?"

"The Americans took him away four days ago, interrogated him, and returned him to his tent the day before yesterday. His face was battered, this big." Ming raised both hands around his head showing a doubled size.

"He's still going to repatriate, right?" I asked.

"Yes. But two days ago, just an hour after he was sent back, some GIs went to take Commissar Pei away."

"Where did they take him?"

"First to the Second Battalion's headquarters in Compound 86. They interrogated him there for a whole night. Afterward they put him into the water jail, and now he's in solitary confinement."

"So you think Wanlin informed on him?"

"He's a suspect."

"How could he be a traitor? If he betrayed Commissar Pei, why would he still want to go back to China? It doesn't make any sense."

"I'm just saying he's one of the suspects. Don't worry." Ming kept clicking the heels of his high-top shoes, which were the same kind worn by GIs. But his pair didn't look like mates, one with its tongue hanging inside out.

I described my conversation with Woodworth. Ming was pleased to hear that I had no contact with the chaplain anymore.

It was a cold morning, the ragged grass crusted with hoarfrost and the north wind billowing, and nobody basked in the sun outside the tents, so we two talked longer than usual. He told me how the enemy had treated Commissar Pei. Pei had been interrogated by Frederick Johnson, an American colonel known in the camp as the

Sinologist, because he spoke standard Mandarin and had a scholarly demeanor, never losing his temper or showing his true emotions. Johnson had been a college professor in Virginia before the war. In this prison camp he often had copies of ancient Chinese classics delivered to important POWs as a gesture of "goodwill." But we knew all along that he must have a special mission here. Now he had finally come to the forefront, personally interrogating Commissar Pei. Yet no matter how hard they pressed him, Pei refused to admit his true identity, insisting he had been a cook. This was futile because the enemy had a file on him. Owing to his high rank, they didn't physically abuse him at this point. After the interrogation he was put into a single-room hut. Toward the evening five Chinese men came, pulling a hand truck loaded with a huge earthen vat, and they put the vessel in his room. Then another three men arrived, each carrying two buckets of hot water, which they poured into the vat. Following them was another man, who held a folded towel and a change of underclothes and a shirt. The head of this group told Pei, "Phew, you don't know how dirty you are. You stink like a wild goat. Colonel Johnson wants you to take a bath."

"I don't need a bath," Pei said.

"You're ordered to get into the water," said the leader, a small rotund man.

"Who gave me the order?"

"Colonel Johnson."

"Tell him I don't take orders from him."

"Screw you! You still think you're a bigwig here, eh?" With a wave of his hand the man told the others, "Dip him into the water and scrub him!"

They hauled Pei to the vat, began tearing off his clothes, and tried to heave him up and drop him into the steaming water. But the commissar gripped the rim of the vessel and wouldn't let go, shouting, "My soul's clean, I don't need a bath!"

They began slapping him, kicking his buttocks, striking him with the shoulder poles, and pulling his hair. Still he wouldn't give in. In the midst of the scuffle an American sergeant arrived and helped them tear off Commissar Pei's pants. Pei turned his head and bit the GI's hand. This brought more blows on him; yet he wouldn't budge, clasping the rim of the vat like a life ring. He kept shouting, "Even if you kill me, I won't bathe myself. Hit me, yes come on, see if your granddad will ever use this bath!"

After another round of punching and

kicking, they gave up and decided to take the vat away. Two men scooped the water back into the buckets, all the while cursing Pei, saying he was a mean ass, an expert in histrionics. One of them stabbed his finger at him and said, "We spent a whole afternoon preparing this bath for you. We should've boiled you alive instead."

The enemy took Pei's blustery response to the bath for some kind of hydrophobia, so the next afternoon they put him into the water prison, which was molded after those built by the Japanese army. I had seen a few such cells in China; the one here was a similar type. It was in a cellar set half underground, in which there were two pools, a large one and a small one, both encircled by barbed wire attached to steel bars and containing three feet of murky, foul water. The small pool was for solitary confinement, whereas the large one could hold five people at a time. In either pool you had to remain on your feet constantly. Eventually you were too sleepy to stand up, fell on the barbed wire, and had your flesh torn. In winter the cold water soaked you to the bones and made you shiver with a livid face; in summer insects bit you without cease and your skin began to rot within half a day. Usually a regular POW was put in the larger pool for five or six hours at a stretch, but Commissar Pei was jailed in the small pool for a whole night. They moved him out only after he tried to drown himself. The next day they resumed interrogating him. However hard they pumped him, he wasn't responsive and often fell asleep, having to be kicked again and again to remain awake. One of the officers threatened to send him to the torture chamber, but Pei replied, "Why not take me to the execution ground? I don't care, I've had enough." Convinced that they could get nothing from him, they put him away in solitary confinement.

In the art of inflicting pain, the Chinese and the Koreans were much more expert than the Americans. When GIs beat you, they would kick and hit you, and they would break your ribs or smash your face, but they seldom tortured you in an elaborate way. This isn't to say that they were not cruel. They did burn some inmates with cigarettes and even tied a man up with electric wire and then cranked a generator. But the Chinese prisoners, especially some of the pro-Nationalist men, were masterful in corporal punishment and even took great pleasure in inflicting pain on others. They knocked your anklebones with a special stick that had a knurl on its end; they shoved a water nozzle into an inmate's anus and then turned on the hydrant (one man was killed this way); they tied your hands up and rubbed chili powder into your eyes; they forced you to kneel on sharp-edged opened cans; they slashed your flesh with a knife and then put salt on the wounds, saying this was a way to prevent infection; they sharpened matches and inserted them under your fingernails, then lit the other ends; they kept you upside down in an empty vat while scratching your soles with brushes; they tied you to a bench and filled your stomach with chili water; they tore off your clothes and put you into an oil drum containing broken beer bottles, then sealed the drum and rolled it around. In contrast to the pro-Nationalists, the Communists were less creative and more blunt. If you were in their way, they either beat you half to death to teach you a lesson or just killed you. They would knock you down and drop a sandbag on the back of your head to smother you. They did everything secretly, perhaps because they were in the minority and had less power in the camp.

One morning, about a week after Commissar Pei's torture, a party of prisoners was dispatched to load rocks onto trucks at a quarry, which was just a mile to the north. The men of our compound were sometimes detailed to do urgent jobs at the wharf and nearby construction sites, usually at a moment's notice. Although escorted by South Korean guards, who were rougher with us than the GIs were, we enjoyed leaving the camp to work; it gave us the feeling of a change and some freedom. Though my leg couldn't stand heavy weight yet, I had begged our company chief, Wang Yong, to let me go out once in a while. By now I felt I was strong enough to do some light work and had grown restless, eager to test my leg. Wang had said there was no job that suited me and that he ought to follow the doctor's instructions and not to count me as a worker, but today somehow I was included in the group heading out. I was glad for this opportunity. To be fair, Wang had treated me decently, not in the way he handled the other prisoners who wouldn't follow him to Taiwan. To date I had never been made to do anything against my will, and I didn't even have to ask permission if I wanted to go to another tent within our compound. Wang allowed me to run slowly in the yard so that I could build up the strength of my injured leg, though with our poor diet I didn't have the energy to exercise every day. Several times he had invited me to share food (mainly bread, canned fruits, and sausages) and a drink with him. I did join him in his office, but I wouldn't stay more than half an hour. I would accept only a cigarette or a candy he offered me. I hadn't touched any of his alcohol or food, though I was very much tempted.

The front gate was opened and we started out for the quarry. It was a warm day, the whitish sky a little overcast. On the roadside, grass sprouted here and there like tiny scissor blades. The rice paddies, deserted by the villagers who had been forced to leave the island to make room for the prison camp, were coated with a layer of algae. Some mallards were busy eating insects and plants in the fields. The air smelled of manure, stinging my nostrils. I was excited, nervous as well, unsure if I could work normally. As we were rounding the southern corner of the prison stockade, the procession suddenly grew disordered; several men turned their heads to the barbed-wire fence and whispered, "Someone's dead." A guard shouted *Kasseyo!* ("Move!"), but we stopped to watch.

There on a thick fence post hung a man, bony and bareheaded. His tongue fell out all the way to his chest. One of his sleeves was missing and displayed his bruised arm, whose blood vessels and tendons were visible under the yellow skin. As I lifted my eyes to gaze at the face closely, I recognized him — Wanlin! I collapsed in a swoon.

Two men helped me to my feet. Heedless of the orders a guard was shouting, I rushed toward the dead man, unable to reach him because of the fence between us. I burst into tears. "He was my friend. He nursed me in the hospital!" I kept telling them.

Nobody tried to hold me back. Instead, they watched in silence, a few men lowered their eyes, and some sighed. They respected anyone who cherished friendship and mourned the dead with abandon, especially in the presence of many people. The four guards reassembled the fifty inmates and the whole team continued on their way, leaving me behind alone. The Korean sergeant in charge had ordered me to rejoin them at the quarry, which was already in sight, about seven hundred yards to the north. The reason I had suddenly given way to my emotions was complicated. I felt betrayed. I knew that the Communists must have masterminded the murder, but I doubted that Wanlin had been a traitor. Even if, under torture, he had revealed Commissar Pei's true identity, they didn't have to kill him. He was a good man with a kind, innocent heart and would never hurt anybody on purpose. The Communists must have meant to make an example of him.

I observed Wanlin again. His bluish face was slashed and even his eyelids were swollen. There was no doubt that they had beaten him up before hanging him. His hands were bound from behind, and his bare feet, on which bluebottles were crawling and feeding on blood clots, swayed a little.

About fifteen minutes later I resumed my trip to the quarry. Now I was alone, free to go anywhere I chose. None of the guards had bothered to stay with me, not in the least afraid that I might escape. In fact, the Chinese POWs, once outside the prison camp, had always been docile, so there was little guarding for the GIs and the South Koreans to do. A few months ago a trainload of Chinese captives had arrived at Pusan from the front without a single guard on it, accompanied only by an

American doctor. The truth was that most Chinese were so gregarious and so dependent on one another that very few of us tried to get away. We could not endure the loneliness. We believed that as long as we stayed together, we would be less vulnerable. Unable to speak Korean, we had no idea where to get food or how to disguise ourselves. So even though we talked a good deal about escaping, few of us could summon up the courage to put the idea into action individually. By contrast, the North Korean prisoners wouldn't think twice about running away whenever an opportunity came up. That was why they were seldom allowed to work outside their compounds. Like any ordinary Chinese, I was also afflicted with timidity, so I dared not steal away.

I walked slowly toward the quarry near the seaside, my mind laden with questions and grief over my friend's death. Passing Compound 81, I saw the North Korean prisoners doing morning drill; they were shouting slogans as they marched. Some of them carried thick bamboo poles whose ends had been cut on the slant, pointed like javelins; some held wooden sticks and pitchforks; a few shouldered spades sharpened into halberds; the four men at the front of the column toted aluminum spears made from stretcher poles. They were so spirited that they didn't look like prisoners at all, more like a detachment of militia. No wonder Ming had told me that the Koreans were much better organized than we. Their secret force had infiltrated the camp and controlled many parts of it. I had heard that most compounds holding Korean inmates had a smithy and a security unit of hundreds of men armed with self-made weapons. Commissar Pei had once instructed us to learn from the Korean comrades, who had demonstrated more mettle.

But we were in a situation different from theirs. Besides having no difficulty in communicating with the civilians, they had secret contact with the guerrillas who operated in the mountains. Even though many Koje inhabitants had been removed elsewhere, there were still numerous prostitutes around, who were indispensable to the GIs. These women kept the channel of communication open between the Korean POWs and the guerrillas. Moreover, some of the South Korean guards served as agents for the North. As a result, the Korean prisoners had become rather at home here, even more so than the Americans.

When I arrived at the quarry, the work was well under way. Two trucks were being loaded while the other ones had left. My fellow inmates knew I had a bad leg and was in mourning, so they let me carry smaller pieces of granite. They also told me not to step on the rocks, which were slippery. Yet whenever I lifted a rock, I felt a numbing pain in my thigh, as though I was about to collapse. I regretted having asked for such hard labor, fearful that I might snap my femur. Some of the boulders were too large for two men to lift, so a thick board was leaned against the back of a truck, and several prisoners together pushed a giant rock from behind while with a jute rope another four men pulled it upward from within the back of the vehicle. The boulder went up little by little until it got settled in a corner on the truck. I couldn't help but marvel at the men's strength. If only I were as strong.

Fortunately the shipment was small, and we finished the loading in an hour and a half. Then twelve men were assigned to go with the two trucks, six on each, to unload the rocks at a construction site. The rest of us were allowed to stay on the beach to have a smoke. This was the best reward for the work, something that made you feel a little like a free man. I lay down with my back against a large boulder and closed my eyes, inhaling the sea air deeply while my mind again turned to my friend's mutilated body. Tears stung my lids and cheeks.

A few barefoot boys loitered around us, each carrying a shoeshine box with a canvas strap across his shoulder. Their calves, mud-spattered, were as thin as sugarcane. They accosted the guards but left us alone, knowing we had no money. Annoyed, a Korean soldier yelled at them, *"Carra! Carra!"* That probably meant "Go away." Meanwhile, the prisoners just lolled about, enjoying the fishy air and watching the boats on the sea.

8. A DINNER

"Why did they kill Ding Wanlin?" I asked Ming when we met the next morning.

He was taken aback, then forced a smile that creased his face. "He betrayed Commissar Pei," he muttered.

"How could you be so sure it was he?"

"We analyzed all the suspects and concluded that he must've been the one."

"Who are the 'we' you're talking about?"

"I can't tell you that, Yuan. I know Ding Wanlin was your friend. I'm sorry."

"He was tortured by the enemy. Why didn't you take his suffering into account? Who wouldn't have cracked under that kind of torture? You should've at least given him a chance."

"Yuan, I wasn't involved in making the decision. It was decided by the Party. Our struggle here is a matter of life or death. How could we let anyone betray us with impunity? If we don't stop this now, there'll be more traitors."

"Who represents the Party here?"

175

"I can't tell you."

"Then why do you bother to meet me?"

"Because we're friends. Frankly, I don't feel comfortable about some decisions made by the Party either. We're both college graduates and can understand each other better. But forgive me, you're not a Party member yet, so I can't tell you everything."

The honest look in his broad eyes mollified me a little. He went on to say I should be careful because the screening would take place soon, at which every prisoner would have to decide whether to return to mainland China. The Party leaders predicted that violence might flare up before and during the screening; therefore all the comrades must unite and help one another.

From our conversation I gathered there must be a Party committee in the camp. Very likely Commissar Pei headed it, since he was the highest-ranking officer caught by the enemy. But I wasn't sure whether it was he who had issued Wanlin's death warrant, because he, in solitary confinement, might not have been in contact with others. Ming had mentioned they were trying hard, but so far in vain, to communicate with him, so there must have been a group of Party members functioning as a leading body here.

Two days later, on the evening of March 26, 1952, I was summoned to our company's office. When I stepped into the hut, I heard noises in the inner room, in which some people were gathered. They didn't raise their voices, but I could smell alcohol and hear the clink of tableware. Wang Yong, the company chief, sitting at his desk alone, beckoned me to sit down. In front of him stood a mug of steaming cocoa, whose rich scent aroused a pang in my stomach. With a smile on his lumpy face he said, "Brother Feng, we don't have a lot of time to play this game anymore. Tell me who you were."

"I was just a company secretary."

"Stop faking. We know you enrolled at the Huangpu Military Academy. Am I right? Ha-ha, got you." He tossed his head and chortled.

Flustered, I remained silent, wondering where he had obtained this information. Did Wanlin betray me too? Unlikely. I couldn't have been so important as to constitute a question for him in the interrogation. I scrambled to say, "How can you prove that? I never went to college."

"Then how come you know English?"

"I learned it from a missionary."

"Come on, stop pulling this old man's leg. I can tell you how I came to know your background. One of our cooks used to work in the kitchen at your academy. He recognized your face but didn't know your name. He was positive you studied at the Huangpu. See, I'm fair and square with you."

I didn't know what to say and kept my eyes fixed on the warped desktop.

He went on, "Brother Feng, I like you a lot. You're such an innocent, good-looking man that I bet you haven't slept with a woman yet. Why should you tie yourself to the Commies? Most of them may never make it back alive. It's not worth dying for them and being buried in this rotten appendix of northeast Asia."

That was the first time I had heard that expression used to describe Korea. Somewhat amused, I said honestly, "I'm not a Communist, Chief Wang, but I have to go home. I have a sick old mother and a fiancée on the mainland." I took the snapshot of Julan out of my pocket and showed it to him.

He glanced at it, apparently unimpressed, and said, "We all have parents and siblings in China, but a real man should set up his home where his heart is. As for your woman, what you said doesn't hold water."

"How come?"

"I served in the Communist army and know their rules. You're not allowed to live with your woman until you reach the rank of battalion commander. When will you ever be qualified for that? Can you stand that kind of separation from her? Remember when you were at the Huangpu Academy and could pick a girl anytime you liked? This is a big difference, isn't it?"

"My fiancée is a college student in Chengdu City where my division stayed, so we can live close to each other even if I'm not an officer."

"My, you're so naive and single-minded. Your division was already liquidated by the Americans. It doesn't exist anymore. How can you go back to Chengdu? And with whom?"

A sharp pang compressed my chest, but I managed to say, "I'm engaged and obligated to go home."

"Forget about that, brother. There're lots of pretty women in Taiwan. I promise you that once we get there, I'll take you to a pleasure house at my expense, and you'll be so happy that you'll forget where your home is." He paused as though having

..aught himself. "I'm sorry," he said. "You know I'm not a gentleman and can express myself only in a crude way. In fact, I never went to middle school and never read a book in my whole life. I shouldn't have used those coarse words just now, but I meant good."

"If this is why you had me here, I'm grateful, chief. Can I leave now?"

"Wait a second, we haven't gotten to the real business yet." He lurched up and came around the desk while saying, "I'd like to invite you to dinner this evening so we can chat a bit more."

Without waiting for my agreement, he clutched my elbow and took me into the inner room, where seven men were gathered, all apparently his underlings and buddies. The moment we stepped in, applause broke out. "Welcome, Officer Feng," one of them addressed me. Then the others greeted me respectfully too, as though I were their superior. Obviously they all knew I had been a cadet at the Huangpu Academy.

The air in here was acrid, gray with tobacco smoke. Five tall lamps stood on the dirt floor, the harsh light casting gigantic human shadows on the gray walls. Apparently they had arranged this dinner for me.

The high-wattage lamps were intended to keep the room warm. On the round table in front of the men were four courses — a basin of fried squid, a pot of sautéed cabbage with dried clams, a mixing bowl of kimchee, and a roast pork shoulder, which must have weighed at least fifteen pounds, in a rectangular iron pan. Beside the dishes stood a jar of wheat liquor and two bottles of brandy; there was also an aluminum washbasin containing rice covered with a napless towel. The tableware was assorted: bowls and plates of different sizes and colors, army mugs, coffee cups, knives, forks, spoons, and chopsticks. I was somewhat overwhelmed by the sight of the copious dinner, from which I had to force my eyes away. This was the first abundant meal I had seen in a year. Where did they get so much good stuff? Small wonder many prisoners complained that their leaders engaged in graft.

Wang Yong announced: "Today we got together here for two purposes. Number one, to let our brothers get to know each other better. Number two, to celebrate the good news that we're going to depart for the Free World soon!"

They all applauded and I also clapped. Then they began talking about what

.aiwan was like and how to restart their lives there. At this point most of them were just drinking, and nobody seemed eager to start eating, though I noticed some of them stealing glances at the pork shoulder. I sipped the brandy in a mug, wondering what I should do — stay or leave? I knew the risk of being here: if one of them took a photo of me at this table, I would be done for, because they could publicize it as evidence of my collaboration with them. Then the Communists would surely punish me. Then again, I doubted if they had a camera.

"Officer Feng," a man with a smooth oval face asked me, "are you going to Taiwan with us?"

"No," I said calmly as all eyes turned to me.

"Then to the U.S.A.?"

"That country doesn't take in Chinese prisoners like us, you know that."

"Where will you go then?"

"Back to the mainland."

"Why? I don't understand. Why are you so loyal to the Reds? What can you get from them?"

"Officer Feng," a freckled man put in, "don't miss the boat. If you don't go with us this time, you'll kick yourself for the rest of your life."

"Come on," chimed in another man, "think about it, Officer Feng. How many men graduated from the Huangpu Military Academy? And how many are still alive after all the battles with the Red Bandits? You'll be a treasure to the Nationalists once you reach Taiwan. Generalissimo Chiang always treats the graduates from the Huangpu like his own sons and grandsons. You'll have a great future if you follow us."

"You may be right," I said, "but I have an old mother at home. I can't abandon her."

Wang Yong said to them, "All right, we just drink and eat today, no more politics. Let's chat about friendship and something happy, no other irrelevant topics." He poured a cup of wheat liquor for me. "Brother Feng, I know you usually don't drink, but this may be our last gathering here. At the least you should take a drop to acknowledge our brotherhood."

He looked so sincere, even humble, that I lifted the cup and took a swallow.

"Drink up!" urged a voice.

"Glass dry!"

"Yes, down it like a man."

Some of them were draining their bowls and mugs while the others attacked the

..shes. I stood up and said, "Please forgive me, I can't stay any longer."

"No, you haven't drunk from my bowl yet," said the oval-faced man, already tipsy.

"You can't go!" A beefy man jumped to his feet, grabbed the front of my jacket, and pulled a dagger out of his belt. He placed it at my throat. Then another man punched me in the face and I fell backward on the floor.

Wang Yong helped me up. He turned and slapped the beefy man, ordering, "Put that thing back, you brute. You're not drunk yet."

More incensed now, the man stamped his feet, brandishing the dagger. He yelled, "Feng Yan, you've never appreciated our elder brother's kindness! You look down on every one of us. Who are you anyway? You're just a fart bag from the Huangpu Academy. You've followed the Reds like a dog, and you're a traitor to our Nationalist cause. Think about this: we've never forced you to join any group, never tattooed you, we've given you all the privileges a POW can have — but you abused our kindness. You — you — I have to get a piece of your flesh today. I don't believe we can't teach you how to behave!" He plunged the dagger into the table, and with a thud it stood beside a bottle.

"Damn you, get out of here!" Wang Yong shouted at him. A few hands dragged the man into the office and put him on a cot in a corner.

Silence fell over the room while my heart galloped.

"Sit down, everybody," said Wang. He turned to me after we were seated again. "Truth be told," he went on, "brother, I really like you, like your ability and your looks. They alone promise a great career, a top-ranking officer. Also, because I can see that you're honest, I want to make friends with you. I'm a coarse man, no manners, only three years' schooling. By making friends with someone like you, I mean to get above myself. I might as well spill out everything here — we want to take you to Taiwan so that we can get help from you one of these days."

"From me?" I was amazed, wondering if he was drunk too.

"Yes, from you."

"How?"

"You graduated from the Huangpu, and beyond question Generalissimo Chiang will promote you to a high position soon after you get to Taiwan. But who are we? Just a bunch of peasants and clods. None us even finished elementary school. On the mainland we were treated like garbage, and in Taiwan it'll be the same story all over again. You're different. So I always thought when you become a general, you might still remember a coarse man like me, who once treated you like a friend. Feng Yan, you're so young, but your heart is poisoned by the Commies. Why can't you go to Taiwan with us? Without an able man among us, no one here will get anywhere, and again we'll be dumped to the bottom of society." He covered his face with both hands, sobbing brokenheartedly. The other men tried to calm him down, but he cried harder, like a small boy. Obviously he had drunk too much.

Touched by his candor, I said, "Chief Wang, you shouldn't be so upset. As you always say to me, every man has his own choice. Believe me, I'm not a Commie. I want to go home only because I miss my mother and my fiancée. How could I enjoy life in another place if I abandoned them?" As I was speaking, tears streamed down my face too. I stood up and lifted the cup of liquor. "Chief Wang, I cherish your friendship and will never forget this night. Let's drink up."

They all got to their feet and downed the

alcohol in their mugs, bowls, and cups. Then I said, "Forgive me, brothers, I have to go now." I turned around, went into the office, raised the canvas door curtain, and stepped into the cool night.

Stars were rubbing one another in the indigo sky while the moon resembled a face grinning and baring its teeth. A dog yapped in the distance, and a ship sounded its horn from the sea like a crazed bull. My head ached; my temples pounded. Never before had I drunk so much that I felt like vomiting. As I staggered around the corner of a large tent, a shadow leaped out. "Who is it?" I asked.

Then a heavy object hit the back of my head and I dropped to the ground.

When I woke up in our small tent, to my horror I saw two English words tattooed on my belly, right below my navel: FUCK COMMUNISM. Dajian and a few fellows sat near me, sighing and cursing the pro-Nationalists. A folded wet towel lay on my forehead, but I still felt woozy. The tattoo terrified me. With these words on me, how could I return to China? Tears gushed out of my eyes, though I squeezed my lids to force them back. As if stabbed in the heart, I blacked out again.

I don't know whether Wang Yong ordered them to have me tattooed. He might have or might not. I was too devastated to place the blame, frightened by the thought that I might never be able to erase the words from my skin.

Two days later Dajian was abducted by Wang Yong's men. They tied him to a chair in the company's office and tattooed these words on his right arm: FIGHT COMMUNISM OPPOSE RUSSIA. He was devastated too, weeping and saying he was done for. Yet to a degree, we were lucky — they hadn't marked on us a hog, an animal they used to identify a Communist. By contrast, on a pro-Nationalist they often tattooed a map of China below a slogan chosen by the man himself, the map including all of Mongolia and a part of Siberia. Neither Dajian nor I knew what to do about our tattoos. He relied on me for a solution. I told him not to lose heart and that there must be a way to exonerate ourselves, but in reality I too was at a loss.

9. BEFORE THE SCREENING

I showed my tattoo to Chang Ming across the barbed-wire fence. He didn't seem surprised, though he wondered why they had used English instead of Chinese. "Do you think I can have this removed eventually?" I asked him.

"A surgeon can get rid of it, I'm sure."

"What should I do now? With these words on me, how do I dare to return to the mainland?"

My last sentence seemed to startle him. He said gloomily, "We didn't anticipate that they'd tattoo our men."

"Can you ask Commissar Pei what I should do? Maybe he can give us instructions."

"We still haven't gotten in touch with him yet."

"How about contacting him through the Koreans? They must have a secret channel."

"We'll try."

"You do it soon, otherwise we'll be lost.

189

really don't know how to deal with this if the screening starts tomorrow."

I had Dajian on my mind too; that was why I ended up using the pronoun "we." Ming promised to let me know what to do in two days. He seemed underslept lately, his eyes dim and tired and his cheekbones more prominent, but he was quite optimistic and assured me that there must be a way to cope with this. He even joked that if he had been me he would have stuffed himself with the pork roast and fried squid before saying good-bye to Wang Yong. He said I should be more tactful, not just act like "a rigid intellectual."

The truth was that Ming couldn't walk in my shoes. Though he was a college graduate too, unlike me he had never been involved with the Nationalists. To the Communists he was a clean man, whereas I carried the heavy baggage of my past. If I had dined with Wang Yong's men, the whole company would have known of it. Then, facing the Communists' accusatory fingers, how could I have absolved myself? Wouldn't they punish me as a traitor too? Fortunately I hadn't touched the dinner, or else, compounded by the horrible words on my belly, I would have become too entangled with the pro-Nationalists to clear myself.

Like me, Dajian had been in low spirits ever since he was tattooed. He broke into wretched sobs from time to time. Once he even asked me whether we should sign up for Taiwan. I told him not to think this way and that we mustn't give up hope so easily.

Two days later, Ming and I met again at the northwestern end of the barbed-wire fence. He said we shouldn't worry too much about the tattoos and must adamantly insist on repatriation at the screening. I asked him, "Did you get this order from Commissar Pei?"

"No, we still haven't gotten in touch with him yet."

It was Hao Chaolin, the former artillery director of our division, who had given the instructions and who seemed to lead the Communist force now. Through Ming, Chaolin assured us that the tattoos could be removed. He provided convincing evidence as well: a few years ago, Warlord Yan in northwestern China had gotten a whole division of his troops tattooed with reactionary slogans on their chests; later many of these men had surrendered to the Communist army, whose surgeons effaced the words for them. This information comforted me some and bolstered my resolve to repatriate. With excitement I told

Dajian the story, but it didn't cheer him up. He just said he'd follow me wherever I went. He was suffering from dysentery these days, passing blood and mucus, but he wouldn't stay at the hospital, afraid he might die there alone. I made him drink a lot of boiled water to prevent dehydration, and he took some medicine prescribed by a Korean doctor. The pills helped him and reduced his trips to the latrine, though his recovery was slow.

Spring in Korea was longer than in inland China, or to be more accurate, it was more distinct as a season. Indigo swallows and petrels appeared in the sky. The wind changed too, mostly coming from the Pacific, warm in the daytime but nippy at night. There were more fishing boats on the sea now, bobbing between the clouds and the water like large birds. Sometimes I watched them for hours on end, as though I knew some people on them. I even imagined myself making a living as a fisherman on the ocean — yes, I would love to do that. I was still young and could start my life afresh. I would prefer any kind of life to this confinement, my heart full of longing for an untrammeled life.

On the morning of April 8 an American sound truck came to the gate of our compound and began broadcasting the policy for the screening, first in Korean, next in Chinese, then in English. The statement, repeated many times, moved and disturbed a lot of inmates. The Chinese part sounded smooth, firm, and clear. An amiable male voice announced:

. . . According to international law, both sides should return captured personnel as soon as possible. Repatriation will not be denied because some prisoners were forced to write their confessions, to have words or signs tattooed on them, or to have done what they would not do under normal circumstances. We understand that they were made to do things against their will. Therefore, we promise we will not hold them responsible. We wholeheartedly welcome every one of you back into the arms of our motherland. Brothers and comrades, your parents and families are expecting you. Please come home and rejoin them to live in peace and to participate in the construction of our great country . . .

After that statement, another man declared in stiff Chinese the United Nations' position on the screening. This voice represented the prison authorities and also urged us to repatriate. It declared:

The U.N. Command can offer no guarantee whatsoever on the ultimate fate of those of you who refuse to return to your own people. Therefore, before any of you decide irrevocably to resist repatriation, you must consider the consequences of your decision for your family. If you fail to go back, your government may hold your family accountable. On top of that, you may never see them again . . .

Hearing those words, many POWs became tearful. Some men drifted back into their tents and buried their heads in blankets, weeping. Wang Yong flew into a fury. "Fuck the Americans!" he cursed. "If I had a grenade I'd blow up that sound truck."

But the loudspeaker kept on: "Please also consider this possibility: if you refuse to go home, you will be held in custody here for at least several months longer. The United Nations cannot feed you forever, will make no promise about your future, and will not guarantee to send you to any safe place . . ."

Indeed, the broadcast was undermining the work the pro-Nationalists had painstakingly accomplished, and it made some prisoners more homesick. Worried about their future, some wanted to change their minds about going to Taiwan. The English part of the announcement also encouraged the captives to return home. It emphasized that the United Nations would keep only those who "forcibly resist repatriation." It sounded like the Americans were not interested in detaining POWs at all. Perhaps they didn't want to embarrass China and North Korea with a huge number of nonrepatriates, which would complicate a POW exchange and getting their own men back. Besides, it must have been an enormous burden to have tens of thousands of prisoners on their hands.

As soon as the sound truck pulled away to blare at a neighboring compound, our battalion was assembled in Liberty Hall. Han Shu, the chief of our regiment, came to speak to us. He was a slim, soft-spoken man, who in every way looked more like an official than an officer. Without Liu Tai-an's help, Han Shu could not have ruled the compound. But somehow the Americans liked him and had put him in the top position. Pacing the platform back and forth with his hands clasped behind him, Han Shu seemed lost in thought. We watched him silently. Then he lifted his intelligent face and said to us, "I have had a question on my mind for a long time." He pointed at Dajian standing in the front row. "Now, brother, I need you to help me figure out an answer. Yes, you. Come up here. Don't be nervous."

Dajian shuffled onto the platform. Han Shu continued, "Actually, my question isn't that hard to understand. We were all in the Red Army once and know the answer in our hearts. Now, my friend, what's your name?"

"Bai Dajian."

"Tell me, Brother Bai, what is the Seventh Article of the Conduct Code of the Communist army?"

Dajian wheezed out, "Never surrender. Never let yourself be taken prisoner even at the cost of your life."

"Correct. Please say it loudly so that everybody can hear you."

Dajian repeated it to the audience.

"Good, you can go back now." Han Shu turned to us. "This is what I want to talk about today. You all know the Communists' discipline and understand what will happen to you as a returned POW. If you still mean to repatriate, you must prepare to go through denunciations, corporal punishment, prison terms, and executions once you're back in our homeland. Even if the Communists let you remain alive, I can assure you that you will be the dregs of their society for the rest of your lives. Brothers, you all know I'm speaking the truth, which some of you are too afraid to face. So I have to bring it up now. History has shown that the Communists always treat their enemies more leniently than their own people. Only by becoming their significant enemies can you survive decently. I'm your chief here and ought to be concerned about your safety. Once you have set foot in this camp, you'll never be able to exonerate yourselves from the blame the Communists will pin on you, because they believe you have brought shame on China. They'll punish you ruthlessly in order to maintain discipline within their ranks. You may protest and say to them, 'But I've always been loyal to our country!' They'll counter, 'Then why didn't you kill yourself to keep our honor intact?' What can you say? Admit you're a coward? You may have to do that. If you're really a brave man, you can take your life now, right here in front of us. Then they'll be informed of your heroic deed and will publicize your story, name you a Revolutionary Martyr, and turn you into a big hero to inspire others.

"Brothers, we're all human beings, made of the same flesh and blood, so we dread pain, hunger, and death. We're often driven by the instinct for self-preservation. Like every one of you, I miss home a lot and often dream of my parents and siblings, soaking my pillow with tears at night. But I don't want to be tortured and butchered like a worthless animal, so I've decided to leave for the Free World, to wander as a homeless man for the rest of my life. Our tragedy is that our homeland is no longer a place where we can live decently like human beings. Then why should we return? The truth is even if you're a Communist and act as one here, your former comrades back home no longer count you as a Communist. To them, you're all cowards and goners and shouldn't exist anymore. So bear in mind that your decisions tomorrow will be a matter of life or death to yourselves. Now, you're dismissed."

The audience remained motionless, transfixed by the bold speech, which no one had expected the reticent Han Shu to be capable of delivering. Liu Tai-an wielded his club and shouted at us, "Return to your tents now."

On our way back, both Dajian and I walked unsteadily, dazed by the brevity of the meeting and by Han Shu's words, which were like awls jabbing at our insides. Many men in our platoon turned downcast, knowing there was a good deal of truth in Chief Han's speech. Dajian and I felt at a loss how to wriggle out of the pro-Nationalists' clutches, and at the same time we dreaded the punishment that might lie in store for us on the mainland. As for the Communists in our platoon, they'd also been shaken by Han Shu's remarks, and some of them remained taciturn.

That afternoon, about five hundred of us would-be repatriates were gathered in the front yard. Around us stood over two hundred "policemen," each toting a club as thick as a baton, but twice as long. Liu Tai-an said to us, "Brothers, the ships sent by Generalissimo Chiang have arrived at the port to take us to Taiwan, where you will live a free and happy life. Tomorrow every one of you will have to decide where to go. I urge you to pick the right way and cut your ties to the Commies once and for all." Liu was a squarish man with a large gold incisor. When he spoke, he kept his left hand inserted in his belt while his right hand held a club.

Suddenly a voice boomed among us, "We want to go back to China. Taiwan is not our homeland."

"Who said that? Step out!" ordered the battalion chief. Seeing that nobody stirred, he added, "If you were fathered by a man, you ought to have the guts to meet me face to face."

To our astonishment, a bulky man, whose head was shaved bald, went to the front and admitted calmly, "I said that, and it's the truth."

"Lin Wushen, I fuck your ancestors! You say that again." Liu Tai-an was so furious that his square face darkened to the color of an eggplant. He seemed to have known the man long before. He thrust his fingers at Lin Wushen's face as though intending to poke out his eyes.

The large man, not intimidated, said, "My home is on the mainland. Why should I go to Taiwan? According to the Geneva Convention, every prisoner has his right to choose where to go. What's wrong about expressing my true intention? We're all prisoners and shouldn't interfere with each other's decisions."

Liu Tai-an lifted the front of his new jacket to show that this wasn't a piece of prison issue with *P* and *W* on its patch pockets or sleeves. He said, "I'm not war trash like you. I'm a free man, an officer appointed to command this battalion."

"Sure, after kissing some American ass," said Lin Wushen. A few men snickered.

Enraged, Liu Tai-an went up to him and ripped the left sleeve off Wushen's jacket, exposing his upper arm. On it was a tattoo, a drawing of the sun shedding a circle of rays — the Nationalist emblem. The chief said, "You've already expressed your anti-Communist attitude in this sign; why did you change your mind?"

"You had it needled on me. It doesn't show my true feelings. I want to go home."

"Damn you, if you really want to return to the mainland, you must leave this tattoo here."

"All right, I have no use for it anyhow."

To our surprise, Liu Tai-an seized Wushen's arm and raised the jade-handled dagger, saying, "For the last time, tell me where you want to go."

"To the mainland."

With two strokes Liu slashed off the flesh occupied by the black tattoo. "Ouch!"

Wushen covered the cut with his hand and was biting his lips to choke his voice, his eyes aglow like tinder as tears gushed out. Blood dripped on the leg of his pants and on the sandy ground. People gasped as a few guards went over, grabbed Wushen's arms, and pulled him away.

"Take him to the classroom," ordered Liu Tai-an. "I'm not done with him yet."

At the education center they had already locked up more than twenty men, who were regarded as die-hard Commies who might undermine the screening and even instigate a riot. In fact, some of these men were not Communists; they were only determined to go home at any cost.

A commotion was going on at the front of the crowd. Having seen Wushen's blood, men began voicing their resentment. Emboldened by collective anger, some were spoiling for a fight. Liu Tai-an looked alarmed, but regained his composure and said to us, "Lin Wushen is a good example for you. If any of you want to go back to the mainland, then leave with us the patch of your skin bearing our words and our drawing. This is fair, isn't it?"

Both Dajian and I stood in the front row of the crowd. He was trembling and squeezed his eyes tight; tears trickled down his colorless cheek. I was petrified too and for a moment lost my speech. All I could do was tug his sleeve to remind him that he mustn't draw attention to himself. Looking sidelong at him, I saw a fat louse in his hair.

"Brothers and friends," Liu Tai-an said loudly, "now it's time for you to make up your minds. There'll be an additional study session this evening in the auditorium, at seven o'clock. You're all required to attend it so that you'll be clear about which course to choose at the screening tomorrow. Now you're free to go."

Before dinner Dajian and I talked about what to do, knowing Liu Tai-an would kill you without blinking an eye if you decided against his will. I was still determined to go back to China, and Dajian said he would follow me. Yet both of us were shaken and wanted to avoid showing our intention overtly as long as we could. In my heart of hearts I was uncertain whether I could endure physical torture, as some Communists would do, without changing my mind. Dinner was good that evening, stewed pigs' intestines mixed with spinach and cellophane noodles; and for the first time we could have a full bowl of rice and a large ladle of the dish besides. Some of those who meant to go to Taiwan even drank saki, which they had come by probably through exchanging their blankets and boots with South Korean guards. Some men opened their only tin of Spam, saved for a special occasion. They seemed to be celebrating this day as the eve of a new life. By contrast, those of us who wanted to repatriate were gloomy and quiet.

After dinner, when the twilight turned smoky and festive with many knots of men chattering and with a bamboo flute trilling from one of the large tents, we set out for our compound's Civil Information and Education Center, which consisted of two spacious classrooms and the auditorium. In front of that place flew the U.S. and the Nationalist flags. At its entrance knelt concrete statues of Stalin and Mao Zedong, both with hunched shoulders and bowed heads like a pair of criminals. Their faces and heads were glazed with patches of dried phlegm and snot. When we arrived the study session had already started. The guards at the door, who were Wang Yong's men, let us in without cursing us for being late. I could feel the intensity of the atmosphere in the auditorium, where people, all sitting on the dirt floor, were so attentive that nobody took note of our arrival. The men confined in the classroom in the afternoon had been hauled onto the low stage in the front. Liu Tai-an looked more resolute than three hours ago and spoke like a real commanding officer.

"To put it in a nutshell," he said, "those who follow the Communists will come to a bad end, because we won't let them get away unscathed." He then turned to Lin Wushen, whose hands were tied from behind. "We begin with you. Now, Lin Wushen, tell me, for the last time, where will you go?"

Without looking at him, the large man turned to us and cried, "I was born in China. Where else should I go!"

Silence ensued, the air as if frozen.

Liu Tai-an barked, "All right, you want to go to the mainland, I'm sending you there now." Grabbing Lin Wushen's neck with one hand and waving the dagger in his other hand, he hissed, "Let me ask you one more time, where will you go?"

Lin Wushen glared at him silently, then looked at us. Suddenly he shouted at the top of his voice, "Long live the Communist Party! Long live our motherland!"

Liu Tai-an stabbed him in the chest and twisted the dagger. Without another word

Lin Wushen dropped on the floor. Immediately Liu bent down and cut his stomach open while the dying man's feet were still kicking. His blood and intestines spilled out, and a few men at the front began retching. With a sidewise slash, Liu slit his chest, then pulled out his lungs and heart, all the organs quivering with steam. He cut out the heart and skewered it with the dagger. Raising the heart, he brandished his bloody free hand at us and said, "Look, this is what I meant when I said we wouldn't let you leave unscathed. If anyone else wants to go back to the mainland, I'll have to see the true color of his heart first." He turned to give the corpse a kick.

For about a minute there was no sound in the auditorium. The air seemed thickened with the smell of the blood. I was stunned not only by the ferocity of Liu's act but also by his skill in disemboweling the man, as though butchering human beings had been his everyday business.

"Let's continue. Next," Liu Tai-an ordered, still holding the heart on the tip of his knife.

The man they dealt with next was an acquaintance of mine. He was Yang Huan, a scrawny fellow with large, intense eyes and a massive scar on his cheek, who was also a graduate of the Huangpu Military Academy. But he had matriculated a year before me and was kept in another company here, so we hadn't had a chance to talk at length when we ran into each other. I vaguely remembered that he had been very active in leading the revolt against the Nationalists in our alma mater. Probably he was a Communist.

They dragged Yang Huan to the center of the stage. Then a lanky man walked up to him and asked, "Brother Yang, do you still know me?"

"Mei Lufu, why are you here?" Yang Huan looked baffled.

"My friend, I came to help you. We lived in the same dorm at the Huangpu for three years, and I can't forget how kindly you helped me, so now it's my turn to pull you out of the Commies' trap."

"I don't need your help."

"You and I are both graduates from the Huangpu, and we're students of Generalissimo Chiang, who treated us like a father. But I can't comprehend why you want to return to the mainland. What made you so loyal to the Reds?"

I was bewildered. Although Mei Lufu said he was our schoolmate too, I couldn't remember him. Yet without question the two men had once been roommates and buddies. Yang Huan answered, "China is where my home is, why can't I go back?"

"Give him one on the mouth!" ordered Liu Tai-an.

Dutifully Mei Lufu slapped his former friend.

"Turncoat!" Yang Huan cursed loudly. "Scum of China, we'll get even with you sooner or later."

"Goddammit, you're a traitor! You betrayed Generalissimo Chiang's love and expectations." Mei Lufu began punching him. "Take this. How dare you call me a turncoat?"

Then a bunch of guards fell on Yang Huan, who kept yelling, "Long live the revolution! Long live Communism!"

Clubs and iron bars landed on him while he was still mumbling, "Long live . . . long live . . ."

Within a minute they beat him to the brink of death. A heavyset man pressed the heel of his boot on Yang Huan's throat and stamped down forcefully. Yang Huan twisted a little, then stopped moving. I was shuddering all over, never having thought that an educated man like Mei Lufu could be as vicious as Liu Tai-an. At the same time I was amazed that the two Communists they had just butchered had seemed entirely unafraid of death. Like me, Dajian was utterly terrified; he placed his hand on my shoulder to steady himself.

Liu Tai-an said to the twenty men on the stage, waving the bloody heart, "You're lucky today. I spare you for now to see how you'll behave tomorrow." Then he turned to us. "Let's end here for today, although I still mean to collect the tattoos from some of you. Brothers, please don't follow the bad examples of Lin Wushen and Yang Huan. You're free to go now."

Both Dajian and I were alarmed, having realized that as graduates of the Huangpu Military Academy, we also must have been targets of the pro-Nationalists. They would use every means to coerce us. Unlike the Communist Party members, we didn't feel we should sacrifice our lives for repatriation. We talked briefly on our way back and agreed we should act according to circumstances and shouldn't openly refuse to go to Taiwan. Above all we had to survive. As long as we were alive, there would be an opportunity to get back to China.

Though many prisoners hated Liu Tai-an, some pro-Nationalists loved and revered him, and some even regarded him as a hero. At the sight of him, even some staunch Communists couldn't refrain from quaking, let alone regular inmates like Dajian and me. It was this small muscular man who had started the slogan "We must go to Taiwan!" It was this savage man who had poured a large bowl of saki, bitten his middle finger to drip his blood into it, and thus inspired some POWs to follow suit: they mixed their blood in the liquor and drank it together to forge the bond of brotherhood. To be fair, Liu Tai-an was generous to pro-Nationalist inmates. As the vice chief of the regiment and the leader of our battalion, he was entitled to eat special meals like Han Shu, but he wouldn't use this privilege and always ate the same food as the other prisoners. One day the kitchen couldn't serve the midday meal on time because it had to cook for the officers first. Liu Tai-an went in and knocked over the cauldron of boiling millet and the pot containing stewed clams and potatoes. After that, even those officers who enjoyed special mess would avoid him during mealtimes. Another day, an illiterate prisoner played truant after signing up for a literacy class. Liu Tai-an knelt down and begged him to treasure this opportunity to learn how to read and write. For Liu, good and evil were as clear-cut as black and white — his mind wouldn't tolerate any ambiguity. It seemed to me that although he had only an elementary education, he must have been a sick man whose mind was warped by the image of the macho hero in classical Chinese novels, embodied by wild figures like Zhang Fei and Li Kui, who wouldn't hesitate to kill an evil man, eat his flesh, and guzzle his blood. In fact, many pro-Nationalists did compare Liu Tai-an to those fictional heroes, and he was proud of the analogy and relished his ability to inspire terror.

Back in our tent, we couldn't stop cursing Liu Tai-an. One said that the Communists should have finished him off, referring to an incident one night the previous winter when a group of Communists had beaten him to his knees and made him beg for mercy. Some regretted they hadn't formed their own armed force. Now without access to weapons they had become meat for the pro-Nationalists to hack at will. Some said that once they returned to China, they would get hold of Liu Tai-an's and his lackeys' families and relatives and wipe them out. Dajian told them that Mei Lufu's younger sister lived in Tianjin City and worked at a newspaper, and one man declared he would settle accounts with her one of these days. As we were talking, both Liu Tai-an and Wang Yong arrived with the police force. They ordered us to get out of the tent immediately.

When we had lined up and stood at attention, Liu Tai-an said, "Those of you who have a tattoo on you step out."

About thirty men moved forward, and Dajian and I followed them. Liu began to speak to us. "Don't think I'm forgetful. I came to collect the tattoos like I told you. If you ate the U.N.'s food, you ought to leave a bit of your flesh in the U.N.'s camp. Whoever wants to return to the mainland, let me know now, and we'll get the tattoo off of you. Now, lie down."

The thirty of us dropped to the ground, face down and with both hands stretched out. Liu shouted, "Those of you who want to go to Taiwan raise your right leg."

Hesitating for a few seconds, I raised my leg. Following me, Dajian did the same. But about half of the men didn't do this. Liu Tai-an pointed at the first of them in the line and ordered his bodyguards, "Pull that bastard up!"

The moment they got the man on his feet, Liu Tai-an asked him, "Mainland or Taiwan?" He flashed at his face a specially made knife — a toothbrush with a razor blade affixed to the end of the bone handle.

"Mainland," muttered the fellow. Two men were holding his arms from behind.

"Say it again."

"Mainland."

"All right, let me take this off."

"Ow!"

Liu began cutting the tattooed words off his chest. The man started groaning, but still speaking clearly. "Yes, get rid of these damned words for your grandpa."

In the corner of my eye I saw a "policeman" holding a short piece of iron wire that had impaled on it about a dozen pieces of bloody skin, each almost half an inch thick. Obviously they had just finished collecting tattoos at another tent. Beside Liu Tai-an stood a boyish man holding a white enamel pail, which contained several pieces of flesh stained with ink. Now I realized that all the prisoners tattooed by force had been the pro-Nationalists' targets. They had marked two kinds of people among us, those who would be valuable to them and those who were their deadly enemies.

Liu Tai-an waved the piece of flesh he had just cut off from the man, and his other hand flipped open the glass case of a kerosene lantern held by one of his body-guards. He burned the flesh over the flame, and it sizzled for a few seconds, scorched yellow. Then he put it into his mouth, munching it ferociously. I was so flabbergasted that my stomach started churning. He said through his teeth, "Even if I kill all of you Reds and eat your hearts and livers, my hatred won't come down."

A heavy hush fell over us, and Dajian began sobbing. As they went on collecting the tattoos, pulling those unyielding men to their feet one by one and forcing them to answer the question, more cries and moans rose from the line. Several men who hadn't raised their legs originally now changed their minds and said they would sign up for Taiwan. Having held up my leg, I didn't expect they would pull me up too. I was trembling and could hardly speak. A pimply-faced man put a bloody knife against my belly and said, "Now, my scholar, tell me where you'd like to go."

"I'll follow you," I mouthed.

"Say it out loud," Wang Yong broke in.

"Okay, I'll go to Taiwan."

Dajian was picked up from the ground too, and he followed my example. The minute they were done with us, Wang Yong had the new "converts" moved to a large tent that was roomy and clean inside. Yet I couldn't go to sleep until the wee hours, listening to those men in the small tents groaning and cursing incessantly. I felt ashamed and reluctant to talk with Dajian, who tossed from side to side too. By following me, he made me bear the guilty conscience alone. Deep down, I wished I could have been as brave as a genuine Communist, who, crazed and fanatic, viewed death without flinching.

10. THE SCREENING

We ate breakfast at six the next morning, then packed all our belongings onto our backs and waited outside Liberty Hall. I had only a satchel and a blanket roll; some men had nothing but the ragged clothes on them, having gambled away everything else. The screening started at 8:00 a.m. Group by group we were led into the hall, where we waited to be called individually to meet the arbiters. We were to walk through a side door and into one of the three white tents, pitched specially for the screening, in which we would be asked whether we wanted to repatriate. After that, we would be sent to join either those going to Taiwan or those returning to the mainland. When our group had entered the hall, I couldn't stop fidgeting, unsure where I was going to wind up. In a corner of the room the bodies of the two men killed the night before were still lying under rice straw. The iron bars hidden in the sleeves of the Chinese "policemen" scared me, and from outside a voice rang out,

"Catch him! Smash his skull!" I closed my eyes and tried not to think.

A U.N. official came in to check our ID tags against his record and made us sign our names on a ruled manila envelope. About a dozen U.N. guards, all empty-handed, showed up too, so the hall quieted down some.

Meanwhile Dajian, standing behind me with several men between us in the line, kept looking at me and asked with his sluggish eyes what we should do. I turned my head away, not wanting to face him because I had no idea either. Out of the corner of my eye I caught him shaking his chin at me a few times, but I didn't respond. Besides, our battalion's police didn't allow anyone to talk, so I couldn't go up to him and say that all we could do was act as the circumstances required.

A pebble hit my back, signaling it was my turn. With shaky steps I moved to the side door. I walked slowly so as to see what it was like outside and to assess the situation. Some GIs stood at the entrances to the white tents, all having *MP* painted on their helmets and on their dark blue brassards. An idea finally came to mind: if the arbiters forced me to go to Taiwan I would rush out of the tent and beg the GIs to send me to the group heading for the mainland. If I spoke to them in English, they might help me, I guessed.

After entering a tent, I was ordered to sit down in front of two American officers, with a folding table between us. One of them was a Caucasian, tall with a long face and in a pea-green shirt; the other was a stocky Chinese. The white man, a captain, began speaking to me about the Geneva Convention and the consequences of my decision. I was amazed that he could speak Mandarin, while the other officer, who was a lieutenant, kept smiling knowingly. Once in a while the Chinese man put in a few words in Cantonese, which I couldn't understand.

I must have looked absentminded, for the white officer grew impatient and said to me, "All right, tell me now, do you want to go to Taiwan or mainland China?"

"To the mainland," I replied firmly.

He looked me in the face for a moment, as though in disbelief. Then he handed me a card, saying, "Go straight to the front gate and give this card to the guards."

With tears on my face I bowed to both of them and said, "Thank you," then hurried out toward the gate. The card in my hand was five by three inches, bearing these words: "The People's Republic of China."

I handed it to the GI standing at the middle of the gate with a rifle hung across his chest. He glanced at the card, grabbed my shoulder, and shoved me out of the compound. Near the sentry post was parked a truck whose back was under canvas. A GI beckoned me to get onto the vehicle by the ladder at its rear. Climbing up, I turned around to look at the white tents in hopes that Dajian would be following me.

"Don't look around, you motherfucker!" another GI yelled and pushed me into the back of the truck. There were only about a dozen men in it, most of whom looked unfamiliar to me. I grew more anxious. If only I had given Dajian an eye signal just now! I felt awful for having left him in the lurch.

About ten minutes later the truck rolled away toward a new compound, number 602, where all the would-be repatriates were assembled. Later I heard from a fellow who had joined us in the afternoon that after Dajian returned to my former company, he kept asking others, "Where's Feng Yan? Did you see him?" They all shook their heads. For hours he wept quietly alone. What had happened that morning was that before entering a screening tent, he was sandwiched between two pro-Nationalists, who told him I had just made "the wise choice." So Dajian declared to the arbiters that he would go to Taiwan too.

11. COMPOUND 602

As we were approaching Compound 602, which was just a few minutes' drive from Compound 72, I saw a piece of reddish cloth dangling atop a bamboo pole. Coming closer, I recognized it as our national flag, self-made and with five golden stars on it. The sight of the flag excited us, and we realized this place must be controlled by the Communists.

More than four thousand men had already been here for days, all determined to return to our homeland. This meant we had come back to the ranks of our comrades. Indeed, this place differed greatly from Compound 72. All the tents were the same size and we shared the same mess. Most men looked cheerful and congenial, ready to help others. Later I heard that this place was nicknamed the Mainland Compound and that such an establishment had been achieved only through an arduous struggle. Many of these men had demonstrated and written letters, demanding that they be separated from the nonrepatriates.

They sent delegates to negotiate with the prison authorities and the pro-Nationalist representatives for three days to little avail. Finally two Swiss from the Red Cross stepped in and mediated a settlement, and thus the Chinese POWs were separated according to our different destinations.

Out of the eight thousand men in Compound 72, only about seven hundred made it here. The rest of them all remained in the old barracks, eagerly waiting to board the ships sent over by Taiwan, as they had been told. But that was a lie or an illusion. No ship whatsoever had come to fetch them.

On the day of my arrival at Compound 602, I was delighted to run into Chang Ming, the editor of our former division's bulletin who had met me regularly across the barbed wire. He and I hugged and broke into tears. He gave me a pack of Korean cigarettes, whose brand I couldn't make out but there were two dolphins printed below some red words. He said we might not be here for long; the Americans hadn't even bothered to organize us into units and everything had been left in our own hands. This state of affairs indicated that the compound must be temporary.

"Where did you hear this?" I asked him,

taking a short drag on my cigarette.

"It's just my observation."

"Boy, you're sharp."

He seemed much more experienced and hardened than before, yet his thick lips and broad eyes still betrayed a lot of innocence and good nature. Like an editor, he carried a stout fountain pen in his breast pocket. I asked him how he had managed to keep that. He grinned, and said actually he could not use it for lack of ink. He invited me to join him in his tent, saying that before all the men were put into different units, we had better stay together. I was happy to do that. We two walked to the third tent in the first row of the barracks, in which I was given a mat spread below an opening that served as a window. The air in there smelled grassy — the tent must have been pitched recently. I put down my blanket roll, pleased with the daylight I could use when staying indoors. Ming left for a meeting as soon as I settled down. He must have assumed some kind of leadership in this compound.

That same afternoon I bumped into Hao Chaolin, who didn't greet me enthusiastically. He told me that he had been busy helping Commissar Pei organize the comrades here. Perhaps because he had held a much higher rank than mine in our former division, he was reluctant to be too convivial with me. In any case, I was glad to hear that Commissar Pei was also here and had taken the leadership. I wondered why the Americans had let him join us. This was like releasing a dragon into its native water. What a blunder.

On the other hand, I was saddened to see that there were many more wounded men in the new compound than in the other ones, men missing an arm, men wearing eyeshades to cover their empty eye sockets, men who had lost their hair, ears, and noses to napalm, men who had gone deaf and had to communicate by signs, and men without legs who moved around with the help of crutches and with thick wooden sticks affixed to their stumps. The thought came to me that no country would want these men, who were mere war trash and had no choice but to go back to China, where they still had their families. They had to follow the Communists home.

Dinner was the same stuff, boiled barley and soy sauce soup, but people were equal here and even friendly. There was no fighting over food, and officers didn't get special meals. That evening I went to see Commissar Pei in the tent that served as the headquarters of the compound. Many people lounged on the grass outside that tent, smoking and chatting. They looked relaxed and hopeful, as if we were to depart for home within a few days. This was another reason I wanted to see the commissar, to find out when we could head home. Inside the tent a meeting was in full swing, so a guard stopped me at the entrance, but he announced me without delay.

A minute later Pei came out with measured steps. "Aha, Yu Yuan, we meet again," he said, stretching out his hand, which I held with both of mine. His palm was still smooth and soft as in the old days.

"When can we go home, Commissar Pei?" I asked.

"Can't wait anymore?" A smiling twinkle appeared in his eyes.

"Honestly, no. If only we could fly back!"

"We may have to remain in prison for a while. But don't worry. Here we're among our comrades, and you won't suffer again like in Compound 72."

I pulled up the front of my shirt and showed him the tattoo. "Commissar Pei, do you think I can get rid of this?"

Observing the words, he said, "I heard

you were tattooed, but I didn't know it was in English. I know what 'Communism' means, but what's the meaning of the other word?"

"Screw."

He tipped his head back and laughed. "Don't worry. Perhaps you shouldn't have it removed now. Let me think about this, all right?"

"Sure. It really bothers me."

"I understand. But it won't do you any harm for the time being."

He couldn't stay with me for long because of the meeting, so I took my leave and promised to come to see him again. Before I turned back, I glimpsed the scene inside the tent through the flaps spread by his hands. Most of the faces in there looked familiar; they must have been some of the Communists who had served in our former division. Obviously Pei was in firm control here. Officially he held no position whatsoever in this compound, whose chief was Zhao Teng, a rugged, popular man, who had once been a company commander in the 540th Regiment; but it was clear to most that Zhao was just a front man for Commissar Pei. Hao Chaolin was the vice chief of the compound and actually had more say in most matters than Zhao Teng.

Probably due to the temporary nature of this compound, the Americans had just appointed the few top leaders and let them organize the prisoners here. Our captors seemed too understaffed to worry about this sort of thing.

Within two days, a repatriation regiment was formed, into which every man here was included. Pei was elected its head, and Chaolin became the chief of the First Battalion, while the other two battalions were also led by officers from our 180th Division, one by Zhao Teng. In addition to the army units, they also set up an office called the Secretariat, which was in charge of confidential work (codes and documents), communications, diplomacy (including translation and interpretation), propaganda, education, and entertainment. Both Ming and I were put into this office, where our colleagues were all educated men, more than a third of them college graduates. Without much difficulty the leadership at all levels was established and began to function. Now I realized this was another reason for our men to demand that we be separated from the pro-Nationalists: to create a new space in which the Communists could restore their control system, especially at the levels of platoons and squads. Once the leadership was in place, we could again function like an efficient unit. Obviously our captors hadn't discerned this hidden motive.

Following the military organization, a political union was also formed, which was called the United Communist Association. There were not many Party members among us and the Communists needed to attract as many people as they could, so the association was designed to draw many prisoners into it. Working in the Secretariat, I read its constitution, which was as follows:

1. PRINCIPLES

The United Communist Association is an underground organization composed of the Chinese Communist Party members and revolutionary soldiers among the POWs in the U.N. prison camp. In the light of our unique circumstances, our association holds the following principles:

We believe in Communism.

We shall organize and lead the prisoners in protecting the honor of the Communist Party and our motherland.

We shall coordinate our actions with our country's military struggle and the Panmunjom negotiations.

We shall expose the enemy's conspiracy to retain prisoners.

We insist upon returning to China.

If the Panmunjom talks fall through, we shall try to break prison and liberate ourselves.

2. ORGANIZATION

We follow the regulations stipulated in the Constitution of the Chinese Communist Party. Every level of our association must maintain revolutionary integrity and struggle bravely but in an underground way. We must conceal our organizational structure, keep our leaders in a low profile, and make our members communicate with the association through the one-and-only-one line. The cells within the association must not contact each other, and we will not hold any conference for all members. The leaders at every level should follow the principle of democratic centralism, but owing to our special situation, all the leaders will be selected by their superiors except the chairman of the association, who must be elected by the directors of the branches. In principle, new members must be inducted individually, not in groups.

3. MEMBERS

The members of the association are the backbone of our struggle against our enemy. Anyone who acknowledges the Constitution of the Chinese Communist Party, has a clean history in the prison camp, and is willing to fight for the principles of our association, regardless of whether he is a Communist Party member or not, can be a candidate for our association. His induction should be recommended by at least one member and approved by the sub-committee. If the case is complicated, it should be approved by the general committee. Every member is obligated to participate in the association's regular activities, has the right to criticize and expose his leaders' misdeeds, must put the interests of the revolution before his own, must guard secrets, and must not be afraid of confinement, torture, or death.

4. DISCIPLINE

Our disciplinary actions consist of four kinds: advice, warning, dismissal from leadership, and revocation of membership. If a member has lost his revolutionary will and won't change after repeated warnings, the case should be reported to the higher level for his expulsion from the association. But to avoid unexpected occurrences, a member will be assigned to keep in touch with him. Our association does not set up an office for implementing disciplinary actions, which are left in the hands of the security officers at all levels.

As soon as the association was established, it put forward three tasks for all the prisoners: unite closely, struggle against our enemy, and study hard. More than half of the men here were illiterate, and nobody would question the meanings of these tasks. Most of them began to buckle down to the three tasks, which had suddenly become the purpose of their lives. At bottom, they must have been afraid of the absence of strong leadership, without which they might again suffer as they had in the compounds ruled by the pro-Nationalists. Besides, though the Panmunjom negotiations were in progress, we were uncertain whether they would succeed. We believed that if they fell through, the Americans might begin killing us or shipping us to the copper and coal mines in Alaska, so our only way out was to break jail. According to our intelligence, Marshal Kim Il Sung had issued secret orders that the Korean POWs must find ways to liberate themselves. We might have to do likewise. Such an undertaking would be impossible without powerful leadership and unified effort. That was a major reason why many men were willing to join the United Communist Association.

Like them, I also applied for membership. I wanted to abide by its principles, because I believed in socialism, which I felt was the only way to save China. I had seen how my country had been ruined by the Nationalists. Inflation, corruption, crime, poverty, all the evil forces had run amok in the old China. I remembered that a distant uncle of mine had once ridden a bicycle loaded with two sackfuls of cash to a grocery store and spent it all, but returned with only forty pounds of sweet potatoes. How could common people have continued to live under that regime? By contrast, shortly after the Communists came to power, people in dire poverty were relieved, usury and market cornering were banned, and criminal gangs disappeared. For better or worse the Communists had brought order and hope to the land.

To my surprise, one afternoon Ming said to me about my application for membership in the United Communist Association, "They may not let you in." This implied that they had been instructed to turn me down.

"Why?" I asked.

"Probably because you translated hymns for Father Woodworth. Also, some people said you often read the Bible alone."

"For goodness' sake, you know I just meant to improve my English. I stopped having anything to do with Woodworth the moment I found out his true colors."

"Relax. I told them the same thing. Don't worry too much. Just explain everything clearly when they ask you. I'm sure they'll reconsider your application. By the way, I almost forgot, Commissar Pei wants to talk to you this evening."

"When?"

"Eight o'clock in his tent."

In the evening, after the front gate had

been locked, I walked along the barbed-wire fence alone. The ground felt doughy, scattered with patches of new grass. For half a year I had never been so free, yet a heavy feeling sank into my heart. I was tormented by the thought that I was an outsider among my comrades. In the distance a trail wound up a hillock, below which a hamlet was still inhabited by some fishing families. Cooking smoke went up from straw roofs that resembled a clump of huge mushrooms. Life seemed tranquil in that village; every once in a while, a donkey brayed. Beyond those houses spread a bluish bay, only a part of which was visible, its water motionless as if frozen. Somewhere a bird tooted rapidly like an alarm. From time to time the cool sea breeze wafted in, bringing a light puff of fishy smell.

I had placed my fate with the Communists, but would they ever trust me? To them I had always been a marked man with a problematic past. But didn't my deeds on the battlefield and in the wilderness prove that I was trustworthy and loyal to our motherland? Unlike most of the graduates from the Huangpu Military Academy, I was one of the dozen former cadets who had followed the Communists

234

to this compound. What else did they need to verify that I was as reliable as the other prisoners? True enough, I had helped Father Woodworth translate the hymns, but I had quit in time, no harm done. Some men here had continued going to the Sunday sermons after I stopped. Why were they not singled out?

Then it dawned on me that to the Communists, my association with Father Woodworth must have amounted to a moral relapse, which revealed my "petty bourgeois outlook," a phrase they often used to criticize an educated individual like me. However, I wasn't applying for Communist Party membership but only for that of a mass association. There was no reason for them to reject me. On second thought, I wondered why I was so eager to seek their approval. Why worry so much about joining that organization? Perhaps I dreaded isolation and had to depend on a group to feel secure. Why couldn't I remain alone without following anyone else? One should rely on nobody but oneself. If Dajian hadn't followed me, he wouldn't have gone astray and remained in Wang Yong's grip. I'd better stay away from the herd.

No. If I mean to return to China, I have

to take part in the pro-Communist activities; otherwise I'll cause more trouble for myself. Whether I join them or not, they'll never leave me alone, so I mustn't stand aloof. Either you become their friend or their enemy. The Communists don't believe anyone can remain neutral . . .

"You may leave now," Commissar Pei said to his orderly at the sight of me. Then, smiling, he gestured for me to come over and sit near him.

"I've thought about your belly, Yuan," he told me the moment I sat down.

"My belly?"

"Yes, the tattoo, I mean."

"What should I do about it?"

"Nothing."

"Leave it as it is?"

"Correct."

"Why?"

"There's no doctor here who can take it off for you."

"But some comrades had their tattoos reshaped into different words or into something like a flower."

"I'm aware of that, but you're a special case."

"How come?" I was slightly upset by his remark. Why did they always treat me differently?

He said with a mysterious look on his face, "You're not an ordinary prisoner. We may need you to deal with the Americans, and a tattoo like yours can help you, don't you think?" As he grinned an elongated dimple formed on his left cheek, though his face was emaciated.

"I don't know," I said.

"Trust me, there's no hurry to have your tattoo removed."

"What if I get punished for it after we go back to China?"

"I'll explain to the Party, I promise. This is necessary for our struggle."

"In that case I'll continue to wear this damn thing. But I have a question for you, Commissar Pei."

"Yes, say it."

"According to you, I'm needed by the Party, but why was my application for the United Communist Association turned down as though I were a reactionary? It's just a progressive mass organization."

"I know that. Some comrades still have reservations about you, to tell the truth. In fact, this is another matter I want to talk about. There'll be a study session, at which you may be asked to do self-examination."

My head expanded with a swoon, because this meant they would denounce me.

I managed to ask, "What did I do to deserve such treatment?"

"Don't be so quick-tempered. All the other comrades will do self-examination as well."

"But I'm a special case, right?"

"Yes, you may have more to say than others."

"Because I helped Woodworth?"

"That's a part of it."

"You know I'm not religious."

"But you often read the Bible."

"That's only because I have nothing else to read. Believe me, if I had a copy of *Das Kapital*, I'd study it every day. Most men in Compound 72 gambled all the time. Do you think that was better than reading the Bible? At least I tried to improve my English and make myself more useful."

"I believe there's more to it than learning English. You must feel lonely, so you want to seek refuge in the Christian God's world."

His acumen stunned me, and I realized I must indeed have some religious longing in me, which must have been awakened by my contact with Woodworth. After a moment's silence, I admitted, "Sometimes I feel better when I read the Bible. I don't know why. It makes me feel less helpless."

"Genuine help comes from your comrades and the Party, not from God. No God can save us. See, you think differently from others. That makes you special."

"I've never claimed I'm a Communist, much less that I think like one. But I believe that only socialism can save China, and I'm willing to follow the Communists. That's why I'm here."

"Well said. I like your candor."

Encouraged by his words, I let my tongue go looser. "I admire the Communists' enthusiasm, dedication, and discipline, but I can't completely accept the logic of your working method."

"What do you mean?"

"The Communists treat every person just as a number. One plus one equals two. One hundred people have united, then you get the power of one hundred men, as though humans are horses. For me, this is too simple. I believe there must be a power much larger than an individual, like a multiplier. If you tap that power, you can multiply yourself. You can become one hundred or one thousand, depending on what the multiplier is."

"You're quite thoughtful, Yuan. So you've found God is that power?"

"No, not yet, but there must be such a

multiplier available for human beings."

"I have found it," he said firmly.

"Really?"

"Yes. It's Marxism," he replied in whole-hearted sincerity.

For a few seconds I didn't know what to say, then I mumbled, "That's why you can act with so much certainty."

"Right."

"That can help you overcome a lot of difficulties, too."

"Yes, it's the Communist ideal that multiplies our strength and courage."

I said with full respect, "I wish I were like you."

"You should try to be. Tomorrow when your comrades criticize you, try to remain calm and patient. They only mean to help you, no hard feelings."

"I'll remember that."

Lying on my mat that night, I went over my conversation with Pei. What amazed me was that he thought of Marxism not as a sociological theory but as a kind of religion. This religious feeling might explain why so many Communists, some of them uneducated and unable to grasp Marxism at all, were so fanatic and so dedicated to their cause. To some degree I was pleased with my talk with the commissar, who seemed to understand me.

Since the Secretariat had a staff of only twelve, we were assigned to study with the kitchen squad that cooked for the regimental headquarters. In the afternoon twenty-five of us sat on the dirt floor of the cooks' tent and began our self-examination. Six or seven men by turns talked about their experiences in different compounds, all saying they wished there had been more of the Party's leadership in those places so that they could have fought the reactionary forces more actively and with a clear objective. When my turn came, I admitted my mistake in translating the hymns and my negligence that contributed to Bai Dajian's remaining with the pro-Nationalists. I had thought my admissions might preempt some criticism, but they wouldn't let me pass so easily. Questions were shot at me one after another. How had I acquired the Bible? Why did I read it every day? What made Father Woodworth pick me to translate the songs? What else did I do for him? Their voices grew so stern that I began losing my patience, telling them bluntly that I had read the Bible because I wouldn't fritter away my time by gambling like some of them.

"But why do you still read it now?" asked one of them.

I wanted to retort, I like to; but I remained speechless, unable to think of a suitable answer.

They made me feel like a traitor under interrogation. This was ridiculous, and I couldn't help but wonder why we were doing the self-examination. If only our captors had put us all to hard labor so that we wouldn't have had so much energy for these meaningless study sessions. My patience snapped and I said, "Look, I'm your comrade, though I'm not a Party member. I suffered no less than any of you and I have never betrayed our country." I lowered my head so that they could see the dark spot on my scalp inflicted by one of Wang Yong's men.

Then a staff member, Li Manyin, raised his hand and was allowed to speak. With his round eyes riveted on me, he asked almost jokingly, "I heard that you were quite thick with an American woman in Pusan. Can you tell us about this special relationship?"

A few men snickered. I got angry and said, "That was a doctor who saved my leg."

Another man put in, "Didn't you hold her hand teaching her how to write Chinese?"

Astounded, I didn't answer, wondering how they had come to know so much. Did my friend Ding Wanlin betray me? That was possible. No, there was nothing worth reporting about my relationship with Dr. Greene. Then where did they get the information?

"Comrade Yu Yuan, please answer the question," said Hao Chaolin. He was presiding over the meeting, though he didn't say much. He must have made sure beforehand that these questions would be brought up.

"She was a doctor in charge of my case," I said. "She had grown up in China, so she treated us well. In fact she was very kind to every patient there."

"But she's an American, isn't she?" the kitchen squad leader asked.

"Yes, she is."

"Didn't you teach her how to write an ancient poem?" another cook said.

"My goodness, this is like a cross-examination! Do you think we were lovers? Ludicrous, I don't even know her first name. I taught her how to write the characters, all right. There was no secret about it. I used the poem as a sample. Commissar Pei told me to remain close to her so that I could get information from her."

"How close?" another man asked.

"Yes, what did she give you?" chipped in a third voice.

"Chocolate bars?"

"Condensed milk?"

"Cereals?"

Some of them chuckled. Chang Ming stepped in, saying with a solemn face, "We shouldn't spend too much time on this. Commissar Pei did want him to keep a friendly relationship with that woman. Comrade Yu Yuan also got some good paper from her for Commissar Pei."

A few cooks hee-hawed. But Ming's words saved my neck, and I couldn't help looking at him gratefully. Though a college graduate, he knew how to deal with these men, who liked and respected him. So his words quieted them down. I noticed a dark shadow cross Chaolin's scabbed face, but he let them move on to the next man.

We had to wrap up the meeting earlier than the other groups because the cooks started working at 3:30 p.m. Before we ended the session, Chaolin proposed a motion — I should turn in my Bible to the higher-ups — which was voted for overwhelmingly. I was the only one who didn't raise his hand, and I couldn't dis-obey. So my Bible became the source of writing paper at the headquarters.

I was angry at heart. The Communists were good only at maltreating their own people and people close to them. Some of their men had just been murdered in other compounds, but nobody here had bothered to examine the Communists' negligence in organizing opposition to the screening. Instead, they'd begun to discipline their own ranks. In my mind echoed the words of Han Shu, the chief of Compound 72: "History has shown that the Communists always treat their enemies more leniently than their own people. Only by becoming their significant enemies can you survive decently."

12. STAGING A PLAY

Despite the leaders' efforts to organize and inspire the prisoners, the initial enthusiasm for our union in Compound 602 soon faded away and a lot of men turned moody again. Clearly the Communists had lost the battle of the screening — out of twenty thousand Chinese POWs more than fourteen thousand had refused to repatriate, most of them voluntarily but some against their will. To rebuild the comrades' confidence and revive their spirit, a performing arts troupe was formed, a couple of songs were composed, and several entertainments were provided, including poems, cartoons, and music (played mainly on self-made instruments). Then a group of men collaborated on the script for a play, entitled *The Dream on Wall Street*; it was about how the American capitalists controlled the White House and the Congress, and how they were behind the Korean War, striving to rule the globe. The play consisted of three acts and five scenes. Having read the script, the compound leaders decided to have it staged. To do this, the troupe needed a platform, props, and costumes. But how could they come by those things here?

To my surprise, some men began building an "open-air theater." In front of the barracks was an open field with bumps and sunken areas in it; toward its northern end the ground bulged a little, a foot or two higher than the rest of the field. Each battalion sent over sixty men to level the ground and heap up earth to make a stage, so that all of the audience sitting in the field could see the performance. Within three days a large platform was built out of oil drums, rocks, crates, tent poles, water pipes, and canvas. In spite of the mishmash, the "theater" looked quite impressive, as good as most stages improvised in the countryside back in China, where after the fall harvest villagers would hire troupes to perform for them. I wasn't interested in the play, which was more like a propaganda skit, but I was impressed by the men's ingenuity in staging it. They overcame one difficulty after another and created all the structures and props needed for the performance. They undid flour sacks, washed them clean, dyed them with tincture of Mercurochrome or that of gentian violet, basted them together, and hung the pieces up as curtains. They also used olive green blankets to make Western suits and American officers' uniforms. The battalions sent over some electricians to install lamps. To adjust the intensity of the light to the drama, they managed to control the electric current with an ad hoc resistor — salt water in a junked porcelain sink. Most of the props were made of wood and burlap sacks, variously painted. Drums were improvised out of bottomless oil cans tightly sealed with rain cloth at both ends. Two violins were created as well — the makers used bamboo and wooden boards and unraveled some nylon shoelaces to get the sturdy strands, then twisted them into strings.

The director of the play was Meng Feihan, a man who had lost his right foot. Before joining the Communist army, he had been a college student in Hong Kong. A talented musician and also a composer, he taught the prisoners how to sing more effectively and how to read music. He never seemed to tire of teaching others; three men were busy learning how to compose from him. Though crippled, he was more active than anybody else. Whenever he finished working on a scene, he would be bathed in perspiration. I guessed he hadn't fully recuperated from his injury yet. He was very strict about rehearsals — if one thing wasn't right he would make the actors repeat it again and again until he was satisfied. He insisted that every one of them learn his lines by heart. Yet however stern he was with them, the inmates respected him.

After a week's preparation, the play was ready for the stage. Ming took the role of Harry Truman. He was good at acting and often made people howl with laughter at the rehearsals. Since most of the characters were Caucasians, the actors would have to put on makeup to transform their Asiatic features, but there was no eyebrow pencil or putty or paint available. From Dr. Wang, Ming got some aspirins and exchanged them for makeup with two South Korean guards. They gave him powdered dyestuff, chewing gum, vanishing cream, paraffin wax, and an eyebrow pencil. To prepare the makeup, the actors mixed the colored powder with Vaseline given them by a medic. The gum was used to enlarge their Chinese noses. Two men were assigned to chew it, then to wash the lumps clean; it was not only pliable but also stickier, much better than putty, the conventional material used for this purpose in the theater.

On the evening of April 21, *The Dream on Wall Street* was shown to the six thousand POWs of Compound 602. Among the main characters were Harry Truman, the special envoy John Foster Dulles, two senators, and a corpulent banker on Wall Street. The play was quite amusing, though on occasion marred by propagandistic gibes. The music, played on the shabby self-made instruments, wasn't very effective, but it helped enliven the performance, especially the washbasins used as gongs and the two pot covers, one bigger than the other, serving as a pair of cymbals. Even the lights were managed well, going brighter or dimmer according to the development of the drama. Most amazing was the talent of the actors, particularly Ming, impersonating Truman, and Jin Shang, who played a fat billionaire. Their manners and dialogue were funny, at times slapstick, but always potent enough to bring out a roar of laughter from the audience. Even the GIs watched the play from the guard tower, and some of them were apparently entertained.

Ming, wearing steel-rimmed glasses, was too tall for the role of Harry Truman, so he kept his legs bowed all the while, his feet fanning out to form a V. This made him clownish. He said to the banker, "Paul, we need another billion dollars."

The capitalist, in a top hat and a tailcoat, answered with one hand on his potbelly, "Mr. President, we don't have much left in our bank. We gave you two billion last year." He twirled a walking stick while speaking.

"That wasn't a gift, it was a loan."

"But we've already shared the cost of the war, haven't we?"

"Come on, we're talking about this year. Can't you give us another loan?"

"At this rate, the war will soon bankrupt us, sir."

"Give me a break! You guys always make tons of money whenever there's a war."

"But we have to reserve a certain amount of capital to make profits."

"Darn it! I'm your capital, I'm your investment, I am the president of the United States!"

"But a billion dollars is astronomical to us."

"Of course it's a huge sum. We have to maintain a large army on the Korean Peninsula."

Their exchange was interrupted by the

unannounced appearance of two senators, one mustachioed and the other partly bald. Then the conversation resumed, and after another round of argument, the billionaire yielded and granted the loan at high interest.

As the scene proceeded, suddenly a GI shouted from the guard tower, "Hey, Officer Feng, you goddamned buffoon! Stop making fun of our president!"

That startled me because I thought he was yelling at me. Then I realized he knew Ming only by his alias, which was Feng Wen, close to mine. Another GI thundered, "Get your ass off the stage, Truman!"

A third cried in a joking tone, "Hey, Truman, you're fired! If you don't get off of the stage, I'm going to open up on you."

But to their credit, they didn't interfere further with the performance other than a few shouts, and remained a good audience for the rest of the play. More earnest than the Americans, the South Korean guards gathered outside the fence, along the barbed wire, watching attentively. Some of them even applauded when the curtain fell.

During the next few days, a number of Americans mentioned the performance to me. They wondered how it had been possible for the prisoners to stage a full-length play and where we had gotten all the theatrical props and costumes. I told them that some of the prisoners had been professionals, specifically the director, Meng Feihan, who had specialized in the performing arts. They were more impressed. One said, "Never thought there were artists among you." I was surprised that they would use the term "artist" so loosely. To us Chinese, only a maestro should be called that.

The Americans had taken us to be an army of peasants, more like cattle than men. The play seemed to have changed their perception of us a little. Later I noticed that the guards would treat the few actors somewhat differently from the regular prisoners, with more respect. They would no longer curse them. This amazed me, because to most Chinese an actor was just an entertainer, and however talented he was, he still belonged to the lower strata of society. His job was only to please others, so he wasn't as important as an officer or an official.

13. AN UNUSUAL REQUEST

Since we had moved into the new compound, the GIs guarding it had treated us less harshly. This was mainly because we kept our tents clean and were not as belligerent as the Korean prisoners. A group of U.N. inspectors visited our barracks and was satisfied with its order and sanitary conditions. As the inmates got to know the American guards better, some of them often went to the front entrance to bum a cigarette off the GIs or watch them taking coffee ladled out of a large cauldron on a kerosene stove set behind a shack. A few men asked me what coffee tasted like. "Bitter. You can't drink it without sugar," I told them. By regulation the GIs were forbidden to talk with us, but many of them did anyway.

I often went to chat with them, because I had been assigned to do so. Although our headquarters had access to *Stars and Stripes*, the U.S. Army newspaper, we couldn't get it regularly enough to follow events outside the camp. A number of our men were in charge of cleaning and maintaining the GIs' quarters, so whenever possible, they'd secretly bring back the newspaper. My job was to read the news and translate the useful information for Commissar Pei and his staff. This was a good, rewarding job, which I enjoyed. My role as a translator enabled me to read a lot and made me feel important. From the newspaper we learned more about the Panmunjom peace talks, at which the issue of the POWs had been raised. An article reported that China had its own air force now, which often engaged American planes over North Korea, though not effectively, because our pilots were inexperienced. There were about a dozen air force divisions in our country, all equipped with MiG-15s. But we had no idea how many planes made up a division, so the prisoners often argued about the exact number — some said one hundred while others insisted on seventy-two. I also read that the American soldiers were eager to go home and that normally they stayed in Korea for no more than one winter, whose harshness intimidated them. One article implied that desertions among the U.S. troops had increased considerably in recent months, and that some GIs had even invalided themselves out of the front line by inflicting wounds on themselves.

There was some news that might have disheartened our comrades, so I didn't translate everything. For example, it was reported that North Korean and Chinese servicemen had occasionally shot prisoners who were too weak to keep up with the other captives in their march to prison camps. Another report said that a secret investigation was under way in the People's Volunteer Army, intended to "ferret out those disguised counterrevolutionaries," the primary targets of the scrutiny being the new recruits with unclear political backgrounds and the defectors from the former Nationalist army, like myself. I didn't mention this to anyone. But I told Commissar Pei that Chairman Mao's eldest son, Mao Anying, had been killed in an air raid. Pei was stunned and couldn't speak for a long while.

"This doesn't seem like a pure accident," I hazarded. "How could the American bombers be so accurate? He was in a shelter when they went to attack."

"Don't let anyone else know of this," Pei said.

"I won't."

"Our Chairman's other son is demented.

This must've been a heavy blow to the old man, who must hate the American imperialists all the more. I'm afraid we won't see the end of this war soon."

My ability to control the flow of information in Compound 602 gave me a sense of power, which, to be honest, I relished. Yet what pleased me most was the opportunity to improve my English and the access to the kind of news regular Chinese publications wouldn't carry. Each issue of the newspaper consisted of more than twenty pages and many photographs, and I read every word of it.

Soon the GIs noticed that our men were pilfering their paper, so they stopped tossing it around. Our supply of *Stars and Stripes* became more erratic — sometimes we got five or six copies of the same issue, but then we wouldn't have any for an entire week.

So I was assigned to chat with the guards as often as possible to collect information from them. I found that most of the Americans were quite talkative. Almost without exception they enjoyed being listened to, especially by an enemy soldier who could understand their language. Sometimes after a bout of talk they would return to the sentry post; then a few minutes later they'd stroll back to me and start talking again. They too seemed lonesome and hated this place intensely. So I often listened to them talk, and from them I gathered useful bits of news.

I wasn't the only information collector. There were numerous other sources as well. The night soil team did a remarkable job in smuggling newspapers and magazines back into the compound; they stank so repulsively that few GIs would bother searching them. Most often, the guards, holding their breath, just waved the whole group past. Every morning over a dozen inmates cleaned the latrines here, carried buckets of night soil with shoulder poles to the beach, and dumped it all into the ocean. A mild-tempered GI, Jim Baker, a stout, light-skinned Negro, escorted them back and forth; they called him Sergeant, though he was just a private. He treated them kindly and had a soft spot for flattery, which they would lavish on him. They went so far as to say that he was the most handsome black man they had ever met, and that some Chinese girls would be swept off their feet by his big smile. Even when they called him "Turtle Egg" and some other names, he didn't take offense, always smiling with his bright white teeth.

He knew the meanings of those swear-words, since he had been learning Chinese from a member in the night soil squad. Besides collecting information, these latrine men also passed messages on to other compounds, especially to the Korean prisoners, who had their night soil teams too.

There was a corporal, Richard, who had deep-set blue eyes and freckles on both sides of his prominent nose. His last name was Randell or Randal, if I remember it correctly. He was on guard duty in the morning on weekdays. He looked older than most of his fellow GIs, and had a girl-friend back home. Before coming to Korea he had been a technician in a farm-tool factory in Detroit. One day, he was telling me how he and his girlfriend had camped on a lake, building a fire and frying trout and whitefish in bacon grease. I somehow could no longer control my emotions and squatted down, covering my face with both hands. I wasn't crying, I just felt miserable, and didn't want him to see my woeful face.

"It's tough, man. I know it's tough," he kept saying with some feeling.

I didn't know how intimate he had been with his girlfriend. His talk reminded me of Julan, who was more than a fiancée to me. Two days before our division left Szechuan, she had asked me to make love to her, saying she wanted to have my baby. I guessed she was afraid I might never return from the war, so a baby could become something of mine for her to keep. For a whole night we made love again and again, almost desperately; it was as though I meant to pour all of myself into her so that a part of me would remain home. With furious hunger she received me, also with hot tears and silent spasms. The next morning she broke her white jade barrette in two and gave me a half, saying with her eyes lowered, "From this day on I'm your wife. Remember, even if I'm dead, my ghost shall be with you." I promised her that I would return to her as long as I was alive. Since that day I had carried the broken jade with me. Whenever I was about to be searched, I would hide it behind my belt or in my shoe. I didn't know if Julan was pregnant, though I had written to her once and alluded to it. I dared not ask her explicitly because I was sure that the mail was monitored. There was a mailbox by the front gate of every compound, into which we dropped our letters once in a while, but nobody among us had ever heard a word from home.

Little by little I began to become friendlier with Richard. He would give me cigarillos and lemon drops. If he had a newspaper on him, he'd slip it through the barbed wire to me. He seemed quite smart, often smiling cynically. One morning he asked me, "Can you do me a favor, Feng Yan?"

"Sure, if I can." I was surprised, wondering how I, a helpless prisoner, could be of use to him.

He said with a small grin, "If this damn war heats up again, I may see action at the front. Can you help me get a safety certificate?"

"What's that?"

"You don't know?"

"I really don't."

"I've never seen one either. But I'm told it has some Chinese or Korean words on it, saying, 'Don't kill this guy, he's our friend.' Something like that."

"What's it for?"

"You Chinese shoot prisoners, you know. I heard that an officer shot more than forty U.S. POWs because he'd lost his regiment on the front. If you get me this piece of paper, I can show it to them if they catch me, and they may not kill me."

261

I was surprised by his candid words, but I made no comment and just promised to help. To some extent, I admired him for speaking about his fear without any shame or embarrassment, so I pulled the bottom of my shirt out of my belt and showed him the tattoo — FUCK COMMUNISM. He laughed and said, "Man, you got that right!"

His request made me think that my tattoo might serve as a "safety certificate" if need be, depending on how I used it. But on second thought, I was already in the prison camp and my life didn't seem in danger. Then why did Commissar Pei say my tattoo might help me? How could it do that? I couldn't imagine.

I reported Richard's request to Commissar Pei that afternoon. In the evening an emergency meeting was held at the headquarters, which I attended. The leaders decided to come up with something like the certificate Richard had described, though nobody had ever seen such a thing. They assigned Ming to take care of it. That night Ming set about designing one. He cut a square of white paper, the size of his palm, and with a pencil stub he drew a star at its top, then wrote these words in the official script:

SAFETY CERTIFICATE

Dear Comrades-in-Arms — the Chinese People's Volunteers and the North Korean People's Army:

This U.S. soldier surrenders of his own will and is our friend. Please treat him well.

> Revolutionary Salute,
> Comrades on Koje Island
> April 24, 1952

When I handed the scrap of paper to Richard the next day, he, without looking at it, put it into his shirt pocket beneath his jacket, then raised his hand, his thumb and index finger forming a circle. I guessed it must mean good or excellent. I was surprised that he didn't even ask me what the words meant. What if the certificate fell into his superiors' hands? Wouldn't he be court-martialed? I was sure that if a Chinese soldier was found in possession of such a thing, he would be jailed, if not executed.

Then one morning Richard wore a long face, as though he had just been crying. I asked him why he looked unhappy. He said, "I got a Dear John from home."

"What's that, a gift?"

He grimaced. "It's a good-bye letter from my girlfriend."

"I'm sorry."

"It came out of the blue."

"Is there another man involved?"

"I have no idea."

I sighed. "A serviceman's life is unpredictable, and a woman usually wants a stable life."

"It's all because of this damned war!" He shook his head, his nostrils flaring.

"That's true."

"I don't see why I'm here. Fighting for what?"

I wanted to tell him that I knew why I was standing on Korean soil — to defend my country — but I refrained. He was so upset that we couldn't chat more that day.

There was another black private, Frank Holeman, a tall angular fellow with a mop of wiry hair, who was from Louisiana, shy and good-natured. He often chuckled with a snorting noise. Like many GIs, he had glassy eyes as a result of smoking marijuana, which grew wild in Korea, also in Manchuria. Neither Chinese nor Koreans liked the weed; we mainly used it to make rope and we preferred tobacco. I chatted with Frank several times and he would answer my questions as though I were not a prisoner. Once I mentioned *Uncle Tom's Cabin*; he shook his head and said, "Never heard of it. I don't read no books."

I was surprised. I had wanted to ask him whether the slaves really could eat chicken, turkey, ham, and biscuits, so I said, "The author wrote that the black slaves ate chicken wings and drumsticks and salt pork. Did they eat such good food in the South?"

"Sure."

"Can you eat chicken every day if you want?"

"Chicken's cheap back home, you know. Most folks can afford it."

"What's expensive food then?"

"Steak. Rich folks go to restaurants for a steak. Seafood is pricey too."

"You mean shrimp?"

"Yeah, also salmon, crawfish, oyster, and lobster. Man, my mouth is watering."

I had no idea what a lobster looked like, though I knew the Chinese meaning of the word — dragon prawn. To my mind it must have been a kind of giant shrimp. But I was a little surprised by his mention of oysters as an expensive food, because I had seen street peddlers selling shucked oysters for five cents a pound in a coastal city back in China. I disliked oysters and wouldn't touch them even for free. I told Frank that to the Chinese, chicken was the best meat and that in the southern provinces like Canton and Fujian even chicken feet were served as a kind of delicacy in restaurants. He whistled and said, "Man, if it ain't for this war, I'd be in the chicken business making tons of dough out of you Chinamen."

"To be the first black millionaire, eh?"

"Why not?"

We both laughed.

I also mentioned to him the antislavery movie entitled *A Shipload of Slaves* that I had seen in China, but he hadn't heard of the film either. His ignorance of books and movies didn't prevent us from having something to talk about. He often gave me chewing gum, for which I wished I could have given him something in return. Once he offered me a joint, which I inhaled but didn't like. Later he asked me to help him get a certificate like the one Richard had. Within two days I handed him a similar one, which pleased him a lot.

Because blank paper was in short supply, we couldn't produce this kind of certificate every time a request came up. If paper was unavailable, we would give the man a red star, our former cap insignia, which might help him some. During the rest of our imprisonment, including the year we stayed on Cheju Island, altogether we issued over one hundred safety certificates to GIs. No South Korean ever asked us for such a thing.

14. A TEST

One evening in the late spring we were sent to unload a ship. Usually we didn't work at the wharf. The men in Compound 70, nicknamed the Labor Gang, would unload cargoes and transport them to the warehouses. Some of them also repaired roads, felled trees, quarried stones, built barbed-wire fences, dug foundations, and laid bricks. Today was an exception because the work was urgent and the ship would raise anchor the next morning. On the way to the quay we sang "The Guerrillas' Song." The guards couldn't understand the words, so they didn't interfere.

There were numerous sentries at the wharf. A pair of searchlights scraped the ground and the sky, while strings of lamps lit almost the entire area. It was a warm night, so warm that you felt drowsy as though drugged. We were divided into four groups, three of which unloaded the ship while the other stacked the cargo on the shore. With my weak leg, I couldn't tread the quivering planks leading to the ship's deck, so I worked with the fourth group piling stacks. From time to time we poked a hole in a sack or a box to see what was inside — corn, rice, peanuts, cigarettes, straw paper, medicines. Among the cargo there were also sacks of cement and bundles of used clothing.

As we slaved away, from the north came some female voices singing ditties that sounded mawkish and lighthearted. We had heard that a number of restaurants and brothels were in that part of town. We couldn't help but look in that direction now and again. The women's voices stimulated me. For the first time since my injury I felt a strong sexual stirring. Even the air I breathed seemed to be sharpening my nose, as if from a distance of over three hundred yards I could smell the flesh and scent of women. My temples were tight and my pulse raced. Though a little giddy, I was happy to feel the throbbing of my blood, because this meant I had physically regained my strength. I was amazed that even subsisting on inadequate food, I had recovered miraculously. I was still youthful, still full of vitality.

In the cabins and on the deck of the ship and among the stacks on shore, the prisoners were busy lifting and shouldering parcels, boxes, and sacks. We were all soaked with sweat and often panted for breath. Yet a GI, a florid-faced man, kept barking at us, *"Pahly, pahly!"* which means "hurry" in Korean.

A tall inmate dropped a clothing bundle on a stack and cursed in an undertone, "Son of a bitch!" He then sneaked away, probably to take a breather.

Curious, I rounded the corner of the stack to see what he was doing. He had opened his fly and was peeing on a roll of canvas, his urine producing a muffled tapping sound. The second he was done, an American officer emerged from the darkness about fifty yards to the north, humming a tune he must have learned from the Korean geishas. He seemed drunk, didn't notice us, and veered unsteadily toward the rows of houses below a water tower, wearing a pistol at his flank. To my surprise, the tall prisoner came out from the stacks and followed the officer at a distance of about a hundred feet. I wondered what he was up to. Did he want to kill him? Or simply to escape?

Not daring to stay there for long, I went back to work, taking care to pick lighter items to carry. Busy as I was, I couldn't stop wondering what the tall man was doing. If only Ming had been here, so that I could ask him. Then I saw Chaolin talk with two men in whispers while the three of them were piling bundles of barbed wire. He was the leader of the two hundred men here. Like me, he wanted to get out of the compound as often as possible, always saying, "I need to stretch my limbs." He and I had never been close, so I didn't go up to him and report on the disappearance of that inmate.

About twenty minutes later the tall man came back, panting hard, his eyes shining. He said to Chaolin that an American officer had gone to sleep without locking his door and that there was a pistol in his room. "Should I go back and take it?" he asked Chaolin.

"Why didn't you just snatch it?" a man butted in.

"I wasn't sure if it was a right thing to do, so I came back to ask permission."

Chaolin said, "We must get the gun, but you shouldn't go alone. Yuan, why don't you go with him?"

"Me?" I was taken aback as several pairs of eyes turned to me.

"Yes, you go with him. Let him stay outside the house to keep watch while you go in for the gun."

"What if the officer wakes up?" I was puzzled why he picked me for the job.

"Kill him with this!" another man said and handed me an iron bar about two feet long.

I realized Chaolin meant to give me a test, which I had no choice but to take. So I agreed. But we couldn't set about the task right away because the sentries at the wharf were still alert. We had to go on working.

After ten-thirty the guards began yawning, whereas many prisoners had grown more spirited, gathering around them, asking questions or complaining that we were too hungry to continue. The inmates wanted to share a sack of peanuts, but the duty sergeant wouldn't let them. While they were begging him, I set off with the tall man, whose name I now knew was Wang Yabing. We sneaked behind the stacks and slunk away, avoiding the lights along the quay. My heart was fluttering as if a rabbit had been trapped in my chest, and my steps were shaky. Within five minutes we reached a low house that looked like a civilian home with a ceramic-tiled roof. Indeed the door wasn't locked and it opened at a light push. Then came the officer's soft snoring. Thank heaven, he was sound asleep.

"You go in now," Wang Yabing whispered to me. "If someone's coming, I'll meow like a horny cat."

With the iron bar under my arm I tiptoed into the room. The table lamp was still on, covered by a shade made of fawn paper. The sleeper, a small man with a graying mustache, had his clothes on, his bristly face toward the dark ceiling. He stirred a little, clattering his teeth as though munching something. Suddenly he chuckled, saying, "Oh dear, what a mess. Can you give him another fork, Cathy?" I froze in my tracks. A moment later he resumed snoring. Beside his pillow lay a grimy Colt pistol and a black flashlight. Shivering all over, I picked up the gun and stepped backward until I reached the door. The instant I turned around, the iron bar fell on the stone steps with a clanking noise, but I didn't stop to retrieve it and just tore away into the darkness.

Wang Yabing caught up with me a moment later. He clutched my shoulder and gave me a shake. "What happened?"

"I don't know." My face was sweaty and my tongue wooden.

"You look as if you've been chased by a ghost."

I was still gasping for breath. He asked again, "Did you get it?"

"Yes." I showed him the pistol.

"Great!" He took the gun and waved it as though to fire into the sky. Together we headed back.

Our men were wrapping up the work when we returned. Chaolin was so elated to see the pistol that he wore it in his belt while listening to me report how I had stolen it. Although I admitted I had left behind the iron bar, nobody took it as a mishap, so I stopped worrying about it. Then a problem I hadn't anticipated arose: how could we smuggle the gun back into the compound? Having talked briefly with Wang Yabing, Chaolin decided to let me carry it through the gate, because I was familiar with most of the guards.

I unloaded the five bullets and gave them to other prisoners, one apiece, to take back. This was easy for them — they could put the bullets in their mouths before going through the gate. I used a long shoelace to tie the pistol to my good thigh; the ends of the string were attached to the waist of my underwear. Most of the time the guards wouldn't touch my thighs.

On our way back the gun chafed my groin badly, but I pretended everything was normal. Still, I couldn't help walking bowleggedly. Some prisoners laughed at my discomfort and even imitated the way I waddled. Chaolin stared at them, eye-signaling them not to attract the guards' attention. Thanks to my injured leg, which always gave me a limp, the GIs didn't notice anything unusual.

The front gate opened and two guards began frisking us. When my turn came I stepped forward with a forced yawn. The GI touched my front and back, from my neck to my ankles, but he didn't feel elsewhere. I passed the gate, then strode toward Chaolin, who was awaiting me inside the compound. The moment we got into the nearest tent, I untied the pistol and handed it to him.

My thigh and scrotum were chafed, but the medic was already in bed, so I had to wait until the next morning to have the sore treated. My muscles were strained too, owing to the awkward walk back from the wharf. Yet I was happy and went to bed without further delay. In a state of half sleep I saw myself in the American officer's bedroom again, looking for his pistol but unable to find it. He yelled suddenly, "You can't have it!" I woke up, my heart palpitating and the front of my shirt damp with sweat. In spite of pain and fear, I was glad I had passed the test in the way a soldier should, though in my mind a shadow of doubt was thickening. I was unsure whether the test had just been improvised by Chaolin or whether there had been a decision within the Party to give me such an ordeal. Later I asked Ming, who said confidentially that a week ago the Party had indeed decided to test my loyalty should such an occasion arise.

The next morning, a company of GIs came into our compound and ordered all the prisoners to get out of our tents. With their bayonets thrust here and there, they rummaged through all the barracks, over-turning our mats and knocking down our makeshift furniture, but they found nothing. In fact, they couldn't possibly have recovered the pistol, which had just been smuggled out of the compound by the night soil team, who had hidden it among rocks on the beach. The Americans were unsure who among us had worked the night before, though they grabbed hold of Chaolin, who claimed he couldn't re-member all the faces and names. So they ordered some of our men at the front of the crowd to step out. Unprepared for such an order, the inmates obeyed. From the back of the crowd I watched them with a pounding heart. The men who had stepped forward were innocent and most of them hadn't gone out the night before. After inspecting them, the officer in charge, a tall man wearing two hand grenades on his chest, one on either breast pocket, picked four prisoners and had them taken away to a truck parked outside the gate. One of the four men turned colorless and hollered, "I didn't do anything wrong! What's this about?" The GIs couldn't understand him and just hauled him away.

I was frightened, unsure if any of the four inmates knew about the pistol. I wondered why the officer wouldn't have Chaolin dragged away too. Probably he was aware that Chaolin was a die-hard Communist from whom they couldn't extract any information. I was also worried that the Americans might be in possession of the iron bar I had dropped, which could be a piece of evidence and from which they might obtain my fingerprints. A sweat broke out on my neck and forehead, but I dared not lift my hand to wipe it for fear of drawing attention. I kept a low profile, remaining in the crowd, while Ming stood at the front serving as an interpreter.

In the meantime, frustrated and unable to focus on the search, the officer began cursing us and threatened to throw some of us into solitary confinement if we didn't tell him the names of the people involved in the theft. "I'll try the lot of you. D'you hear me?" he shouted. "You bunch of thieves! You don't dare to face me like a man!"

Ming didn't bother to translate those words. We all remained silent as though nobody had understood the officer. Many looked at him with genuine confusion. Half an hour later the Americans withdrew. But before leaving, the officer warned us that this was just the beginning of the investigation.

Toward midafternoon two squads of GIs came in again, carrying shovels and pickaxes, and they also delivered to us the inmates they had taken away. The four men were all battered, their noses stuffed with bloody cotton balls and their faces swollen like loaves of bread. One had a black eye with sealed lids. They were so fear-stricken that they could hardly speak, merely nodding or shaking their heads when others talked to them. I felt awful, though none of them looked trustworthy. If they had known I was the thief, they might have given me away.

While we were busy helping the returned men, the GIs went on digging and poking around. They called us all kinds of names for causing them such drudgery, but some prisoners whistled and waved their caps at them. This annoyed them more.

They didn't find any weapon, not even one of the five bullets, but they got hold of two pairs of pliers, which was a minor loss to us. That evening I was informed that the Party Committee here had cited me for brave service. The citation was of the third class. I was pleased, hoping that from now on my life would be easier and that they wouldn't test me again.

The pistol was never used in our later struggle. It was passed on to the North Korean prisoners, who already possessed some small firearms.

The Communists always tested the men they suspected. I knew a number of such cases in the camp. One man was instructed to burn a warehouse storing provisions for the POWs, and under cover of darkness he torched not only the main house but also two stacks of timber nearby. The flames sprang up fifty feet high, and four fire engines raced back and forth to get water from the seaside, but everybody could see that the fire was inextinguishable. The man was awarded a special merit citation by the Party Committee afterward. Luckily for him, the Americans, after questioning many of us, gave up searching for the arsonist. Another man was ordered to steal a crate of Spam from a storehouse at night. He didn't make it because a searchlight spotted him as he was crawling back through a hole in a fence, and he was shot dead. The guards must have thought he was either cutting the fence with pliers or attempting to blow it up with a box of explosives, which the crate of Spam might have resembled. Indeed, we had planned to breach the fence all along. In the compound there were about a dozen pairs of pliers and pincers, all smuggled in by the prisoners. The enemy knew that and often came to hunt for them. These tools would be indispensable if it came to the point where we had to break jail, so our leaders often ordered someone they meant to test to steal a pair.

15. MEETING WITH MR. PARK

There was frequent contact between us and the compounds controlled by the Korean Communists. Commissar Pei wore a steel-strapped Swiss watch offered to him by our Korean comrades. On April 30 we received a secret message from them, which requested us to send two representatives to attend an important meeting. Pei let Chaolin and me go. Initially I was excited about this assignment, assuming the Party had begun to trust me now that I had stolen the pistol; but on second thought, I realized I'd become a side-kick to Chaolin in this mission mainly because I spoke English. Nobody among us knew Korean, and Pei wouldn't want the Koreans to think we were ignorant of any foreign language, so he sent me along to save face.

The Korean POWs had been here longer than we had and possessed more resources. They were better supplied than the civilians and in a way fared even better than the South Korean troops, who didn't have enough medicine and often starved. Our North Korean comrades could always exchange clothing for kimchee and soybean paste with the villagers, and their underground channels kept them in touch with their national leaders.

As a rule, when a multicompound meeting was to be held, all the attendees from different compounds would feign illness so as to get permission to go to the Sixty-fourth Field Hospital, where a meeting would take place. Many Korean medical personnel worked there, and the Communists controlled a good part of the hospital. On May 1, Chaolin and I got permission from Dr. Wang of our compound, so the guards let us out. Chaolin knew the camp well because he often left our compound to meet with the prison authorities. He looked runty, like a starved chicken, but he had a steel will and often quarreled with the Americans, since as the vice chief of Compound 602 he spoke on behalf of six thousand men (Zhao Teng, the nominal chief, was slow of words). Chaolin was also good at giving speeches that could sway a large audience. I respected him for his eloquence and experience, though whenever I was with him I would feel tense, wary about what I'd say and do.

The hospital was within the camp and served the POWs only; it consisted of eight tents, two small houses, and three sheds. Behind a cottage we were received by two Korean men, both in their early thirties, one with a fleshy face, which was rare among the Koreans, whereas the other looked quite feminine, delicate and slender. We sat down in the backyard, where laundered sheets hung on iron wires stretched among drooping willows, obscuring the yard considerably. A swing swayed gently in the breeze as if there had been children living in the cottage. Chaolin had met the officers before and introduced them to me as Lee and Choi, saying they were both colonels in the Korean People's Army. Choi, the fleshy-faced man, happened to be a college graduate, had majored in history, and could speak some English and Russian. Lee was less educated, but he spoke Chinese beautifully, having lived in Manchuria as a guerrilla fighting the Japanese for over a decade. They looked healthier than regular prisoners and seemed at ease. On our way in I had noticed two young Korean nurses folding sterilized bandages in an office at the front of the house; in reality these women were keeping guard for us. Now and then they hummed a song; their laughter sounded carefree. Their pleasant voices distracted me from time to time.

The meeting was short; it wouldn't be safe to stay in the backyard too long. But we were shocked by what the officers told us: the Koreans planned to kidnap General Bell, the U.S. commandant on Koje Island. They wanted our compound to cooperate with them.

"How can we assist you in carrying out this bold plan?" asked Chaolin.

They said we should ease the general's vigilance by inviting him to our compound and talking with him without arousing his suspicion; after that, they would ask him to visit their barracks too. Chaolin suggested that we seize General Bell ourselves if he came to our compound, but Lee, the feminine man, said they had already made arrangements and had more "armed force" than we did. He explained, "We shouldn't let you bear the brunt again if the Americans retaliate. You've already sacrificed enough." He must have been referring to the fact that we had come all the way to Korea to fight our common enemy. Chaolin didn't insist and promised to participate in their plan.

Before we left, they took us into a side

room in the cottage, where we were introduced to Mr. Park, who was the top leader of the Korean POWs. Sitting on the glossy floor, Mr. Park was a short but muscular man in a tweed coat. His face was pale and his eyes piercingly bright. Around him sat several officers. He shook hands with Chaolin and me and gave us each a cigarette, which we lit and smoked ravenously. I was amazed that he had Lucky Strikes, the American brand. He spoke to us while Lee was interpreting for him. He thanked us for letting them have the pistol I had stolen. Then he said, "From the bottom of our hearts we are grateful to the Chinese Communist Party and the People's Volunteers. You're our closest comrades-in-arms. You have made great sacrifice and suffered for us. We salute you."

Chaolin replied that we shared the same enemy, the U.S. imperialists, and that by coming to Korea we actually fought to protect our country as well. I was impressed by his ease in adopting an aggrandized role, as if he were equal to our host in rank. Then Mr. Park talked about the significance of capturing General Bell — this event would shock the world. He said that Marshal Kim Il Sung had ordered them to open "a second front" in the prison camp and that we must embarrass our captors and expose their lie that we were all treated humanely. Also, the success of this operation would help our negotiators at Panmunjom as well. Chaolin promised that he would brief our headquarters about their plan and that we would help them in any way we could. When we were leaving, Mr. Park embraced us and said we would definitely meet again, very soon.

Seeing us off, Colonel Choi told me in English that Mr. Park had studied in Moscow and had been the governor of the North Yellow Sea Province in Korea. Here in the camp he was their commander. We asked Choi how Mr. Park had been taken prisoner if he was such an important official. Choi wouldn't explain, just smiling mysteriously. I had the impression that Mr. Park still lived and functioned like a provincial governor here, well preserved and thoroughly protected. He had an air of serene confidence, as if he were the boss in this camp, not the Americans.

That evening our headquarters held a meeting, over which Commissar Pei presided. He sat at a "table" built of eight upturned cardboard cases covered with a blanket. Now and again he tapped the tip of his cigarette over a rusty enamel bowl.

The veins on the back of his hand stood out; a healed scar marked the end of his thumb. He didn't seem enthusiastic about the Korean comrades' plan and looked thoughtful, his face a little wrinkled. Whenever his brown eyes gazed at me, I felt as if he could see through me. He didn't express his opinion, though before the meeting he had said about the Koreans to Chaolin and me, "They're so bold. I hope they know how to deal with the consequences." I was puzzled but dared not ask him what he meant exactly.

People got excited about our report on the Koreans' plan. The commissar instructed us to demonstrate the next day and then go on a hunger strike. Meanwhile, the Secretariat must gather evidence for the crimes committed by our captors so that we could charge General Bell when he fell into the Koreans' hands. After the meeting, Ming went about writing two letters, one addressed to our delegates at the Panmunjom talks and the other to the International Red Cross, exposing the maltreatment the POWs had suffered and demanding that the Americans return all the bodies of our comrades killed on the battleground, that they stop backing the pro-Nationalist force in the prison camp, and that they take measures to stamp out violence and bring the murderers to justice. The first of the demands surprised me, because I remembered the dead our former division had buried along our way to the front in the spring of 1951. Hundreds of men had been killed in air raids and left in the wilderness, and I was sure none of their bodies would ever be shipped back to our homeland.

Ming and I both worked as translators in the compound. I spoke English better, so I was present most of the time when we met with the Americans. He was a Party member and attended their secret meetings, for which I wasn't qualified. We two got along well and often compared notes, so I knew quite a bit about the happenings within the Party.

16. MEETING WITH GENERAL BELL

The next afternoon we presented to Lieutenant East, the officer in charge of guarding our compound, a formal letter that demanded the improvement of our living conditions and also a face-to-face talk with General Bell. I had spent a whole morning putting the letter into English. Ming, who seemed to have infinite connections, had bartered an American army overcoat with a South Korean officer for an English-Japanese dictionary. Since in many cases we could guess the meanings of Japanese words without knowing the language, this dictionary was quite handy. Without it I couldn't have rendered any document accurately into English.

Having gotten no response to our letter, we demonstrated in the compound the following day. Three groups of men, each six hundred strong, by turns went to the area close to the southern fence, shouted slogans, and raised pieces of hardboard that carried words in both English and Chinese, such as "Uphold the Geneva Convention!," "Treat Us Like Human Beings!," "Stop Violence in the Prison!," "Punish the Murderers!" The guards were nervous, but some of them mocked us and gave us the finger. One shouted, "Okay, if you want us to treat you better, tell Chairman Mao to sign the Geneva Convention first."

I didn't translate those words for my comrades. I had read in *Stars and Stripes* some time ago that neither China nor North Korea had signed the convention, and that the United States had signed it, but its Congress hadn't ratified it yet. On Capitol Hill there had been a debate over whether the U.S. Army should actually abide by the convention. Few of the Chinese prisoners knew the truth, which would be hard to explain to them, and which our leaders, believing ignorance was strength that could enable their men to fight bravely, wouldn't want us to know.

Toward three p.m. a short officer showed up, accompanied by the gangly Lieutenant East. The small man introduced himself as Major Leach and said to us, "I represent General Bell and you can talk to me. He's busy at the moment." Somehow his narrow face reminded me of a possum.

"We will speak only to General Bell in person," said Danwei, the head of the third group of demonstrators.

I translated his reply. Then to whatever the major said the prisoners wouldn't respond. The six hundred men just stood there, arms folded on their chests. After half an hour's coaxing and blustering to no avail, Major Leach left in a huff.

The next morning a hunger strike started in our compound, but no demonstrators got to the yard, and only two dozen pickets stood near the front entrance. Some mess tins and bowls were hung on the barbed-wire fence to express our determination not to eat. A truckload of barley, spinach, and radishes was delivered at midmorning, but our pickets blocked the vehicle, so everything was unloaded and placed outside the gate. Chaolin and I went to talk with Lieutenant East. We asked him to inform General Bell that only by meeting our representatives personally could this crisis be resolved, and that we trusted nobody but the general because only he could guarantee our safety.

Lieutenant East spat out some tobacco juice and said, "Who gives a fuck if you eat or not? Starve as long as you like. I won't pass him your word."

We were worried about his refusal, but Commissar Pei told us to be patient, saying the lieutenant wouldn't dare suppress our request without reporting it to General Bell. Both Ming and I felt frustrated and talked about this matter in private. Why couldn't the Koreans just execute the kidnapping by themselves? Why did this have to be so elaborate and involve us? They could have just invited the general to their compound and seized him there. Probably they were apprehensive and wanted a broader base of support for their plan. Then why wouldn't they adopt a less risky form of protest? They might get more than they bargained for.

Sure enough, as Commissar Pei predicted, the next morning a jeep appeared at the gate. In it were seated General Bell and Major Leach; behind them followed about twenty GIs in a ten-wheeled truck. I was summoned to our headquarters while Ming set off to inform the Americans that we would like to talk with the general in the tent of our Secretariat. A few minutes later Ming returned with a message from Lieutenant East, who insisted we go to the front entrance and speak with the general there. So Chaolin, I, and six other men approached the gate, behind which we were ordered to remain.

Lieutenant East went up to the jeep to brief General Bell. Bell was a robust man with a ruddy complexion, in his mid-forties, wearing shiny boots and a diamond ring, which made him look rather urbane. Below his cap a bit of gray hair was visible. He seemed to have spruced up for this occasion, and even the insignia on his cap was shiny. Following him was the short major with a briefcase under his arm and a thick book in his hand. All the GIs had jumped down from the truck and stood in a fan shape, holding M1 Garand rifles. Chaolin said to me, "They really believe we're going to hurt him, don't they?" Then we stepped closer to meet the officers.

Through the barbed wire on the gate, Chaolin said, "Welcome, General Bell. Thank you for taking the trouble to come personally."

I translated his words. Bell nodded with a complacent smile and said, "I respect you Chinese. And your compound is a model of discipline and cleanliness. You can let me know your gripes now."

Chaolin smiled and said again, "We'd like to invite you to inspect the malnutrition most of the inmates have suffered here.

Many wounded men are bedridden and need medical treatment, but we don't have enough medicines and staff to help them. Most of the prisoners in this compound suffer from night blindness, scurvy, beri-beri, skin disorders, and other diseases because we haven't eaten enough vegetables. We hope you will observe the Geneva Convention and treat us decently." Chaolin's description of the inmates' physical condition was true on the whole. Some prisoners could see nothing but a wall of darkness at night, and some still had running wounds.

The general cleared his throat and said, "We have always abided by the Geneva Convention and tried our best to honor all the articles, although I don't have enough staff and materials at my disposal. Let me ask my aide to read some paragraphs from the convention to refresh your memory."

Solemnly Major Leach opened the big green book and began reading in a bass voice. I didn't bother to translate, because Chaolin was familiar with the Chinese version of the relevant articles. Meanwhile, General Bell looked absentminded, shifting his weight from one foot to another. To my amazement, he took nail clippers out of his jacket pocket and picked his nails with the tip of the file. The backs of his hands were bristly with brown hair.

We knew those articles by heart, so none of us listened to the major. To the Americans' credit, I should mention that they had posted the relevant clauses of the international law in every compound, in both Chinese and Korean, and that they also issued to every platoon a booklet containing the text. Before seeing the booklet, we had only heard of the Geneva Convention but hadn't known its contents. Having studied the document thoroughly, our leaders concluded that the Americans had contravened Article 118, which stated: "Prisoners of war shall be released and repatriated without delay after the cessation of hostilities." However, when the regulation had been drafted three years before, the world had been less complicated and none of the participating countries had been able to imagine our situation — in which more than two-thirds of the Chinese POWs wouldn't be going home. Still, whenever possible, we would confront our captors with their violation of Article 118, and most of the time we could get the upper hand.

In addition to the issue of repatriation, our leaders also accused the American side of some other serious violations of the convention. To be fair, I didn't feel that our captors treated us very badly. At least we were sheltered and had food. Most of the wounded prisoners had access to medical treatment, though conditions still had room for improvement. About six thousand people had been crowded into a small compound, with no disease springing up, because sanitation had been adequately maintained. Some inmates had even gained a little healthy color, especially some cooks whose cheeks had grown thicker. We often joked that the latrines in the compound were better equipped than those in our barracks back in China. Seats had been installed in them, and at the centers of the rooms were washing facilities — faucets for running water and metal basins set into round concrete tables. On the whole, I had to admit that the Americans were generous, at least materially. Besides food, each POW was given at least one pack of cigarettes a week, and sometimes two packs. I saw with my own eyes that American medical personnel treated injured civilians at the Pusan prison hospital. Here in every compound the United Nations had set up a program for civilian education that distributed books among the inmates, offered courses in mechanics, science, and Christianity, and often showed movies. Unfortunately our compound, controlled by the Communists, wouldn't have anything to do with such a program. Whenever a prisoner reported that he had lost his blanket or mat, he would be issued another one, since there was always a surplus of these things within the compound. Sometimes this would even apply to uniforms. Such replenishment was unthinkable in our own army, in which you would be disciplined for the loss. Back in China I had never heard of a soldier losing his bedroll.

Chaolin had a sharp tongue. The moment the major finished reading, Chaolin said, "Obviously our treatment falls short of the standard set by the convention. For example, we Chinese don't eat barley, which is fed to livestock back home. But you have made barley the staple of our diet, and most of the time there isn't enough barley for everyone. Each man can have only two bowls a day, and the calories are way below the minimum need of the body. What's worse, there's very little vegetable in our diet, and meat is absolutely a rarity. If your country has difficulties, please notify our country. I'm sure China will send over shiploads of rice, meat, and eggs to keep us from starving."

What he had said about barley wasn't true. No Chinese would feed animals barley, which we didn't like as much as rice but which tasted better than corn and sorghum, the principal foodstuffs in northern China. Having heard my translation, General Bell reddened and said, "I will take your unusual Chinese dietary habits into consideration and try to solve this problem. If you always feel hungry, I suggest that you stop the hunger strike now, which will just increase your fellow men's misery and waste food. As for the medical conditions, I will see what I can do."

Chaolin replied, "We appreciate that. If you agree to take steps to improve our living conditions, we'll be glad to end the hunger strike."

General Bell straightened up and promised, "I give you my word."

Chaolin and the other men looked at one another for a few seconds. Then he said, "We're willing to believe your sincerity, General Bell. Please accept our gratitude for coming to meet us personally."

"Does this mean you will call off the hunger strike?"

"Yes, we shall do it today."

"Very good, I'm glad we've met and talked."

"Thank you, General."

Bell nodded with a satisfied smile and then headed back. He got into his jeep, which pulled away, splashing muddy water from a puddle.

Not far from the gate, a middle-aged woman in a ruffly white dress was squatting on her haunches at a garbage dump, digging around with a mattock about two feet long. She was blind but came here every day to rummage around for edibles. On her neck was a healed gash. Beside her were a large gourd bowl and a small girl, four or five years old, whose hair had been cut straight across at the upper ends of her ears. The child held a bunch of grasshoppers, all strung through the mouths by a straw of dogtail grass. Now and then she ran away from her mother to catch a grasshopper. For a moment I was lost in a memory of my childhood, when my pals and I had often gone into the wilderness to catch insects and roasted them to eat. Cicadas and grasshoppers had been our favorites. My reverie was cut short by the woman's calling to her daughter, asking her what she herself was holding in her leathery hand. It was a piece of turnip peel, the child told her. The woman raised the thing and smelled it, then with a faint smile put it into the gourd bowl.

No matter how awful our situation was, there were always others who had it worse. The image of this blind woman would come back to haunt me for many years. Sometimes when I was losing heart, my mind would return to this war-mangled woman and to her eerie smile at a mere turnip peel. Then the desire for life and the will to continue would again stir in my chest.

"Hey, let's go," Chaolin said, bringing my mind back to the camp. Together we returned to the headquarters to give an account of the negotiation.

All the men who heard our report got excited, and some believed General Bell was a jackass. Yet to me he seemed to be an honorable man, perhaps somewhat naive; he couldn't possibly see through our ruse. I felt rather sad, because Bell's promise to improve our living conditions would come to nothing if he was kidnapped.

On a sheet of ruled paper Ming wrote down a brief account of our meeting with the general, particularly his manner and the state of his vigilance. The information was delivered to the Korean comrades that same evening.

17. THE ABDUCTION OF GENERAL BELL

On the evening of May 7 Major Leach arrived in a jeep. He wanted two of our officers to go with him right away, to Compound 76, the one that held Korean prisoners.

"What for?" we asked.

He said General Bell was going to hold a meeting and had invited representatives from different compounds to attend. Chaolin gave me a meaningful grin that revealed his ulcerated gums. We guessed something unusual must be afoot. We hurried back to our headquarters and reported the new development to Commissar Pei. Pei sent Chaolin and me to go with Major Leach because we had met the Koreans and Bell before. We picked up our protest letter and memorandum on our captors' crimes, both written the previous night, and came out to join Leach. With Ming's permission, I brought along the English-Japanese dictionary as well. Before we set off, Commissar Pei's orderly ran out, waving for us to stop. He rushed over and handed us each a service medal, which Chaolin and I put on as the jeep rolled away.

It was slightly windy, gray clouds chasing one another in the north as if following us. The dusk was smoky and flickered with puffs of midges, which brushed my face time and again. A flock of swifts twittered sharply and snapped at mosquitoes and gnats, soaring, diving, and spiraling like miniature aircraft in a dogfight. On the roadside rhododendrons and crimson azaleas bloomed in clusters, and rice paddies stretched in the fields studded with yellow forsythia, though half of the land was unused, overgrown with weeds. As soon as we passed a cattle pond, we saw large crowds of Korean prisoners gathering in various compounds. Most of them stood arm in arm swaying in rhythm and chanting battle songs. Seeing the jeep, a few men waved red flags, most of which were just pieces of shapeless cloth. They also shouted slogans. They seemed to know something extraordinary had just taken place.

Approaching Compound 76, the jeep slowed down a little. The road was lined with American tanks and half-tracks topped with machine guns. Military police and hundreds of marines stood around, all toting rifles. A radioman was shouting into a walkie-talkie that sat on the hood of a light truck, its antenna jittering. As we passed them, I felt almost as if we were their honored guests — all the prisoners and the Americans gazed at us intently. Near the gate to Compound 76 gathered more vehicles and marines, whose steel helmets were reflecting the shifting columns of searchlights beamed from the guard towers. Portable floodlights had been set along the barbed-wire fence, and somewhere a generator was whining. Beside the compound's gate hung a huge piece of white cloth — some sheets sewn together, six by thirty feet — which bore these English words: "WE CAPTURED BELL. AS LONG AS OUR DEMAND IS MET HIS SAFETY IS SECURED. IF THERE IS BRUTAL ACT SUCH AS SHOOTING AND BOMBING, HIS LIFE IS IN DANGER!" The exclamation mark was twice the size of a letter. I was impressed by the Koreans' thorough preparation; the sign must have taken a lot of work to make.

The jeep pulled up at the gate. Major

Leach stayed behind while Chaolin and I walked into the compound. It was bright in there, lamps and torches everywhere. Over a hundred prisoners in their baggy uniforms stood in two lines to welcome us, clapping or waving a few tiny Chinese and Korean national flags made of paper. As we went farther in, people began shouting slogans in stiff Chinese: "Korea and China!" "Kim Il Sung and Mao Zedong!" "Welcome Chinese Comrades!"

We didn't know Korean, but we were so excited that we shouted: "Salute to our Korean comrades!" "Let us unite like brothers!" "Down with American imperialism!" From behind us came the swearing of the marines, reminding me of all the guns trained at us.

We were taken into a tent that had been prepared for the representatives from different compounds, among whom, to our surprise, were three young women. We shook hands with one another and even hugged some men as though we had known them for a long time. The tent was humming with chattering voices, Korean and Chinese. The noise made me slightly giddy; I was excited to be here, affected by the euphoric ambience. Everybody looked jubilant and friendly. For the next half hour Colonel Choi described to the representatives how they had caught General Bell.

By May 7 the men in Compound 76 had been demonstrating for two days, demanding a face-to-face dialogue with Bell. At 1:30 p.m. the general finally came, escorted by a platoon of GIs. Major Leach accompanied him. Together they went over to the front entrance to talk with the Koreans. As they came toward the gate, the GIs all followed them. The Koreans pointed at the troops and asked Bell, "What's this about? We don't understand why you, an American general, are afraid of us unarmed prisoners." Bell looked at his men for a moment, turned to glance at the inside of the compound, then motioned the GIs to move back and keep some distance from the gate. Only Leach stayed with him.

The Koreans enumerated the prison authorities' violations of the Geneva Convention and then demanded that Bell plead guilty. In the beginning the general was quite serious. He told his aide-de-camp to read out some articles of the convention, and then he tried to refute the prisoners' accusations. But as the Koreans continued to rail at him, he grew impatient and tired, so he stood aside and let Major Leach answer questions for him. He lit a cigarette and smoked absently; every once in a while he shook his head in frustration. Gradually the GIs, fifty yards away from the officers, slackened their vigilance, whispering to one another and standing in disorder.

At that point a team of latrine cleaners appeared from within the compound and headed for the front entrance, each man carrying two large buckets of night soil with a shoulder pole. The gate was opened for them. The American officers stepped aside, hands over their noses. When the last bucket of night soil had come out, suddenly these latrine men, all members of the compound's shock unit in disguise, dropped their loads, grabbed the general and Major Leach, and dragged them back into the prison. Leach shouted to the GIs for help, clutching a brace on the gate with both hands, so the Koreans let him go. But General Bell, not as quick as the younger officer, was pulled into the compound. The prisoners immediately bolted the front gate.

The whole thing had taken place so suddenly that the GIs were too dumbfounded to react. When the idea of a kidnapping had finally sunk in, they rushed to the gate, but it was too late. All they could see was four husky men hauling the general away toward a nearby tent. Bell turned his head and shouted at his troops, "Help me! Goddammit, help me!"

"Halt! Halt!" Major Leach cried at the prisoners. The guards raised their rifles.

Two Koreans ran over, displaying the white scroll with the English words on it. Then a battalion of POWs, over seven hundred strong, poured into the yard, holding self-made weapons and ready to confront the Americans. Major Leach ordered the GIs not to open fire, so all they could do was watch their commander disappear from view. At the entrance to the tent, still blustering and swearing, Bell refused to move, so the four men simply carried him, his legs kicking.

Sirens screamed, one after another. Within half an hour marines in tanks and personnel carriers surrounded the compound while a plane circled overhead, ordering the prisoners to release General Bell without delay. The enemy, too confused to deal with the situation, seemed unsure whether to contact the kidnappers or just stay put and wait.

About an hour later an inmate went to

the gate and presented a sheet of paper signed by General Bell to one of the American officers. The letter had apparently been composed by the Koreans. It read:

I order you never shoot POWs, so we can prevent the expansion of this crisis and keep my safety. I agree to hold the conference that includes representatives of prisoners from other compounds. Also agree to discuss the possibilities and search for solutions of the problems. Let our troops leave Compound 76. Stay away, please!

General Matthew Bell

But all the vehicles and GIs remained where they were. Forty minutes later came another slip of paper, a genuine letter bearing Bell's handwriting. He ordered them to have a phone line connected to the barracks of Compound 76 and to follow his instructions closely from now on. He gave a list of things to be delivered without delay. Among them were blankets, canned meat, rice, pencils, pens, writing pads, brand-name cigarettes, folding tables and chairs, and a few things he needed for his personal accommodations. The acting commanding officer, General Fulton, who had just rushed here to take Bell's place temporarily, was Bell's friend, both having graduated from the Virginia Military Institute, so Fulton granted whatever Bell requested. Several jeeps were dispatched to different compounds to fetch POW representatives. Then a truck arrived to deliver the personal items for General Bell — there were even some bottles of spring water and a toilet. Later in the evening a larger truck came, loaded with supplies for the conference.

Behind a row of barracks a special tent had been pitched for the general. In front stood eight self-made red flags rippling in the breeze, each carrying a red star in a white circle. Dozens of pickets were posted around the tent, toting clubs, sharpened bamboo poles, long picks, shovels. One man, obviously a team leader, wore a shiny sickle in his belt. Chaolin and I were allowed to go in and have a look inside. A guard opened the door flaps for us. My goodness! I was struck by the fancy interior, which was thoroughly furnished and partitioned into four or five separate spaces; the entire floor was covered with army blankets. Even the walls were lined with blankets too, since it could still get chilly at night.

Toward the back of the tent, a white curtain shielded an area for the bathroom. In the center of the front section stood a glossy desk and four chairs; on the desktop was a beer bottle holding a bunch of wild lilies, white and saffron, so fresh that some of the blossoms were still closed. In a screened corner were a cot and a tiny cabinet, on which perched the general's reading glasses and his cap. The curtain was not drawn. We could see Bell lying on the bed with his eyes closed, his face longer and flabbier than before. He looked old. Chaolin and I didn't disturb him, though I was sure the general knew someone had come in.

In meeting and mixing with the Korean soldiers, I had noticed that they did things more elaborately than we did. For instance, the distinction of rank among their officers was immediately visible, marked by the bars and stars on the shoulder tabs. Even their enlisted men's ranks could be identified by the stripes on their sleeves. Their officers' uniforms were much more formal than ours — peaked caps with cockades, jackets with brass buttons and large epaulets, high patent-leather boots, and green or blue breeches whose legs had red stripes along the seams. They imitated the Russians as much as possible. In contrast, our officers didn't wear any insignia, and there was little sartorial distinction between them and their men. At most our colonels and generals donned woolen jackets and trousers and maybe leather shoes. As for the enlisted men and junior officers, our quilted uniforms, felt hats with tied-up flaps, and canvas-top shoes were so crude that the GIs on the front called us "laundrymen." At least many of us looked less skinny in our winter outfits.

General Bell was so impressed by his accommodations that the next morning he said to General Fulton on the phone, "I'm living like an emperor here." Indeed, the interior of the tent resembled that of a royal Mongolian yurt, perhaps even more luxurious. What's more, his cook was going to come three times a day to deliver his meals, and two American orderlies were allowed to do housekeeping for him here every morning. Bell looked as if he were on vacation, camping on a lakeside or a mountain, though his face was grim.

As Chaolin and I were wondering whether we should go forward or withdraw, General Bell opened his eyes. But he didn't get up and seemed lost in thought. He closed his eyes again and we stepped closer. His large body weighed down the cot noticeably. Two top buttons on his jacket were missing, and his right epaulet, with one star on it, was ripped, barely attached to his shoulder by a few stitches of thread. How different he looked from the spruce general who had spoken with us just a few days ago.

"We should talk with him," whispered Chaolin.

We stepped over, but the general still didn't stir. I tried to guess why he acted this way. Out of anger? Or out of arrogance or contempt? More probably out of uncertainty. Like his men outside the compound, he too must have been at a loss how to deal with his kidnapping. Chaolin and I looked at each other again. He smiled and stuck his tongue out, which was heavily furred. He tilted his head, meaning I should start. I bent down a little and said, "Hello, General Bell, we came to see you."

"Oh, thank you, thank you." He opened his eyes, whose whites were bloodshot. He sat up, combing his sparse hair with his fingers, and shifted his legs out of the bed so as to get to his feet.

"Please remain seated," I said. "We are the representatives of the Chinese prisoners. We met four days ago."

"Really? Oh yes, I promised you I'd solve some problems."

I was surprised that he hadn't recognized us. Chaolin said through my interpretation, "Now we want to see your deeds. We don't want the same result again — where the problems remain unsolved while your men pitch gas grenades into our barracks and even fire at us."

"That has never happened here." Bell wasn't wrong; that kind of violence had occurred in some camps on the Korean mainland, not on this island.

"But your men often beat the inmates," Chaolin pressed on.

"In that case, I should have kept better discipline among my troops."

"What do you think of the way we treat you here?"

The general looked puzzled, not having expected that the Korean prisoners represented us Chinese as well. I too was a little surprised by the collective pronoun "we." Then Bell realized the meaning of the question and muttered, "Yes, I can say the Communists have accommodated me well."

"We're glad you understand this. If only General Ridgway were here to take the same lesson."

"I can pass the message on to him and —"
Catching himself, Bell looked abashed.

"We'll talk more about the treatment of the prisoners at the conference tomorrow. Meanwhile, take it easy and rest well."

"I will."

"Good-bye now."

"Bye." He stood up, and his hand moved but didn't stretch out.

The moment we came out of the tent, Chaolin burst into laughter, holding his sides with both hands. I joined him in laughing too. A Korean officer, who had been at the entrance to the tent during our meeting with Bell, remarked in English, "American general is just so-so, a paper tiger, like Stalin says."

I don't know where Stalin said that. Amused, I translated his words to Chaolin. That brought out more laughter. Without further delay the Korean officer led us to a tent at the back of the barracks, where we were to meet their top leader.

At the sight of us Mr. Park got up from a reed mat and came to hug us. He said in barely comprehensible Chinese, "Ah my friends, welcome!"

He gestured for us to sit down on the mat. I noticed that unlike the others, he sat on a sheepskin, its white fur mottled with black blotches. With ease we entered into conversation. The slim Colonel Lee sat beside the leader, serving as his interpreter, so I could relax now. Mr. Park showed deep concern about our living conditions and asked us how well we were organized in Compound 602. Chaolin reported to him briefly on the newly founded United Communist Association. Mr. Park was impressed by the intention to include as many people in the organization as possible while maintaining the Party's leadership and principles at the core. He said, "I always admire the Chinese Communist Party. You have more experience and more strategies. I'm sorry we haven't given enough support to your struggle."

Chaolin seemed touched and replied, "Under your leadership the Korean comrades captured General Bell. This is an extraordinary event in the history of warfare, and it dealt a crushing blow to our common enemy. It has also inspired us tremendously. We must learn from our Korean comrades' courage and bravery."

"Well, without your help we couldn't have done it at all," said Mr. Park, smiling. "So half of the victory belongs to you. The Chinese comrades showed us how to stage a hunger strike and how to lure Bell to our compound, otherwise we couldn't have brought him in. This victory is only a part of our two peoples' joint struggle."

He turned aside and whispered to an aide. Lee winked at us and said, "Mr. Park would like to invite you to dinner."

"Please don't treat us like guests," I said.

"You are our honored guests," replied Lee, smiling meaningfully. He got up and went out, apparently to make arrangements for the dinner.

I wondered what kind of food Mr. Park could offer us in such a place. Maybe a bowl of white rice and a bit of kimchee, at most accompanied by a few pieces of dried fish or some baked squid. My thoughts were interrupted by the hearty laughter from both Chaolin and our host. Mr. Park inquired after Commissar Pei and sent him his regards, which Chaolin promised to convey. I forced myself not to think of the promised dinner so as to remain in the conversation.

Then a young man stepped in, carrying a large cauldron lid filled with steaming dumplings made of wheat flour, quite thick. We were flabbergasted — this was the best Chinese food a host could offer! Where on earth could they get the stuff for such a meal?

Mr. Park smiled and opened his arms almost mischievously, saying, "Help yourselves, please."

"Let's eat together," said Chaolin, motioning for them to sit closer.

"No, we already ate."

"How can we thank you enough for this?"

"Stop talking and eat. You don't have to thank us. Everything came from the Americans. If they hadn't delivered the flour and the meat, we wouldn't have known what to come up with. So enjoy yourselves. Excuse me for a moment." Mr. Park stood up and went into a corner to discuss something with a group of officers.

We each picked up a wooden spoon and began eating. The fillings were made of corned beef mixed with young cabbage. There was so much meat in the dumplings that they dripped oil whenever we took a bite. I tried hard to eat slowly while Chaolin grinned at me and went on licking his lips. He said, "After we go back home, I'll tell my wife to make dumplings every weekend."

"This is the best meal I've had since we crossed the Yalu," I said with a catch in my throat.

"I know. Come on, don't be too emotional, Yuan. They're watching us."

I checked my tears. Despite enjoying the food, I wasn't happy exactly. My emotions were mixed, evoked by Chaolin's mention of his wife. I remembered the crabmeat wontons my mother and my fiancée had cooked for me the day before I left home. But I broke my reverie and forced myself to smile and not to think about my family in a situation like this. It was embarrassing to let your personal emotions interfere with your work. From now on I must build a closet in my heart, in which I would lock up my personal thoughts and feelings so that they couldn't crop up at the wrong time.

What happened after dinner was even more astonishing. We were led into a secret basement in the back of the tent. It was like being inside a bunker, but it was well lit, and on a small dais of earth covered with a piece of hardboard sat a radio — a glossy case made of grained oak, about two feet long and one foot high. Colonel Lee told me that they had exchanged canned food and blankets for this machine with a grocer and had it smuggled into the compound. As I was wondering if they had radio contact with the North, Mr. Park placed his hands on Chaolin's and my shoulders, saying, "My dear comrades, only because we seized General Bell could we invite you over. But we have nothing special to entertain you with, so I thought perhaps you might like to listen to the voice of Beijing."

Heavens, they could hear broadcasts from China! We hadn't heard a single sound from our homeland for more than a year. Hurriedly we bent over and turned on the radio. Through the rasping static came a female voice, crisp, clear, and warm. It announced:

More donations were received lately. To support our army on the Korean front, two and a half million people participated in the public assemblies held in the capital last week, condemning the American invasion of Korea and championing the anti-imperialist cause. The actress of Yu Opera, Chang Hsiang-yu, donated a large sum for a jet fighter. The painter Huang Ran offered five of his paintings. A party of famous writers sold their manuscripts. All the proceeds are going to our army in Korea . . .

The news seemed as distant as if it were coming from another planet. At the same time it was so close that it was tightening my scalp, contracting my chest, and shaking my heart. Tears were coursing down Chaolin's and my faces. The air was so charged that nobody made a sound for a long while. Noiselessly we let our tears drop on the damp, yellow, foreign earth. Colonel Lee wept too.

There was to be a preparatory meeting at the Koreans' headquarters attended only by the key leaders. Chaolin stayed on for the meeting, so for the rest of the night I was free. As I walked out of the tent, large emotions were still surging in my chest. The salty breeze stung my still-wet face, and my heart was filled with home-sickness and love. If only we could be heading home tomorrow! If only the moon were a transmitter that could send a tele-gram to my mother and Julan! But I curbed my fantasies and walked on, taking care not to get near the barbed wire, be-yond which a group of GIs stood. They were smoking and jabbering, their guns emitting flecks of bluish light, their shiny helmets dulled by the string nets over the steel.

Somehow in my mind echoed the words of the Russian revolutionary novelist

Nikolai Ostrovsky: "The most valuable thing to man is his life. Life belongs to him only once and should be spent this way: when he recalls his past, he will not regret having wasted any time or feel ashamed of having accomplished nothing. Thus he can say on his deathbed: I have devoted my whole life and every bit of my energy to the most magnificent cause of humanity — the struggle for the liberation of mankind." Like many others, I had committed to memory this passage from *How the Steel Was Tempered*, but now it was resonating more in my mind. I felt for the first time that I was a useful man, and that my life had finally been shaped by a goal. How small an individual was. Only when you joined a cause greater than yourself could you expand your individual role by a "multiplier." For the time being, maybe the struggle against the American imperialists was the "multiplier" I had been seeking. Even though my role at this conference made me feel rather aggrandized, I was, after all, a mere translator and didn't even play second fiddle to Chaolin. I got so carried away that I even considered applying for membership in the United Communist Association again.

I found a place in the tent reserved for

the representatives and went right to bed. Tomorrow was going to be a long day, and I'd better rest well for it.

For breakfast all the representatives had *jook,* a Korean dish, which was somewhat like porridge but with meat and diced turnip in the rice. The word *jook,* I thought, must be derived from the Chinese word *zhou,* which means porridge. Every one of us was served a full bowl of it, and a plate of kimchee sat in the center of each table for everybody to share. The Koreans couldn't live without kimchee, which was obviously a rarity here. We ate almost ceremoniously; everyone seemed to make an effort not to rush. Chaolin and I didn't care for kimchee; the chili was too hot for us. But I liked the smell of the cabbage and ate a few cloves of garlic pickled in the sauce. The *jook,* however, was tender and tasty; the meat was from canned beef stew. Again I was impressed by the Koreans' resources.

The conference started at 9:00 a.m. in a large tent. In the middle of the room stood eight long tables grouped together and covered with blankets; chairs were arranged around the tables. At the end near the entrance was the defendant's seat, and at the opposite end was a chair for the head of the conference. On the wall behind this seat spread a Chinese and a Korean national flag. The enlarged committee meeting of the previous night had elected Colonel Choi the chairman and Hao Chaolin and another man the vice chairmen. So Choi took his seat at the head of the table; on his left Chaolin and I sat together. The three Korean women were seated next to me. In all, there were forty-two representatives and witnesses from seventeen compounds.

After everybody sat down, we began to discuss the agenda of the conference, which was approved unanimously. Then we sent for General Bell.

Bell came in with a ponderous gait and sat down in the defendant's seat. Colonel Choi announced that the conference had begun, and that the first major item on the agenda was to allow Bell to listen to the representatives' accusations and condemnations. He told the general in English, "You can defend yourself, but you must respect facts."

Then the representatives began to speak by turns. The Koreans had prepared a good deal of evidence for the abuse and violence they had suffered, and even claimed that some of their comrades had been coerced into joining the South Korean army. They described how their men had been tortured and killed just because they wanted to return to the North. A number of them had vanished, nobody knowing their whereabouts; had they been shipped away by our captors to some remote place as guinea pigs for the experiments in biochemical weapons? General Bell sat vacantly, perhaps because he couldn't understand much of what they were saying despite the joint effort of two interpreters, who spoke English with abrupt inflections and misplaced accents like beginners.

A tall man stood up and spoke in a hoarse voice, tears streaming down his face. He pointed his forefinger at the defendant and kept shouting. The left side of his face was scarred, burned, he said, by hot irons when he had refused to betray his comrades. He pulled up his shirt to display some dark wounds on his chest, which he kept slapping. He said these scars had been inflicted on him by South Korean guards and GIs. There was also a healed knife gash on his stomach in the shape of a horseshoe, which looked at least ten years old. The Korean interpreter was rendering his accusations into broken English that was hard to follow, but the main drift was clear. He was saying how he had been refused medical treatment because he wouldn't speak into a tape recorder.

After him, a squat man spoke. He said an American officer had given him a steel bar and ordered him to murder Mr. Park. He wouldn't do that, so they hung him up on a beam in the torture chamber and thrashed him almost to death. A South Korean sergeant even threatened to cut his anus and feed it to a dog. After this a willowy boy, about eighteen years old, stood up and spoke in a thin voice. He claimed that a GI often groped him when searching him at the gate to his compound.

As the accusers continued speaking, many representatives became enraged and couldn't help but shout at General Bell, who avoided looking at their scowling faces. Every once in a while Bell seemed so absentminded that Colonel Choi would order him to "Pay attention!"

One of the three female representatives, Shunji by name, could speak English. She was a high-cheeked woman of about twenty-five and must have been stout once, but now she looked rawboned with a sunburned face. She stood up and began speaking with emotion. Her voice was clear, though her accent muffled her words somewhat. She said many of the women inmates had been abused by the prison guards, who would beat and curse them at will. Some South Korean men had even burned their faces and chests with cigarettes in the presence of American officers, who had always shut their eyes to all kinds of physical abuse. Shunji lifted her foot, put it on the table, and pulled up the baggy leg of her pants all the way to her thigh, which was rather skinny compared with her large body. Indeed, about a dozen brownish burns dotted her leg, each the size of a kidney bean. She also said that a girl of eighteen in their compound had been raped by four American soldiers before she was delivered to the prison camp, and that later she had given birth to a fair-skinned boy with green eyes. The malnourished mother died of heart disease afterward; now the baby was still in their barracks, as the youngest prisoner.

While she was speaking, the small woman seated beside me started sobbing. Shunji pointed at her and said, "She's been paraded through the streets of Seoul for two days, together with more than thirty sisters. The American imperialists and their Korean running dogs ride in jeeps and on big horses, whip them, and order them to take off their clothes, so all people can see them naked. They call them whores and spit on them. Some throw stones at them and beat them with canes and sticks. One of the sisters is five months pregnant, but no matter how she begs them, they go on whacking her, force her to take off her pajamas and carry an A-frame on her back, so all the passersby can make fun of her. Here's my comrade, she's living evidence of your crimes. Look at her back!" She helped the small, moon-faced woman to her feet, made her turn around, and pulled up her shirt from behind. The woman's back was a mess, marked by scars and blood-encrusted welts.

"Look at her face," said Shunji, pointing to the other woman still in her seat. All eyes turned to that face, spotted with scabs. She was quite young, under twenty, with tender, healthy skin on her neck; her blemished face must have been quite pretty once. She got up too and began speaking through Shunji as her interpreter. She said she had been a guerrilla and had been caught by Americans, who then handed her over to the South Korean police along with twenty of her comrades. They beat her, beheaded several male guerrillas in front of a large crowd, and even forced her to hold her elder brother's decapitated head so that they could take a photo of her. To this day she still had nightmares and often screamed and writhed in bed at night, wrestling ghosts. Why did the police treat human beings worse than animals? Why did the Americans encourage and connive with them? Why did GIs cross the Pacific Ocean and come to this land to ruin their lives? Her voice was growing shriller and shriller as she continued. She was so choked with emotion that her words gradually became incoherent, hard for Shunji to interpret. Finally she stopped in midsentence, then the three women held one another and broke out wailing.

A man jumped up and rushed toward General Bell, his arms flailing wildly; he was yelling like crazy, but two representatives restrained him. He said he and his comrades had also been ordered by Americans to undress completely when they were captured. The GIs thrashed their buttocks with rifle butts and jabbed the muzzles of the guns in their crotches. As a result, one of the men still had blood in his semen to this day.

Like everybody else, I was angry too, as I

remembered how some men had been tortured by the pro-Nationalists. Colonel Choi told us to remain coolheaded, reminding us that Bell was just an officer who had to obey orders given by the real criminals — the U.S. government and Wall Street.

I saw Bell's large hands, hairy and veined, shaking a little. He held the edge of the table to stop them from trembling and fixed his eyes on the teacup in front of him. Now and then he bit his lower lip.

In the afternoon the accusations and condemnations resumed. A Korean officer, who had lost his left arm, accused the medical personnel under the defendant's command of amputating his good hand. He rushed over to General Bell and shouted in English, "Drue or not?" His only fist punched the tabletop, but he didn't touch Bell as we had been ordered not to.

The general stood up and said, "I'm not sure. Some of the awful things you mentioned I know might have happened, but some I don't think are true. I shall look into them nonetheless."

He remained on his feet even after the Korean officer had returned to his own seat. Colonel Choi asked Bell to sit down, and said, "We're Communists and won't treat you the way your men treat us. We respect your human dignity and will not insult and abuse you. But as an American general, you must have the courage to face the facts."

Bell nodded, sweat beading on his domed forehead.

At the midafternoon recess Chaolin and I talked about our prepared speech scheduled for delivery the following day. We felt that although we had written it out, we should present more evidence. Also, it would be impossible for me to translate our lengthy accusation into English that very night by myself; I would need help. So Chaolin went to talk with Colonel Lee and returned to Compound 602 in a jeep after dinner under the pretext of fetching a witness. The truth was that he wanted to report to Commissar Pei on the current state of affairs. At the preliminary meeting the night before, there had been a heated argument over how to handle General Bell should the enemy resort to force to rescue him. Some Korean officers insisted that they fight back with all their might, and that if need be, they should execute Bell and blame his death on the Americans' indiscriminate gunfire. Some people disagreed, saying this suggestion bordered on adventurism. Chaolin argued that we should protect Bell at all events. If the enemy attacked us, we should smuggle Bell into another compound (the Koreans had some kind of underground connection facilitated by their agents among the guards). As long as Bell remained alive in our hands, we would have an edge on the enemy. Mr. Park praised Chaolin's idea, but they were still uncertain whether Bell would cooperate with us. What if he refused to sign any agreement? The answer to this question remained unclear. Chaolin was eager to go back and consult Commissar Pei, who was more experienced and could give us instructions.

An hour later Chaolin returned with Ming and another man, Wu Gaochen, who had witnessed the bloodshed in the Third Collection Center in Pusan during the "screening" a month ago. That night together Ming and I revised our speech for the following day; then we translated the whole thing and the gist of Wu's accusation into English.

While we two were working, I told him that we had eaten dumplings the night before. He slapped me on the shoulder and said, "Damn, I should've come with

Chaolin first. You stole my luck."

"Maybe tomorrow they'll give us some goodies again," I said.

"Hope so." He turned away to check an English word in our dictionary. In fact, for the rest of the conference we ate the same food as the other prisoners.

The next morning the condemnations resumed. Our man Wu Gaochen stood up and spoke. We had given General Bell the English version of his accusation, so there was no need for me to translate Gaochen's words orally. Colonel Lee had our material in Chinese and interpreted it directly from the paper for his comrades while Gaochen was speaking. In a torn voice the accuser described the violent incident that had occurred in the Third Collection Center about a month before. He told this story, which he had rehearsed twice the previous night:

"On the evening of April fourteenth two battalions of GIs surrounded our compound. Together with them were six Sherman tanks. Through a loudspeaker they ordered us to come out of our tents within five minutes and to go through the screening, which was held just outside our compound. But five minutes passed, and nobody went out. The loudspeaker ordered us again and gave us another five minutes. When the time was up, still no one had come out. They repeated the orders several times. Then about an hour later they took action. Two tanks rolled into the compound, followed by a platoon of GIs. They came to move us by force, and we resisted them with whatever we could lay our hands on. In the scuffle we beat up some GIs and grabbed two rifles from them. Because there were more prisoners involved in the fight than they'd expected, the GIs were scared and withdrew from the compound. Even the tanks turned back. This enraged their commander, who ordered another attack twenty minutes later. They fired machine guns and threw grenades at us. Instantly, thirty-four comrades were killed and more than fifty wounded. Since it was impossible to resist them with bare hands, about two hundred of us agreed to submit to the screening. Also, many of us were ill and starved and couldn't fight back at all. Their gas bombs nauseated us and stung our eyes, and we couldn't breathe and vomited repeatedly. So the Americans rounded us up and took us to the screening area.

"Both my cousin and I were among the

two hundred men. Before this massacre, we two had talked about what to do if we were forced to go through the screening, and we were both determined to return home at any cost. Now all the men lined up, but we were allowed to go up to the screening desk only one at a time. When my turn came, an American officer asked me, 'Do you want to go to Free China?' 'Where's that?' I said; I truly didn't know what country it was. 'Formosa,' the man said. 'No, I want to go back to mainland China,' I told him. He handed me a card. 'Go there and join those men,' he said and pointed at a door. That's how I avoided going to Taiwan. But afterward I searched through the crowd in the yard and couldn't find my cousin. Someone told me that he had betrayed our motherland. That was impossible! We had sworn to go home together. I was so worried I burst into tears. What happened was that he had mistaken Free China for mainland China, so he'd said yes to the question. As a matter of fact, another four men from our group had made the same mistake and all had landed in the enemy's hands.

"Now, General Bell, you tell me, why did your American army force us to go through the screening? And why did you purposely set the trap for us at the screening desk? Two of the four men were loyal Communists and couldn't have been willing to join the Nationalist ranks at all, but they were tricked into the demons' den. Before I came to Korea, I had promised my uncle and aunt to take care of my younger cousin. Now he's gone, what can I say to his parents?" Gaochen broke into noisy sobs, which made his words unintelligible. A Korean man handed him a towel.

His accusation seemed to affect General Bell, who sighed, chin in palm, his elbow resting on the table. "There're lots of crimes in the war, but I can't be responsible for all of them," he said in a low voice.

In fact, Gaochen's story of the massacre wasn't the entire picture. He had left out the immediate cause of the incident: the Chinese prisoners had planned an uprising at night, to break prison, attack an American company nearby, seize some weapons, then flee to a mountain where they would carry on guerrilla warfare. But a traitor among them stole away to inform the guards. That was why such a large force came to subdue the prisoners. Of course, when preparing the accusation, we were told to expunge the cause of the incident.

Neither General Bell nor the Koreans could know the whole story.

Now it was my turn. I spoke in English, describing the persecution in Compound 72 — how Liu Tai-an had disemboweled Lin Wushen and how my former schoolmate Yang Huan had been cudgeled and strangled to death. After giving an account of how the pro-Nationalist officers in that compound had cut some men to collect the tattoos they themselves had inflicted on them by force, I pulled up my shirt and displayed the words on my belly — FUCK COMMUNISM. To my surprise, General Bell chuckled. He immediately checked himself; yet his large nose still gave out a snuffling sound. I banged the table with my fist and shouted, "You think this is funny, huh? Damn you!"

"No, that's not what I think," he said. "I can't imagine they'd play such a prank."

"Prank?" I cried. "With these words on me, how can I live a normal life in my homeland?"

Red patches appeared on his face. "I hadn't thought of it in that light." He lowered his head and pressed his lips.

"This is a crime, isn't it?" I asked.

"Yes, of course."

"This took place in one of the com-

pounds under your charge. Are you not responsible for it?"

"Maybe in part, I would say," he muttered.

"Those prison chiefs were trained in
Japan and Taiwan, and then sent back by
your government to help you run the
camp. They murdered and beat us at will.
Isn't the American government responsible
for their crimes?"

"If what you say is true, our government
didn't do a great job. To be frank, I have
no idea who trained them."

His equivocal answer infuriated me. I
lost self-control, shouting at him hysteri-
cally, "Stop dodging! You think you're
clean? Let me tell you, you too are a criminal whose hands are stained with Chinese
and Korean blood. You think you can pre-
tend you don't know what crimes your men
committed? You think you can bend our
will and force us to betray our motherland?
Do you know what the true Chinese spirit
is? Let me tell you, if we're alive, we're Chinese men; if we're dead, we're Chinese
ghosts. Those bastards under your protection can never change us by mutilating our
bodies. Let me say this to you —"

Ming grabbed me by the shoulders and
dragged me out of the tent to cool me

down. "Boy, I never thought you could be so emotional," he said. I too was surprised by my outburst, which began to embarrass me.

When we had returned to the tent after a smoke, Colonel Choi asked solemnly, "General Bell, are you responsible for the crimes committed by your men or not?"

"Maybe for some of them."

"Are you guilty or not?"

After a long pause, Bell answered, "Perhaps partially."

Chaolin stood up and spoke in a voice of some authority. By now I had calmed down, so I translated his words to the general.

Chaolin said, "We understand that as an officer, you have to obey your government's orders. Yet what you have done is to sow the seeds of hatred among peoples. We believe the American people love peace and hate war, just like us Chinese and Koreans. We hope you can do something to make amends."

Bell nodded and said, "Thank you for your wise words. Trust me, I won't forget this experience, or this lesson. I shall try my very best to correct our mistakes." There was a slight tremor in his voice.

In the afternoon we went about working

on two documents. The first one was called "The Korean and Chinese POWs' Accusations," which listed the major crimes perpetrated by the prison guards and would be released to the world (General Bell's kidnapping had already drawn international attention and some reporters had arrived at Koje Island). The second one was entitled "The Promise Made by the American Prison Authorities" — it was meant to be signed by Bell, so that we could get decent treatment and have our living conditions improved.

After a brief meeting we unanimously agreed on the four prerequisites for Bell's release: first, the prison guards must stop using violence on the inmates; second, the prison authorities must abandon the policy of the so-called "Voluntary Repatriation of Prisoners"; third, they must call off the screening of the North Korean and the Chinese soldiers; fourth, they must recognize the union of the POWs as a legitimate association and cooperate with it.

Now everything would depend on whether General Bell would accept these preconditions. If he did, he'd be set free and the victory would be ours.

We wondered how the enemy would respond to our demands. Their new commandant, General Smart, who had arrived the previous night to replace Fulton and take full command of the camp, had already issued six ultimatums, ordering us to release Bell unconditionally, but we had ignored them all. As our discussion continued, the telephone rang. Colonel Lee picked up the handset and passed it to a Korean interpreter. I sat nearby and could hear the voice at the other end. The caller was General Fulton, who wanted to speak to Bell.

An orderly was sent for the general. Two minutes later Bell stepped in. Choi told him, pointing at the phone, "Fulton wants to speak to you."

"Hello, this is Matt," Bell said into the mouthpiece.

"How are you, Matt?" asked the other end. I craned my neck so that I could overhear the whole conversation.

"I'm okay, Charlie."

"Listen, Nancy has arrived from Tokyo. I went to see her just now. She was crying, this is hard for her. She's so emotional that I haven't told her yet that we have phone contact with you. But she may call you soon."

Bell furrowed his brow. "Please tell her I'm fine, no need to worry."

"Matt, tell me, have they insulted or tortured you? We're very concerned."

"Believe me, I'm okay." Bell glanced at Colonel Choi and went on, "In fact they've been respectful."

"Thank God! Do you know how long they'll keep you? Tell me what I can do to help."

"I've no idea, maybe when their conference is over. Don't press them. Just let them go on with their conference."

"All right, I'll stay around here. Call anytime you need me."

"Thank you, Charlie. This means a lot. Let's hope we'll meet soon."

"Yes, I'll keep my fingers crossed, Matt. Good-bye."

"Good-bye."

I was amazed by the phone call, not having expected that the American generals would talk in a casual, personal manner in the midst of such a crisis. They had treated each other as friends, not as comrades who shared the same ideal and fought for the same cause. They hadn't mentioned any ideological stuff. What a contrast this was to Chinese officers, who, in a situation like this, would undoubtedly speak in the voice of revolutionaries, and one side would surely represent the Party.

After dinner Chaolin and I went to see General Bell. The previous evening Commissar Pei had instructed Chaolin to mediate between the Koreans and the Americans and make sure that Bell signed the agreement. The commissar also said that he would organize demonstrations in Compound 602 to support our struggle, and that we must remain composed and reasonable, because a victory could be earned only through careful planning and patient negotiation. Our Korean comrades tended to be too hot-blooded and would even refer to themselves as Great Stalin's soldiers who wouldn't share the same earth and sky with the American imperialists. Many of them lost their temper easily.

General Bell looked exhausted, but he seemed pleased to see us. After we sat down, Chaolin told him through my translation, "General, we do want you to return to your family safely. That's why we came to talk with you."

"Thank you. I appreciate your good intentions," Bell said.

"We understand that your wife is here, and your children must be worried about you too. So please sign the agreement tomorrow. If you don't, we're afraid our Korean comrades may lose their patience. To tell the truth, we've been trying to keep them from running berserk."

"Well, I'll have to see what's on that paper before I sign it."

"We understand that. If you can't accept some parts of the agreement, talk with them. Don't just turn it down categorically. I'll try to persuade them to revise it. In short, don't lose this opportunity for peace."

"I shall keep that in mind."

"Good. Have a restful night."

"The same to you."

We went out and felt relieved. It was overcast, and soundless lightning slashed the northern sky and silhouetted the ridges of the distant hills. We parted company because I had to join Ming in preparing the documents for the following day.

Early the next morning, a copy of our preconditions was delivered to General Smart. While waiting for his reply, we held the ceremony of signing the agreement. On the ground outside the tent sat over seven thousand men in neat lines, though some of them were carrying self-made weapons, whose wide variety precluded the uniformity of the formation. They were waiting to hear the final outcome of our three days' struggle. Meanwhile, inside the tent the atmosphere was solemn and tense. Colonel Choi announced that this was the last part of our conference and that now we were going to test the sincerity of General Bell's attitude toward his crimes. With a wave of his hand he summoned an interpreter to read this agreement to our captive:

I promise to immediately stop our barbarous behavior, our insult and torture of Korean and Chinese prisoners, such as forcing them to write reactionary letters in blood, threats of solitary confinement, mass murdering, rifle and machine-gun shooting, using poison gas, germ weapons, experiments with the prisoners for the A-bomb.

I also promise to observe the Geneva Convention, humanely treat my prisoners, the Brave Soldiers of Great Stalin, give good medical service, human food, new clothing, and stationery. I shall follow international law and let all POWs go back to their home country safely.

I also promise to stop "Voluntary Repatriation" and screening prisoners, and to punish my soldiers who beat and curse prisoners.

Brigadier General Matthew Bell

While listening I felt the hair on the nape of my neck bristle. My head was reeling. The previous afternoon we had discussed what this document should include, and nobody had mentioned stationery, new clothing, or the A-bomb. How could our Korean comrades have produced such a wild piece of writing?

The interpreter went up to Bell and with both hands presented the sheet of paper to him. Bell put on his reading glasses and looked through it. He said calmly, "There's no way I can sign this."

"Why?" asked Colonel Choi, whose small eyes turned triangular.

"The language is inappropriate, and I'm not authorized to respond to some of these demands."

Chaolin stepped in, "Do you wish to revise it?"

Bell thought for a moment, then shook his head. "This is impossible to revise. It has to be rewritten."

When the Korean interpreter had translated his words, all eyes glowered at the general. Bell flinched but added, "If I signed this, it would constitute treason. I'm an honorable man and won't commit such a crime against my country."

A Korean officer slapped the table and

yelled at him. Shunji, the woman who knew English, interpreted his words to Bell: "No signature, no go back!"

Quick-witted, Chaolin said to the general, "How about this — you write something that covers the essence of our demands and is also acceptable to yourself?"

"Well . . ." Bell fingered his mustache and seemed reluctant. Then he said, "All right, let me try."

He picked up a ballpoint and wrote on a pad of yellow paper:

With regard to your demands, I admit that there were instances of abuse and bloodshed in the prison compounds on Koje Island, and that some POWs were killed by other inmates and injured by the U.N. guards. As the commanding officer I am partially responsible for the loss of lives. I can assure you that in the future the POWs here will receive humane treatment in accordance with international law. I will do everything in my capacity to prevent violence, bloodshed, and corporal punishment. If such incidents occur again, I should be called to account.

He looked through the statement carefully and stopped at a spot for a long time. He picked up the pen, then put it down. He handed the pad to us.

I roughly translated the contents to Chaolin. He lowered his head and mulled them over for a few seconds, then asked, "This is acceptable to us, don't you think?"

"Yes, it's pretty good," I said.

We passed the statement on to the Korean interpreter. He began translating it to their officers and representatives, some of whom got angry, shaking their heads and shouting. Chaolin went over to Choi and talked with him. He insisted that despite the absence of most of the details they had put in, the statement in principle conveyed the spirit of our original demands, especially where Bell mentioned he was partially responsible for the crimes. As for the issue of screening the prisoners, Bell indeed might not be in a position to respond to it. Both Choi and Lee nodded in agreement; probably they realized there was no other way to break this deadlock.

So we told Bell that we would go along with his version. He signed it willingly, then took off his glasses and rested his arm on the back of the chair, gazing at us almost emotionlessly. He closed his eyes, perspiration gathering on his forehead.

All the people in the tent stood up and applauded. Bell got to his feet, clapping lightly too. Chaolin and I went up to him. We shook hands with him for the first time. His grip was heavy and damp.

Then came a storm of hurrahs from outside. From Compound 76 the news of our victory spread through shouts to other compounds, which began celebrating it as well. Meanwhile, a group of prisoners painted two sentences, as though directly quoted from General Bell's promise, on white sheets and hung them on the front fence for the Americans to see: "WE WILL NOT KILL AGAIN!" and "WE WILL TREAT POWS HUMANELY!"

After lunch the new American commandant, General Smart, showed up at the front gate to receive Bell. He had been sent over to cope with the crisis, because the commander of U.N. forces, General Ridgway, was unhappy about the way General Fulton had handled this incident, especially about his allowing us to hold the conference. We took Bell to the gate and handed General Smart a receipt to sign. Smart was a stocky man with a firm paunch, a muscular face, and rheumy eyes.

We could tell he loathed us and was disgusted with the piece of paper, which read:

Today I received an American brigadier general Matthew Bell from the fearless Korean soldiers in Prison Compound 76. After careful examination, Bell is good in every respect, no trace of insult and physical damage. I prove this statement!

The Highest American Commander on Koje Island

Signature_____

May 11, 1952

With a grunt General Smart signed his name. Then we shook hands with Bell again. He got into a blue sedan, and many of us waved good-bye to him. In spite of General Smart's glum face, Bell doffed his cap a bit as the car drew away.

At 2:00 p.m. a celebration started in Compound 76. After Colonel Choi summarized this episode and its importance to the seven thousand men, Chaolin delivered a speech too. He thanked the Korean comrades-in-arms for this great victory and said we Chinese would learn from their heroic spirit and bravery. He concluded by declaring forcefully, "The Chinese people will remember this great historical deed forever!"

I was moved, intoxicated by the euphoria over the victory, to which I had also contributed my little share. In joining the great struggle, I felt as though my life had finally gained a purpose.

In the midst of loud applause, Ming went to the front and belted out "Song of the Guerrillas on Mount Halla" in Korean. He had just learned this song from one of the three women. He was such a splendid singer that the audience encored him, so he sang a snatch from the Chinese opera *The White-Haired Girl.* After that, the three women performed a short dance and then chanted "The Spring Song." And finally, a group of prisoners acted out a skit, "Capturing General Bell Alive."

Besides the men of Compound 76, the POWs in a nearby compound also watched the performances from across a narrow road. Altogether there were more than thirteen thousand spectators. Even the American military police and the South Korean guards couldn't help but keep their eyes in our direction.

18. AFTER THE VICTORY

As we were celebrating our victory, hundreds of GIs sealed Compound 76, and no representatives, except for the three women, were allowed to return to their compounds. So the four of us Chinese got stuck there. On the same day General Smart revoked the agreement Bell had signed, declaring it illegal, made under duress. He announced that he would take all necessary measures to restore order in the camp, including the use of force. Soon we got word that Bell and Fulton had both been demoted and had left Koje Island. From the radio we heard that Pyongyang and Beijing had widely publicized our victory, which had provided ammunition for propaganda and some leverage for our negotiators at Panmunjom. Yet I began to feel uneasy about this victory, which had caused us to be trapped here and might bring more trouble to the Korean prisoners.

From mid-May on, the American troops harassed the POWs. They fired rifles, pitched tear-gas bombs into different compounds, and drove tanks up to some fences to spew fire from flamethrowers onto the slogans and the portraits of Stalin, Mao, and Kim Il Sung erected by the prisoners. Every day the guards would fire at the inmates in Compound 76. Within three weeks about two dozen men had been wounded. Obviously the enemy intended to provoke the inmates so that they would have a pretext for punishing us.

After a few meetings among the leaders of Compound 76, to which Chaolin and Ming were both invited, a conclusion was reached: the enemy must be planning to take revenge, so we must prepare for it. In addition, General Smart might have another object in mind — six compounds controlled by the Korean Communists had repeatedly refused to be screened by U.N. personnel, so he might be intending to solve this problem as well. Very likely the enemy would attack Compound 76 to set an example for the other bellicose compounds and intimidate them into obedience. Therefore the leaders decided to organize for self-defense, preparing for the impending violence; at the same time, we must not give the enemy a handle for any large-scale attack, so we should avoid acting rashly and know where to stop. The Korean prisoners responded to the leaders' call enthusiastically and organized themselves into different task groups. An assault brigade was formed: its members were armed with self-made weapons — cudgels, gasoline bombs, and long spears made of pieces of steel ripped from oil drums, sharpened, and tied to the tips of bamboo poles with iron wire. They also began digging trenches within the tents to protect themselves from gunfire. We, the four Chinese, all joined them in building defenses.

On the early morning of June 12, about forty tanks and armored personnel carriers and twelve hundred GIs surrounded Compound 76. The snarling of the vehicles woke us up, and we watched them from within our tent. General Smart supervised the operation on the spot, wearing a steel helmet, a pistol, and binoculars on his broad belt. We saw all the gun barrels pointing at the barracks inside the compound. A battalion of GIs, looking ghostly in their gas masks, all raised their bayonets, ready to charge.

Inside the compound the prisoners got into the trenches to defend our position.

At eight sharp a gunshot shattered the silence. At once two columns of personnel carriers and tanks plunged forward, knocked down the front gate, and rolled into the compound. Following them, all masked, the foot soldiers ran in, seven or eight as a group. Without delay flame-throwers started launching torrents of fire at the tents; rifles and machine guns burst out crackling; grenades and gas bombs went off here and there. The explosions thundered while greenish gas was billowing all over the place.

As Chinese, the four of us were not allowed to take part in the combat; ten men had been assigned to protect us. While I was wondering how the Koreans could possibly fight such an unequal battle, the members of the assault brigade sprang out of their trenches, wielding their spears and cudgels, and charged the enemy. They shouted *"Mansai! Mansai!,"* which means "long live" in Korean, an exclamation somewhat like "hurray." As they were attacking, machine guns began raking them. A few men got close enough to stab at the GIs, but most were shot down before they could reach them. Several of their gasoline bombs hit the personnel carriers and tanks, which started burning, though the brief fires could hardly have done much damage. Meanwhile, all the other prisoners were chanting the "Internationale" — "Rise up! slaves of hunger and cold. Rise up! you who won't suffer anymore . . ." We joined them in bellowing the song. Strange to say, this felt more like a demonstration than a battle.

Some Koreans sang their army's fighting song while confronting the GIs, who charged at them with bayonets and even fired at them point-blank. Many of the prisoners shouted in English, "Death to GIs!" and "Down with Truman!" Within five minutes all the men of the assault brigade had fallen, lost in the dark smoke and the greenish gas. Crazed by the sight, Wu Gaochen was about to leap out to join the battle, but two Koreans pulled him down, saying if he got killed they would be punished.

About twenty minutes later the gunfire subsided. The GIs began rounding us up. They came into our tent, pulled us out of the trench by the collars, and forced us to go to the front yard. When we got there, I saw that most of the tents had burned down; two were still standing but in flames. There were numerous scorched spots on the ground, and everywhere were cartridge cases, shrapnel, bamboo poles, shards of glass, and dead and wounded bodies, from which blood was still flowing. The air was so heavy with nauseous gas, smoke, and diesel fuel that we couldn't breathe without coughing. A few of us stepped aside to help our wounded comrades, but the GIs stopped us. The assault brigade had consisted of about four hundred men, the best among the Koreans; they were all lying on the ground, scattered like bales of rags, some still smoldering. At least half of them had been killed. A few were screaming for help like small boys crying for mama. One of them managed to sit up; he seemed to have suffered a concussion — his eyes, ears, and nose were bleeding. Wordlessly he was flailing his arms in every direction as though blind.

Meantime, a group of medics wearing Red Cross armbands were busy treating the wounded GIs, carrying them away on stretchers or bandaging them on the spot. None of the medical personnel bothered about the wounded Koreans until every GI had been helped.

With the aid of a Korean prisoner, the Americans singled out us Chinese and took us to a corner where about thirty Korean representatives and officers were sitting on their haunches. They made us squat down in the same manner. Toward noon they ordered us to line up, all with our hands clasped behind our heads. Then they put us on a truck, which shipped us to "the top jail" on Koje Island. They told us that we had become "war criminals." On the way I saw smoke and fire rising from the hamlet on a hillside in the north. The enemy had found out that some of the villagers had collaborated with the POWs, so a unit of South Korean troops had been sent there to plunder the village. A breeze wafted over the cries of women and children, which sounded shrill, like the long chirps of insects. Gunshots broke out from there now and again. Soldiers were taking away buffaloes and sheep while dogs barked explosively. Later I heard that most of the civilians had been removed to Pusan.

"The top jail" confining us was a standard prison house surrounded by a high stone wall capped with rolls of barbed wire. Inside the jail it was dark, cold, and damp; the cells were guarded by GIs around the clock. All the new arrivals were shut in solitary confinement here. We were not allowed to stand up or lie down in the daytime. All day long each of us had to sit on a reed mat, four by seven feet, that almost covered his entire cell floor. I was given a tattered blanket, which I wrapped around my legs during the day. Having nothing else to do, I often rubbed the wounded area in my thigh to help the blood circulate.

I was afraid I might develop arthritis in such a damp, cold place, so I often sat on my heels. Some guards would snarl at me when they found me in this posture, and would order me to sit down fully on the mat. Sometimes when they were not around, I would do a few squats.

Although we were "high-ranking prisoners" now, our food was the same — two barley balls a day, with a ladle of soy sauce soup in which sometimes floated a few bits of cabbage leaves or mustard greens. In a corner of my cell sat a toilet pail with a lid on it; the pail was collected every morning by a Korean man. There was no lamp in my one-windowed room, so as soon as dusk fell, I had to go to bed with my head on my shoes stacked together as a pillow. The cell was teeming with fleas, which would torment me viciously until around midnight, after which they'd subside. I guessed they must have become sluggish after they were engorged. But little by little I grew accustomed to them and could go to sleep soon after I lay down.

My enthusiasm about the collective struggle had begun to wane. At heart I was starting to doubt the wisdom of abducting General Bell. True, we had created a piece of international news and provided ammunition for the Korean and the Chinese governments, but at what cost? Our living conditions had definitely deteriorated, and hundreds of men in Compound 76 had been killed or wounded. Why hadn't we thought about the consequences beforehand? Was any news story worth so many lives? Who would get credit for the "victory"? Of course the Communist leaders here, not those men buried underground. The enemy was brutal, yet we could have avoided being hurt by them. The real task for the leaders here should have been to make sure that all the POWs survived unharmed. Any effort other than that must have had ulterior motives. Lonesome and miserable, I felt I had been used too, though compared with the dead and the wounded, I was lucky.

In this special jail corporal punishment was commonplace. I often heard prisoners scream while GIs hit them with sticks and belts. I was not often beaten or kicked like others, because I didn't talk back. One morning I was taken out for interrogation.

I wouldn't tell the Americans how we communicated with the Koreans, so they led me into a windowless room. In came two strapping GIs, one toting a rifle while the other hauled a fire hose. "We're going to do some cleaning today," said the one holding the nozzle, smirking. He then turned it on. A column of water hit my stomach and hurled me backward. My head banged into the wall so hard that I blacked out instantly.

When I came to a moment later, the water was still hitting me. I huddled into a ball by embracing my knees, with my back toward the men. The water struck my spine and lower back until my pants were ripped from behind. They laughed and wound up the session by giving me a few kicks in the buttocks.

"Get up, gook!" ordered one of them.

I was shivering, my chest and head aching. I managed to turn over but couldn't stand up.

They pulled me to my feet, dragged me out of the house, and left me in the small courtyard to dry my clothes for a while. I sat in the warm sun, still queasy, watching the seagulls sailing beneath the clouds. My face felt puffy and my eyes smarted. I wanted to weep but checked myself, aware that some eyes were observing me. Far away in the east, toward the beach, a bell was tolling, and a group of men were chanting a work song in Chinese. I turned my head to listen closely, then I caught sight of Mr. Park behind the grilled window of his cell. He was waving at me, raising his thumb and clasping his hands to congratulate me for having thwarted our enemy's attempt to extract information from me. A Korean officer in the next cell even saluted me. I waved back, trying hard to smile.

That evening the one-eyed Korean man doling out food handed a bowl of barley to me through the steel bars on the door of my cell. I forced myself to eat some. To my surprise, beneath the coarse grain were about a dozen small meatballs made of pork and onion. Hurriedly I turned away from the door so that the guards couldn't see the meatballs while I ate them. Evidently there were agents among the Korean workers here. Mr. Park may often have been given this kind of meal. Although grateful to him for having the meatballs smuggled in for me, I was bothered by the fact that even in this prison for "war criminals" he still enjoyed privileges like a top official. It was simply impossible for our captors to take full control.

One morning a tall American officer passed by my cell, and I recognized him — Lieutenant East, who had commanded the guards at Compound 602 when I was there. I had once relayed to him our demand for negotiating with General Bell in person. He seemed in charge of nothing here. As he returned from the other end of the corridor, I moved to the door of my cell. Dressed rather slovenly — half of his buttons undone and one of his shoes unlaced — he shuffled along the hallway as though deep in thought.

"Lieutenant East," I said.

"Yes." He stopped.

"Do you remember me?"

He shook his head, his gray eyes staring at my face. Then he recognized me. "Yes, you were the Red spokesman at Compound 602."

"No, I was just an interpreter. How come you're here?"

"None of your business. Damn you Reds, why did you help the motherfucking Koreans kidnap General Bell? You got me into trouble too."

"Like I said, I was just an interpreter, not involved in any decision making. As a soldier I didn't have a choice, I just obeyed orders."

"Let me tell you something," he said with sudden anger, jabbing his forefinger at my face. "General Bell is a good man. He played baseball with us. He's a powerful pitcher. Many guys here miss him. He treated you Reds well, didn't he? When you wanted to talk, he came to meet you. After you complained about barley and night blindness, the next day he called around to get more rice and vegetables for you. But what did you do in return? You conspired with the Koreans. You abducted him. You ruined him! That man is a husband and a father and had an honorable career. Now he's totally humiliated, busted to colonel. How come you Reds pulled such a dirty trick on him?"

I hadn't expected this lean-faced man would defend his superior so passionately, and I was a little bewildered by his judging the general on the basis that he was a good baseball player. What did Bell's character have to do with sports? This fellow in front of me hadn't grown up, like a big boy. Still, somewhat touched by his words, I mumbled, "I'm sorry for him. Also for the hundreds of Koreans killed in Compound 76 and for the villagers whose homes were burned down."

He stared at me, as though amazed. For

about half a minute we remained wordless, looking at each other. Then I averted my face and he walked away.

Lieutenant East's remarks upset me. What surprised me most was that he hadn't thought of the incident in the way an officer should. He took it personally, thinking of General Bell as a specific individual. That made East different, though he still regarded me as no more than a Red. His words had jolted me into a sudden realization. Before the conversation with him I had felt misgivings about the wisdom of confronting the vengeful enemy with force, but my thoughts had remained vague in the back of my mind. Now they had crystallized. To be able to function in a war, an officer was expected to view his men as abstract figures so that he could utilize and sacrifice them without any hesitation or qualms. The same abstraction was supposed to take place among the rank and file too — to us every American serviceman must be a devil, whereas to them, every one of us must be a Red. Without such obliteration of human particularities, how could one fight mercilessly? When a general evaluates the outcome of a battle, he thinks in numbers — how many casualties the enemy has suffered in comparison with the losses of his own army. The larger a victory is, the more people have been turned into numerals. This is the crime of war: it reduces real human beings to abstract numbers. This was why, ever since I'd been treated by Dr. Greene, I had wished I could become a doctor like her, who dealt with individual patients in a war and didn't have to relish any victory other than the success of saving a limb or a life.

A few days later both Wu Gaochen and I were sent back to Compound 602. I felt lucky that we two returned on the same day. Had I left the top jail alone, my comrades might have suspected that I had worked out a deal with the enemy or had confessed to them. We both went back on June 26, and without prior agreement we told Commissar Pei the same story; that is, the enemy had let us out because we were not as important as the other "war criminals." Lieutenant East had said to me that they needed the solitary cells for real officers. After six weeks' separation, I was glad to rejoin my comrades.

19. THE APPREHENSION OF COMMISSAR PEI

The Chinese POWs in Compound 602 had been informed that we were going to move to Cheju Island, which is more than a hundred miles farther south in the Yellow Sea. This news unsettled the inmates, and I could feel the suspicion and fear among them. Rumor had it that some Nationalist troops from Taiwan had already gathered on Cheju Island, getting trained before they joined the U.N. forces on the Korean mainland. (This hearsay proved to be wrong.) So most of the men here were reluctant to leave for Cheju, fearful of falling into the Nationalists' hands.

I went to see Commissar Pei in the evening. He was pleased to have me back and asked about Chaolin and Ming, saying he felt crippled without them around. Then he told me his thoughts on the imminent move to Cheju Island. He believed the enemy's purpose was twofold: first, to separate us from the Korean prisoners, and second, to shake our determination to return to mainland China. "But we haven't planned for any resistance yet," he said. "The enemy just destroyed Compound 76 and they may turn on us at any moment, so we shouldn't give them any excuse for using force." He looked tired, though his rugged face still showed resolve. He had a sprinkling of gray hair now.

Encouraged by his discretion, I reported to him how the GIs had burned and flattened Compound 76. I got so carried away that I even said, "I don't know if it was really worth the sacrifice for the Koreans to kidnap Bell. Their entire shock brigade was wiped out by the Americans, at least four hundred casualties."

"To make revolution means to sacrifice," he said seriously. "Of course for such a victory the price is high, but we reached our goal of embarrassing the enemy internationally and exposing their lie that we were all unwilling to return to our motherland."

I realized I had said too much, but in spite of myself, I kept on: "I just feel sorry for those Koreans, who were all brave men charging at the tanks with bamboo poles."

"The Koreans can be fanatic sometimes." He chuckled, lifted a green enamel mug, and took a gulp of hot water.

Then I told him my impression of Mr. Park and how the Korean Communist force had even infiltrated the jail for "war criminals." I gave him more details of our stay in Compound 76; he seemed amused by the way we had been treated, unconsciously licking his upper lip while listening to me describe the beef dumplings.

Early the next morning a jeep topped with a stout loudspeaker pulled up at the front entrance to the compound. A man shouted in Chinese, "Pei Shan, if you were really fathered by your dad, get out of your hole, or we'll make all you Red Bandits suffer."

I was puzzled why they didn't just come in and take Pei away. Perhaps they were unsure what he looked like now. Even though they had the commissar's photo, they might not be able to identify him, because his features had changed considerably; he was bearded and much thinner than a few months before. I was told that the jeep had come and given the same order every morning for almost a week.

The loudspeaker blared again, this time in English, "Pei Shan, you come out right away, or we'll handle you differently when we come in to nab you."

There was no response from our headquarters, wherein the commissar sat smoking and talking with others. He had held a meeting three days earlier to discuss how to deal with the enemy's demand. He even said he'd follow the decision made by the leaders of the United Communist Association. If they believed he should surrender himself to the enemy, he would do that to save the compound from destruction. Of course nobody wanted him to turn himself in. They decided to ignore the enemy's bluster, which suggested that the GIs might not dare come in to search for the commissar at this moment. The massacre in Compound 76 had just raised an international outcry, and a group of European inspectors had come to visit the burned barracks, shooting photos and even interviewing Korean POWs. So the enemy might have pulled in their horns for the time being. On the other hand, we feared that if Commissar Pei fell into their hands, they would keep him here, probably in the war-criminal jail, so as to paralyze our leadership before we were moved to Cheju Island. In other words, the enemy might be planning to isolate our top leader from us.

Commissar Pei was aware of the possibility that he might be taken away and kept separate from us. He had prepared two sets of leaders among us in case more of them were snatched away or the enemy divided us into groups. He also organized the Party members into small sets that could assume low-level leadership if necessary. As for the position of the top leader, if Pei was gone, the man to replace him was Zhao Teng, a flat-faced warrior with a hot temper. If we lost Zhao, Zhang Wanren, a slow-witted but dependable man, would step in. Now I saw that Pei really needed Chaolin and Ming badly; they would have been more capable leaders.

In another three days it would be July 1 and the Chinese Communist Party's thirty-first anniversary, so the leaders in the compound decided to hold a demonstration, not a large one, just a symbolic act to show the enemy our strength and to remind the prisoners of the Party's presence. Commissar Pei assigned me to write some English words on placards, such as "Long Live Communism!," "We Must Go Back to Build Our Country!," "Down with American Imperialism!," "Follow the Communist Party Forever!"

But on the evening of June 29, as plans for the demonstration were in the works, General Smart arrived. As soon as his jeep pulled up at the front gate, he announced through a bullhorn, "All the prisoners in Compound 602, I order you to leave this place tomorrow morning. Two ships are going to take you to Cheju Island, where you'll live in brand-new barracks. If any of you resist moving, we shall evict you by force." A middle-aged interpreter translated the orders to the inmates, who listened without response.

After Smart left, an emergency meeting was held in our headquarters, for which I served as secretary. Without blank paper I just jotted down a few notes on the margins of the Bible I had once owned, so that we could keep track of who said what. The leaders were deliberating whether to depart for Cheju Island peacefully. Commissar Pei said, "Perhaps we shouldn't resist this time, just to save our strength for future struggle."

Several men disagreed, feeling our country might lose face if we yielded to the enemy without a fight, because the Koreans had just scored a huge victory and were watching us. They argued for collective resistance, or at least for creating some difficulties for the Americans.

"I can see your points," the commissar said. "But we don't know anything about the situation on Cheju Island. Who will guard us there, Americans or South Koreans or the Nationalist troops from Taiwan? Are we going to be the only POWs in the camp? Are there other armies on the island? There're so many unknowns that we should be cautious about any action now, not to waste our energy."

"I'm afraid the enemy has another ax to grind," put in Zhao Teng, the compound's nominal chief, licking his gold teeth.

"That's true," another voice added.

"What if they take away our leaders before they put us on the ships?" asked a third man.

The commissar's eyes brightened. "I've thought of that. That's a possibility. Let's talk about it."

"I believe we must refuse to move," Zhao Teng said. "First, we should show the enemy our determination to fight, so when they come to search for you, they'll understand that even if they find you, they might not be able to take you away without causing lots of trouble for themselves."

"I don't want to get our men into danger," said the commissar, blushing a little. This was the first time I had ever seen his face change color.

"We know that, but this is a part of the struggle we cannot avoid."

A bald man chipped in, "This is also an opportunity to create a scandal for the Americans. If they open fire and burn our tents, they'll be condemned by the whole world."

More men argued for resistance. Commissar Pei seemed in an awkward position because his personal safety was also at stake. He was much less resolute than before. After another hour's discussion, he finally gave way, but he specified some conditions: "Tomorrow morning we won't move unless they come in to take us out. But we must make sure none of our men will be hurt and there'll be no bloodshed. We should exhaust the Americans' patience so that they'll expose themselves to the eyes of the world."

After the meeting I mulled over Pei's words. He had never been so cautious, so unwilling to risk the lives of his men. I was impressed by the compromise plan he had made. Then the thought occurred to me that he might have argued for peace for personal reasons. A full-blown confrontation would have put him at a disadvantage. If he fell into the Americans' hands, they might punish him more for the resistance he had masterminded. Enraged, they could cripple or even kill him and then blame it on an accident. In other words, he must have been fearful, worried about his personal safety, knowing that without thousands of men around him, he would be at the enemy's mercy. So I had mixed feelings about his attitude. On the one hand, I was totally for a peaceful departure, and on the other, I felt that by nature Pei wasn't a peaceful man — he had only been frightened into supporting a relatively passive resistance.

At eight the next morning, six truckloads of GIs arrived at our compound. Their officer, a craggy-faced man, ordered us to come out with our blanket rolls and line up on the front yard, but none of us moved. The GIs were waiting. A hush enveloped the compound, as if all the men were sleeping. The officer shouted his orders again. Still nobody stirred. The barracks were so quiet that you could hear bursts of static coming from the megaphone and a flock of orioles chirping in the crown of a crooked elm.

The GIs waited about half an hour. Then the gate was opened and they came in, advancing while pitching tear-gas canisters at our tents. In no time the compound turned cloudy and people began coughing.

"Get your damn asses out!" shouted the officer.

Now balls of dark smoke started rising from two tents at the west side. Surely it was our men who had set fire to their quarters, to make it look like the GIs' doing. A few minutes later we filed out of our tents, each carrying his blanket roll, and many men covered their noses with wet towels. We formed up in the yard while a company of GIs surrounded us. The officer ordered some three hundred prisoners to go fight the fire. He kept hollering, "Damn it, I'm gonna try you all for arson!"

Two fire engines arrived, and without difficulty they extinguished the fire.

Then a squad of GIs led us out of the compound, with more guards escorting us on both sides. As we were leaving, about a hundred pro-Nationalist prisoners appeared outside the gate. They rattled sticks and threw pebbles at us, calling us all kinds of names. Some of them even shouted: "Feed them to sharks!" "Work them to skeletons in the coal mines!" "Dump them into the ocean!" "Commies, your final hour is coming!"

I had never met any of these men before and wondered which compound they came from. Suddenly one of them, a young boy, sprang out of their ranks and sprinted toward us, yelling, "I want to go home. Let me go with them!" Surprised, we stopped to watch. The boy looked fourteen or fifteen. I thought it bizarre that he believed we were headed for China. A beefy man was chasing him, brandishing a self-made machete and barking, "Little rabbit, I'm going to chop you to pieces." Still the boy was dashing toward us for all he was worth.

Richard, the corporal who had been sympathetic to me, stood close by but watched amusedly while the other GIs were whooping and whistling. I cried, "Richard, help him please!"

He strode over and thrust his rifle at the chaser. "Halt!" he ordered.

The man stopped short, then protested in Chinese, "That little bastard is a Commie. I must let him have it." He slashed the air with his machete and stamped the ground.

Ignoring his explanation, Richard pointed his rifle at the man's chest and said, "You go back now." He jutted out his chin in the direction of the other harassers.

Deflated, the man returned to his party near the fence while the boy, having joined us, was still sobbing, his face crumpled. With his index and middle fingers held together, Richard saluted me, and I returned him one.

Our long procession continued toward the shore. Some crippled men couldn't go fast and were supported by their comrades. I walked beside Commissar Pei, who looked wearied, his thick lips cracked. He said he hadn't slept well the night before and had gotten a migraine. The steady breeze from the sea, fishy and warm, wafted over the smell of burned firewood from a village. The yellowish ocean came into view, on which some gray sails were bobbing. The willow bushes and cypresses on the hills looked tired of growing, as if stunted by the salty wind. To our left the rocky bluff, brightened by the rising sun, was still wet, while dewdrops on the overhanging shrubs glistened, sending out tiny flashes. On the roadside, puffs of cobwebs were scattered here and there on the grass like miniature jellyfish. I could sense the agitation in the procession. It was rumored that some POWs had been shipped to Canada as guinea pigs for chemical-weapon experiments and that hundreds of prisoners had been forced to labor in a gold mine on an island near Japan. Once we got on the ships, God knew where the enemy would take us. They might have lied to us about Cheju Island all along.

At the fringe of a sloping pine grove, a knot of small boys, barefoot and in baggy shorts, were flourishing slingshots and hunting tits, sparrows, wrens. One of them carried about a dozen dead birds strung together on a wicker twig pushed through their mouths. Still there were a lot of birds warbling in the woods. Another boy, the smallest of them, waved a whittled branch, to the tip of which was affixed a ring of iron wire covered with many layers of spiderweb; he used this tool to catch dragonflies, which would be fed to chickens and ducks. I kept watching the boys until they faded into the forest.

Once we were clear of the hill slope, the muddy beach appeared, spreading like a long strip of unplanted paddy fields. At its northern end, at the beginning of the wharf, were anchored two large black ships, the sides of their prows painted with white Korean words that none of us could understand. They were cargo ships, whose tonnage must have been over three thousand, and each had a pair of tall funnels puffing out dark smoke. On the beach hundreds of armed GIs had already assembled; General Smart, in a helmet, was also there waiting for us. Together with him were a group of junior officers and about twenty Chinese men in the uniforms marked with *PW.*

We were made to form up into eighteen lines on the beach. Each of the junior officers took one of the Chinese helpers to the head of a line and began checking us one by one. "Turncoat!" somebody cursed one of the collaborators. Obviously they were searching for Pei, who was standing next to me. These Chinese helpers had all served in our division and had met Pei before; perhaps they could recognize their commissar, whose face might be memorable to them for his bright eyes, stout nose, and fat ears. I wondered what we should do if they identified him.

The two men in charge of our line were moving closer. I stared at them and forced myself not to show any fear. The second they passed me, the mousy Chinese man lifted his hand to point at Pei. The American officer turned and yelled, "We got him!"

Dozens of GIs rushed over. The commissar stepped out of the line, turned around to wave at us, then walked away with them without a word. I was amazed by such a peaceful apprehension. Had this happened to Mr. Park, the Koreans would definitely have gone berserk and broken ranks to fight with the GIs.

"Well, Mr. Pei, we finally meet," General Smart sneered, his arched upper lip curled.

The commissar didn't respond and stood sideways to us as though to keep his face partly out of our view. Somebody poked my back and I turned around. It was Zhao Teng. He whispered to me, "Go to the front and tell them we won't board the ships unless Commissar Pei comes with us."

I hesitated, unsure whether the GIs would allow me to get there. Zhao Teng pushed me. "Go now!"

I stepped out of the line and walked toward Pei. "Turn back!" a sergeant shouted at me.

"I have an urgent message for General Smart." I raised both hands above my head. He came over, put his big hands on my stomach, and searched me; then he stepped aside and let me pass.

I went up to the heavyset general and said, "I was sent over to inform you that none of these men will board the ships without Mr. Pei coming along with us."

He turned to look at the swarm of dusty,

emaciated faces. I too gazed at my comrades. I could feel their fear and anger. They were tense, their eyes all fastened on us. I repeated, "General Smart, they won't get on the ships if you take Mr. Pei away."

"Who are you?"

"I'm just a regular serviceman who happens to know English. Just a messenger."

"Tell them, Don't bluff me!"

Suddenly a voice boomed in Chinese, "We won't board the ships!" That was Zhao Teng.

Most of the six thousand men followed him to shout in unison. The GIs were stunned by the sheer volume of the voices; so was I. I realized that my comrades were frightened and desperately needed Commissar Pei as their protector. To their minds, he was the only man capable of leading and organizing them, and without him they'd be lost. He embodied the Party to them.

"Return Commissar Pei to us!" a voice shouted. Again they roared together.

General Smart smirked, but he too realized the seriousness of the demand. Although unarmed, we outnumbered the GIs by fifteen to one. If a fight broke out, for sure there would be a disaster for both sides. Smart summoned a photographer over to take a picture of Pei. He then turned to talk with an officer who seemed to be his aide-de-camp. Meanwhile, the prisoners went on shouting our demand.

When the photographer arrived, Pei motioned for me to come over. He wanted to take the photo with me. General Smart frowned, but didn't interfere. So I went up to Pei and stood beside him for the picture.

That done, Smart straightened up and said to Pei, "All right, we never meant to harm you, and you can go to Cheju with them. But we'll keep you separate from the crowd from now on."

I translated his words to the commissar, who nodded, apparently pleased.

So he was taken away to the second ship, and I rejoined the crowd. We all saw him go down into a cabin near the stern ramp. To us this was a victory, though I doubted if the Americans had ever intended to keep Pei on Koje Island. Zhao Teng patted my shoulder and said, "Great job, Yuan!"

Then we began boarding the ships.

20. ARRIVAL AT CHEJU ISLAND

Although we had been shut into the cabins, the ships didn't weigh anchor until two hours later. The cabin I was in was swarming with about five hundred men, some sitting and some standing. Every bit of space in here was taken; it was impossible for anyone to lie down. A line of lamps behind glazed glass affixed along the walls shed dim light on the prisoners' faces and rendered them more sallow. Fortunately I was pushed against a wall, so I managed to settle down in a corner. The dust on the floor was at least half an inch thick. In the air there was a strong odor of dung — the ship must formerly have carried fertilizer or guano. Ten yards away from me, a man with a trampled leg was whimpering. There was no medic among us, so nobody could help him. Two men, exhausted from standing, even sat on the injured fellow's good leg, but they got up after others objected. I was angry at the way the Americans were transporting us. Why couldn't they use more ships or move us batch by batch?

Gradually the cabin began to stink with human stench. Curses went up here and there, even louder than the roaring of the engine. Those men who had to stand on their feet tired out, and grew clamorous and aggressive, jabbing their elbows at one another. Against the aft wall of the cabin stood a line of oil drums, all sawed in half, which we called "honey buckets" because they served as night pails in the camp. At the beginning of the trip some men vomited into them, but soon some began to use them to relieve themselves. Whenever the ship rocked, the half dozen oil drums would shift and even career. Eventually two of them tipped over, the liquid stuff spilling on the floor; yet people had no choice but to remain where they were, some of their blanket rolls soaked with urine. Unless you were unable to hold it any longer, you wouldn't fight your way to reach one of those buckets to relieve yourself, not because of the shame of urinating or doing a BM in front of so many eyes but because you couldn't possibly regain your spot once you had left and would have to stand all the way afterward.

I rooted in my corner and closed my eyes to shut out this hellish sight. In a dazed state of mind I drifted off to sleep from time to time. I don't know how long I had been asleep before a metallic thud from above woke me up. The hatch on the deck was opened and a gust of air rushed in. Ah, fresh air! I inhaled it ravenously. Then an iron bucket tied to a hemp rope came down, overflowing with cold rice. All at once people near the opening began scrambling toward the food, and abuse was tossed out in all directions. As they were shoving and tussling, another few buckets of rice were lowered down, but it was impossible for most men to reach the food; as a result, only about a third of the prisoners actually had a bite. I was too far away from the rice buckets, so I gave up trying.

Following the food came five buckets of water, most of which spilled over the men below the opening. The rice and the water were our dinner. In fact, even if I could have reached a bucket I would have had second thoughts about taking in anything, for fear of having to relieve myself afterward.

I tried to block out the horrible scene by mulling over what had happened on the beach that day. Before we boarded the ships, two leaders, Zhao Teng and Zhang Wanren, had sidled up to me when the GIs had turned their eyes to a fight between two prisoners, staged to divert their attention. Both of them congratulated me on my "negotiation with Smart," calling it a great victory. Wary of the term they used, I told them what the general had said to Commissar Pei, "You can go to Cheju with them. But we'll keep you separate from the crowd from now on." They were both nonplussed. And for a good while we racked our brains to fathom the implications of Smart's words. He had seemed to say that Pei and we were all going to stay on Cheju. This was good news in a way, because it implied there might indeed be a prison camp on the island. General Smart's words might also suggest that the Americans were not going to finish us off somewhere in the middle of the ocean. So we felt somewhat relieved.

The ship lurched and a man nearby retched. I closed my eyes and let my mind continue to roam. I wondered why Pei had grabbed me to be photographed with him on the beach. I was sure he hadn't done that out of kindness or appreciation of my service, but I couldn't figure out his motive. Probably he had done it from habit, following his instinct for acting in such a situation. Then it dawned on me that my presence in the picture could at least provide a date and context for it, so that the enemy couldn't easily distort it for propaganda and thus Pei's superiors could not suspect him of cooperating with the enemy. In other words, he had used me as a potential witness to his innocence. What a smart man. I was impressed, though I felt uneasy about being used like that.

Tired of thinking, I tried to doze away. Now and then misgivings would rise in my mind about where we were headed. People around me talked about whether the Americans would make us work like coolies or send us to a battlefield, so I couldn't help but think about all the possibilities too. Luckier than many of the men who had to fight to keep their spots, I was safe in my corner niche and managed to sleep several hours before the engine finally stopped grinding.

Toward daybreak we dropped anchor at a wharf on the northern side of Cheju Island. We were let out of the cabins and then disembarked. Four men, seriously trampled, were left on our ship, accompanied only by an orderly. For the moment few of us gave a thought to them, because everyone was desperate to breathe fresh air and stretch his limbs. After we stayed long enough on the shore, some men were sent back to carry the injured off the ship. The beach here was sandy and the sea was much less yellow, almost aquamarine. One by one they laid the injured men on the sand. "Water, who has water?" a man shouted through his hands cupped around his mouth. Soon a half-filled canteen was passed on to the spot where the four fellows were lying and groaning.

About half an hour later an ambulance came to carry them to the hospital. The shore was still wrapped in fog. A macadam road stretched along the whitish beach and faded into the milky clouds. Through the haze we could see a few bulldozers parked at a construction site nearby, motionless and dark like miniature reefs. By now Commissar Pei had gotten off the other ship too, but two GIs were guarding him. After we all assembled on the beach, the sun finally came out, dissipating the fog in the southeast, where a few miles away rose some rugged hills. In front of us the contour of the prison, Camp 8, was growing clear on a gentle incline. It was an immense enclosure, encircled by three rows of barbed wire. We were told that this place had been specially built for us, the would-be repatriates. Within the camp numerous barbed-wire fences surrounded clusters of sheds that were the barracks for the prisoners. Along the exterior fence of the camp stood some guard towers on wooden pillars braced by slanting battens as thick as beams, a pair of searchlights mounted on the handrails of each tower. At the middle of the other end of the camp, near the main entrance, sat a brick house, which was the guards' office. Unlike on Koje Island, here such a house was within the enclosure. The Americans seemed to have a different way of running this place.

The frail boy Richard had saved hadn't stayed in the same cabin with me, but he caught sight of me on the beach. Wordlessly he came over as if to claim a special relationship. His long-lashed eyes were still intense, fastened on me. I patted his shoulder and asked, "What's your name?"

"Shanmin," came his clear voice.

"Have they put you into a squad yet?"

He shook his head. I said, "Then stay with me."

He nodded eagerly.

Our procession walked a long distance around the fence to reach the front gate. When we had entered the camp, I saw why there were so many barbed-wire fences in here. Within the enclosure were ten compounds, each containing about ten sheds and surrounded by barbed wire almost fifteen feet high. These compounds, arranged in two unequal rows and guarded individually by GIs at the gates, were divided by a large open field, to the west of which were four compounds, about one hundred yards apart from one another, and to the east of which lay six compounds, a shorter distance separating them, about eighty yards. This layout made it impossible for any barracks to have direct contact with its neighbors. In addition, there was a small prison, a stone house at the edge of the sea, over a thousand feet from the northern fence of the camp. The enemy seemed to have learned from the abduction of General Bell the importance of dispersing the POW leaders, so they meant to keep us in smaller groups from now on.

We were divided into ten units, each having about six hundred men. Shanmin and I were put into Compound 6, whose conditions were not as bad as I had feared, its facilities new and adequate on the whole. The compound was at the northeastern end of the camp. In it, eight long sheds stood in parallel, all built of dark volcanic rocks with asphalt-felt roofs. At its southeastern corner stood the kitchen, with a dwarf chimney, and at the southwestern end was the latrine, similar to the residential sheds in shape, though smaller in size. What made the privy unusual was that its urinal had been installed outside, a long concrete trough slanting alongside the fence at an angle of fifteen degrees. In between the kitchen and the outhouse was the recreation area, a small playing field as large as four basketball courts placed together. All the other nine compounds basically had the same layout.

Although each shed here held more than seventy men, it was much less crowded than the tents in the camp on Koje Island. In it two long plank beds had been installed along the walls; on either bed forty people could sleep. This was not bad at all. Shanmin and I were assigned to the first shed, near the kitchen. The moment I unpacked my bedroll, a commotion rose from outside. I went out to take a look. Oddly enough, Commissar Pei strolled into our barracks, smiling and waving at the men around. At once people broke out shouting, "Long live Chairman Mao!," "Long live the Communist Party!," "Fight the American imperialists to death!" Those slogans were their way of expressing their joy. About two thousand men were still waiting in the field to be assigned to their compounds; they saw our top leader and began shouting too. Immediately the commissar gestured for them to hush for fear of attracting the enemy's attention. The guards must have forgotten General Smart's instructions that Pei must be kept separate from us. How else could they have let him come back like this? A GI walked over and handed two cans of Spam through the barbed wire to a prisoner in our compound, saying, "Those guys over there asked me to give you these for the brass." He was referring to Pei and the inmates outside Compound 7 waiting to be led into their quarters. Evidently Commissar Pei's appearance had boosted the prisoners' morale. Some men even shed tears, as though a god, or a guardian angel, had suddenly appeared among us. They regarded Pei as the embodiment of the Communist Party here. These men had no gods to worship, so they could only project their religious feelings on a leader, a human being, whose return to us might have been a fluke. And even Commissar Pei himself said to me, "I don't know why the Americans let me come back."

When he had settled in, he sat down beside me, and putting his large hand on my knee, praised me for speaking to General Smart on his behalf. "You're a brave man, Yuan," he said, and slapped at a horsefly landing on his face. "If you hadn't intervened yesterday, they would've kept me on Koje Island for sure. Then heaven knows what would have happened to me."

"It was Zhao Teng who told me to deliver the message," I admitted.

"But you spoke well to Smart. I was impressed by your composure. You made me realize our Party needs many more intellectuals like you. Don't you think you're a tough soldier now?" He tossed his head back and laughed heartily.

"Maybe. I feel I've developed a little."

"More than a little. It's remarkable that adversities have toughened you so much. To be honest, I used to consider intellectuals unreliable, but you've made me think differently."

I was pleased by his praise, but didn't know how to respond. He then told me that the Party had awarded me another merit citation, first class this time, in addition to the one I had earned for stealing the pistol. I felt proud of myself. Actually I could see that people respected me more than before. By now I had been imprisoned for almost a year and had indeed become a stronger man, though sometimes I still felt isolated and lonely.

Toward midafternoon, a squad of GIs came in and took Commissar Pei away to the prison house on the beach, into which the camp authorities had originally intended to put him. That was the top jail on Cheju Island, where Pei was to be confined from now on.

21. COMMUNICATION AND STUDY

In mid-July a GI on a guard tower was struck in the head by "a message stone" hurled by an inmate from our compound. A gun was fired in response, but the fellow dashed into a shed nearby and was not hit. The stone, with a message tied to it, had been aimed at Compound 7, which was eighty yards away. Because of the long distance, such a stone could be hurled only with a string attached to it, whirling it first, and as a result it often flew astray. Yet since our arrival at Cheju Island, this sling-a-stone method had been the main channel of communication between most compounds.

Now that the enemy had a message of ours in their hands, our leaders were afraid that they might crack our self-made code. Fortunately, our code men, following the rule of changing the code monthly, had altered it a week ago by partly substituting three numerals with alphabetic letters, which made the code more irregular and harder to break. Unable to identify the slinger of the message stone, the guards took away Zhang Wanren, the chief of our compound, and interrogated him for a whole day, but Wanren played the fool and insisted he was unaware of any attempt to contact another compound. He kept wagging his head at the message they showed him and saying he didn't know what to make of it. In the end, the Americans told him that from now on they'd view stone hurling as an act of provocation and would react with gunfire. So we had to abandon the sling-a-stone method and rely more on signaling by semaphore.

Each compound had two or three signalmen who could perform the semaphore, so all the battalions could communicate with their neighbors. A system of hand signals had been invented recently, corresponding to numbers, which worked as follows: right hand on the chest meant 1, left hand on the chest — 2, both hands on the chest — 3, right arm akimbo — 4, left arm akimbo — 5, both arms akimbo — 6, right hand touching the ear — 7, left hand touching the ear — 8, both hands touching the ears — 9, and both hands covering the face — 0. After a set of numerals was transmitted, both hands would fall down to mark a pause; if there was a mistake, the sender would shake his right foot to indicate a restart. Four numerals always formed a unit standing for a word, which could be deciphered through the code.

Though the semaphore was ingeniously designed, it was too slow, too arduous, to handle long messages. Besides, it couldn't be used between the compounds divided by the central field, the distance in between being too far for the signalmen to read the gestures. Soon another semaphore system was invented, called the Large Gesture Telegraph, which required more extended movement of the limbs and was used only between the east and the west sides of the field, though it tended to draw the guards' attention.

Whenever there was a long message to send, the night soil teams were employed. Those latrine men were allowed to go to the seaside only one group at a time, but they dumped the excrement at the same spot. On the way they'd take a breather at a patch of wattle bushes and could leave a message for another team under a rock or some other object there. The secret spot had been specified beforehand to the other barracks through the semaphore, so the message could be picked up smoothly most of the time.

Although there had always been communications among the compounds, we couldn't find an effective way to contact Commissar Pei. He wasn't far away, in the prison house on the beach, and we could see him whenever he was let out for exercise or was basking in the sun in the afternoon. He usually stayed in the open air for twenty minutes, walking by a long sandbar, against which nestled a shack that served as several Chinese men's living quarters. Those men were also POWs but willing to collaborate with the Americans, so they had been detailed there to maintain the prison house and keep watch on the special prisoners jailed in it. In addition to confining "the war criminal," the prison also took in "troublemakers." At times Commissar Pei and we waved at each other, but the long distance prevented him from hearing our voices. If only we could have communicated with him more.

This absence of communication with Pei also meant that there was no paramount leader in the camp. Zhao Teng, designated as Pei's successor long ago, was now in the Fifth Battalion, at the southwestern corner of the camp, beyond the reach of the men in the compounds east of the field. Owing to the absence of the Party's central leadership and any rival pro-Nationalist force, for weeks the camp was peaceful, though many prisoners had grown restless, as if they'd lost their bearings.

Zhao Teng, who was a good warrior but a poor strategist, just ordered us to carry on the three tasks stipulated three months ago in Compound 602 on Koje Island: unite, struggle, and study. Now that we had been isolated into groups, the first task was out of the question. Nor had we any clue how to "struggle," since there was no pro-Nationalist force here. So the only feasible task was "study," to which the inmates devoted themselves earnestly. A slogan began circulating among the battalions: "We must make ourselves more useful for the revolution."

Somehow in early August both Hao Chaolin and Chang Ming were shipped to Camp 8 too. I was delighted to learn of their arrival. I didn't see Ming in person, but Chaolin went to Compound 7, adjacent to ours, so we waved at each other from time to time. He wrote a message in uncoded words and had it passed on to us by the night soil teams. From it I learned that Ming had been sent to the Fourth

Battalion, west of the field. With both of them in the camp now, the leadership would become effective again. They were much more capable than the rest of us. Since it was difficult for Zhao Teng to communicate directly with every one of the six compounds east of the field, Chaolin assumed the leadership of this side of the camp while Zhao Teng was in charge of the four western compounds. The two leaders would communicate first, and then if necessary each would contact the other battalions on his side. Chaolin fully supported the study movement, knowing we might have to stay here for a long time.

More than half of the prisoners in my compound were illiterate, and several educated men, like myself, began teaching them how to read and write. There was no paper, but this problem was easy to solve. Some construction was still in progress outside the camp, so whenever we went out to work, we brought back scraps of cement bags, which we could use in class. Pens were hard to come by, but some men made nibs out of strips of tinplate cut from cans. For ink they used diluted tobacco tar or juice squeezed out of grass. Rain cloths were nailed to walls as blackboards, on which you could write with a toothbrush soaked with the solution of tooth powder. Without enough kraft paper, some men practiced their writing in a layer of sand spread in cardboard boxes. We, the instructors, set a basic goal: every one of the illiterate men should know at least five hundred written characters in three months. This seemed implausible at first, but to our amazement, most of these men were bright and eager to learn. Intuitively they understood literacy would improve their lives, so they applied themselves avidly. In our battalion there was a copy of James Yen's *Thousand Character Lessons* distributed by the U.N. Civil Information and Education Center on Koje Island. This Chinese primer, intelligently compiled, was very handy and served as the basis of the lessons we prepared for the illiterates. James Yen was a Yale graduate and a leading expert in mass education. He had taught Chinese coolies in Europe in the early 1920s and obtained funding from the United Nations for his education project. In fact, Mao Zedong once briefly attended his class in Changsha City, but Yen was barred from entering China after the Communists came to power. In addition to the literacy class, we also offered courses in arithmetic,

401

geography, history, calligraphy, and general knowledge.

As for the literate prisoners, the instructors taught them mainly through telling heroic stories and explicating lines of ancient poetry. I didn't join them very often in the story sessions, which were usually held between noon and two o'clock, when the guards were relaxing or napping. But I was impressed by the number of talents among us. One man, Yiwen, transcribed from memory chapter after chapter of the Russian novel *How the Steel Was Tempered*, and also *The History of the Communist Party of the Soviet Union*; another man, Minshen, could recite most of the pieces from the classical anthology *Three Hundred Tang Poems*; another fellow, whose name I cannot recall, knew dozens of folk songs and taught others how to sing them; a man with only one eye left, who had been a political instructor of a machine-gun company, even wrote a booklet on the history of the Chinese Communist Party. But I was most impressed by my young friend Shanmin.

Shanmin was sixteen and had been an artillery fire-direction man before he was captured. Although illiterate, he was quick at learning things and had good eyesight, so his battalion had trained him to observe the enemy's positions. He often climbed to hilltops alone, carrying a twelve-power telescope, a pistol, and a two-watt walkie-talkie that weighed thirty-five pounds. One day a senior officer in the U.S. Twenty-fifth Division announced to his men that he would give a week's leave to anyone who caught an enemy soldier alive. So a lot of GIs went out hunting for Chinese orderlies and stragglers. They would cut a telephone wire, wait for a repairman to appear, and catch him. They also ambushed cooks going to the front to deliver meals and hot water. A black GI spotted Shanmin, who was busy reporting to the commander of a mortar battery from the crest of a hill. The black man knocked him out from behind, threw him on his shoulder, and carried him down to their headquarters to claim his vacation. Because he had left behind Shanmin's pistol and walkie-talkie, his superior at first couldn't believe that this fifteen-year-old was a soldier. But the telescope with a coordinate axis and numerals on it helped them identify him. They didn't beat the petrified boy; instead they tied him to the side of a tank heading for their rear base. He was frozen half dead, unable to speak, when they got there.

Now after a year's imprisonment, Shanmin was bonier than before, like a bundle of firewood, but he had grown taller, to almost five feet four. He looked younger than his age, as though in his early teens, and had a pallid face and large sensitive eyes. Often underfed, he was languid most of the time, lying with his hands clasped behind his head. When he walked he seemed too tired to lift his feet. However, he came to life with the study movement. He was bright and spared no effort in learning how to read. He enjoyed the story sessions immensely and simply worshiped the raconteurs. I liked seeing his enchanted smile, which was innocent and heartfelt, revealing his crowded teeth. From the first day when we became shed mates, he had been fascinated by my reading *Stars and Stripes*. He once asked me, "Is it hard to learn American words?"

"No, Chinese is harder," I replied.

"How many years have you studied the foreign language?"

"More than ten years."

"Ah, if only I could be so well learned."

"Of course you can. Besides, I'm not as knowledgeable as you think."

"I hope I'll go to school when we're back in our country again."

His words saddened me. At such a tender age, he shouldn't have been here. His parents had lived in the countryside in Henan Province and had been too poor to send him to school, so he had joined the army and ended in Korea. He had three younger brothers and one elder sister, he told me. None of them had any schooling.

Shanmin never asked me to teach him anything, as though such a request would offend me or diminish his respect for me. One day in late July I offered to give him lessons individually. He was overjoyed and said he would be my student all his life. From then on I taught him ten words a day and also the ways phrases and sentences are formed. He had a remarkable memory and never forgot what he had learned. I soon noticed that his appetite for knowledge was quite voracious, though he seldom showed it. One night I overheard him murmur the words "combustion" and "momentum," which I had taught him that afternoon. As I knew him better, I began to add two or three idioms a day. I also taught him multiplication and division. Having served as a fire-direction man, he had a little rudimentary arithmetic, but his knowledge was fragmentary. In just two days he memorized the entire multiplication table. His ability astonished me and made me wonder what he could have accomplished had he had the opportunity to attend school and college. I told him to keep a diary, and he wrote it dutifully every day, sometimes three or four sentences and sometimes a long paragraph. I would check the homework and correct the errors. I also taught him how to use an abacus, which we had made by stringing together some broad beans and then dividing all the strings horizontally with a split chopstick.

He helped me whenever possible. He'd clean mud off my shoes, wash my clothes, and sometimes pour hot water into my mug. He made no secret of his respect and affection for me. He also resoled my shoes with four strips of rubber cut from a discarded tire; he had learned to do this from a prisoner who had been a street cobbler. I enjoyed teaching him; it made me feel like a more useful man.

The other inmates were all fond of Shanmin too, treating him like a younger brother. I don't mean the prisoners were all kindhearted. No, many of them were hardened by the miserable life they had led and were almost unfamiliar and uncomfortable with tender feelings. Quite a few, whose paths I avoided crossing, were plain scoundrels. Yet Shanmin had such a lovable nature that no one could help being brotherly to him. In the beginning his jacket had been too long, almost reaching his knees like an overcoat. A bearded man, whose place on the plank bed was next to Shanmin's, cut the bottom of the jacket with a razor and hemstitched it for him. Weiming, a round-headed fellow from Canton Province, came across a half-filled, soft-covered notebook while cleaning the GIs' quarters, and brought it back for Shanmin. He wrote on the first page, "Little Brother: May wisdom always accompany you!" Another man gave him a used pencil, which the boy cherished so much that he never left it anywhere except in his pocket. When the pencil was worn down to an inch, another man folded a piece of tinplate into a short pipe for him so that Shanmin could insert the stub into "the cap" and continue to use it. During his imprisonment on Cheju, for the progress he achieved in his study he received two medals: a pair of large stars made of iron sheet and coated with red paint.

One day by chance I found him smoking. He stood outside the kitchen and looked silly with a cigarette clamped between his cracked lips, two coils of smoke dangling under his snub nose. Like all the others, he was given a pack of cigarettes a week. I went up to him and said, "Stub it out! You're too young for that."

He obeyed me and lifted his foot, scraping the tip of the cigarette against his rubber sole, but he looked hurt, his eyes misting. I softened and said, "I'm not a meanie, Shanmin. Tobacco will damage your lungs, which are still tender. If you were over eighteen, I wouldn't interfere."

"I understand."

"You don't want to become a consumptive, do you?"

"Uh-uh."

"You still want to study with me?"

"Of course I do."

"Then you mustn't start smoking now."

"I won't light a cigarette again."

He kept his promise. From then on, whenever he was allocated a pack, he would exchange it for food or stationery with others. The inmates all smoked the same kind of cigarettes that had no brand. On one side of the white pack was printed three scarlet words: LIBERTY, JUSTICE, PEACE; on the other side was the moon half hidden in the clouds. Cigarettes were a kind of currency among the prisoners.

Sometimes Shanmin gave a few to others, and this made them like him more.

I still remember how amazed I was to see that he could read an article in a Chinese newspaper just three months after he had enrolled in the literacy class. One day he came upon a scrap of *Ta Kung Pao*, a Hong Kong daily, which must have been subscribed to by the Chinese translators working for the prison administration here. Sitting in a corner, Shanmin was poring over a report on a race of dragon boats. From time to time I glanced at his engrossed face. His lips went on stirring and once in a while a smile flickered on them. When he finished, I asked him, "Any new words?"

He beamed and shook his head. I wanted to congratulate him, but my voice caught. I was so happy for him.

Shanmin even wrote a skit about the South Korean president, Rhee Synman. After a little editorial help from the others, his play was staged in our compound and was well received. It would be inaccurate to say that the war and imprisonment ruined this boy, as they did destroy millions of lives. His was an exceptional case. He flourished in the camp. How mysterious, tenacious, and miraculous life could be! If

Shanmin had stayed home, he might not have had an opportunity to learn how to read and do sums, and might have had to work the fields to help his parents raise his siblings, or might have gone begging from town to town. But in this prison he thrived and even got some education, which helped him grow into a capable man eventually.

Many years later he wrote me a beautiful letter, saying he had become the accountant in his home village, where no one but he could use the abacus. He thanked me for having taught him so well and was proud to inform me that he still didn't smoke. His handwriting was clean and handsome.

22. THE PEI CODE

Colonel Kelly, the commander of the guards at Camp 8, informed us that we must provide two men for Commissar Pei, one to be his cook and the other his interpreter. Both of them were to live with the commissar in the same cell inside the prison house. The cook was easy to find; several men volunteered because the work promised better food. A fellow named Hailin was picked for the job. But choosing the interpreter was more difficult. There were a number of men who knew English, and each compound had at least one interpreter as its spokesman. For us, though, the officer about to join Commissar Pei had another task, which was to establish communication between the prison and the compounds. I knew English better than the other interpreters, so I was one of the candidates for the job, which I was not especially keen to take because the interpreter would have to suffer the strict confinement of the prison too. Chang Ming, whose English was second only to mine, was

411

also a candidate. After an exchange of messages among the leaders of the different compounds, mainly between Zhao Teng and Chaolin, Ming was detailed to go there. This was an appropriate choice, because he was more resourceful than me, and besides, he was a Party member, able to assist the commissar in matters other than translation, especially the Party's secret work.

Chief Zhang Wanren, a balding man with carious teeth, was pleased that I remained in Compound 6, saying I was indispensable to him. He often talked with me about the affairs of our compound and sought my opinion. That was why I knew so much about the workings of the leadership in the camp, where most men had no idea what was transpiring, having strictly followed the order "Do not question what you are told, and do not listen to what you are not supposed to hear." I guessed probably Pei and Chaolin had said some good words about me to Wanren, who treated me like a leader of sorts and had kept me at the battalion headquarters. Wanren once even asked me whether I would like to join the United Communist Association, which had been inducting new members ever since we arrived at Cheju Island. I told him that Commissar Pei believed I should go through a longer period of testing. He couldn't check this with Pei, so he didn't press me again. The truth was that after my application had been turned down four months before, I had vowed I would never apply for membership again, unless Pei himself invited me to do it. This was a way to protect myself from being humiliated again. Besides, I didn't believe in Communism. Why should I change just to suit their requirements? I should be loyal at least to my own heart.

There were only two rooms in that prison house near the beach, roughly the same size — twelve by sixteen feet. One jailed troublemakers and the other held the war criminal; the two cells were separated by a stone wall. A number of men had been confined there as troublemakers, usually for two weeks at a stretch, so, through their accounts, we knew the interior layout of that cell. Ming went to the prison charged with the task of digging a hole through the wall between the two rooms. It took him a whole week to fulfill this mission. He found a stone that looked removable in the southern upper corner of the wall. With the help of the cook and Pei, he managed to pry that stone off, and after some digging by turns, they bored a hole, which became the channel of communication. Whenever we wanted to get orders from the commissar, a trustworthy man would be instructed to pick a fight with someone or yell and make obscene gestures at GIs so that he would be sent to the trouble-makers' cell, where he could take orders from our top leader through the hole in the wall. When released, he would return with the oral message. However, this method of communication was extremely slow, unreliable, and cumbersome, because usually a troublemaker was imprisoned there for at least five days, sometimes as long as three weeks. Often by the time the messenger came back, the orders no longer applied to the changed situation in the camp. Still, up to early September this method was the only one available.

The Pei Code wasn't created according to a plan; it came about by a stroke of luck. One day toward the end of August, I was sent to the prison house because a guard had found in my pocket a slip of paper that carried "Song of the Three Tasks," composed by some men in another compound. Zhao Teng had asked me to pass it to our battalion chief. Colonel Kelly interrogated me for half an hour, but I insisted that I had copied the song myself from the in-

414

mates repairing the road outside the southern fence of the camp. They were mostly from Compound 9 and could sing the song. The colonel didn't believe me, saying I had attempted to relay a secret message, so he had me taken to the prison. I wasn't very upset at this turn of events, because now I could finally communicate directly with Commissar Pei and Ming.

Two men were already in the troublemakers' cell when I was slammed in. One of them had been a telegrapher in our army, a large fellow named Mushu, and the other, Little Hou, our code man. Mushu was jailed because he had been caught in the act of semaphoring from Compound 10, and Little Hou was here for hiding bullets in his cap; a GI at the gate to our barracks had found the two rounds. They punched and kicked him, then hauled him away. They interrogated him for a whole evening, but didn't believe what he told them — there was no gun in our hands, which was true. He'd kept the bullets just in case we might use them someday. The next morning they sent him here. He was our battalion's only code man, so his absence from the compound had done us some damage — for the time

being we were unable to read any semaphore messages.

Little Hou and Mushu were both
pleased to see me, saying it was boring in
the dark room. The cell had a dirt floor,
walls built of volcanic rocks, and a window
facing the ocean in the north. It was damp
inside because the room didn't get any
sunlight until late afternoon.

On my first day there we tried to while
away time by wisecracking and telling
stories. But we were bored soon and began
to doze off. Toward midafternoon we were
ordered to get out to walk a little, relieve
ourselves, and breathe some fresh air. Behind the prison stretched a low sandbar,
along which I walked with my face toward
the window of the cell that contained
Commissar Pei. In no time I saw Ming
gazing at me and waving behind the steel
bars. He looked shaggy and dirty but in
high spirits, his face vivid and whiskered.
Not allowed to get close to that window, I
only nodded to acknowledge that I had
seen him. There was a shack nearby, in
which lived the POWs maintaining this
place. Undoubtedly one of their tasks was
to eavesdrop on us and report to the
Americans on our conversations, so I
wouldn't talk about anything serious with

my two cellmates in the open air.

Mushu became restless after we came back in. The room was so damp that he wouldn't sit down on the dirt floor immediately. He kept pacing back and forth while Little Hou and I sat huddled together in a corner. The wind was picking up outside, and the tide was rising, smoky water crashing on the reefs rhythmically. After every six or seven steps Mushu had to turn around; this pacing was maddening him.

Tired of remaining on his feet, he sat down. We began chatting and bantering idly. But our chitchat became earnest as we continued. We talked about what we should do while we were here. By no means should we just sit around wasting time "like a bunch of sea cucumbers," an expression coined by Mushu. As long as we joined hands we could do something useful. We decided to form a fighting group, and they both wanted me to be its leader because I was a kind of officer and older than they. Although embarrassed by this sort of rank pulling, I accepted my leading role. We knew that the most urgent problem our comrades in the camp were facing was how to communicate with Commissar Pei efficiently. So what could we do to improve this situation? Both Mushu and Little Hou believed we could devise a new method of communication. Ignorant of signaling and codes, I just listened to them talk and argue. Every once in a while I put in a question.

We talked for three hours on end, but couldn't figure out a way. After dinner, which was boiled sorghum and a few pieces of salted turnip, the door opened and the last light of sunset flooded in, reddening my fellow inmates' faces. In came a custodian, a hollow-cheeked man who had once been in our army and now was a turncoat, a name Mushu called him to his face. A collaborator though the man was, he might have given in to the enemy only under unbearable torture, so I felt uneasy about the hostility my cellmates showed him. The man dropped a blanket onto the floor for me, then put a bucket in a corner as our toilet pail and took away the one already used. Little Hou and Mushu glared at him, but he dared not look at us and kept his head low.

The door was closed and the room turned quiet again. Mushu couldn't help but resume pacing back and forth, while Little Hou and I, eyes shut, tried to drop off, though I didn't feel sleepy.

Night came. A trapezoid of moonlight fell on the wall, sliced by four parallel lines of shadows. Tired of chatting and thinking, I soon began drowsing. Suddenly something hit the wall from the other side. We all heard the thumps, which sounded carefully measured, so the three of us sat up at once; Mushu's large eyes glowed in the darkness while Little Hou pressed his ear against the wall. Then came four more knocks, all equally spaced. There was no mistake now! Little Hou knocked on the wall three times in reply. We all held our breath, listening.

From somewhere near the ceiling, in the southern upper corner of the wall, came a rasping sound. We stood up and moved over to look. Slowly a lumpy thing emerged in the corner. None of us could reach it, so Mushu squatted down and let me step on his shoulders while Little Hou held my leg to keep me steady. I stretched out and pulled the thing in through a rift between the ceiling and the wall. It was a parcel wrapped in a piece of waterproof cloth. Hurriedly we opened it — inside were a block of cooked rice and six baked squids, each about four inches long. On top of the food was a slip of paper bearing Commissar Pei's handwriting in pencil:

"Keep fighting, take care of your health, stay alert, and we'll be in touch soon." We wolfed down the war criminal's food, which was much tastier than ours. We were very touched by the message, which was passed among us several times. We were so excited that for hours we went on talking about what we could do. For most of us, Commissar Pei seemed like a lighthouse that could guide our foundering ship home.

Then Little Hou said, "Why don't we use the time here to create a special code, to open a channel of communication between Commissar Pei and the camp?"

"That'll be great if we can," said Mushu.

"But I don't know anything about the code stuff," I put in. "Can we do it only with the three of us?"

"Probably he can." Mushu pointed at Little Hou, who hiccuped, chewing something vigorously. Mushu continued, "Keep in mind, it was this fellow who made most of the general code used among the battalions."

Little Hou said to me about Mushu, "He was a signalman in Compound 10, he can help me."

We three looked at one another, then hugged tightly. I told them that I would obey any orders they gave, despite my leadership. They laughed. I still couldn't imagine how they could possibly open such a channel of communication, though I knew I ought to encourage them. After we broke the work into separate parts, we ran into difficulties we hadn't expected. To begin with, we needed paper and a pencil. How on earth could we get those things in this hellhole? Little Hou regretted not having brought along his pencil stub. I told him, "Forget it, even if you had taken it with you, you might've lost it to the guards."

Mushu nudged me in the ribs and said, "Look at that." He pointed at the window-sill, on which was a whitish wad. I rushed over and grabbed the thing — ah, a roll of toilet tissue! "The Americans are so con-siderate!" Mushu laughed. "I never used such fancy toilet paper back in our country. Comrades, I bet none of you did either."

"Uh-uh, not me." Little Hou shook his chin with a straight face.

We cracked up, though subduedly. So we had solved the paper problem. But what should we do about the pencil? This beat us, and we agreed to ask for help the next morning.

I slept well for the rest of the night, whereas neither of them could sleep a wink. When I woke up six hours later, they told me that I had snored like a pig. Before daybreak, as the stars were fading and a fine mist was rising from the ocean, we knocked on the wall. Instantly the other side responded. I got on Mushu's shoulders and talked to Ming through the hole. "This is Yuan," I whispered.

"Ah, I was so happy to see you yesterday." His voice was brisk but half suppressed.

"How's Commissar Pei, and yourself?"

"We're fine."

"Listen, we're planning to create a code for you to use to communicate with the camp. But first we want to get permission from Commissar Pei. Can you ask him for us?" We ought to inform the top leader beforehand in case a similar project was already afoot.

"Certainly," Ming said.

Both of us got down to give our bearers a breather. Two minutes later I stood on Mushu's shoulders again. Ming told me, "Commissar Pei is delighted. He appreciates your initiative in this matter. He says he'll wait for the news of your success. Can we do something to help?"

"We need a pencil. Do you happen to have one?"

"We do have a short piece here. Wait a second, I'll hand it over."

Seeing that a wet patch had emerged on Mushu's back, I asked him if I should step down for a moment.

"No, I'm all right." He patted my leg. Little Hou squatted down beside him and asked me to put my right foot on his shoulder, but Mushu pushed him away. They were both excited because a pencil was available.

A moment later another package was pushed over through the hole. This time it contained some rice together with a pencil. Little Hou grabbed the three-inch stub, kissed it, and pressed it against his chest.

Without delay we began to work. There were two parts to the project: first, the code, and second, the method of transmission, that is, a special way of sending and receiving encoded messages. According to Little Hou, the code wasn't very hard to make, and he had already started on it. Neither Mushu nor I had any clue how it was formed exactly, so we focused on the method of transmission, which was the difficult part, having to be invented entirely by ourselves. Alas, I couldn't be of any help. If messages could not be transmitted properly, the code would be of no use however ingeniously it was devised, but all the methods Mushu could imagine were unsuitable. For example, the semaphore of gestures employed among the compounds couldn't be distinguished from a distance of over three hundred yards. How about light? That wasn't feasible either. In the first place, we had no flashlights. Even if we'd had them, they would have been too dangerous to use, since the enemy could see the light and might fire at the signalman.

What should we do? Mushu began pacing the cell again while we were both thinking hard for a solution. Although I was a layman, I could tell we wouldn't find an adequate method very soon, so I suggested we focus on the code first, giving thought to the transmission part whenever we could. During the day I stood at the window most of the time keeping watch on the guards and the maintenance men. We had divided the safety measures among ourselves. If a GI or a custodian came in, I would go up to him and block his way by speaking to him, and Mushu would drop his pants and crouch over the toilet pail so as to prevent the intruder from searching the cell while Little Hou would put the piece of toilet paper he was writing on into his mouth. Little Hou always kept the penciled sheets underneath his shirt. With great caution we went on working at the code.

Day after day we racked our brains, but still couldn't find an adequate transmission method. Little Hou was truly a smart fellow and engrossed in the code work most of the time. When he was eating or taking a break, he would mention to us one possibility and another, but none of them would work. Then one morning he hit on a brilliant idea, namely to simplify the Morse code as much as possible, to the degree of letting one dot or one dash stand for a numeral. This would not only speed up the transmission but also reduce confusion. Based on this conception, he and Mushu created the Walking Telegraphic Method: the sender of the message would stand behind the window of the war criminal's cell. If he walked to the left side, it meant a dot; if he moved to the right, it denoted a dash; if he hunkered down below the window, that indicated the beginning of a new group of numerals. One dot meant 1, one dot plus one dash — 2, two dots plus one dash — 3, two dots — 4, three dots — 5, three dashes — 6, two dashes plus one dot — 7, one dash plus one dot — 8, two dashes — 9, and one dash — 0. As a rule, every four numerals represented a word. After the receiver jotted down the numerals, he passed it on to the code man, who could decipher them with the aid of the codebook Little Hou was making. In the reverse order to our cell, the war criminal's room had a window facing Compound 6, so they could send and receive messages from within the room. This method would definitely resolve the problem of transmission. How excited we were! We wanted to shout for joy, but we didn't dare. We only lifted Little Hou on our shoulders and walked a few rounds in the cell. Then he returned to working at the code.

When the lead in the pencil was worn down, Mushu would bite the tip sharp. As the main worker, Little Hou didn't get enough sleep, his eyes bloodshot. We were worried about him, but couldn't do much to help. Without a dictionary, we couldn't remember all the essential words, but we managed to come up with over eight hundred common characters. This wasn't bad. The code shouldn't be too elaborate; otherwise it would have been difficult to master. So we aimed at fewer than one thousand characters. Whenever an often-used word came to mind, we would tell Little Hou. The penciled pages looked complicated and incomprehensible to me, but Little Hou could trace what he had done to avoid repetition. We continued to work for five days.

Finally a booklet — loose sheets of toilet paper bound by a shoelace — was completed, which listed all the codes and gave instructions about the Walking Telegraphic Method. We put a title on the cover: *The Pei Code.*

The work done, we reported our success to the other side. Immediately came Commissar Pei's congratulations. He wrote: "Dear Comrades — You have accomplished a spectacular deed, which demonstrates your sense of revolutionary duty and astonishing talent! It is hard to imagine how much the code will contribute to our future struggle. I hereby notify you that each of you is awarded the first-class merit citation. On behalf of the Community Party, I thank and salute you!" I could see the excitement in his vigorous handwriting, which was less formal than usual. I was amazed he had another pencil.

We hugged one another again, proud of our achievement.

Then came a problem we hadn't antici-pated: How could we take this code back to the barracks? The original codebook was going to be handed over to the other cell; normally we would duplicate a copy, which wasn't hard to do. But none of us would be able to smuggle such a thing back into the camp, because we'd have to go through at least two searches before we could rejoin our comrades there. Looking at one another and clutching at our hair, we were at a loss. Silence filled the room.

Ten minutes later, Little Hou said, "I'll memorize the whole thing. They can't search my brain, can they?"

Jailed in the cell longer than Mushu and I, he might be returned to the camp before we two. I said to him, "There're more than nine hundred words and you may not have many days to stay here. Are you sure you can memorize them all?"

Despite my misgivings, I knew this was the only solution. Mushu slapped Little Hou on the shoulder and said, "Boy, if you can remember the entire code, I'll give my citation to you."

We all laughed. From then on Little Hou started to learn the codebook by heart. For two days he did nothing but memorize the numerals and words. He had to seize every moment because he could be sent back anytime. Except when he had to eat and sleep, he sat in a corner, now looking at the thick booklet and now closing his eyes to rehearse what he had read. His mouth moved continuously.

As time went by, I noticed that he looked at the codebook less and less often. Toward the end of the third day he said to us, "I'm done, you can test me now."

We all moved close to the window, since it was already dusk, and began checking his memory. At first his response was rather slow, but accurate. As we continued, he matched the characters with the numerals much faster. Indeed, he had memorized the whole thing. There wasn't a single mistake. We were amazed!

Mushu said to Little Hou, "I always thought you were a bit flighty. Now I know I can't judge a man only by his appearance."

We two raised Little Hou above us, imitating the Americans and the Koreans, shouting Hurray! and *Mansai!* The moment we put him down, he fell asleep.

Before Little Hou was released from the troublemakers' cell, we passed the codebook on to Commissar Pei. From then on Ming became both the signalman and the code man in the war criminal's jail.

Later Mushu often told the story of our devising the Pei Code to other inmates. Little Hou also bragged about it. He made a codebook with kraft sheets, which nobody but he could use in the camp. Yet he wasn't happy about Mushu's claim that he — Mushu — had conceived the idea of the Walking Telegraphic Method alone; Little Hou often accused him of stealing his "patent." In any case, our success became a legend, a major piece in the inmates' story repertoire.

The code worked effectively. Now our Sixth Battalion had become the hub of communication, because we alone had transmission contact with the prison house, which directly faced our compound. All the messages going to the top leader would be transmitted by our staff. To illustrate the efficiency of the Pei Code, let me give you an example. One day an inmate in the Eighth Battalion working at the wharf chanced upon a page of *Liberation Daily*, a major Chinese newspaper published in Shanghai. On the page was a brief report on how the Chinese People's Volunteers in Korea helped the civilians till their fields, rebuild their houses, repair the bombed dams and dikes, and dig irrigation canals. The article was about 120 words long. Within a day it was transmitted in its entirety to the prison house through the Walking Telegraphic Method, though we had to skip seven words the code didn't include.

Now that the Pei Code had been established, the commissar resumed his command of the six thousand men in the camp. Actions among the battalions became coordinated, and there was more certainty and purpose in our dealing with the enemy.

The Americans had been trying to suppress our communications all along. I heard from a South Korean officer that an expert code breaker had once been flown in from Hawaii, who had boasted that he could crack our "bush code" after seeing three messages. There were a number of messages in the enemy's possession, but the American expert, after perusing all of them and racking his brains to unravel the logic of the codes, simply couldn't do a thing. He didn't even know there were two codes in use now — one was for intracamp communication and the other was the Pei Code. He kept saying, "This is so messy, absolutely unprofessional." Indeed our codes were highly irregular, following our code men's own whims and improvisations. So they remained uncracked.

23. THE VISIT OF A
YOUNG WOMAN

One evening, two days after Mushu was returned to Compound 10, I was alone in the troublemakers' cell. It was drizzling and the sea had disappeared from view, buried in gray mist. My fingers were twisting the pencil stub, though I wasn't scribbling anything so as not to waste the lead. From behind the house came the drone of a motor.

I put the pencil into my pants pocket and went over to see what was going on outside. To my surprise, a jeep driven by an American officer and carrying a young woman skidded to a halt before the prison house. On the beach stood Ming and the cook. I wondered why they had been let out again; two hours ago they both had done their daily exercise in the open air.

The woman and the eagle-nosed officer got off the jeep. After he whispered something to her and patted her on the shoulder, she headed toward the door of the war criminal's cell alone. She looked under thirty, with long, loosely bound hair, wide eyes, and a heart-shaped face. At first I thought she was Korean. But when she came closer, I could tell she was Chinese, though definitely not from mainland China. She was petite with a slender waist, wearing an orange silk skirt and a cream-colored wraparound top. In her right hand she held a tiny brown leather bag, which looked overstuffed. Her backside swayed a little, throwing ripples down the skirt, while her high-heeled sandals kicked up a bit of white sand. As she turned the corner of the house, her profile displayed the fine curvature of her bust and hips. She wasn't pretty, but attractive in a coquettish way.

Gazing at her, I felt my neck going stiff and the blood pounding in my temples. I hadn't seen a young woman for half a year, and the excitement set my heart throbbing. Why did she come to see Pei? Obviously the guards had purposely taken Ming and the cook out so that she could meet with our commissar alone.

I hurried to the southern end of the cell to get close to the rift in the corner. I turned over the empty bucket and stood on its bottom so that I could hear them better. The tide had subsided on the beach and it was windless, but at first I couldn't catch all they were saying. I attuned my ears and little by little began to pick up their words.

"My, you're mending your shirt!" she said with a soft lilt in dulcet Mandarin.

"A serviceman has to do many things by himself," Pei replied lukewarmly. "In fact I'm doing this for my cook."

"It's very hard, isn't it? This kind of needlework doesn't suit a man like you. It's a woman's work. Can I help you with it?"

"No, you're a guest. I mustn't let you touch this smelly thing, infested with cooties. I'm already grateful that you came all the way to see me."

"I've wanted to visit you for a long time."

"I'm sorry I don't even have a seat for you, and I let you stand like that."

"It's all right. Can I take a photo of you?"

"No, don't waste your film. No, no, if you raise your camera I'll have to cover my face with this shirt."

"All right, I won't do it then."

"Tell me, why did you want to see me? I don't think we've ever met."

"Nothing special, I just came to see how you're doing. Don't you miss home?"

"Of course I do. But thousands of my men miss home too."

"You want to go back to China?"

"Yes."

"Can't you go to another place?"

"Like where?"

"The Free World."

"Where's that?"

"Formosa or America or Europe. How about this? We go to the Free World. I mean you — you and me together."

"What do you mean exactly?"

"I'll accompany you wherever you go as long as you don't return to Communist China."

"But I *am* a Communist. Where else should I go?"

"You can always change."

"You mean to be a traitor?"

"Uh-huh."

"Then my parents would disown me and even my kids wouldn't call me dad." He chuckled and resumed, "I knew you didn't come here for yourself. You represent the Americans and Chiang Kai-shek. Please go back and tell them that I'm too old to be malleable. They'd better give up on me, just to save them all the trouble."

"Mr. Pei, you're too narrow-minded."

"How do you mean?"

"The world is so vast that you can go anywhere. I don't care where I'm buried as long as I'm happy when I'm alive. A real man should set his mind on distant seas and lands."

"How about this, you come with me back to China?"

"No! How can you say that?"

"A good woman should follow the man she sets her heart on." He gave a belly laugh.

"I don't want to mix with the Reds, period."

"But you said you like me."

"Only if you agree to go to the Free World."

"All right, then let me tell you what I think of you." His voice turned serious. "You're an overseas Chinese and seem to be a reasonable person. Why would you serve the American imperialists this way? Or maybe you were sent here by the Nationalists in Taiwan. Either way, how much do they pay you for trying all your tricks on this old man? Are you not worth more than that?"

"Knock it off! Save this load of crap for the other Commies. Don't talk to your grandma like this."

"Oh-oh, I didn't think you'd blow up so soon."

"Enjoy the jail then."

"Take back your present, will you?"

The door was slammed. Immediately I stepped down from the bucket and rushed to the window. She came out of the corner of the house in a huff. A stout tin landed behind her with a thud, but she paid no mind to it and made for the car. Waving her hand, she said loudly to the American officer, "No go. Such a diehard!"

The officer stretched his neck and shouted at the war criminal's cell, "Damn you, I'll get your balls one of these days!"

They got into the jeep. In the murky, humid twilight the car rolled away along the coast toward the east, where the South Korean army's training center was.

I thought the orange tin must contain candies or nuts. A maintenance man strode over and picked it up. He opened it, pulled out a piece of pastry, and took a bite. "Hey, moon cakes stuffed with red bean paste and sesame!" he cried at another man who was digging for clams on the beach, then ran toward him, waving the tin all the way.

The Moon Festival must have been around the corner or just over. Without access to the lunar calendar, I didn't know on what date the holiday fell this year.

The next morning I was returned to Compound 6. Some inmates had seen the jeep carrying the woman to the prison and asked me about her visit. I described to them the exchange between Commissar Pei and her. They were all impressed by our leader's wit and ability to resist female charms. Soon different versions of this story began circulating in the camp. Some of them were extravagantly enlarged. One went so far as to claim that the woman had opened her arms to embrace the commissar, who repelled her by showing her a fat louse caught behind his ear. I noticed that whenever the prisoners talked about Commissar Pei's meeting with this woman, they tended to poke fun at women in general in order to make themselves appear more macho. They couldn't help bragging about themselves while holding up our top leader as a model.

The truth was that nobody in the commissar's place would have dared to accept the woman's favors. His cook and interpreter were outside within earshot and I was on the other side of the wall, also able to hear the conversation. Besides, the maintenance men were all watchful. Only a fool would have gotten entangled with her then and there. I dared not explain my thoughts to my barracks mates, who seemed eager to create a hero worthy of their worship.

After I saw that woman, to be honest, I thought about her for several days. What kind of person was she, bold enough to offer herself that way? Whatever her motivation, it must have taken a lot of nerve to do that. I was bothered by the fact that she was willing to become intimate with a strange man she must have despised in her heart. Did she do that only for money? Probably so. What a tough job she had, trying to seduce a dedicated Communist like Pei. At bottom I was a little disappointed, because she looked like a decent woman in appearance, not that cheap.

On the other hand, she might not have been serious about her offer at all. If the commissar had agreed to go to the Free World with her, she might have dumped him even before they reached there. Perhaps Pei had discerned this ruse; otherwise he mightn't have dealt with her that flippantly. Perhaps he had just put on a show for me and Ming and the cook to witness, so that we could tell our comrades about it.

24. RAISING THE
NATIONAL FLAG

On the afternoon of September 25, 1952, a message came from the prison house, which ordered: "Every battalion must raise our national flag on October 1 to show our spirit and resolve."

The leaders of the ten compounds passed the order down to the ranks. Most of the prisoners got excited. Bored and restless, they were eager to do something on October 1, our National Day. The immediate difficulty was how to make flags and long poles, and how to hoist the flags and protect them from being destroyed by the enemy. In our battalion people were thinking hard about how to get a piece of cloth, but nobody could come up with a suitable solution. That evening, Wenfu, a spare fellow with sleepy eyes who was the battalion chief's orderly, struck on an idea. "Can't we use a piece of rain cloth?" he said.

"You mean to get rid of the rubber part?" asked a company leader.

"Yes." Wenfu narrowed his eyes and seemed to know how to do that.

The Americans had issued us each a piece of waterproof cloth, which we could put on as a rain poncho. It had white nylon fabric on one side and coated rubber on the other.

The next morning Wenfu heated an oil drum behind the kitchen and spread his rain cloth on it. Without much difficulty he peeled off the rubber. We were all impressed. Next, we needed to color the white cloth red. But where could we get the dye or paint? One man pierced his finger with a safety pin and smeared his blood on the white nylon, but soon the blood turned brownish, so this wouldn't do. Then we remembered Mercurochrome, and a man was dispatched to get some from the medic. The antiseptic worked much better, so we decided to use it as the primer for the flag. That resolved, we had to come by five stars. Somebody suggested cutting them out of tinplate. Without delay a few fellows got hold of a pair of pliers and went about making the stars. Meanwhile, the nylon fabric was cut into a rectangle and hemmed along the edges.

Then the five stars — one twice as big as the rest — were sewn to the cloth. Many hands were busy helping with the sewing, which was done within an hour.

The finished flag looked quite impressive. Now the next problem was how to make a pole, which had to be about thirty feet long. This proved easy. There happened to be a pair of stretchers left in our compound, which the Americans had not collected after we had used them to carry two sick men, so we dismantled them and tied the poles to one another. We had enough rope, but we needed to fix a small pulley to the tip of the pole so that we could hoist the flag. Since it was impossible to come by such a device, we substituted a self-made iron ring for it. Amazingly, all the preparations took us just one day.

Although I participated in making the flag, from the outset I had a foreboding that something horrific would happen. I knew Commissar Pei well enough to see that besides shattering the enemy's claim that the Chinese POWs were unwilling to return to China, he might have something else on his mind. I couldn't guess his motives yet. Somehow my thoughts kept turning to the fact that our national flag was actually in its infancy, not even three years old. My comrades were unlikely to have developed a staunch attachment to it, not to mention devoted love. Then why had they all of a sudden become determined to fly it at any cost?

Most prisoners got carried away with the plan. Many applied for the shock team and the flag protection group; some even wrote pledges in their own blood; one of the hotheads was so worked up that he broke his little finger in front of others to show his passion to fight this battle for raising the flag. Meanwhile many of us were exchanging our home addresses back in China in case we got killed on October 1. On the surface we appeared courageous, but in reality our resolve was mixed with desperation.

We all felt ashamed of becoming POWs because we should have died rather than submit to capture. Many even believed our captivity had impaired our country's image. I often heard some men say they had "smeared soot on Chairman Mao's face." The guilt weighed heavily on their consciences. That was why ever since our arrival at Cheju, the Party leaders in the camp had propagated this slogan as the principle of our action: "Through our struggle we shall remove our shame and win back our glory!" Those words struck a chord in most inmates' hearts. Now Commissar Pei's order gave them a chance to vent their pent-up emotions, and many men couldn't wait to fight. Some even believed it would be better to fall in a heroic, if ill-fated, battle than to be jailed like animals. So all at once the compounds turned hectic — the prisoners were busy preparing to confront the enemy. They picked up stones and piled them in places, filled bottles with urine, gathered wooden sticks and cudgels, made knives out of the steel sheets torn from oil drums, forged and honed daggers. There was some kerosene used for cooking in the kitchen, so they poured the fuel into empty cans, inserted short pieces of shoestring into them, then sealed the tops with soap to create nine bombs. To use such a weapon, they'd light the string, then pitch it.

The inmates seemed suicidally blind to the resources the enemy had. I was agitated but dared not say anything, fearing the accusation of cowardice.

On September 27 Commissar Pei issued another message, ordering us to "strike at the enemy," specifically to kill one or two top American officers. After an exchange of views among the battalion leaders, it was decided that every compound prepare to murder Colonel Kelly, the commandant here, should such an opportunity arise, and that if possible, Major MacDonald, the camp's executive officer, should also be removed. Our neighbor, Compound 7, was much more active than we, and I could hear hammers hitting hot iron in their kitchen and makeshift smithy continually. In total, they forged more than a hundred daggers and machetes. They also drilled their men in different formations for a whole afternoon on September 28. But that night a traitor slipped out of their barracks and informed the Americans of their plan.

Early the next morning Major MacDonald, a colossal man with tawny hair, came with two companies of GIs and three light tanks. They forced all six hundred men in Compound 7 to assemble on the central field and one by one searched them. Whenever they found a dagger they would slap and punch the weapon carrier or butt him with rifles. Altogether they seized about twenty machetes and seventy daggers. Throughout the search Major MacDonald, holding his pistol, stood away from the prisoners to avoid being attacked.

The Seventh Battalion was thrown into disarray. Should we proceed with our original plan? Some of our leaders began wavering, afraid that the enemy would disarm the other compounds as well.

As we wondered about what to do, Commissar Pei issued the final instruction: "Go ahead and raise the flags tomorrow. Whoever disobeys this order will be dealt with as a deserter from battle." I was unsettled by this message, which seemed to reveal a note of desperation.

Without delay we transmitted the order to the other battalions, and that very evening all the prisoners were informed of it. People turned active, itching to have a go. The atmosphere in the camp grew intense. In our compound, besides the assault unit and the flag protection group, we also formed a rescue crew and a logistic platoon. The men in the Seventh Battalion seemed apprehensive, having just lost most of their weapons. They feared that the enemy might turn on them again, because they had become the weakest of the ten compounds. But they were still determined to fight a battle if need be. They organized a large shock team, over eighty men strong, and a flag protection group, composed of fifteen of their best soldiers, whose task was to prevent the enemy from getting hold of the flag. If their force couldn't stop the GIs, the fifteen men would take down the flag and burn it. Our battalion's flag protection group was larger than theirs, consisting of forty people, but our assault unit comprised only thirty men. This implied that Wanren might not want a bloody battle for our battalion.

Under cover of darkness we rolled out three oil drums to the middle of the backyard, filled them with dirt, then planted the flagpole into the gap among the drums and stuffed the hole with gravel. After the preparation we returned to our sheds. I was anxious and fearful and couldn't stop trying to fathom Pei's motives. Perhaps he wanted to draw the Party's attention to Cheju, a small island hundreds of miles away from China. Indeed, ever since we'd landed here, we had lost communication with the outside world. There were not many Korean servicemen in the camp, so we couldn't find the right contact with North Korean secret agents. Even Father Woodworth, who would visit prison camps in different places, had never come here to preach. Commissar Pei must have felt isolated and eager to create an incident so as to catch outside attention and remind his higher-ups of our existence. In fact, even the GIs here could hardly endure the isolation. Although they often saw movies in their mess hall and always had books, newspapers, and magazines to read, they got bored and frustrated. One night, returning from the hospital after taking a patient with acute appendicitis there, I had seen three American officers standing at the brink of a stream, firing pistols at the full moon. I asked the guard escorting me, "What are they doing?"

"They're just having some fun," he said. I was surprised they could waste ammunition with impunity.

By now I was certain I had divined Commissar Pei's motives, which also revealed his weakness. He seemed to have lost his composure and patience and could no longer wait. He wanted to be considered by our negotiators at Panmunjom without further delay. There was another element in his anxiety which wasn't easy to discern, namely that like a regular prisoner here, he too was at sea about what to do. The POWs all looked up to him, depending on his directives and believing he was their backbone; what they didn't know was that he needed a lot of backing himself. In other words, Commissar Pei must have been anxious to get instructions and assurance from his superiors. The more I thought about his motives, the sorrier I felt for the soldiers who were going to fight doggedly the next day. They were being used, though most willingly.

Another thought also occurred to me about Pei's fear. He must have been afraid that his captivity had tarnished his image in the Party's eyes. Probably he needed a battle to achieve something that would change the Party's opinion of him. In every way, a timely battle was an advantageous move for him personally. I wondered what kind of role Ming had played in this decision. A perceptive man, he could see through Pei for sure.

At six sharp the next morning, when the eastern sky was just pinkish with light, we all gathered in the backyard. All the men in the other compounds had come out of their barracks too. Our battalion chief climbed on top of one of the oil drums to deliver a speech. "Comrades," Wanren said, his narrow eyes glittering, "today is our National Day, a sacred day celebrated throughout our motherland. So we're going to join our people back home in celebrating our country's third anniversary, and also to show the enemy our indomitable spirit. Come what may, our national flag must fly high in this prison camp, and we shall fight to our last breath to defend it. Also keep in mind that our flag bears the color of the Revolutionary Martyrs' blood. We must protect the purity of the flag and never let it lose color in our hands . . ."

Choking with emotion, he couldn't speak for long, so he jumped down from the drums. Quietly we were waiting for the other battalions to wind up their prebattle mobilization. I heard Chaolin delivering his speech to the men in Compound 7. His voice was strong, but I couldn't make out his words. His hands went on chopping the air as he spoke. Finally done speaking, he shouted, "Defend our national flag with our blood and lives!" In unison his battalion roared. Then, thrusting up his small fist, he cried again, "We shall fulfill our glorious mission!" His men again followed him in one voice. That might have also referred to the execution of the other part of Commissar Pei's orders — to kill Colonel Kelly and Major MacDonald if possible.

It was six-thirty now, and our battalion began singing the "Internationale" while slowly our flag was raised. I looked around and saw many faces enraptured and bathed in tears. The flags in the other barracks were rising too. All the battalions were chanting the same song, though the chorusing was out of sync.

After the "Internationale," we started to sing our national anthem. By now hundreds of GIs had assembled at the front gate to the camp. We saw a column of tanks turning the northwestern corner, coming our way. On the guard towers machine guns were aimed at us while the GIs were talking wildly with one another or into telephones. Then came Colonel Kelly's voice through a bullhorn, ordering us to haul down our flags and return to our quarters immediately. "If you don't obey, we're going to make you," he announced.

In response, we shouted slogans: "Down with American imperialism!" "Long live our motherland!" "We won't stop without a full victory!" "Defend our honor with our lives!" "Send us home!" "Observe the Geneva Convention!"

Eight light tanks, M-24s, were lined up at the front entrance now. More than five hundred GIs had assembled outside the camp, ready to come in. A few minutes later two guards opened the front gate and the tanks rolled into the central field, followed by the GIs, all in steel helmets and some in gas masks. They toted rifles with fixed bayonets, wearing grenades and tear-gas bombs on their belts. A dozen of them carried on their backs flamethrowers, each of which consisted of three steel cylinders hooped together. Colonel Kelly dispatched two companies and four tanks to the western side of the camp, then directed most of the remaining force to Compound 7, but he also posted trucks and half-tracks topped with .50-caliber machine guns at the entrances to the other compounds. After all the GIs were in position, the paunchy colonel issued his ultimatum that we must take down our flags immediately. He shouted, "You're out of line, I tell you. My patience is wearing thin. If you don't listen to reason and pull down those rags now, I'm going to kick your butts."

Still we ignored him. The red flags, though fluttering now and again, drooped in the damp daylight, weighed down by the metal stars.

Through the bullhorn Colonel Kelly ordered the officer leading the troops assembled at the gate to Compound 7, "Proceed as planned!" From a window of our shed Shanmin and I watched them, my heart palpitating. I wished our leaders could have talked with the enemy. Even though it might not have resolved the crisis, it might at least have reduced the enemy's momentum and kept violence at bay. About eighty GIs rushed into Compound 7 and cautiously closed in on the rows of barracks, at which all their M1 Garand rifles were pointed. Although that compound was as quiet as if deserted, I saw some prisoners crouching in a ditch behind a shed. Heavens, they wanted to ambush the fully armed Americans! This was suicidal. Why were Chaolin and the other leaders of that battalion letting their men act so recklessly?

As I was wondering, the GIs got within twenty yards of the sheds. Suddenly the shock team jumped out of the ditches, shouting "Kill!" and charging at the enemy with stones, clubs, kerosene bombs, bottles of hot water mixed with bleach. Meanwhile, the men in reserve shouted slogans and hurled all kinds of objects at the GIs — tattered boots, clods, rocks, fragments of bricks. The enemy was taken by surprise, its formation thrust out of order, and some of them paused. A bottle of urine crashed on a GI's helmet and set the man screaming — he must have thought the stinking liquid was acid. Several of them were scalded by the bleach water, howling for help. Indeed the hot solution terrified them, because they took it for some kind of chemical weapon. So they withdrew immediately but kept firing at the men charging forward. About two dozen prisoners were shot, lying in the yard. Some of them were motionless while the others were moaning, kicking their legs and flailing their arms. Two or three of the Americans were wounded. An enemy platoon commander had been hit in the face by a stone; he took off his helmet and wiped his bloody nose with a wad of bandage. He couldn't stop swearing and stamping his feet as a medic dressed his wound.

The moment the prisoners had carried their casualties back into the sheds, the GIs came to attack again. This time they first pitched about three dozen tear-gas bombs and concussion grenades, then four flamethrowers launched torrents of fire at the sheds, whose roofs burst into flames, forcing the inmates to flee in all directions. Machine guns and rifles broke out rapping. The Seventh Battalion's assault team, about to charge again, was at once rendered defensive. Their second echelon, already fully exposed and without any fortifications, was drawn into the battle now. Wave after wave of men dashed toward the GIs and were mown down. The yard was littered with bodies and puddles of blood while dark smoke rose and drifted away toward the ocean. Behind the sheds the flag hardly swayed, as if frozen.

I was sure Commissar Pei and Ming were observing the clash from the prison house. Why hadn't Chaolin had some deep trenches dug in the barracks, as the Korean prisoners had done on Koje Island, if he wanted his men to fight such a battle? Even though it was the commissar who had initiated this whole operation, Chaolin should be held responsible for the heavy casualties, I thought.

Suddenly, fifteen prisoners sprang out of the last shed and dashed toward the flag-pole; only one was armed, with a short spade. A group of GIs were headed toward the flag too; believing that the approaching inmates intended to charge at them, they opened fire. Some of the prisoners were struck down, but none of them turned back. One was shot in the thigh yet still hopped toward the flag. I counted the bodies in their wake: seven fell before they reached the oil drums. Fortunately the enemy held their fire. Hurriedly the prisoners pulled down the flag and set it ablaze. At once the flames engulfed the nylon cloth, which blackened, shrank, then vanished.

The enemy commander took this to be a gesture of capitulation, so he withdrew his troops from the compound. Soon a team of American medical personnel arrived to help the wounded POWs, some of whom were crying loudly and waving at whoever was nearby. But the doctors and medics ignored them and checked the motionless ones first. Near the wall of a shed lay an American soldier, entangled with the bodies of several inmates; they had all been knocked out by concussion grenades.

During this part of the battle, a fight had also broken out in Compound 5, which was too far away for us to see. All we saw was black smoke going up in columns and puffs in the southwest, and we also heard guns clatter sporadically. Unable to do much to help their comrades in the two compounds, the other eight battalions just went on shouting slogans and throwing things at the GIs, who ignored them.

Toward midafternoon we received the report on our casualties. Fifty-three men had been killed in Compound 7, and another six had died in the hospital. There were 109 men seriously wounded, most of whom had been carried away by ambulances. In Compound 5 four prisoners had been killed and twenty-one wounded.

Among the dead was their chief, Zhao Teng. His death saddened me. He had been a good man, hot-tempered but honest. The year before, in his former unit, he had shot a platoon leader because the man had raped a Korean girl. He and I had never been close, but I had respected him as an officer who would take the lead in anything he ordered his men to do. His men had loved him.

We got an odd message from the Seventh Battalion that afternoon, saying they had scored a great victory. Why had Chaolin made such a foolish claim? This was beyond me. Obviously he hadn't taken into account the heavy losses. What kind of leader was he? Under normal circumstances he ought to have been reprimanded, if not punished. I was dismayed, but dared not express my thoughts to anyone, not even to my friend Shanmin.

More surprising was that toward evening we received congratulations from Commissar Pei. I had seen Ming walking left and right behind the window of the war criminal's cell, busy sending out a message. He appeared rather stooped and coughed into his fist from time to time. In addition to congratulating us on "the glorious victory," the message declared that all the comrades who had sacrificed their lives today were named Hero Fighters, that every man in the Seventh Battalion had earned a second-class merit citation, that every member on the shock team was awarded a citation of the special class, and that on every wounded comrade in both compounds was conferred a first-class citation. Pei also called on us to salute the men of the Seventh Battalion and to learn from the example of their mettle.

I was more dubious about this business of the citations now. Indeed, a senior officer like Pei was entitled to issue a few awards once in a while, but definitely not so many of them. Why had he acted as though all the citations had been in his pockets and he were at liberty to hand out as many as he liked? I had been awarded three already, but never had I seen a medal, and I couldn't help but doubt their value. Accompanying each major citation — the first or the special class — one should also receive a raise in both rank and salary, but never had that been mentioned. These awards might just be a hoax; I truly doubted if Pei had even kept a record of the hundreds of citations he had bestowed on us. Who had ever heard of every member of a battalion being given a second-class citation? This kind of award inflation seemed fraudulent, but the men were not skeptical of them. They tended to take the citations as something that might reconfirm their loyalty to our country and the revolution, and therefore as something that could reduce their shame. Some men in our barracks even envied those in Compound 7.

The next day Chaolin presented to the Americans a written protest on behalf of all the prisoners in the camp. In the letter we demanded that Colonel Kelly let us send a representative to the Panmunjom armistice talks. Kelly thought we were crazy, in his words "a bunch of loonies," and he dismissed our demand, saying this was beyond his power. Commissar Pei had a long cloth banner hung out from his window — a white sheet bearing these words in English: "Stop Butchering My Comrades!" A squad of GIs went there, ripped the sign away, and thrashed the three men in the cell with rifle butts.

Not until six days later were we allowed to gather in front of the barracks within each compound and hold a memorial service for the dead, who had all been buried on a hill slope used as a graveyard by the island natives. After some argument, the

459

Americans let us choose five representatives from each battalion, who went to lay wreaths at the graves of the dead comrades. I remember that one of the wreaths was draped with two strips of white paper that bore two lines of ancient poetry:

Yearn not for native soil —
Your loyal bones can lie in any green hill.

25. ANOTHER SACRIFICED LIFE

Gradually I figured out why, despite the massacre, the leaders considered the flag-raising battle a victory. They ignored the casualties and cared only about the news value of the incident. The more people got killed, the more sensational the event, and the more reverberant the victory would be.

To Commissar Pei, the ideal aftermath of the massacre would be some strong response from the Chinese government and from our delegates at the Panmunjom talks. He must have believed China would take advantage of the incident to start another propaganda campaign to embarrass the United States. I too felt that some international repercussions would follow the sixty-three deaths.

Week after week we expected some news, but nothing happened. No reporter came, and no change could be noticed in the Americans, as if this island were a deserted corner forgotten by the world. The feeling of isolation must have become all the more unbearable to Commissar Pei. By contrast, most of the POWs didn't seem to feel isolated at all; they bore the monotony of prison life with vegetative patience. As long as the top leader was with them, they could set their minds at ease — he was their mental mainstay. They couldn't see that like themselves, Pei too was apprehensive, probably more so than they were, because he had no superior to rely on. On the other hand, he understood that to many of them he embodied the Party, so he had to appear resolute and full of certainty. In mid-October a GI shot a prisoner, a latrine man, who had accidentally tripped and splattered a bucket of night soil onto the jeep the GI was driving. The man bled to death before the ambulance came. Yet even such gratuitous violence didn't kindle any disturbance in the camp. Commissar Pei seemed to be sinking into deep lassitude.

This situation agitated me. In appearance I was calm, like an experienced officer, but at heart I was afraid that our country had forsaken us and that the commissar might wage another full-blown battle to create another newsworthy incident. Some time ago I had read in *Stars and Stripes* that the U.S. delegates at the Panmunjom negotiations had made the issue of POWs their top priority, whereas the Korean and Chinese generals had refused to consider the issue first — instead, they wanted to focus on the territorial dispute. I hadn't told the news to anyone, not even to our battalion chief, Wanren.

Later, some years after we returned to China, I came across an article that reported that the top Korean delegate at the cease-fire talks at Panmunjom, General Nam Il, had launched a protest about the massacre in our camp at General William Harrison on October 4, 1952, but the Chinese side had remained reticent. Clearly the POWs were not an urgent item on our generals' agenda, though as usual, our delegates demanded that all the Chinese prisoners be repatriated, including those who refused to go home.

Leaves began dropping from elms and oaks, and grass was turning yellow. In the morning the ground was often sprinkled with patches of hoarfrost, and in the south Mount Halla, over six thousand feet tall, which was said to be the highest in Korea, had lost its green cover; more rocks were visible on its rugged ridges now. Cheju Town was in the east, tucked away from the turbulence of the war. It had several two-story buildings and hundreds of houses that all had hip roofs and latticed windows covered with white paper instead of panes. From the distance they looked like a swarm of hayricks. I had passed that town once with a group of prisoners in a truck. Unlike the houses on the Korean mainland, the homes here were all built of volcanic rocks. Their thatched roofs were fastened with hemp ropes, evenly criss-crossed, to keep the rice straw from being blown away by sea winds. Viewed from nearby, the roofs brought to mind turtle shells, convex and neatly checkered. As an interpreter I had the opportunity to leave the camp once in a while. One day, standing at the shoulder of the eastern knoll, I had gazed at that town, whose sun-drenched tranquillity moved me. The rice paddies beyond a thin brook reminded me of the countryside near the Yangtze River, where my paternal grandparents had lived. Though strewn with rocks, the land here was pretty and peaceful, dotted with clumps of daylilies and wild chrysanthe-mums. Pampas grass spread everywhere, its long flowers like fluffy rabbit tails rip-pling in the breeze. If not imprisoned, I wouldn't have minded living for a year or two in such a place, away from the turmoil of the world. If I had not been engaged to

Julan or had my old mother at home, I could have imagined myself marrying a Korean woman and settling down here forever, just like many Chinese who had emigrated to Korea before the war. Women on the island were cheerful, hardworking, and tolerant of men; they made devoted wives, I was told. What else should a common man like me want besides a comfortable home filled with children and a good woman? What's more, the island climate was mild, with distinct seasons. Although it was often windy and rained in torrents, there were not the biting winds and the snowstorms of the northern winter.

I was surprised by thoughts of this kind, which I hadn't dared think before. I realized I was more capable of enduring loneliness now. Indeed, I was quiet and preferred to be solitary whenever it was possible.

We were positive that there were guerrillas on the island, because we had heard gunshots several times coming from a hill in the south, on which there were bunkers and tunnels left by the Japanese army garrisoned here during the Second World War. But no Korean comrades had ever contacted us. We were indeed like a batch of lost souls, whose fate the outside world seemed no longer to care about. "This is worse than Siberia, where at least some people would go visit," I often said to myself. If only we could know what was in store for us. If only there were a radio set with which we could hear news.

Ever since the October 1 incident, the Americans had stepped up security in the camp. They often came to search the compounds and made a shambles of our barracks. We knew they wanted to get hold of the self-made weapons we had hidden away. One afternoon in late October, a company of GIs suddenly arrived and ordered us to get out of our living quarters. Our battalion was gathered on the shriveled grass outside the barbed-wire fence. Every one of us was made to turn his pockets inside out and put all his personal belongings in front of him on the ground. While the guards looked through our stuff, we couldn't help but watch the GIs poking and digging around in our barracks with shovels, picks, and spreading forks. By regulations, they were not supposed to take guns into the compounds unless their lives were threatened, so only the guards searching us outside the fence were armed. Captain Larsen, the head of the guards at our compound, was leading the hunt, directing the GIs to rummage through our sheds and kitchen. He was a burly man, over six feet tall, slightly whiskered. He barked at a sergeant, "Hey, Walt, don't let them get smart with you."

"I won't, sir," cried back the sergeant, who was listening to a complaining prisoner.

Suddenly a GI burst out of our headquarters, shouting, "I got it!" He was holding our flag, which we had secreted in a wall. The find excited the Americans so much that some of them whistled. One did a jig with the flag wrapped around himself while others flung their heads back guffawing. Captain Larsen took the flag, raised it above his head, waving it at us, then started tapping his heels.

Although enraged and restless, we had no idea what to do. Most of us thought that at all costs we must not let them take our flag away. Some still remembered the self-sacrifice of the comrades in the Fifth and Seventh Battalions, so they were spoiling for a fight. Stealthily a few leaders went over to Wanren so that they could work out a plan of action. They talked and decided to let Shenning, a stout man who was the head of the Second Company, lead a group of prisoners to get the flag back. Without delay Shenning went to rejoin his men and tell them what to do.

When the Americans had finished searching, we were filing back into our quarters. Outside the fence the guards looked relaxed, while inside the compound their spoils were still on display — besides the flag there were daggers, spears, pliers, flashlights. Captain Larsen gave us a sneering smile that bared his long teeth to the gums. Slowly I was moving toward the gate, anxious about what was going to happen. I could feel the tension in the air. Many eyes were fixed on the flag held by the captain, who somehow didn't sense any danger. As Shenning and his men were approaching the gate, another group of inmates turned up, led by Little Hou, as if they too were coming to charge at Larsen. Shenning hesitated for a moment, wondering why Hou's group had appeared. Little Hou, our only code man, was under special protection and shouldn't participate in such an action. Inquiringly Shenning looked at Little Hou, who just nodded at him without a word. More prisoners entered the gate now. Passing Larsen, Shenning cried, "Get it from him!" In a flash a dozen men surrounded the captain and some grabbed the flag, struggling to pull it away. But Larsen held the other end of the flag with both hands and wouldn't let it go. He yelled at his men, "Give me a hand!" A short tug of war ensued, which scared us — if the GIs outside the fence came in with their weapons we wouldn't be able to continue the tussle. Little Hou bent down and bit the back of Larsen's hand. "Ouch!" the captain yelled and loosened his grip. With the flag in his hands Shenning dashed away, but, unclear where to go, he just ran. One of the GIs grabbed a shovel and set out chasing Shenning, who was frantically bolting along the fence.

"Put that down, you bastard!" the GI roared. Shenning kept running and running. How frightened we were! The armed guards outside the fence might have opened up on him, but luckily they didn't. Instead, they seemed to relish the scene, some smirking and some laughing.

Gradually the husky GI caught up with Shenning, who rolled the flag into a ball and threw it to Wenfu, the skinny orderly. Wenfu in turn pitched it into the opened window of the kitchen; immediately a cook removed a cauldron and spread the flag over a stove, whose flames at once engulfed the fabric. With the shovel the GI began hitting Shenning, who was rolling on the ground but didn't scream.

"Yeah, let him have it good!" yelled Captain Larsen, with both hands on his hips.

We all shouted at the GI, but he wouldn't give up thwacking our man. One blow hit Shenning's face and he stopped moving instantly. Meanwhile, Larsen ordered his men to round up all those who had participated in retaking the flag. Little Hou, Wenfu, the cook, and many others were singled out and forced to leave with their hands clasped on their crowns. The GIs prodded them with bayonets all the way to a truck parked outside the front entrance. They shipped them away to a large pit behind the fuel depot west of the prison camp. Later that evening Shenning was also sent there, directly from the hospital. Altogether they had seized eighteen prisoners.

Our leaders were worried, but mainly about the safety of Little Hou, without whom the camp's communication with Commissar Pei would be disrupted. How could we get him back? They thought hard for a solution, but couldn't find one.

Afternoon darkened into evening at the fuel depot, but the enemy still wouldn't release the detainees. Having eaten nothing, the eighteen men were shaking with cold and huddled together in the pit, which was actually a collapsed bunker. Above it stood more than a dozen GIs, all fully armed. A pair of searchlights formed two long, luminous cones atop the pit throughout the night. The prisoners were soon tired out and some fell asleep. Toward daybreak, the GIs began throwing stones into the pit, and several sleepers were hit and injured. One chunk of cement tile struck the cook in the forehead and opened a cut about two inches long, and blood spurted out. But the prisoners knew the enemy hoped to have a pretext for shooting at them, so they didn't respond to the provocation. Nevertheless, half an hour later, a submachine gun fired at them. A bullet struck Wenfu's head and killed him on the spot. The detainees raised a shirt soaked with blood, which stopped the gunfire.

The lieutenant in charge came over with five GIs and saw the body of our orderly. "Damn, it was so accurate," he muttered, then strode off to call for an ambulance.

A van came twenty minutes later and carried Wenfu's body away, together with four wounded men. The rest of them couldn't leave the pit until late that night. They had been starved for more than thirty hours. Our kitchen cooked millet porridge for them, because in such a state it was dangerous for them to eat solid food right away.

The same thing happened again: Commissar Pei sent his condolences and awards — on Wenfu was conferred the title of Revolutionary Martyr and the first-class merit citation, which was also issued to Shenning, Little Hou, and the cook — Huang Jian. Now that the battalion chief's orderly was gone, Shanmin was chosen for the job. I told my young friend that from now on he should give his cigarettes to Wanren, who could protect him. Wanren was a decent man and had never taken anything more than his own rations, so he might appreciate the extra cigarettes.

I was ambivalent about the attempt to reseize the flag. On the one hand, I admired the courage our men had displayed, and in a way I'd been awestruck by their passion and bravery, which I have to admit I didn't share. On the other, I doubted whether it was worth losing a man's life for the sake of a flag, which, symbolic as it might be, was just a piece of nylon cloth. I had noticed that there was a kind of religious fervor in some of these men, who were capable of laying down their lives for an idea. However silly the idea might be, the act of self-sacrifice made them truly remarkable. Potentially many of them were heroes.

26. KILL!

All the prisoners in our compound were angry at Captain Larsen, believing he was responsible for Wenfu's death and for the injuries inflicted on the other four fellows. Every evening a duty sergeant would assemble us in the front yard to conduct the head count. Sometimes Larsen would do it personally. I don't know how this got started. One evening in early November, after Larsen's count, when he said, "You're dismissed," suddenly dozens of prisoners shouted in Chinese, "Kill!"

Perplexed, Larsen looked around, then grabbed hold of Shanmin, who couldn't make off fast enough, and asked him what they meant. The boy told him to his face, using the few English words I had taught him, "Kill that bad egg."

At once Larsen's face dilated with rage, his nostrils flaring. He stretched out both hands, flapping them toward his chest as though able to embrace the whole yard into his arms. He lifted his voice and ordered us, "Halt! You all come back and form up again!"

Reluctantly we reassembled in front of him. He told us, "We're going to do this one more time. I want you to leave without a peep, got it?"

I translated his order, but nobody responded. A lull set in as two dogs yapped from a straw shack on a hill slope in the southeast, followed by a pair of magpies that cried sleepily from the wild orange grove beyond the fences of barbed wire. In the south the half moon was hardly visible, obscured by billows of rusty clouds. Larsen jerked his neck and announced, "Now you're dismissed."

"Kill!" roared most of the men, then we all started for our living quarters.

"Damn it!" Larsen exploded, throwing up his big hands. "You all come back and line up again." He stamped his foot while the GIs behind him were grinning as if they had been bystanders.

Wordlessly we regrouped before him, but everyone seemed to have brightened up some. Larsen blustered, "I want you to disband quietly. Everybody keep your mouth shut when I let you go. If you don't follow my orders this time, I'll cut your rations for a week."

I told the crowd his warning, but they just stared at him without betraying any emotion. Then I saw a smirk cross Wanren's stubbly face; he seemed at ease, wanting to let this confrontation continue.

"Attention!" Larsen called.

Some of us clicked our heels. The captain coughed, then shouted, "Now you're dismissed."

"Kill!" all the prisoners thundered in one voice.

Larsen turned around and ordered the squad of GIs, "Take a few of them to my office."

His men rushed over, some brandishing pistols, grabbed three inmates, and dragged them away. We hadn't expected he would make arrests indiscriminately. Nor had we thought the GIs carried handguns underneath their jackets; if they had been unarmed, some of us might have charged at them to rescue the three men. Before we recovered from the shock, the GIs had taken the fellows out the front gate, shoving them and prodding their backs with handguns. All the other prisoners could do was call Larsen names, which he didn't understand anyway.

Without delay the heads of the companies gathered at our headquarters to discuss the situation and make plans of action. I was unsure whether it was wise to be so confrontational. No doubt the three detainees were going to suffer for us, so we shouldn't let the hostility escalate. In any event we must prevent Larsen from hurting them. Yet there seemed no way to make the enemy relent if we didn't resort to some kind of pressure or force. Words alone wouldn't be sufficient. While the leaders were arguing, I sat on an upturned crate listening without expressing my view. The new orderly, Shanmin, was sitting next to me, but he just went on slapping at flies with a self-made swatter, a scrap of perforated leather affixed to the end of a bamboo stick. He had a theory about swatting flies, which, according to him, couldn't take off without shifting position first, so you should strike at them only when they were on the move or rubbing their legs. I saw a black mosquito on his neck working so hard that it looked as if it were standing on its head, so I swatted it. Shanmin was startled, then relaxed, seeing the bloodstain on my palm.

Soon the leaders reached a consensus: we would go on a hunger strike and demand to talk with Colonel Kelly in person. Since it was already too dark to contact the prison house and the other compounds, they decided that we should go ahead and act on our own the next day.

The kitchen was ordered not to make breakfast, so the cooks happily slept in the next morning. As soon as it was light we signaled our decision to the other compounds and then to Commissar Pei. The guards on the tower noticed that few inmates stirred, so they asked us why the compound was so quiet. Having learned about the hunger strike and our demand, they reported the situation to their superior without delay, but Captain Larsen ignored us.

For a whole morning our barracks lost its daily activity; most prisoners lounged in bed doing nothing. Nobody was allowed to leave his shed unless he had to go to the outhouse. Our leaders had told us not to make any noise, because they intended to affect the guards with our silence. After ten-thirty, the time for the cooks to prepare the midday meal, none of the chimneys in the ten compounds spat smoke, and all the kitchens remained locked. This unnerved Larsen, who hadn't expected that the entire camp would participate in the hunger strike. He came to our front gate and stood beside the three gunnysacks of barley and a huge hamper of turnip greens, delivered by a truck two hours ago but rejected by our cooks. From time to time Larsen beckoned to inmates passing by, probably meaning he'd like to talk with them, but they ignored him. He lit a cigarette and chatted with the guards for a while. Then a GI handed him a megaphone, through which the captain yelled at us, "I order you to eat lunch. The vegetable is rotting in the sun, and I won't tolerate this kind of waste."

His words amused some prisoners, who laughed, saying, "As though he owned our mouths."

This was the first time that all the compounds had gone on a hunger strike in Camp 8. When we were on Koje Island, this kind of protest had been commonplace and the prison authorities had known how to cope with it, but here Colonel Kelly, somewhat disturbed, readily agreed to meet with the chiefs of the battalions. We were encouraged by his agreement, though uncertain whether he really intended to resolve the crisis.

Toward midafternoon Wanren and I, representing our compound, went to the guards' headquarters. In the lounge outside Kelly's office, more than a dozen prisoners were already seated on folding chairs, but the colonel himself was not in. Chaolin nodded at me and I waved back. I went over and sat down behind him. Yet we couldn't chat freely because Interpreter Peng, an officer from Taiwan working for the camp administration, was within hearing, his rear end resting on the windowsill. Chaolin turned around and said to me, "I've heard you did a great job in helping others." He was alluding to my assistance to Wanren.

I replied, "In a hellhole like this we ought to help each other." I noticed that Interpreter Peng was all ears, so I switched the topic and asked Chaolin, "Are you ready to spend the winter here?"

"Sure, we each just got another blanket."

That was news to me; our compound hadn't received additional clothing for the coming winter yet. A surge of sadness gripped my heart, but I managed to ask him again, referring to the dry socket on his upper gum, "What happened to your tooth?"

"A GI knocked it out of me last month."

"Does it still hurt?"

"It's all right now."

So he had lost an incisor in the battle for raising the flag, and the loss didn't seem to bother him.

Captain Larsen went to the front and clapped loudly to cut short our chattering. He said, "When Colonel Kelly comes in, everybody must get up, okay?"

There was no response. I sat next to Wanren, fascinated by the rhythmic clatter of a typewriter in a room down the hall. In the opposite corner of the lounge stood a cluster of dwarf bamboos set in an earthen pot. Beside the plant was a coffeemaker on a metal desk, gurgling staccato. The door opened and Colonel Kelly stepped in, but none of us stood up, whereas Captain Larsen and Interpreter Peng both sprang to their feet. Anger distorted Larsen's face.

The colonel stopped in front of us, a pistol on his brass-studded belt over which hung his beer belly. He bunched up his lips and said to us, "I have only twenty minutes, so just tell me why you started the hunger strike."

We had figured out our demands beforehand, which Chaolin began to present to him. As Chaolin's interpreter, I wondered if I should stand up, but decided not to, seeing that he remained seated. Then Colonel Kelly motioned for me to stop because he wanted Peng to do the translation. This was all the better for me.

Chaolin told Kelly that we had two demands: first, Captain Larsen must release our comrades; second, the camp authorities must investigate the death of Wenfu and punish the murderers. To our surprise, Kelly smiled and said, "The three prisoners will be sent back. There's no reason for us to keep them. Actually they may be already on their way back to the compound." He fixed a stare on Larsen as though annoyed by his inability to handle us by himself. Then he resumed, "But the investigation of the death will take time, and we cannot reach any conclusion before the process is complete, so I can't promise you what I'm going to do."

"Do you agree to investigate or not?" challenged Chaolin.

"Of course I do. I'll have to write a report to my higher-ups on this case as well, so I'm going to look into it."

"Will you let us know the result of the investigation?"

"That's something we can talk about."

"We want the murderers punished."

"Let's not jump the gun, all right? What you should do now is call off the hunger strike."

"But we want you to promise you'll investigate the murder case and punish the guilty party."

"Like I said, I'm going to look into it and if somebody's guilty, we'll handle him accordingly. Now, you must stop starving yourselves."

"Are you going to share the result of the investigation with us or not?"

"I shall do that only if you end the hunger strike."

"Is this a promise?"

"Yes."

"In that case our kitchens will cook again."

"When?"

"Today."

"Good, I'm pleased to hear that."

I didn't expect the dialogue to be so reasonable. Somehow Chaolin and the other chiefs didn't raise more questions. They should have asked the colonel approximately how long it would take him to finish the investigation and when we would hear from him, just as Kelly had pressed Chaolin for the exact time the hunger strike would be called off. I didn't remind them of this negligence because I wanted the crisis to end as soon as possible.

Before we left, the colonel even shook Chaolin's hand as though they had known each other for years. I was surprised by his cordiality, which made Chaolin so uncomfortable that he grinned at us tightly.

The three detained men had been returned while Wanren and I were away at the guards' headquarters. One had suffered a smashed hand and the other two had swollen faces. Although we agreed to eat dinner that day, that same evening we again shouted "Kill!" when Larsen dismissed us at the end of the head count. Crimson-faced, he got hold of Wanren and said, "Will you please stop this silly trick?" I translated the question.

Our chief answered, "You beat up my men and we must get even."

Larsen put on an innocent look and said, "I didn't touch them, I swear. It was those guys at the central office who mishandled them. I protested to them already and said they just made my job more difficult. Will you stop your men from shouting that silly word?"

His explanation seemed convincing to Wanren, who had heard from the three injured fellows that some strange Americans had whacked them. Slow of words, Wanren didn't counter with the fact that it had been Larsen who ordered their arrest. Instead, he argued, "We have freedom of speech, don't we? We've done nothing wrong."

I translated this a little differently, saying, "Captain, you shouldn't get annoyed. In our army we often use the word 'kill' as an exclamation, like 'hurray' or 'whoopee.' You wouldn't make us give up our language, would you?"

"That's not what I meant."

"You respect freedom of speech, don't you?"

"Sure we do."

"So no hard feelings."

He sighed, shaking his lumpy chin. From then on we would continue to shout "Kill!" whenever Larsen conducted the head count, and he would turn a deaf ear to it.

Colonel Kelly didn't keep his promise. We never heard from him about the result of the investigation, which perhaps hadn't taken place, and we knew for a fact that nobody was punished for the death of Wenfu. Wenfu hadn't had any close friend among the prisoners, so nobody mentioned him again.

27. A TALK WITH CAPTAIN LARSEN

One morning in early December Wanren came back from the guardhouse, holding a paper bag that contained a dozen cans of smoked sausages. At the sight of the cans the men at our battalion headquarters all got excited. Wanren told us, "Larsen gave me these."

"Why was he so generous today?" I said.

"I have no clue. He asked me to come into his office and then he let me take these cans."

This was bizarre. "He didn't want you to do anything else?"

"Nothing but a signature."

"For what?"

"For the cans."

His answer sounded odd, but I didn't question him further. The men around were disappointed that our chief wouldn't open a can of sausages for everybody to try. Instead, Wanren declared he would give the cans to the wounded men who hadn't recovered yet. When everybody had turned away, I said to him, "I have a question for you, chief, but it might offend you."

"Fire away. You know I don't like men who keep their opinions to themselves."

"All right then, on what kind of paper did Larsen have you sign your name?"

"A large writing pad."

"Was it blank?"

"No, there were some words on it."

"What did they say?"

"I have no idea. Probably a record of how he distributed the food."

"Are you positive about that?"

"No, I'm not. It could be a receipt too."

"Don't you think he might have made you sign an important document?"

He blushed, his lips quivering. "Well, he was smiling all the while, very friendly. To be honest, that thought never crossed my mind."

"He might have wanted your signature on something that he can use against us."

"It didn't look that serious. Every word was handwritten on a piece of lined paper."

"To the Americans as long as your signature appears on paper, it will be good legally. They don't use a personal seal like us."

"Well, what should we do now?" He looked a bit flustered, twitching his nose.

He was slow-witted, an able warrior but not an exceptional leader. How could the enemy take him in so easily? I was quite sure that the signature was intended for something else. Captain Larsen must have sensed Wanren's inadequacy, so he dealt with him exclusively. Still, I felt for Wanren, who obviously had been so eager to get the sausages for the wounded men that he hadn't thought twice about putting his name down.

For the whole afternoon he and I considered what to do. Should we discuss this matter among the officers in our battalion? Or should we report it to Commissar Pei and request instructions? Or should we just go ahead and make amends by ourselves?

Wanren, at a loss, said we probably should let Chaolin and Commissar Pei know right away. I didn't feel it was a wise idea. "Look," I said, "don't you think they may take you to task? Besides, we're not clear what Larsen has been hatching exactly."

"Tell me what we should do, Yuan." He

looked dejected, rubbing his stubbly chin with his palm.

I was just an interpreter, the compound's spokesman, and should not be advising him in such a matter. But I believed we shouldn't let too many people know or there might be another battle, with more men butchered. What Wanren had signed must be something about the incident a month ago — perhaps Captain Larsen felt uneasy about the death of our former orderly and wanted to clear himself by making it look as though we were to blame for the loss of life. If this was the case, it implied that Colonel Kelly had indeed started an investigation. At least Larsen must have thought Kelly would act on his promise, so he had taken steps to protect himself. I said to Wanren, "I can give you some suggestions, but you're the chief and have to decide what to do on your own."

"Sure, let me hear your opinion."

"To me, the fewer people we let know of this, the better the outcome. We should resolve it by ourselves quietly."

"But how?"

"How about this. Tomorrow we'll go to Larsen and invite him to inspect the sanitary conditions of our compound. If he comes, we'll have him detained and demand that he return your signature to us."

"Shouldn't we inform our men of this plan?"

I gave thought to that and said, "I don't think so. Just let our Security Platoon know and prepare to detain him. That should be enough. Besides, Larsen may not take the bait. Even if he comes, we may not be able to hold him if the situation isn't favorable to us. We should be flexible. Above all, we mustn't lose any life."

"You're a smart man, Yuan."

I felt uncomfortable that he used my real name. He was the only man who did that in our compound; apparently he had come to know my name through Commissar Pei. I said, "Don't tell others that I'm involved in making the decision. I should serve as your interpreter only."

"Sure, this is just between us."

At nine o'clock the next morning he and I went to the guardhouse to see Captain Larsen. We were led in without waiting. Larsen was sitting behind a metal desk, smoking a cigar and reading a magazine, on the back of which was the picture of a young woman in a frilled swimsuit and high heels. I was amazed to see a plaster bust of Larsen himself on the utility shelf behind him. The figure resembled him on the whole, a full forehead, a heavy chin, bell cheeks, and downcast eyes, but there was something distinctly Mongoloid in it — the face was a bit too round and the lids too thick. I remembered that Dr. Wang was fond of sculpting human figures in his spare time. A medic had once told us that an American officer had asked the doctor to make a plaster bust of himself. That officer must have been Captain Larsen. In contrast to most of the Americans, he looked urbane and often wore a sneer on his lips, but I hadn't thought he was so vain and narcissistic. Then I sensed something more about the statue, something juvenile, a boy's longing to become somebody, a significant man or a hero. This realization touched me a little; I guessed that deep inside, Larsen might be similar to many of our men, most of whom hadn't mentally reached manhood yet.

Wanren bowed and thanked the captain for the sausages he had received yesterday, then asked for a box of corned beef or any kind of canned meat. I translated his request to Larsen, who lifted his eyebrows in disbelief. Wanren pressed on: "There're dozens of wounded men suffering from malnutrition in our compound, and some still have festering wounds. A man is what he eats, you know. The regular prison food can't help them recover. The sausages you gave us were great, but not enough to go around among the wounded men. Please let us have some more."

"No way," Larsen said. "You took away a dozen cans yesterday."

"Captain," I said, "we mean to cooperate in any way you want us to. We understand you'd like to make our compound a model for the entire camp, so we cleaned our quarters thoroughly yesterday, just to show our gratitude to you."

"Well, how clean are they?" He grinned, the corner of his mouth tilting. "No flies in the latrine?"

"No."

"No lice and nits in the seams of your underclothes?"

"Of course not. We deloused everyone last week."

"I'm not a fool, you know."

"You can inspect our barracks right now, but on one condition. If you're satisfied with our cleaning, you will give us a box of corned beef, twenty-four cans."

"I don't cut deals with my prisoners."

"Look, we're not requesting this for ourselves. You can go ask the wounded men in our barracks whether they ate sausages yesterday."

A doubtful smirk emerged on Larsen's face. His glossy eyes blinked; his brown pupils contracted a little and then relaxed. I could see that he took us to be a bunch of corrupt officers, so I added, "On our word of honor, we didn't take a single bite of the sausages. If you are fair, you're obligated to come and ask the wounded men. Your doubts about our officers' integrity are an insult to us."

I felt I couldn't continue any longer, because I was just an interpreter and shouldn't take over the role of the requester. Wanren meanwhile seemed content to let me do the persuasion and remained silent. To our relief, Larsen stood up, stubbed out his cigar in a stainless steel ashtray, and put the unused half into his breast pocket. Together we all left the office. But Larsen went in another direction, toward the PX, saying he'd arrive at our compound in an hour or so and personally question some wounded men.

Without delay we returned, told some prisoners to begin cleaning the yard, and deployed the Security Platoon inside the shed where the wounded men lived. After midmorning Captain Larsen came, accompanied by a first lieutenant who carried one shoulder higher than the other. They sauntered through the gate, both in good spirits, chewing gum and bantering with each other. A few prisoners, as instructed, smiled and waved at them. Everything seemed normal, and some men lounged around, sunning themselves. I went up to the two officers and said, "Thank you for coming to inspect our barracks. Would you like to see the wounded men first?"

They nodded and followed me to the shed beside whose door hung a Red Cross sign. The second they stepped in, the door was shut behind them. Larsen took alarm, but before he could say a word, our battalion chief shouted, "Hold them!" More than ten men sprang at them and twisted their arms behind their backs.

"Hey, hey, what's this about?" cried the spindly lieutenant.

"Jesus!" Larsen hollered. "I'll give you five crates of corned beef, all right? Just let us go!"

Wanren went over, about to slap him, but I held the chief back, whispering, "This isn't what we have them here for." That cooled him off a little. I turned to the American officers and said, "We invited you here just for a serious talk. Yesterday morning, Captain Larsen, you misled our chief into signing his name on a piece of

493

paper. It was dishonest of you to take advantage of his ignorance of English. Now we demand you return his signature. The moment we get it back, we'll let you go."

"I have no clue what you're talking about."

"Of course you know."

We took them into the inner room that served as our office. Both of them sat down, still sputtering. Calmly we began questioning Larsen. At first he dodged the issue, saying, "Officers, you're too paranoid. Let Charlie and me go, okay?"

"Not until you give us the signed page." I pointed at him, trying to isolate him from Charlie, the lieutenant.

"I already dumped it along with the trash," said Larsen.

"Then we have to keep you here."

"You're too greedy. I shouldn't have given you the sausages to begin with."

"This isn't about the cans, Captain. We want the signature back."

"I've lost it, all right? It's gone. You want me to plow through the entire trash dump outside the camp? You can go do it yourselves. You have my permission."

"In that case we'll have to keep you here."

"Jeez, how can I make you understand? This is nuts!"

By now the GIs at the front gate had sensed that something had gone awry. They called their central office, which sent over a platoon within twenty minutes. All of a sudden the situation turned more dangerous than we had anticipated. It was impossible to keep the inmates in the dark anymore, so I said to Wanren, "Please tell our comrades the truth and get them to help us."

"That's a good idea." He went out immediately. In a hoarse voice he summoned all the men in view and ordered them to stop the GIs from coming in to rescue the two officers in custody. He told them that Larsen had stolen our document, which we must get back. At once about two hundred men swarmed to the front gate, confronting the armed troops.

Inside the shed I said to Larsen, "If your men open up on us, we can't guarantee your safety."

He and the lieutenant looked at each other, both faces misshapen. I said to Larsen again, referring to his fellow officer, "Let him go tell your men to retreat so that we can resolve this peacefully."

"I can see that you're scared, Officer Feng," he said to me. "Our men can storm in and level the whole place."

"Keep in mind that I'm just a spokesman, not a real officer. But frankly, if your men attack us, we can't guarantee your life. You don't want to get killed first, do you?"

He hung his head. I went on, "Captain, we don't need any bloodshed for such a trifle. Just let Charlie go tell them to withdraw so that we can talk this out."

He thought for a moment, then told the lieutenant to deliver the message to the GIs outside. Meanwhile, some officers of our battalion came into the shed. They had no idea what had happened, so Wanren explained. He kept saying, pointing at the captain, "That bastard roped me in!"

I said to Larsen again, "At all costs we must head off bloodshed. It's unfair that you played a trick on our chief. Please return the signature to us. The sooner you do that, the better it will be for both sides and for your own safety as well."

Wanren banged his fist on a desk and yelled at him, "I'm running out of patience. If you don't cooperate, we can't let you leave unharmed."

Larsen sensed the volatility of the situation and seemed lost in thought. A moment later he said to us, "Okay, I'll give it to you. But you must promise to release both of us once you get that piece of paper."

"You have our word."

The moment the lieutenant came back, Captain Larsen handed him a bunch of keys. Holding a small brass one between his thumb and forefinger, he said to him, "Go to my office and unlock the left drawer of my desk. There's a writing pad in it. Rip off the top page with a Chinese signature on it and bring it back immediately."

"Yes, sir." Charlie turned and went out again.

While we were waiting, I explained to the leaders of the three companies why we had chosen such a drastic course of action. I insisted that we were still unsure what Larsen had done and that we had just taken preemptive measures. Maybe it was nothing serious at all, so there was no need to let everybody know of this beforehand. Most of the men looked suspicious and some complained that they should have been notified nonetheless. Wanren, red-faced and wordless, was smoking in a corner. He shot sullen glances at me time and again. I too felt embarrassed about this operation that seemed to be getting out of hand. We should have taken into account all the possibilities and made some backup plans.

Ten minutes later the lieutenant returned with the page. I looked through it and was glad it indeed bore a false statement, which said: "On November 22, the Chinese prisoners in my compound attacked the guards and bit Captain Larsen without any provocation. As a consequence, we suffered several casualties, including one death. I, as the chief of Compound 6, am responsible for the incident." Then came Wanren's squarish signature. Several men asked me to translate the words, which I had no choice but to do. Listening to me, some of them gasped. A few went up to Larsen, intending to teach him an indelible lesson. I stopped them, then turned to Wanren and the company leaders, saying, "We promised to let both of them go unharmed the moment we got this page back. We should make good on our word."

They nodded. So the two American officers were taken to the front gate and released. That afternoon we received messages from the other compounds, inquiring about what had happened. We were obligated to inform them truthfully. After dinner the battalion headquarters held a meeting, at which Wanren was mildly criticized by the other officers. But we all felt lucky that we had forestalled the potential trouble peacefully by ourselves. Because the secret operation had been exposed to the whole compound, Wanren seemed mortified and a bit ornery. Probably he feared that he had revealed his incompetence to his men, or that I had stood out as a more capable officer in handling this case. Afterward he was reluctant to talk with me as casually as before.

A week later Captain Larsen was demoted and transferred to a different prison camp. By order of Commissar Pei, a meeting was held among the leaders of our compound, presided over by our political instructor, Manpu. Wanren made self-criticism at the meeting and admitted that his vigilance had slackened. He said he was grateful to all the comrades who had helped him get the signed sheet back, otherwise the enemy would definitely have utilized it to sabotage our victory in defending our flag. But he didn't mention me, because Commissar Pei had awarded me another citation, second class this time, which I didn't really care about anymore. By contrast, Wanren got a disciplinary warning, though he remained in charge of our battalion.

After the detainment of Captain Larsen,

Wanren and I could no longer get along. But now and then we still played chess together, with pieces we made out of cement, each bearing a handwritten name on its face, such as Horse, Elephant, Cannon, and Carriage. He was highly skilled at the game, and I was among the few who didn't have to receive the handicap of a carriage or a cannon as his opponent. Although I was still indispensable to him when he had to deal with the Americans, he wouldn't come to me for advice anymore. He was an honest man, probably above small maneuvers; still, I took care not to give him any handle against me.

28. ENTERTAINMENT
AND WORK

Unlike Compound 602 on Koje Island, in this camp any large-scale cultural project, such as a full-length play or an art show, was out of the question. The singers, actors, painters, composers, and calligraphers had been scattered among the battalions, and there was no way to assemble them. At first this state of isolation caused us some difficulties, but soon every compound formed its own cultural staff. As a result, there were ten groups of "artists" in the camp, around whom many prisoners gathered.

Among the ten groups, the one in Compound 9 had more talents than the others and was most active. Meng Feihan, the composer and stage director who had lost a foot, was there. Besides him, the chief of that battalion had a fondness for cultural work, having once led a song-and-dance ensemble in an artillery division. Every evening you could hear music and songs rising from their barracks. Throughout the camp many inmates took part in musical activities of this kind. I participated too, though briefly. I tried to teach others how to read music, but my voice was so tuneless that whenever I sang to illustrate musical notes, some men would chuckle or cackle. So I gave up.

The POWs also contrived several kinds of instruments, including drums, flutes, violins, and horns. The first bugle was fashioned out of tinplate. A bugler by chance had brought into the camp his mouthpiece, which later served as a casting model for the lead mouthpieces on all the wind instruments here. Drums were relatively easy to produce, and there were several sizes of them; all were made out of sawed oil drums, water pails, and gas cans, covered with rain cloth fastened by rope. My friend Weiming, the short Cantonese man who was very protective of Shanmin, was an expert in making stringed instruments, which were more difficult to create than the wind ones. He was tone-deaf, however, and couldn't read musical notes or play any instrument; but he was more inventive than others. He turned a tin can into the resonator for an *erhu*, a two-stringed Chinese violin; he also used wooden boards, bamboo pipes, rat skins, and other materials. Ignorant of music, he had to have helpers and testers, of whom he had many, since others had lined up to join him. In fact, every instrument the prisoners made was a result of teamwork. There were dozens of instrument-making groups in the camp. They even produced several guitars that had three or four strings. They also created various kinds of violins: resin was obtained from steeped pine chips; the bows were mostly thin iron rods bent on both ends; as for the hair, they unraveled pieces of rope, soaked the hemp in warm water, combed it straight, then picked the sturdy strands to be tied to the sticks. Most "silk strings" came from the jackets and boots they wore, whereas all the metal strings had one source — electric wires, which could be found at the construction sites. By far the Western violin was the hardest to make, because it had four different metal strings that were difficult to come by. Nevertheless, one group managed to come up with a kind of strings, which were entwined with threads to make them sound close to the standard G, D, A, and E strings. It took a great deal of experimentation to create a Western violin.

Throughout the summer, our compound

was like an instrument factory, and some sort of manufacturing was under way in most of the sheds. The prisoners took the work as seriously as if it were their livelihood. In addition, many men had begun to learn how to play the instruments and formed small bands. I often wondered why they were so earnest about such activities. I guessed they were probably bored and just meant to have some fun, frittering away the time that hung heavy on their hands. But I was mistaken. I soon realized that for them this was serious business, a matter of survival. Usually four or five men worked together at one instrument, so the product embodied a kind of collective will and effort. Likewise, a band always belonged to a platoon or company as "a special weapon in fighting the enemy." That was the language the leaders used. I wondered why they applied such hyperbole to a mere band. Perhaps they believed music could bolster the comrades' courage and kindle their hatred and thus turn them into better fighting machines.

On occasion, a skit or a comic talk accompanied by bamboo clappers was enacted in our compound, though none of the pieces was exceptional. Some prisoners tried to write short scripts for the stage and some composed songs, but few of these efforts resulted in passable work. Once in a while they would draw cartoons to ridicule the Americans, who would be given cucumber noses or bloated midriffs. The blackboards in our compound always carried jokes, drawings, and poems. Yet by far the most popular form of entertainment was the songfest.

Whenever a satisfactory song was composed, it began circulating briskly among the inmates, and within two weeks all the ten battalions could sing it. Meng Feihan in Compound 9 was the major composer; in general his music was solemn, strenuous, and high-minded. Two of his disciples were good at singing folk songs, so they blended light melodies into some satirical airs, which became immensely popular, such as "The Loudspeaker Always Lies, Don't Listen to It," "God, I'm Scared," and "Truman Is Done For." The prisoners enjoyed these erratic, uncanny tunes so much that they would croon them even when they were alone, whereas they would sing the serious songs only in groups. The leaders made good use of the musical talents. Whenever something important happened, they would have a song composed to mark the occasion. For instance, to commemorate the fight for raising our national flag, a song was made a week after the massacre. It went as follows:

Red flags fly high on October 1.
Our comrades' blood bears out
The American imperialists' crimes.
However brutal the enemies are,
We shall be more resolute.
Our hands can stop their bayonets
And stones can block their bullets.
Shoulder to shoulder we form a bastion
To defend our national flag
And fight the savage foe.
Our hatred is redoubled —
The debt of blood must be paid in blood.
The evil American imperialists
Cannot escape the hands of justice.
We sons of the new China
Shall make our deeds known to the world
And keep our flags flying for good.
Rest in peace, our brave martyrs.
You will always live in our hearts.

Despite its simpleminded boastfulness, this song became quite popular and served as a fighting anthem for some POWs. I disliked it and never learned to sing it. Yet I was amazed by my comrades' great zeal for songs. Every day there was so much singing in the camp that even some GIs picked up the tunes. One of them, a skinny fellow with red sideburns, would chant at us the line "March, march, follow Mao Zedong" as a kind of greeting.

Gradually I came to understand that singing was a cathartic experience for the prisoners. A song's contents didn't really matter; as long as the men could sing something together, they felt better. Many of them were depressed and cantankerous, so a songfest was an expedient for releasing their grief and anguish and for restoring their emotional balance. We missed home and our former ways of life terribly. This mental state disposed many of us to be sentimental. I saw men weep all of a sudden for no apparent reason, perhaps just touched by a happy thought or by a surge of self-pity. Without question, singing together assuaged their misery and cheered their hearts. More importantly, songfests enabled them to identify with one another emotionally so as to increase their feeling of solidarity, though the affection they felt for their fellow inmates could be momentary.

The singing also eased the prisoners' tremendous dread of loneliness. The inmates were very gregarious, as most Chinese are. Some of them feared loneliness more than incarceration. As long as they stayed together and organized, they felt they had a better chance of survival. Singing provided them with a kind of socialization that not only soothed their aching hearts but also suspended their individual isolation. Frankly, sometimes I wished I were more like them, capable of chanting whatever came to mind with total abandon.

Another question troubled me for some time. Were the arts groups' creative activities truly artistic, as they claimed? In the beginning I had respected the composers and the painters immensely. Unable to play any instrument, I'd look up to whoever could saw a tune out on a fiddle even if he played with assumed bravura. But before too long I noticed that there was a crudeness in whatever they did, as though the idea of perfection had never entered their minds. I daresay this crudeness originated from their utilitarian conception of the arts. They created every piece of work merely for its usefulness, like that of a weapon: each was made simply for the purpose of rousing people and boosting the fighting spirit. These creations had an instantaneous feel, a dash of spontaneity, but invariably ended in a slipshod fashion. Most of the time a man would finish writing a song or a poem at one go, and he'd be proud of completing it "without changing a single word," and even brag about it, as though to assert that the work had come purely from inspiration, which was a mark of genius. Patience and refinement were alien to these young men, who couldn't see that art didn't have to be useful or serve a purpose other than entertainment. Their works could be powerful at times, but never beautiful. So I began to have deep reservations about their efforts and sometimes felt they were just wasting their energy and time. No doubt these men were talented, ingenious, and passionate, but they always stopped at the point to which their cleverness led them, not going beyond into complexity and subtlety, not to mention depth. As a result, however extravagantly they used their talent, they remained like smart hacks, blind to their own shoddiness. There was no way to explain my thoughts to them without risking my neck, so I kept quiet.

Unless I had to, I didn't sing with others. My young friend Shanmin enjoyed singing, and I didn't discourage him. I spent more time reading English-language newspapers.

It was my job to glean information for our leaders, so nobody interfered with my reading. Often tired of news articles, I craved a good book, a long novel or biography. This mental deprivation was more painful to me than hunger. Sometimes I sat alone with an old issue of *Stars and Stripes* on my lap, but my eyes couldn't register the meanings of the words as I sank into thought. This manner of sitting, however, was a safe way to indulge in my own thinking. I felt that when I was alone, my mind would be clearer and more alert. I didn't have to join the inmates in the morning exercises; instead, I would read loudly for an hour to practice my spoken English, which was also my job.

Barely having enough to eat, I couldn't run as often as I wished. Sometimes I did dozens of squats inside the shed, deliberately putting more weight on my injured leg; once in a while I ran a few laps along the fence of our compound. If I had been given enough food, I would have been happy to labor like a coolie every day, because I believed that physical work and fresh air could keep me from rotting away in jail. I wanted to return home healthy and strong. I was not yet twenty-five and should have a long life ahead.

But I wasn't well fit for hard labor. I once left the camp with fifty men to dig ditches in the South Korean army's training base, where recruits were drilled before they were shipped to the Korean mainland. The work was exhausting, though once in a while you could be lucky enough to find a turnip or a sweet potato left in the fields. That morning we set off at eight and dug away for a whole day with only a half-hour break for the midday meal. It drizzled in the afternoon; few of us had brought our rain ponchos, and by the time we returned in the evening, most of us were drenched. I couldn't get up the next morning, aching all over, and remained sick for several days. The doctor forbade me to join the ditch diggers again. My bad leg, not having fully recovered from the injury yet, couldn't stand the long hours of work. Oddly enough, this experience made me see that some of the "artists" stayed in the barracks for artistic creation perhaps because they wanted to shun physical labor, from which only officers and the disabled could be exempted. This realization instilled into me some contempt for those able-bodied shirkers.

Being an interpreter, I was regarded as an officer by the Americans and the pris-

511

oners, who literally called me "Officer Interpreter." So the inmates didn't like my joining them in their work, as if I was a nuisance to them. My bad leg wasn't strong enough for me to carry anything heavier than sixty pounds; this made me a poor hand when we unloaded a ship or truck. Some men often poked fun at me, though good-naturedly, saying they didn't need a scholar around when they were slaving away. But I wasn't a total weakling in their eyes. We had arm-wrestled several times, and I could beat many of them.

The work I liked best was shoveling, which could tone my muscles without overstraining my injured leg. At first, when I used a shovel, I would drip with sweat and have a sore back and hot, swollen hands in the evening. But gradually I adopted a rhythm when shoveling dirt or sand or gravel. I could apply a shovel with a swing of my upper body like a skilled laborer. Whenever there was shoveling to do, I would volunteer to go. Sometimes they took me and sometimes they didn't. Wet mud was much harder to shovel, but because so many hands were available, we would tie a rope to the shaft of a shovel, just above its scoop, and have two men pull at both ends of the rope to help the shoveler lift a pile of mud. This rhythmical group shoveling could be fun if you were teamed with the right men, with whom you could swap jokes.

Behind our kitchen sat a grinding stone, at which we often crushed grain to groats. I would volunteer to rotate the stone by pushing a long rod attached to it. I liked this work very much because it could exercise both of my legs and, working alone, I didn't have to hurry. Most people wouldn't toil at the grinding stone and some called it a donkey's job, so I often did the grinding. At times when I was done, the cooks would give me something to eat, a bowl of pea soup or a piece of dried fish, which made the work more rewarding. Gradually I could see that some men thought of me as an eccentric — they wondered why an officer, a college graduate, would condescend to labor like themselves. I never explained why, just saying I enjoyed it.

There was another advantage in doing some physical work. An educated man like me tended to be accused of having deliberately separated himself from others. If I often worked with my hands, few people could say I had put on airs. In fact, the battalion leaders praised me several times for my integration with our men. They mistook my voluntary labor for an educational task I had imposed on myself, like the kind of education the Party had always called on intellectuals to undergo conscientiously.

One evening my friends Shanmin and Weiming returned from the GIs' quarters, where they had been detailed to plant grass. They told me excitedly that they had eaten their fill in that barracks, where they had come upon a trash can stuffed with cartons that still contained half-eaten bread, roast beef, carrots, and sliced cucumber. "What's this, do you know? Lard or soap?" Weiming showed me a yellowish chunk, the size of a matchbox.

"Cheese," I said. "It's very nutritious, made from milk."

"Damn, we should've taken all the leftovers back," he said to Shanmin. He stroked his belly, on which slanted a scar like a giant centipede. His navel was huge and cavernous.

Shanmin told me, "There were many cubes of this cheese in the trash can. We weren't sure if it was edible."

"We tried it," said Weiming, "but couldn't swallow it, so we didn't bring the rest with us."

"Men, you left behind the best stuff." I was salivating a little.

So he gave me the cheese, which I put into my mouth, chewing with relish, though it was stale. They were both amazed. "You have a diplomat's stomach and can eat anything," said Weiming, smiling and shaking his round head.

29. A SURPRISE

One day in mid-January, two hundred men from our compound were sent to unload a large cargo ship at the wharf. I went with them. We carried sacks and bundles to the shore and piled them on the ground so that they could be transported to the warehouses near the camp later on. For lunch we were each given a hard roll and an apple, so we were happy about the work. There was no wind, and the ocean looked placid and somewhat opalescent, wavelets flickering in sunlight. Though it was wintertime, it was quite warm.

Interpreter Peng, the officer from Taiwan, accompanied the two squads of GIs guarding us. He was a quiet man and seldom spoke a word unless he had to. His English was mannered, slightly British. He seemed lonesome. For a whole day he continually read a dog-eared book under a willow and didn't mix much with the GIs. At the end of the work, we formed up for him to do the head count. He directed ten of us at a time to step aside to join those he had already counted. Done with the last batch of us, he found one man was missing. He demanded that every squad leader conduct a roll call to see who was absent.

Shanmin tugged my sleeve and whispered, "Weiming's not here." I was taken aback; but convinced that our friend would never escape alone, I reported his absence to Interpreter Peng.

Meanwhile Sergeant Harris, the commander of the two squads escorting us, was enraged. And we were worried too, looking around for Weiming. Then I caught sight of his back in the wattle bushes over a hundred yards away. I had heard that he suffered loose bowels these days, and I thought he might be having a movement, so I pointed him out. Interpreter Peng saw Weiming too. "He's there," he told the sergeant.

"Goddammit!" Harris shouted at Weiming, "What are you doing over there? Get your big ass back here." His breath smelled awful, like underarm odor, though he chewed gum constantly.

Weiming didn't respond, as if he had heard nothing. I broke in, "He's suffering from dysentery recently. Let me go get him back." Without waiting for permission I strode away toward the bushes.

The sergeant followed me; so did Officer Peng. When we reached the bushes, Weiming still didn't budge, his naked posterior in clear view.

"Are you deaf?" Harris yelled at him.

Still there was no response. The sergeant stepped over and pulled Weiming's ear from behind, but the squatting man made no sound, as if lost in concentrating on his business. Harris walked around and pinched his cheek; still Weiming didn't say a word, though he winced this time. The sergeant seized his hair and yanked; Weiming shuffled forward a few steps, revealing two dark turds on the sand. At the sight of the solid feces, Harris flew into a rage. He kicked Weiming's backside ferociously and sent him up to his feet. Without wiping himself, Weiming pulled up his pants while the sergeant battered him with his rifle butt.

"Ouch, ouch!" my friend finally said. "I have a stomachache!"

Interpreter Peng told the sergeant, "He has stomach trouble."

To our astonishment, Harris picked up a turd with his bayonet, thrust it to Weiming's mouth, and ordered, "Open wide!"

Weiming was too flabbergasted to say a word. The sergeant yelled at him again, "Eat this! It'll cure your stomach problem. If you don't, I'll finish you off right here."

Weiming looked at me and then at Interpreter Peng, but he wouldn't open his mouth. I intervened, saying, "Sarge, please don't be so —"

"Shut up!" His elbow jabbed me in the sternum. "You fucking liar! You said he had dysentery. Look at his shit, solid like stone. I tell you, if you mess with my job again, I'm gonna make you eat the other piece." He resumed kicking Weiming.

Strangely enough, Interpreter Peng said in his clipped English, "Sergeant, please stop abusing him. He just answered a call of nature. We all do the same."

These unmodulated words seemed to stun Harris, who looked at the interpreter for a moment, then asked, "What did you say?"

"Please stop beating him."

"Who the fuck do you think you are? Get out of my face!"

With trembling lips Peng said, "Colonel Kelly assigned me to accompany you, so I too am responsible for keeping order here. If you don't like my suggestion, you can complain to your superiors."

"You little shit, you think you can order me around?"

"You have been unreasonable."

"Whose side are you on, eh?"

"That has nothing to do with this. You're wrong. Who can eat his own shit?"

"Fuck you, chink! You're helping them Commies. You think I can't see through you?"

While they were wrangling, I dragged Weiming back into the ranks of the prisoners. I was afraid that Sergeant Harris would attack the interpreter. But a moment later they came back, both with sullen faces. Officer Peng didn't walk with the GIs on the way back to the camp; instead, he followed us, alone and rather absentminded. I turned to glance at him from time to time. He looked pensive, his face tauter than an hour ago.

Back in our compound, Weiming described the incident to the other prisoners, who were all amazed, because we had always held in contempt the Nationalist officers working here and believed all they dared to do was say "Yes sir" to the Americans. Nobody had expected that the interpreter would intercede for a POW, an enemy he was supposed to hate. A week later Officer Peng left the camp. Some people said he had been called back to Taiwan, some believed he had applied for a discharge of his own accord, and some guessed he might have gotten demoted. What happened to him? I asked several Americans, but they didn't know either.

I have often thought of this scrawny man. Over the years, his smooth face and close-set eyes have grown more and more distinct in my memory.

30. THE FINAL ORDER

Winter was short on Cheju, though it wasn't over in February yet. Nothing newsworthy had happened since November. It was peaceful on the island, but the peace was not easy for our leaders to take. We had learned that the truce talks at Panmunjom had broken off some months ago and hadn't yet resumed. One day in late February, Colonel Kelly informed us that four of our officers must go to Pusan to get reregistered. Among them were Hao Chaolin and Chang Ming. We all thought they would be interrogated again, and that probably the Americans meant to put them away before the repatriation began. Ming was still with Commissar Pei in the prison house; it might do him good to get out of the confinement for some time, though the reregistration sounded treacherous. I often saw him moving left and right behind the window of that cell, transmitting messages. His movement was slow. His health had deteriorated, and I had heard that he suffered from arthritis. The inside of that prison was extremely damp; it was on the edge of the beach, and sometimes at high tide, seawater would reach the base of the exterior wall.

A message regarding the reregistration was sent to Commissar Pei. The next afternoon he replied: "Feng Wen cannot leave his job. Ask Feng Yan to go for him. The four officers should contact the underground Party at Pusan and build a channel of communication." Ming's listed name was Feng Wen and mine Feng Yan — we shared the same family name. That must have been one of the reasons I was ordered to take his place. Before we received Pei's message, a returned "troublemaker" from the prison house had delivered to us Ming's POW ID tag, which was a card six inches by three, bearing information on his birthplace and date of birth, family members, education, rank, conscript time, and the serial number of his former army unit. At the top of the card was his POW number: 720143. Plainly Pei wanted me to take Ming's tag with me.

Having read the message, I was overtaken by anger and fear. I left my shed without a word and walked along the barbed-wire fence alone. The yard was slushy in places and the mud felt sticky under my boots, but I didn't care and just let my feet go anywhere they wanted. My face was hot, as if I were running a temperature, and I kicked whatever was in the way, pebbles, tin cans, bottle caps, twigs, mule droppings. Soon my boots, caked with mud, felt twice their normal weight. The wind tossed up a couple of tattered leaves, whose ribs and veins hadn't rotted yet; the leaves now tumbled around and now dropped flat. Outside the camp, the ground looked fecund, already pierced by the sprouting grass. In the southeast, nutmeg trees were green with tiny leaves, and their thick boles brightened, whitish in the last sunlight. I was angry about the commissar's decision, my throat aching. Indeed Ming was his interpreter, secretary, code man, and signalman, yet I could easily have replaced him without interrupting the regular work and communication. With a little training, I could learn how to use the Pei Code and how to transmit and receive messages from that cell. At most it would take me two days to master the skills. Why did I have to go in place of Ming?

Then the thought crossed my mind that probably this was because I was not a

Party member; I was, like a regular soldier, dispensable. Perhaps the commissar believed that the repatriation would start soon, and wanted to save his own men. Had he gotten enough use out of me? Was he ready to discard me now? What did Ming think of this decision? Had he been involved in making it? I wondered if he too meant to do me in, just to protect himself.

It also dawned on me that since we were in a relatively safe situation on Cheju Island, none of us wanted to leave this oasis alone, at least for the time being. The less you met the enemy individually, the safer your future was likely to be. When we returned to China, every one of us might face the problem of clearing himself. As long as you had stayed with your comrades constantly, you might avoid the Party's suspicion, because your fellow inmates could testify to your role and activities in the camp. This might explain Ming's preference for remaining with Commissar Pei — he wanted to keep his credentials impeccable for the Party.

When I returned to the barracks, my comrades already knew of Pei's decision. Our battalion chief, Wanren, came up to me and shook my hand with genuine feeling. He didn't even bother to ask if I would go, knowing I had no choice but to obey the order. I handed him my ID tag, which he would surely pass on to Ming. I said, "I'll set out tomorrow."

At those words, Shanmin broke into tears, rushed over and hugged me tightly. "I'll miss you, elder brother!" he said.

A few men sighed. Someone suggested they throw me a send-off party that evening. So after dinner, about thirty men gathered in the headquarters, mostly officers, my two friends, and a few shed mates. The refreshments consisted of a jar of watered-down saki and half a washbasin of roasted sunflower seeds, which I had no idea how they had come by. I tried to remain calm and taciturn, though the air at the party was depressing. They treated me as if they would never see me again. Indeed this could be our last gathering. I didn't say anything and just listened to them talk; some said they'd always remember me, and some advised me not to lose heart. There was always a way out even though you seemed to have reached a dead end, they assured me. Then a tall man started a Russian song, "The Anthem of the Communist Youth League." All the other men joined him in singing and I did the same. Together we belted out, "Good-bye Mother! Don't grieve over my departure. Just wish me a safe voyage." Tears trickled down our cheeks.

Finally I gave way to my emotions, sobbing convulsively, and buried my face in my hands. Shanmin passed me a towel. Then Weiming straightened his neck and recited loudly an ancient couplet, "The wind howls while the river is about to churn; / Our warrior sets out, perhaps never to return." He glowered, as though he were crazed, his round eyes blazing.

This sobered me up some. I was surprised by the indignant edge in his voice, which seemed to convey his understanding that I was being treated as an expendable item. Manpu, our political instructor, interposed, saying that I shouldn't lose hope so easily and that the reregistration might be just a routine thing, so I would come back for sure. If not, we'd meet again in our homeland. He told us, "How could the Americans tell Lu from Liu, or Chiang from Chang? For them, we're all Chinese, so Feng Yan, don't be upset ahead of time. As long as you keep your mind clear, you'll know how to navigate through the process safely. You must take courage."

A man laughed at the back of the room. Manpu's words had cooled us down, though I still believed that in the enemy's eyes the four departing officers were not regular POWs but war criminals.

The party ended at nine. Most of the men left after slipping a few sunflower seeds into their pockets. Together with my two friends I returned to our shed.

That night I handed my work over to the new interpreter, a man who could speak some English but couldn't read it, having not begun to learn the language until he was taken prisoner. After giving him the file of newspaper clippings, I lay down on my pallet and thought about my family. How I missed them. Heaven knew if I would ever see them again. I sat up and fished a pencil out of my pocket, tore a sheet of writing paper in half, and wrote a note on both pieces — one addressed to my mother and the other to my fiancée. In the one for Julan I said:

February 27, 1953

Dear Julan,

It's a pity I cannot go back and marry you, but my death is not meaningless. I have served the cause of our country and sacrificed my life for the peace of the world. Please forget me and go on with your life. May you have a happy family.

Love,
Yuan

PS: Please visit my mother once in a while. I am her only child. She may feel lonely. Thank you.

I put addresses on the backs of both notes and handed them to Shanmin. I said, "If you hear I'm dead, mail these letters for me when you're back in China."

I also gave him all my belongings — a stack of kraft paper, two pencil stubs, a pair of woolen gloves, an overcoat, two blankets, everything except for the jade barrette half tied around my neck. He said to me, "I'll keep all these things for you so that you can use them again when you come back."

"Don't be silly. I won't need them when we meet again."

I slept well that night, whereas Shanmin spent several hours listening to me snoring. In this regard I was truly blessed — however hard I was hit emotionally, I could always get a good night's sleep. I snored loudly too, and often woke up my shed mates. This habit of mine made them regard me more as a soldier than as a college graduate. They even remarked that I slept like a general.

The next morning the four of us officers were taken onto a steamboat. We were put into the cabin below the deck, so that we couldn't see the outside except when we went up to the toilet, to which we could go only one at a time. Eleven GIs escorted us, led by a freckle-faced officer I had never met before. Their number unnerved me because it seemed to reflect our importance, but soon I discovered, through their chattering, that most of them were headed for Pusan to visit friends and to see a show given by a popular singer from the United States. During the trip they wouldn't allow us to talk. Chaolin was sitting opposite me on a maroon leather seat. He was thinner than before, his face hairless and his teeth coated with tobacco tar. But his eyes were bright and intelligent, manifesting some ease and defiance. Whenever he grinned at me, I'd smile back. He seemed more sociable now, and I felt less jittery with him around, since he was a seasoned officer and could advise me if I ran into difficulties. On the other hand, I had to be on my guard when rubbing elbows with this small man who could be the Party's eyes and ears among us. I thought of dropping into the ocean Ming's ID tag, which had his fingerprints on it and could be used against me at Pusan. Without the fingerprints, the Americans might not easily detect my false identity. But I dared not get rid of the tag, for fear that Chaolin might notice its disappearance and report my misconduct to Commissar Pei.

I knew the other two men only by sight. One had been a deputy battalion commander in the Thirty-ninth Army, and the other a staff officer in the Eighth Artillery Division. They both looked downcast. One of them was seasick and vomited continually, muttering that he might spew out his viscera, whereas the other man dozed away almost the whole time.

31. AT THE REREGISTRATION

The four of us were put in a small tent at the Pusan POW Collection Center. Now we could talk among ourselves. I was worried about the reregistration, but Chaolin said this might not be anything unusual, otherwise the enemy would have separated us and posted more guards at the entrance to the tent. Indeed, only one South Korean was standing there. The other two officers agreed with Chaolin, saying if the Americans had meant to kill us, they would have done it by themselves without involving the Koreans. So for the whole afternoon, they relaxed, chatting and wisecracking, though I was still nervous, unsure what to do if my false identity was discovered.

Our tent wasn't far away from the Operating Section of the hospital, which I couldn't help but gaze at when it was still light. I wondered if Dr. Greene still worked there. A few female medical personnel passed the door of the white building, but none of them resembled her. If she could see the way I walked now, she'd be pleased, proud of the miraculous job she had done. After watching for about an hour without recognizing anyone, I went up to the Korean guard and asked him about Dr. Greene, but he couldn't understand English and kept shaking his long face.

The next morning we were taken to the administration center one by one. Chaolin went first, while the rest of us lay on straw sacks, smoking, chatting, and waiting for our turns. We talked about Korean women, most of whom we believed were not as good-looking as women in Manchuria, because they didn't wear makeup. "So many of them have sun-bitten faces," the staff officer said, crinkling his flat nose as though sniffing at something. On his neck was a large purple mark left by a cupping jar.

"Their faces are fine for me, some are pretty," said the deputy battalion commander, who was about forty. "But they have bowlegs, that bothers me."

"How come you know what their legs look like? Don't they always wear long dresses or slacks?"

"We stayed near a village two years ago and I often saw them in the river."

"Bathing?"

"Yes." The older officer laughed with a bubbling sound in his throat and waggled his half-grizzled mustache. "Actually you can imagine what their legs are like by looking at Korean men, who mostly have bowlegs."

"Maybe they sit too much," I put in. "They don't have furniture in their homes and sit on the floors all the time. That may have deformed their legs."

"Probably true," agreed the staff officer.

I went on, "Also, Korean women carry manure baskets and water jars on their heads, so their spines must be compressed."

"Right," said the older officer.

But we all felt that by and large Korean women were good-natured and would make better wives than most Chinese women. We guessed that the majority of them were short because they worked too hard, which had stunted their growth. Few Korean men seemed involved in farming. You often saw old men drive oxcarts, watch over orchards, burn charcoal, cure tobacco, grow ginseng in the mountains, but rarely could you find them planting rice shoots or weeding vegetable gardens. Besides, most young men had been conscripted, so the fields had been left to the care of women, who started to do farmwork in their early teens. But with few exceptions Koreans had strong white teeth, which I had noticed because I was often bothered by my inflamed gums. A Korean doctor had once assured me that kimchee was accountable for their healthy teeth.

Chaolin returned an hour later. He was in good spirits, saying that he was allowed to go back to Cheju and that the reregistration was indeed just a routine thing. He believed the Americans must have lost some files and wanted to reestablish the records. Besides us, there were dozens of POWs who had come from other camps for the reregistration too. I didn't have time to ask him more about the process before the guard took me away.

I stuffed Ming's ID tag into my pants pocket and set off. Passing the central latrine on the way, I told the guard I needed to pee, and he let me enter the roofless privy, where I ripped the ID tag to pieces and dropped it into one of the four hundred pits.

Before I went into the registration office, a clerk, a black man whose neck was as thick as his face, asked me to show him my ID tag. I said, "I don't have one."

"How come?" He looked puzzled.

"I lost it in the camp on Cheju Island. I was ill for some time and couldn't take care of my stuff."

"All right, let me get your fingerprints."

I held out my left hand, and one by one he pressed my fingertips into an ink container and printed them on a card that had five marked squares, one for each digit. He did the same with my right hand. After giving me a piece of straw paper to wipe my hand with, he led me into an office, an inner room in a large tent. Here sat an American lieutenant and a Chinese interpreter, who was apparently an officer from Taiwan, though he wore civvies and tortoiseshell glasses. I was told to sit on a padded chair in front of them. This office looked cozy; a white bookcase stood in a corner, loaded with dozens of books, which I observed for a good while. Among the volumes were novels, manuals, and some brand-new copies of the Bible. The lieutenant must have been involved with the prisoners' education program.

"Your name?" the American officer asked. He was about my age, but with a balding crown. I pretended I didn't know English and waited for the interpreter to translate so that I could think before answering.

"Feng Wen," I said, my heart fluttering.

"Age?"

"Twenty-six." Ming was one year older than me.

"Education?"

"College."

"What school?"

"Beijing University."

Suddenly the black clerk stepped in and put the card of my fingerprints on the officer's desk. He said, "Lieutenant Wright, this doesn't match the one in our file."

Heavens, they'd kept a record of Ming's ID! My head was swimming and my heart pounding while both the interrogators fastened their eyes on me. Except for his baldish head, Lieutenant Wright was quite handsome, with a straight nose, a sensuous mouth, and a chin covered with a curly beard. He said, "Now, you must be honest with me. Evidently you're not Feng Wen."

"I am Feng Wen," I replied in English, having forgotten to wait for the interpreter to translate.

They looked at each other. The lieutenant said sternly, "Then you must explain why your fingerprints don't match our record."

"I have no idea. This must be a mistake. I was told to come and get registered again."

"You speak good English," commented the interpreter.

"I took some English classes at college."

Lieutenant Wright said, "Mr. Feng, or whoever you are, if you can't explain the discrepancy, we're going to keep you in custody until this gets clarified."

"That wouldn't make much difference, I'm already in custody."

"I don't think this is an error, though. What we have here is subterfuge, so we must get to the bottom of it."

I was impressed by his manner of speech. Obviously he was a well-educated man, probably a college graduate. Despite my effort to be articulate, I got rattled, sweat oozing from my face. I lifted my hand and wiped it away.

Wright flicked his fingers and ordered the guard, "Put him into Cell 4."

I wanted to say something, but words failed me. Silently I followed the guard out.

Once slammed into a solitary cell whose window was blocked by an iron grille, I began thinking about what to do. The crucial question was whether I should admit my true identity. Such a confession would amount to treason in the Communists' eyes, but if I refused to own up, the inter-

538

rogators would not let me go. What step should I take then? Should I tell them something but not the whole truth? Maybe I should do that, but how much information should I give them? That would depend on how much they knew about me. If they found out that I had withheld information, I'd be done for.

Hard as I tried, I couldn't make up my mind. The more I thought about my predicament, the more I resented Commissar Pei for sending me here. If Ming had come himself, the whole thing would have ended well without costing him a single hair. The Party just wouldn't risk losing one of its own men.

Unsure what to do, I decided that from now on I'd act according to the situation. In any event I must not get myself hurt. As long as I stayed alive, there would be a way to get back to China.

Early the next morning I was taken to Lieutenant Wright's office again. This time a bulky tape recorder was on his desk. I told myself I must speak carefully. The moment I sat down, Wright handed me a photograph that showed Commissar Pei and me on the beach. Dumbfounded, I couldn't face him.

"Well," he said with a grin, "we know

who you are, Feng Yan. Now you must tell us why you came here in Feng Wen's place."

"They told me to come, but I'm not sure why," I said.

"Who are *they*?"

"The Communist leaders."

"What's your mission here?" demanded the interpreter.

"None, just to sacrifice myself, I guess."

"How do you mean?" asked the lieutenant.

I was so angry about Pei's scheme that I said, "Feng Wen is Pei Shan's interpreter, indispensable to him. That's why Pei sent me here, to be trashed."

"You must speak English better than Feng Wen, don't you?" asked the Chinese man.

"But I'm not a Party member."

"I see."

Lieutenant Wright said, "Let me ask you another question, which you must answer honestly. Then we'll decide how to handle your case. My question is: are you disgusted with the Communists?"

I glanced at the tape recorder, which wasn't on. "Yes," I managed to say.

"You don't sound convincing."

At the spur of the moment I pulled up

my shirt to show them my tattoo — FUCK COMMUNISM. "Look at this. Don't you think this is convincing?"

They both laughed. Lieutenant Wright flung up his hand and said, "I don't know. I can't read your Oriental mind, which is full of duplicity. If you hate the Communists as much as your tattoo indicates, then why did you follow them all the way to Camp 8?"

"I was a soldier and had to obey orders."

"Whose orders?"

Before I could answer, the Chinese officer stepped in with a shrewd smile, "I doubt if you told us the truth."

"Why don't you believe me?"

"That tattoo must've been put on your tummy by the Communists themselves."

"Why would they do that?"

"To make you an effective agent working for them."

"Yes, that's it." Wright's hazel eyes gleamed.

"That's preposterous," I said. "The two words were marked on me by some men in Compound 72 on Koje Island. It has nothing do with the Communists. You can call that compound on Koje, check with the chief of the Third Company by the name of Wang Yong, and ask him whether his men tattooed me last spring."

That held them in check. The lieutenant said, "Okay, we'll contact Cheju Island. Let's stop here for today."

"Why don't you call Koje?" I was surprised.

"They moved to Cheju too."

That was news to me. I had never heard there was a camp for the pro-Nationalist prisoners on the island.

Before I left, I again looked at the bookcase. Wright caught my envious eyes, but said nothing. Back in the cell, I wondered if I had done a wise thing to mention Compound 72. Many of those pro-Nationalists must still hate my guts, and they might tip off the Americans to destroy me. If only I hadn't mentioned Wang Yong. But if I had not, there would have been no way to get myself cleared. I was anxious about what would happen at the next interrogation. To some degree I liked Lieutenant Wright, who seemed decent and unassuming, careful with his choice of words. It was his interpreter who unnerved me. Americans were usually forthcoming, poor at concealing their feelings, so you knew where you stood when dealing with them, whereas some Chinese were hard to assess, rarely showing what was on their minds. I feared the interpreter might plot to hurt me.

My premonition proved right. The moment I sat down in front of the interrogators the next morning, Wright told me, "We have checked with Wang Yong. He remembered that his men had tattooed you."

"So you can let me go back to Camp 8?"

The Chinese officer said, "Why are you so eager to rejoin the Communists?"

"I've told you I dislike them, but I want to go home. I'm my mother's only child."

"Mr. Feng, you're a graduate of the Huangpu Military Academy, a student of Generalissimo Chiang. Why won't you go to Taiwan? We shall return to mainland China sooner or later. It's just a matter of time."

I lowered my head and couldn't respond, unsure what he had up his sleeve.

Wright said, "We believe in deeds more than in words. If you hate the Communists, you must separate yourself from them. Let's get this straight now. I won't tolerate duplicity anymore."

"Well, Mr. Feng, you have to decide where to go," the interpreter added and uncrossed his legs.

It became clear that they would never let me return to Camp 8, so the only way out of this impasse was to go join the pro-Nationalists on Cheju Island. My head was reeling and aching and my windpipe tightened, but I forced myself to remain calm. After a moment's silence I said, "All right, I'll go to Taiwan with one proviso."

"Name it," Wright urged.

"I want you to write a letter saying I am going to Taiwan of my own free will."

"I can do that."

"Then I'll go anywhere you send me."

He picked up a squat fountain pen and began writing on a sheet of stationery. The interpreter meanwhile tamped tobacco into a black pipe and lit it. A puff of smoke obscured his slightly pitted face. The tobacco smelled sweetish, like creamy candy, so it must have been an American brand.

"Can I look at your books?" I asked Lieutenant Wright, pointing at the bookcase.

"Help yourself. Those are not mine," he replied without raising his head.

I walked over and went through the titles — about twenty romance novels, half a dozen military manuals, and more than ten copies of the Bible.

"Here you are," Wright said loudly and pushed the letter to the edge of the desk.

I returned to the chair, picked up the sheet, and read the slanted script.

March 2, 1953

To Whom It May Concern:

In the process of reregistration, we identified Feng Yan, who speaks English fluently, as someone who is unwilling to remain in the prison camp dominated by the Communists. He wants to go to Free China, and therefore we are sending him down to you. Please take good care of him.

Sincerely,
Second Lieutenant Timothy Wright

I was pleased by the letter, especially the last sentence. I folded it carefully and put it into my breast pocket while saying to Wright, "I can't thank you enough for this."

"I'm glad about the result too."

The interpreter put in, "So you're going to Cheju Island this afternoon. We've already made arrangements. You can board the boat heading that way."

"How come I never heard there was another camp for Chinese prisoners on Cheju?"

"It's on the southern end of the island, Camp 13," explained Wright.

Then another thought came to me. I said to him, "One more request before I go, may I?"

"Okay, if it's reasonable."

"Can you give me a Bible? In the Communist-controlled camp they won't let me read any religious books, but I want to study the Bible."

His large eyes lit up. Smiling, he told me, "Pick one then."

I went across to the bookcase and pulled out a chestnut copy, which was a Chinese-English parallel edition, vellum-bound and with a pink ribbon bookmark. I returned and put the book on the desk. "Can I take this one?"

"It's yours." He raised his chin and laughed. So did the interpreter.

"Thank you!" I said.

"Sure. You're free to go now."

When the guard had taken me out of the administration center, I caught sight of a young woman walking toward a medical ward. Viewed from behind, she looked familiar, and her russet hair, like a flaming torch, arrested my eyes as the memory of Dr. Greene flashed through my mind. I begged the guard, "Let me go and thank that doctor, all right? She saved my leg."

He nodded. "You have two minutes."

I ran to catch up with the woman, shouting, "Dr. Greene, Dr. Greene!" She turned around, but to my disappointment, she was a different person, with pink cheeks and wide-set eyes.

"I'm not a doctor, I'm a nurse," she told me pleasantly.

Panting hard, I said, "Do you know Dr. Greene? She operated on my leg." I moved my left foot forward as if this nurse knew my case.

"I've heard of her, but she'd gone back to the States when I came. Most doctors stay here only for a year." She smiled, her lips twisting a little.

"Sorry, I mistook you for her."

"It's all right."

Embarrassed, I went back to the guard, sighing and shaking my head. He took me to a tent full of people, Chinese, Koreans, and Americans, waiting for trucks to take them to the docks or the airport. The officer in charge of the POWs looked through the piece of paper the guard had handed him, then told me, "Go join those guys lying over there. You're going to the same camp with them."

I went over and picked a spot where I could sit down. Lounging against a wooden box filled with assorted nuts and bolts, I began leafing through the Bible, but I couldn't concentrate on the words, because from time to time a miserable feeling overcame me. I was devastated by the prospect that I might never be able to go home to take care of my mother and live with the woman I loved.

32. BACK TO CHEJU

Pusan at that time was the provisional capital of South Korea. In spite of its asphalt streets and neon signs, the city was squalid and crowded; yet the sight of strolling pedestrians and the stands overfilled with merchandise intensified my self-awareness as a captive. The Chinese words on numerous shop signs evoked my memories of China, while the smell of home cooking, a mixture of sautéed scallions and pork, wafted up, bringing me intense hunger pangs. The moment we came out of the downtown area, refugees appeared. There were so many of them that even the bushes and trees were draped with laundered clothing and diapers. Rows and clusters of tents, shacks, and huts sprawled in every direction; even the nearby hills were scattered with them. Many of the civilians wore olive drab clothes made out of American blankets. I was amazed that the Koreans used the army blankets for so many purposes — insulating rooms, making mattresses, unraveling them for the wool with which they knitted socks, shawls, sweaters, mittens, baby clothes. Some men and women just wrapped themselves in blankets, moving about like small mobile tents. I had heard that the North Korean POWs bartered blankets with civilians for dried fish, pickles, alcohol, and medicinal herbs, but never had I imagined the business had reached such a huge scale.

There were automobiles everywhere, but many of them, especially those driven by Koreans, were just rattletraps assembled with parts from American and Japanese models. On the hood of a jeep, parked under an acacia, sat a small Korean boy in a steel helmet, laughing noisily as some GIs gave him Coca-Cola to drink while teaching him how to curse in English. The area smelled awful, the air thick with a stench, an amalgam of carrion and human excrement.

The trip back to Cheju was relatively pleasant. Once the ship pulled out of the harbor, the air became fresh and invigorating. Along the coast clouds of smog were gliding slowly, and some freight trains crawled about like gigantic worms spewing dark smoke. The sea was calm toward evening as the setting sun cast its last rays on the greenish waves. I leaned against the railing at the bow and spotted a school of sharks, each five or six feet long. A few POWs rushed over to watch them, whooping and jabbering as the fish dashed away, blazing a phosphorescent trail. Except for that moment I stayed by myself all the way, reluctant to mix with others. I just watched the ocean, from whose surface small silvery fish skipped out time and again. We were allowed to spend our time on deck, though we had to return to the cabin when it got chilly at night. Because we were all supposed to be anti-Communists, the guards treated us prisoners less severely than before.

Toward midmorning the next day we arrived at Mosulpo, a tiny isle about a mile southwest of Cheju Island. As we approached the rocky shore, I saw some women in black suits and caps and large goggles diving in the bay to gather mussels, sea cucumbers, scallops, abalones, conchs. About a dozen large gourds floated on the water, to each of which was affixed a string bag for the catch. I was amazed that there was no man among them. The women looked cheerful, calling out and waving at one another from time to time. Some of them were not young, close to forty; I noticed their wrinkled chins and necks when their weather-beaten faces popped out of the water.

"*Haenyo,*" a Korean man said behind me, pointing at the women. The word, meaning "sea maids," must have come from Chinese originally. I was quite moved by the tranquil sight of the women, whose livelihood seemed unaffected by the war.

All of the twenty-seven Chinese POWs went directly to Enclosure 3 of Camp 13. I was struck by the enclosure's front entrance. It resembled a grand memorial archway, on top of which rose a pole like the apex of a spire. A Nationalist flag was flying high at the tip of the pole. All the four gate pillars, built of bricks and painted white, bore giant black words. The inner two declared STAMP OUT COMMUNISM and RECONSTRUCT OUR CHINA. Atop each of the pillars perched a weather vane, whose bar was spinning a pair of balls lazily. It turned out that the ten compounds in Enclosure 3 were ready to receive us. A few POW leaders stood at the front gate to meet the new arrivals. The American guards frisked us perfunctorily. I felt lucky that they didn't find the Bible in my satchel, though I knew they wouldn't necessarily confiscate such a book.

"Well, well, well, look who's here," said Wang Yong at the sight of me. He came over and held out his hand, smiling in a rather friendly way, his eyes half shut. Two beefy bodyguards stood behind him.

"How are you, Chief Wang?" I asked after shaking his hand.

"I'm good. Welcome back, Feng Yan."

The thought came to me that he must have requested his superiors to return me to his company. This realization unsettled me because he could be ruthless if offended. I had better take care to get along with him, or else he would make me suffer. I pulled Timothy Wright's letter out of my breast pocket and handed it to him, saying, "Here's my recommendation from the Pusan POW Collection Center."

He glanced through the letter and said, "I don't understand the foreign words. Tell me what it says."

"It's from Lieutenant Wright, who is in charge of registration at the Pusan center. He notifies you that I left the Communist camp because I want to go to Taiwan. He also asks you to take care of me." I forced a smile that tightened my jaw.

"Good. Keep this letter and don't lose it."

His bodyguards called him battalion

chief now, so I congratulated him on his promotion, which he said was just in name. Later I found out that he led the same number of men as before and his battalion was basically the former company. Together we entered Compound 8, all of which was under Wang Yong's charge.

He didn't send me to one of his three companies but instead kept me at the battalion headquarters. I stayed with his orderlies, bodyguards, the secretary, and the mess officer. The compound was in good order. The yard, the barracks, and the outhouse were all clean, and there was no garbage anywhere in sight; apparently the prisoners here spent a lot of time improving their living conditions. Also, they ate better than the year before. I wondered if the Nationalists in Taiwan had subsidized their board, but this turned out not to be the case. The prisoners had grown some crops on their own. I felt it rather eerie to rub shoulders with these men, many of whom donned self-made uniforms and peaked caps similar to those worn by the Nationalist soldiers. On each cap was a large insignia of the raying sun.

That evening I ran into my friend Bai Dajian, who had by mistake remained here. He was a little sturdier than before but had bloodshot eyes. We shook hands and I even shed a few tears, but he didn't seem overjoyed to see me, though his eyes were also wet with emotion. He said, "I heard you were coming this morning. How have you been since you left?"

"I'm all right." I meant to tell him how the Communists had sent me to Pusan in place of their own man, but I held my tongue, unsure how much he had changed. "Have they treated you well here?" I asked instead.

"Yes, they've been good to me."

There was some coldness in his manner. I couldn't tell whether it stemmed from his resentment at my leaving him behind at the screening the year before, or from our long separation, or from his association with these pro-Nationalists whose cause he might have adopted now. He seemed to have grown mentally and become more re-served, more independent, more sure of himself. Later I came to know he had often served as the interpreter of the battalion. His English was functional now; he had hardly been able to speak a coherent sentence when we parted. I was surprised that Wang Yong hadn't found a better English speaker. Per-haps Bai Dajian feared that my presence here might jeopardize his position.

I still dreaded Liu Tai-an, the vice chief of Compound 72 on Koje Island who had cut out Lin Wushen's heart. My fear was eased when I heard that he had left the prison the previous summer, having fulfilled his task of fighting the Communists in the camp. Ironically, he was in the Communists' hands now. The Americans had sent him on a special mission. After three months' training in Tokyo, he was airdropped into North Korea as an agent in the disguise of a Chinese officer, but no sooner had he landed there than the militia caught him. They handed him over to the headquarters of the Chinese People's Volunteer Army, where the interrogators identified him easily because they had kept a file on him. He was taken back to China and imprisoned in a suburb of Fushun City. Five years later, on June 24, 1958, he was executed publicly for murder, treason, and espionage for the United States. Some inmates in Enclosure 3 believed that it had been Han Shu, the chief here, who'd had Liu sent on the suicidal mission, because the two leaders hadn't gotten along and Han Shu had no longer needed Liu Tai-an's help after the pro-Communists were removed. Now with Liu's absence from the camp, I felt less frightened. As long as I stayed on good terms with Wang Yong, I should be safe.

Life here was simpler than in the pro-Communist camp. From time to time a fight would break out among the prisoners, but it was usually over trifles, such as a lost towel, a missing cigarette holder, a magazine torn accidentally. Not staying with the regular inmates, I didn't have to consort with them every day. Wang Yong gave me a desk and a chair made by the carpentry house in the enclosure, which were as good as those you could buy from a regular furniture store. He also issued me a washbasin, a crude iron bowl painted beige. it had been manufactured in the camp too, but it was handy and made me feel privileged. I was allowed to use the radio set in the battalion headquarters. Most prisoners would listen to the Voice of Free China in the evening, when it often commented on the situation in Korea. Several times it addressed us POWs directly, admonishing us to cooperate with our captors and remain loyal to the Nationalist cause. Once I heard Chiang Kai-shek speak on the radio and call on people in mainland China to rebel against the government.

Most prisoners here spent their days gambling, playing chess, cards, and mah-jongg. Some read booklets distributed by the Civil Information and Education Center and the Red Cross. Unlike the Communist-controlled camp, here you could read anything except books about Marxism and the Communist revolution. I spent more time reading the English part of the Bible, and the Chinese translation printed in the left-hand column on each page enabled me to figure out the meaning of any new word. The reading improved my English rapidly. I was glad I didn't have to peruse any newspaper in its entirety to glean information anymore. Newspapers were in regular supply here, mainly back issues of *Stars and Stripes*, and we had several Chinese magazines. Sometimes I came across a copy of the *New York Times*, always five or six weeks old. The prisoners were very fond of the Chinese magazine entitled *America*, which circulated widely in the enclosure. However, the most popular reading materials were the Montgomery Ward and Sears Roebuck catalogues. Besides the fancy merchandise advertised in them showing how Americans lived, there were also photos of women and girls in various outfits and postures. I guessed that this must account for the popularity of the catalogues. Every week a movie was shown in our battalion, and it was always enthusiastically received. I saw *Abe Lincoln in Illinois, Gone With the Wind, King Kong, The Good Earth,* and others.

At the education center there was a noncirculating album containing hundreds of newspaper and magazine clippings. Many inmates thumbed through this bulky book and talked about General MacArthur and General Ridgway. Some of them were impressed by the smooth-faced MacArthur, who, when visiting his troops, had often worn civvies, patent leather gloves, sunglasses, and even a woolen neck scarf; but some preferred General Ridgway, who had combat clothes on all the time, a first-aid kit attached to his left shoulder and a grenade to the right side of his chest, and a pistol and a pair of binoculars on his belt. As for myself, I disliked MacArthur, who often smiled complacently in the photos and obviously enjoyed the war, in which he seemed quite at home and comfortable — as if he were sitting in a stadium watching a game. Dressed in civvies, he looked like a nonparticipant in any battle, like someone who sat high above his men, reluctant to get his hands soiled. He seemed more like a senator than a warrior. The prisoners who worshiped him would disparage Ridgway, who they said was like a hick with a corrugated face and tired eyes. One day I got so impatient I asked them, "Look, as a soldier, under whose command would you like to fight, MacArthur's or Ridgway's?" None would choose MacArthur.

Although Ridgway looked like a peasant, he seemed like a very careful man who understood the soldiers' minds. The way he dressed demonstrated enormous care, confidence, and responsibility. It signaled to his men that he was one of them and would rush to the front when needed. The grenade at his chest emphasized his effectiveness as a warrior, whereas the first-aid kit at his left shoulder suggested his awareness of fatalities — the issue of casualties on his mind all the time. This kind of attention to minute details indicated that he was a responsible, conscientious commander. I never saw a picture in which Ridgway was smiling. His somber face seemed to betray a certain distaste for war.

The album also contained photographs of other celebrities. Among them was a thirtyish combat correspondent from the *New York Herald Tribune* named Margaret Hinton, a tall blonde with the looks of a second-rate movie actress — large vivid eyes, a narrow nose, permed hair, and flashing teeth. She always wore baggy fatigues, aviator sunglasses, tennis sneakers, and an oversize cap. One picture showed she was quite familiar with General MacArthur, whose hand casually rested on the small of her back. Articles about her said that she often got stories other reporters couldn't get and that she had traveled to the front and even slept with the troops on the Inchon beachhead. Wherever Miss Hinton appeared, she would attract gaggles of GIs who hadn't seen a pretty blonde for months. Her jeep was the most popular sight to the troops. She must have been a good reporter, having won a Pulitzer for journalism. She had returned to the United States long ago, but still suffered from bronchitis, acute sinusitis, and recurrent malaria, dysentery, and jaundice, all of which she had contracted during her war reporting. In one of her interviews, she claimed she would not marry until she found "a man who's as exciting as war." Having read those words, I felt sick at heart. For her, the war had been a publicity stunt, a game. She should have been given a rifle and made to fight like an infantryman so that she could undergo the physical suffering and taste the bitterness of betrayal, loss, and madness. One article even concluded: "Korea is her war." Who can bear the weight of a war? To witness is to make the truth known, but we must remember that most victims have no voice of their own, and that in bearing witness to their stories we must not appropriate them.

In our compound few men bothered me, because they knew Wang Yong had taken me under his wing. In return for Wang's protection, I had to do what he asked. I even wrote official letters for him. Compared with the pro-Communists, the pro-Nationalists cared more about formalities, so an official missive had to be elaborate and ostentatiously elegant. They always addressed a superior with his full title; among themselves they used various fraternal terms, like Elder Brother (even if the person addressed was a generation younger), Respectable Brother, and Benevolent Brother. I disliked this sort of decorum, which was feudalistic and ludicrous, but I was familiar with it and could compose the letters with ease. What's more, now that I was here, Wang Yong often took me along, instead of Dajian, when he met with the Americans. Once in a while he would lend me to the regimental headquarters, especially when foreign officials came to inspect the prison. I didn't want to hurt Dajian's feelings, but I had to obey the chief.

Crude and fearsome though Wang Yong was, he worshiped knowledge, especially that from books. Whenever he saw me reading the Bible, he'd cluck his tongue admiringly. He even got me a pocket English-Chinese dictionary, which helped me in my reading. We didn't have any money, so we couldn't buy a dictionary, but Wang Yong had obtained one from a Nationalist officer working for the United Nations here. The book had been published in Taiwan just two years before and had hardly been used at all. I signed my name on its title page and cherished it.

My reading speed had picked up, and now I could read ten pages of the Bible an hour. The progress pleased me greatly. I marked all the new words in pencil and reviewed them later on. Intuitively I felt I would benefit from my ability to use English, so I worked hard.

Outside the barbed wire, in the west, a few cherry trees were crowned with pinkish, fluffy blossoms. Beyond them stretched a dwarf orange grove whose fruit grew more visible week by week. Sometimes cuckoos would cry from the depths of the trees. Frequently as I tried, I never caught a glimpse of the birds. On occasion when I gazed at the grove, a few Mongolian ponies, piebald and bay, would appear, grazing and galloping at will. They were probably wild horses.

Though life was relatively safe here, it was not insulated from political struggle. Our peace of mind was often interrupted by sessions designed to intensify our hatred for the Communists, those Red Bandits. Study groups met regularly, and we were made to read Chiang Kai-shek's *China's Destiny* and Sun Yat-sen's booklet *The Three People's Principles* (referring to nationalism, democracy, and the people's livelihood). Every week we spent a day airing our grievances against Red China and the Soviet Union. The prisoners sat in rows, and one by one we talked about the crimes perpetrated by the Communists. Someone said his uncle had been executed only for selling a bit of opium on the streets. Another claimed that his parents' house, a stone mansion, had been confiscated by the village government, which later had it torn down, its stones used to build a dam at a reservoir. A man, obviously fond of drink, went so far as to claim that the Communists had shut down all the wineries in his hometown. The secretary of our battalion said his father, who had owned just ten acres of land, had been executed by the Communists as a landowner while he himself was serving in the Red Army. His superiors didn't tell him about the execution — they even changed the contents of a letter his sister had written him so as to keep him in the dark.

Story after story, the prisoners indeed had endless grievances. During these sessions, organized mostly by the Oppose-Communism-and-Resist-Russia Association, everyone had to say something to condemn the Reds. A thickset man once argued that on the whole the Communists were villains, but they had done a few good things, for instance banning opium, containing inflation, and treating women equally. The other inmates were furious, saying he was sympathetic toward the Commies, and at night some men got hold of him and beat him up. I felt that these men, though opposing Communism, had been so affected by the Red Army's indoctrination that they couldn't help acting like the Communists in some ways. They had banded together mainly because of their fear of the uncertain future. They had traveled too far on the anti-Communist road to retrace their steps. I suspected that in the eyes of the Nationalist government, they might not be trustworthy either, because they had served in the Red Army, thus having betrayed their original Nationalist masters.

One afternoon in the "airing grievances" session, the medic said something almost incredible, though there must have been some truth in the story. He told us: "When our former division suffered heavy casualties near Wonsan, we rushed over to evacuate the wounded men. There were hundreds of them lying on a hillside. I was naive and just went ahead bandaging those crying for help. But our director told us to check the insides of the men's jackets first. If the insignia of a hammer crossed by a sickle was there, that man must be shipped back immediately and given all medical help. So we followed his orders. All those men who had the secret sign in their jackets were Party members. We left behind lots of ordinary men like ourselves."

The audience remained silent for a good minute after he finished speaking. I knew the medic and didn't think he had made up the story. Wang Yong broke the silence: "The Reds used us like ammo. Look at the GIs, they all wear flak vests on the battleground. The U.S. government cares about their lives. How about us? What else were we wearing besides a cotton jacket? How many of our brothers could've survived if they'd put on the vests like the GIs? Recently I came across an article. It reports that General Ridgway says the U.S. forces could absolutely push the Communist armies all the way back to the Yalu, but he won't do that because he doesn't want to sacrifice thousands of his men. Just imagine: what if the People's Volunteer Army could drive the Americans down to the Pacific Ocean? Wouldn't Mao Zedong sacrifice every one of the Volunteers to accomplish that goal? You bet he would. Didn't he already send us here to be wasted like manure to fertilize Korean soil?"

"Down with Communism!" shouted a man.

The audience followed in one voice and thrust up their fists.

"Reseize the mainland!"

Hundreds of men roared in unison again.

Wang's analogy of us as human fertilizer revived thoughts I had been thinking for a long time. True enough, as Chinese, we genuinely felt that our lives were misused here, but as I have observed earlier, no matter how abysmal our situation was there were always others who had it worse. By now I understood why occasionally some Korean civilians were hostile to us. To them we had come here only to protect China's interests — by so doing, we couldn't help but ruin their homes, fields, and livelihoods. From their standpoint, if the Chinese army hadn't crossed the Yalu, millions of lives, both civilian and military, would have been saved. Of course, the United States would then have occupied all of Korea, forcing China to build defenses in Manchuria, which would have been much more costly than sending troops to fight in our neighboring country. As it was, the Koreans had taken the brunt of the destruction of this war, whereas we Chinese were here mainly to keep its flames away from our border. Or, as most of the POWs believed, perhaps rightly, we had served as cannon fodder for the Russians. It was true that the Koreans had started the war themselves, but a small country like theirs could only end up being a battleground for bigger powers. Whoever won this war, Korea would be a loser.

I also realized why some Koreans, especially those living south of the Thirty-eighth Parallel, seemed to prefer the American army to us. Not having enough food supplies or money, we had to press them for rice, sweet potatoes, any edibles, and sometimes we stole dried fish and chilies from under their eaves, grabbed crops from their fields and orchards, and even dug out their grain seeds to eat. By contrast, the Americans had everything they needed and didn't go to the civilians for necessities. Whenever the U.S. troops decamped, the local folks would rush to the site to pick up stuff discarded by them, such as telephone wires, shell boxes, cartridge cases, half-eaten bread, cans, soggy cigarettes, ruptured tires, used batteries. We thought we had come all the way to help the Koreans, but some of us had willy-nilly ended up their despoilers.

A big-boned man jumped up and declared, "I have lots of bitterness too." The prisoners had nicknamed him the Capitalist, because he raised a hen, for which, when it was a chick, he had exchanged four packs of cigarettes with a Korean peddler. He tethered the chicken to the back of his shed and fed it grass mainly. In the spring the hen began to lay, but it was so underfed that it could produce only one puny egg every other day. Its owner bartered the eggs for food with the cooks.

"Speak," Wang Yong ordered him.

"In Manchuria our company was detailed to load trains. We worked for a whole week carrying sacks of soybeans and peanuts into cargo wagons. I asked our company commander, 'Where's all this stuff going?' He said, 'Russia.' I asked, 'Why? Do they give us something in return?' He said, 'This is a way we show our affection for our Russian big brothers. They'll send us lots of machines in the future.' From then on we worked at the train station on and off for almost a year, but I never saw anything from Russia, not even a nail. Instead, we always shipped stuff to them. From this I reckon the Commies are just a bunch of traitors selling out our country."

After him, another man began talking about how he had been misled into a battle. He said huskily, "I'm a Chinese, but I'm no Volunteer. Before we came to Korea, our leaders told us the Americans were just paper tigers. They were afraid of night fighting. Their weapons were more advanced, but they didn't know how to do hand-to-hand combat. Compared with us, they were just pushovers. So we all wrote our pledges. One fellow promised he'd wipe out twenty GIs, another said he'd catch an officer alive, a colonel, and I said I'd blow up three tanks, because I was good at handling explosive satchels and bangalore torpedoes. Then when we came to Korea and got to the battlefields, all the men who'd written pledges were ordered to charge first. Our company commander said to me, 'Comrade Fan Long-yan, before the battle you volunteered to destroy three American tanks. Now it's time to honor your word.' I had no choice but to charge. That's how I lost my arm."

"Screw the Reds," Wang Yong said. "They always brag. Mao Zedong said the whole U.S. Seventh Fleet was a paper tiger. If that's true, how come the Reds don't dare to cross Taiwan Strait? Everybody can see that they're scared by the aircraft carriers stationed there."

"Yes, there's no way they can break the U.S. naval blockade," responded a man with a swarthy face.

"You can count on the fingers of one hand how many warships the Reds have," added another voice.

"And all those are as obsolete as their mothers' underpants," said a broad-cheeked fellow.

Laughter exploded from the audience. I couldn't help but laugh with them.

In these sessions I also spoke about the horror I had seen in the Red Army. Most of the time I talked about how the Communists valued equipment more than human lives. This sort of endless condemnation was rather crude compared with the way the Communists conducted their political education, in which they always managed to associate people's personal sufferings with the oppression of foreign imperialism, Chinese feudalism, and capitalism so as to amplify the hatred. Once the inmates here got on the track of voicing their grievances, they could no longer hold themselves back. All kinds of accusations were brought up, some of which were true, some groundless. By rule you had to say something, or you might be suspected of sympathizing with the Communists.

I always took care not to speak when a tape recorder was on, because some of the speeches were recorded for propaganda purposes. Deep inside, I felt the Communist government had been more responsible than the old regime; it had done some good things for the common citizens and made China a stronger country. At the same time, though, I dreaded the Communists and the way they controlled people's lives and minds.

There was another kind of political education here that was more harrowing to me. This was known as self- and mutual criticism. We were ordered to admit that one way or another we had helped the Reds and to confess whatever wrongdoing we had committed purposely or inadvertently. We had all served in the People's Liberation Army, so many men would touch on their past perfunctorily and no one would press them to confess. I was a special case, however, because for almost a year I had been away in the pro-Communist camp. Therefore, one morning in our shed, an entire session, attended by more than sixty men, was devoted to me alone. All kinds of questions were fired at me. What did you do in Camp 8? How active were you in the riot last October? What made you change your mind and come back? How can you convince us of your sincerity? Question after question, it was like attending a denunciation meeting.

I was overwhelmed, even as my mind was flooded with thoughts of my own. What's the difference between you people and the Communists? Where in the world can I ever be among my true comrades? Why am I always alone? When can I feel at home somewhere?

To my astonishment, Bai Dajian stood up, pointed at my nose, and declared in a gruff voice, "Brothers, I think this man is an agent working for the Reds."

I scrambled to ask, "Dajian, why are you doing this to me? We used to be good friends, didn't we?"

"You're not my friend anymore because you betrayed our Nationalist cause."

"Confess!" a voice commanded me.

"You're a Commie, aren't you?" another butted in.

"Come on, own up."

"Don't play dumb."

Wang Yong got up, came to the front, and stood beside me. He said, "Brothers, let's stop this dog-bite-dog business. I know how he returned to us. He showed me a letter of recommendation from an American officer based in Pusan. Feng Yan, do you still have it?"

"Yes, I have it here." I took the letter out of the inner pocket of my jacket.

"Read it to them," he said.

I read out the letter in English, then translated it into Chinese. That quieted them down. Still Dajian wouldn't let me off. He came up to me and said, "Show me the letter."

I handed it to him. He looked at it, but

to my surprise, he tore it up and dropped the pieces to the floor. He said through his teeth, "This is a hoax, a fabrication." His face had lost color and the finger stumps on his left hand were quivering.

I stood there speechless, not knowing how to respond. Why had he nursed such intense hatred of me? He used to be a gentle, diffident man. Why was he so hysterical now? He must have been hurt terribly when I left him. Then it dawned on me that he might still be a passive man, and that he was malicious because he regarded me as a rival.

Suddenly Wang Yong bellowed, "I do it to your mother, Bai Dajian! You dare to destroy a document from the top. I talked with the Pusan POW Collection Center before Feng Yan was sent down, and they told me he was coming to join us of his own free will. Everything was done officially, plain like a louse on a bald head. How can you say this was a fabricated letter? What blackened your heart so? Now, you go to the kitchen and stay in there for a week helping the cooks."

The audience rocked with laughter. A few men even applauded. Wang Yong came up to me and pulled up the front end of my shirt to reveal my tattoo. "Look, brothers," he said loudly, "the words we fixed on him are still here. This proves he's been on our side all the time, don't you think?"

"Yeah!" a voice rang out.

More people guffawed. It was lucky that I had shown Wang the tattoo a few days before. He went on, "True, Feng Yan made an awful mistake in leaving us last time, but we should give him a second chance, shouldn't we?"

"Yes, this is benevolence," remarked an older soldier.

"That's the word." The chief took it up. "We're different from the Reds. We must cherish our brotherhood and treat each other unselfishly so that we can unite with one heart and one mind. Brothers, you all know Stalin popped off a few weeks ago. It's time to prepare ourselves for the great cause of toppling the Communist world. We shouldn't just keep our field of vision within our small compound, biting and barking at each other like mad dogs. We must have the vision of a thousand miles so that we can fight all the way back to Beijing and then to Moscow."

"Yeah!" a few voices cried.

To be honest, I didn't fear this crowd all that much, because these were simpler, weaker men than the Communists. They cared more about personal relationships, especially brotherhood and group loyalty; they didn't share any concrete ideals and their actions had little consistency. I turned to face them and said: "Forgive me, brothers. I left you last year only because I had a sick old mother at home. She's very dear to me, and I'd be happy if I could remain with her till the end of her life. I'm her only child, so nobody will take care of her on the mainland. Now I'm afraid that the Reds will punish her because I'm here and going to Taiwan. Like every one of you, I can no longer fulfill my filial duty."

That silenced the crowd. A few men sighed. Somebody cursed the Communists loudly and the others followed suit.

I stole a glance at Dajian, whose cheeks somehow kept changing color, now pasty, now pinkish, now sallow. I interceded for him. "Chief Wang, please don't make Dajian do KP this time. He just got carried away. He must've been hurt by the Reds badly."

"He's a psycho. If he had an opinion, he could talk and argue, nobody would gag him. But he tore the official letter to bits like a madwoman on the street."

In the end, Dajian didn't have to work in

the kitchen. I was grateful to Wang Yong for coming to my rescue, but I also realized that in the long run, if I went to Taiwan, my one year's stay in the pro-Communist camp would remain a hidden reef in my life. There would be no way to free myself from suspicion. Anyone could invoke this problematic period of my past against me.

33. CONFUSION

There were three enclosures at Mosulpo, numbered 1, 2, and 3, which formed Camp 13. Each consisted of ten compounds, held about forty-seven hundred Chinese nonrepatriates, and had the same layout as Camp 8, which was thirty miles away to the northeast. Each compound within an enclosure was now called a battalion instead of a company and contained fewer than five hundred prisoners. That was why Wang Yong had become a battalion chief, though he led the same number of men. However, the gates to the compounds within an enclosure were not strictly guarded, and sometimes an inmate could slip into another battalion, since the GIs couldn't remember everyone's face.

The Americans treated these POWs more leniently than those in Camp 8. They provided them with vegetable seeds and fertilizers, encouraging them to grow sweet potatoes, cabbages, eggplants, tomatoes. The inmates could also gather seaweed and shellfish from the beach. So, though barley and corn were still the basic staples, the food here was better than what I had gotten used to eating in the pro-Communist camp. Some of the prisoners seemed to have gained a little weight. Owing to the absence of the Communists, the enclosures were peaceful on the whole. Classes were offered to illiterate inmates, and over twenty clubs had been formed, such as fellow townsmen's fraternities, mah-jongg leagues, gymnastic teams, a Catholic brotherhood, a calligraphy and painting society, a drivers' association. We had no access to automobiles, but there were a number of former drivers who offered lessons in auto mechanics and in driving skills. For the Chinese, the ability to drive a car was a professional accomplishment. On the battlefield, one headache for our army had been that we couldn't get abandoned American trucks back to our base because few of our men knew how to drive. Very often we ordered the captured GIs to move the vehicles for us, but most of them would say they couldn't handle a truck either. The truth was that they didn't want to be strafed and bombed by their own airplanes on the road.

Sports were popular here. Every company had its basketball and volleyball teams, and every battalion had a gymnastic team. We could go swimming, which I often did after lunch when others were napping. The beach, covered with black sand, was just a few steps from our compound, so when bathing we remained within the guards' view and hearing.

Life was kept as normal as possible here. Each of the three enclosures had its own newspaper, a two-sheet thing folded in the middle, the size of a regular book. It was handwritten, mimeographed, and published once a week; each issue had only some twenty copies for distribution, carrying four or five short articles. Enclosure 1's paper was entitled *Liberty Journal*, Enclosure 2's, *The Vanguard*, and Enclosure 3's, *Survival*. I was invited to contribute to them, but I never wrote anything. Our enclosure also had a theater, which was just a large platform; it regularly staged various local operas and classical dramas. Most of the plays were conventional, though there were propaganda pieces as well. Compared with the prisoners in Camp 8, these men were less enthusiastic about artistic creation, though there was no difficulty in assembling the talents from all the battalions for one project.

There was a madman named Jiafu in Enclosure 1. I had known him in Compound 72 on Koje Island, but at that time he had been sane and docile. Now he would go to the barbed-wire fence every morning, wailing, "I miss my parents. Don't let me die here!" The prisoners used to joke about him, but nowadays few would mention him without sighing. In the summer of 1951 his infantry regiment had moved to the front to fight the Americans. He hadn't seen action before and was scared. One day, his platoon commander rebuked him for carelessly taking off his camouflage, a wreath of tall grass around his head. Then the leader assigned Jiafu to gather firewood in a valley, where he came across a leaflet dropped by an enemy plane. It read: "Friends and Brothers — Please come over to us. We promise to send you to our rear base, where you can rest as long as you wish. We guarantee your personal safety, wholesome food and warm clothing — you will be treated like a U.N. soldier. Please stop wasting your lives for the Soviet Union and Communism. Remember, your families are waiting anxiously to see you back safe and sound."

At those words Jiafu sobbed and then went across to surrender to the Americans, having left behind his raincoat and burp gun. An interpreter came up to help interrogate him, but they couldn't extract much useful information from such a new recruit. He was honest with them, however, and admitted he had capitulated because he was afraid to die and longed for the comfort of their rear base. They said he had to work first. They wanted to send him to the front to broadcast to the Chinese position, but he wouldn't do it, insisting he was gun-shy. So they just shipped him directly to the Pusan POW Collection Center.

On arrival, at the sight of the prison, he blustered and made a scene, accusing the Americans of breaking their promise and not giving him freedom. Of course they wouldn't listen to him and just put him into the camp. Later, in Compound 72, again afraid of being killed, he agreed to go to Taiwan and had himself tattooed.

Never had I expected Jiafu would become such a wretch in this camp. He had gone insane the previous summer when all the pro-Nationalist prisoners arrived here and were ordered to construct enclosures and barracks for themselves. Apparently at that time the Americans treated them with little difference from the pro-Communists, so these nonrepatriates feared that they might never be able to reach Taiwan and even believed they could be delivered to Red China, which wasn't that far away — Tsingtao was just three hundred miles to the west. They even imagined that the Americans might mislead them onto ships and then send them back to the mainland. Their anxiety wasn't totally unjustified. Anything could happen at the Panmunjom talks, and the United States could hand them back to China at any time if there was enough to gain from their repatriation. So all the fourteen thousand prisoners were terrified by the prospect; dreading the Communists' retaliation, some of them planned to drown themselves together in the ocean if they were forced to board ships. Some suggested that if worse came to worst, they would break prison and flee to Mount Halla, where they could live as guerrillas. Many began to make spears, knives, and cudgels. Indeed those first few months here were the nadir of their life in captivity. Several men attempted suicide — one of them plunged headlong into a latrine to drown himself, but he was saved by his fellow townsmen. They looked after him, and he recovered from his depression half a year later. It was during this time that Jiafu went crazy too, but unlike the others, he never regained his sanity.

Sometimes when I passed Enclosure 1, I would stop to speak to him. He had such a vacant face that he must surely have lost his memory, though he still remembered his birthplace and his family, calling to his parents as if they were somewhere nearby. On his forehead was a tattooed Nationalist emblem like a black sunflower. Whenever you asked him whether he wanted to go to Taiwan or the mainland, he would shake his head and croak, "Send me to Haicheng." That was his hometown in Manchuria.

I missed home terribly too. I had written to my fiancée only once since I'd been taken prisoner. Near the compound gate a metal mailbox hung on a pole; yet few men would drop letters into it because most POWs had adopted aliases and believed that both the American and the Chinese authorities would monitor our mail. We were afraid of implicating our families, who would be made to suffer for their sons' staying in the pro-Nationalist camp and refusing to return. It would be better if the government classified us as "missing in action," so that our families could benefit from our absence — by rule they would be treated as Revolutionary Martyrs' families.

In the Communist-dominated camp, the prisoners didn't write home either, mainly because they feared that the Americans would open the mail and find out their true identities. Here, once in a while, an inmate did slip a letter into the mailbox, but often with a nicknamed sender on the envelope, such as Second Ox or Little Pillar or Mountain Boy, to reduce the risk of being identified. Naturally none of us had ever heard from home; nor did we know if our mail had ever reached our families. Through our contact with the Americans, we knew they received letters and parcels regularly. How we envied them!

Whenever I was alone, I would think about how to return to China. I didn't believe the Nationalist army could ever defeat the Communists and regain control of the mainland. I had seen how the People's Liberation Army had crushed them in the civil war. Although they were equipped with American weaponry and originally had more manpower, they were no match for the Communists, who had mustered the people's support. In all probability red flags would be flying over Taiwan in the near future.

I hadn't changed my mind about going

home, but I just couldn't figure out a way. For a whole spring and summer the men in my compound talked about Taiwan, a place none of them had ever been to but had learned about through reading magazines. They imagined the restaurants and theaters they would patronize once they got there. Now the end of the war was imminent, and we all could feel it. Since April, groups of crippled POWs, as reported in the newspapers, had been returned to North Korea and mainland China. This might herald the final departure of all the prisoners.

In late June we heard that the South Korean guards at the camps in the Pusan area had set free twenty-seven thousand Korean nonrepatriates. In just one night all those POWs had vanished among the civilians. Enraged, the Chinese and the North Korean armies launched a major attack on the positions held by the South Korean army and devastated their lines. The release of those prisoners, however, inspired the inmates here, who began to demand to be freed in the same way so that they wouldn't have to face repatriation. The prison authorities ignored the demand, so the prisoners went on a hunger strike, which didn't last long because Father Hu, who often came to the camps to preach, mediated for the United Nations and assured us that we would never be delivered into the Communists' hands. He said this was a matter of principle for the Americans, who respected human rights. Still, three inmates in Enclosure 2 were so depressed and so tired of the long wait that they hanged themselves. I could see that these men dreaded the reprisals in store for them and would do anything to avoid going home.

Toward the end of July, word came that the armistice had been signed at Panmunjom. The war was finally over; this meant our imprisonment would end soon. Again the inmates were tossed into a great tumult, terrified by the possibility of repatriation. But I was on edge for a different reason: if I couldn't find a way back to China, I might have to depart for Taiwan with these men.

Then it was said that all the POWs would be sent to the Korean mainland again to go through the final screening called "the persuasion." This frightened the prisoners, who would do anything to avoid reentering the Iron Curtain. Many of them began talking about a massive demonstration. A few even offered to kill themselves, since they'd be killed anyway if they were returned to Red China. Some planned to jump into the ocean if they were forced to board ships heading that way.

But before any drastic action took place, there came Chiang Kai-shek's letter, read by himself on the radio and broadcast through amplifiers all over the camp. In an elderly voice the generalissimo urged us to trust the United Nations' arrangements, and he promised to bring us to Taiwan safely. The next day we were each given a Nationalist flag, on whose back was printed Chiang's letter in its entirety. He instructed us:

> In order to realize your freedom, you must endure the next few months and must cooperate with the U.N. authorities. In the meantime, your compatriots in Free China will join forces with you to bring about your final liberation. I shall personally see to this matter and ascertain that the United Nations will abide by its principle of respecting the POWs' choice for freedom. In addition, I shall make the United Nations adhere to its promise that it will not send you anywhere against your will, so that you can come to Taiwan, the true China. . . .

This letter pacified the prisoners, though it made me all the more anxious because I wanted to go home. Yet home seemed ominous now — I was unsure what would happen to me if I went back. If only there were a third choice so that I could disentangle myself from the fracas between the Communists and the Nationalists.

In mid-August we heard that many POWs in Camp 8 had left Cheju for China. This meant we might have to depart soon. A recent issue of *News World*, a weekly published in Hong Kong, showed some pictures of Korean women prisoners burning their mats and blankets before they started out for the North. Here the prison authorities informed us that we, the nonrepatriates, would be sent to a place near Kaesong called the Neutral Zone, where we would stay for three months to go through the final persuasion. The Communists insisted that many of us had been coerced into choosing Taiwan, so they wanted us to listen to their representatives explain their policy regarding the returned captives.

Although the Neutral Zone would be guarded by troops from India, a nonaligned country, this news caused a stir here. The prisoners all knew that the Communists were skilled in psychological attacks. Just showing your face to them would give rise to a good deal of consternation, because they could identify you and make your family and relatives back in China suffer. So unrest again spread among the prisoners. What's worse, the Neutral Zone was so close to the Communist army's position, just two miles away, that their forces might storm the camp and wipe us out. Actually they wouldn't have to enter the zone; just an artillery barrage could do the job.

Back on Koje Island I had thought that some of these pro-Nationalists wrote petitions in their blood just for theatrical effect; now I could see that they truly dreaded the Communists, who in their eyes were savage beasts. Many men, encouraged by their leaders, voiced their determination not to set foot on the Korean mainland again. A petition, signed by thousands of men with their blood, was delivered to Colonel Wilson, the commandant at Camp 13, stating that the POWs would fight to the death before submitting to being moved north to listen to the Communists' persuasion. The Americans were disconcerted, and a deadlock ensued.

Then two officers in the Nationalist

army flew in from Taiwan. Secretly they talked to the POW leaders and convinced them to participate in the persuasion after promising them that every prisoner here would get to Taiwan safely. The leaders gave in readily; this was an opportunity to please their future bosses. When they told the rank and file about the inevitable trip, grumbles started rising in the camp, though nobody challenged the decision openly.

To appease the regular prisoners, the leaders took several measures to sabotage the Communists' last-ditch attempt to salvage their loss. The fact that so many men had chosen Taiwan over the mainland must have been a slap in the face to the Chinese government, so its representatives, the persuaders, would make every effort to bring back as many POWs as possible. For a whole week our compound was engaged in mock persuasions, in which some men played the roles of the Communist persuaders, the American observers, and the neutral nations' arbitrators. These rehearsals were mainly meant to prevent the illiterate ones from fumbling at the interview. We were all shown where we'd sit in a persuasion tent, how far away from us the Communist persuaders would be seated, what questions they'd ask us, how we should answer, and how, if rules were violated, we could get help from the arbitrators sitting close by. After the prisoners went through the faked interviews, most of them calmed down. But I was more agitated than before, still wondering how to squirm out of this plight. Whatever happened, I must return to my mother and Julan.

Gradually the mock persuasions evolved into exercises for humiliating the Communists. The leaders had slogans prepared and trained us to insult and curse the persuaders. We were told to berate them freely and that as long as we didn't hurt them physically, there would be no problem. The battalion even held a few spitting sessions, teaching the men how to bring up chunks of phlegm and spit at the Communists accurately. Besides these rehearsals, a cruel tactic was devised, called the Chain Protection, which should have been named the Collective Punishment. The leaders split the inmates into groups of three or four; if one of the men broke his vow and chose mainland China, everybody in the group would be punished. This applied mainly to the regular prisoners, not to the officers, and only our enclosure imple-

mented the Chain Protection. As an interpreter, I was not chained to anyone. Wang
Yong seemed to trust me.

In late August a group of officials from
Taiwan came to see us, but they were not
allowed to enter any compound, so we met
them only at the gate. Toward evening,
through the amplifiers, they spoke to us,
giving advice and warnings. One of them
claimed that the Communists had already
executed many returned POWs. The head
of the delegation said to us:

"When we met today, it became clear to
me that you had all been oppressed like
slaves by the Communists. Why can't we
shake hands and hug one another today?
Why are we not allowed to enter your barracks? Why do we have to strain our voices
to speak through layers of barbed wire between us? All this is due to the Communists, who mean to keep you here forever.
We must remember this and settle accounts with them one of these days . . .
Brothers and friends, Generalissimo
Chiang cares about your well-being deeply.
You're all anti-Communist heroes and
pillars of our nation, so he sent us here to
convey his best wishes to you. He invites
you to come to Taiwan and join us in our
great cause of fighting Communism. After

you arrive, you all can follow your aspirations — you can attend colleges, or continue your military service, or pursue any honorable profession. I assure you that we will do everything to facilitate your way to success."

He coughed dryly to clear his throat and continued: "Soon you will set out for the Neutral Zone, where the Communists will try every trick to lure you back to them. This will be the most crucial point in your lives, so please keep your minds clear and don't agree to return to the mainland. To tell the truth, if you yield to the Reds, they will practice the Policy of Three Heads on you. What's that? you may wonder. Let me explain. First, they will nod their *heads* smiling at you. Second, the moment you leave the Neutral Zone and enter their territory, they will make you hang your *heads* to confess your 'crimes.' Third, when you have crossed the Yalu, they will chop off your *heads*. That's their Three Heads Policy, which is already being implemented. Brothers and friends, don't be taken in by them. Come join us. We'll always treat you benevolently like blood siblings. With our joint effort we shall prevail and retake China."

The officials brought us a lot of gifts.

Every prisoner got a picture of Chiang Kai-shek, a T-shirt with the Nationalist flag printed on its front, a woolen overcoat, a canvas satchel, a box of sugar cubes, two cans — one of stewed pork and the other of pear halves in syrup — and five ounces of green tea wrapped in a plastic bag. In addition, each enclosure was given basketballs, soccer balls, volleyballs, books, pens, magazines, drums, gongs, cymbals, bugles, horns, three dozen sets of playing cards, and chess sets. There were also four bolts of white cloth bearing over 100,000 civilians' signatures expressing their support for the inmates' cause.

Many of the prisoners were overwhelmed by the gifts. Some even wept while chewing bonbons and drinking hot tea, which we hadn't tasted for more than two years. Some said they would never forget the generalissimo's kindness and generosity. What a difference this was from the Communists, who just forced you to charge at the enemy while feeding you like cattle. The inmates talked on and on; everyone was intoxicated. Then to make themselves look more like the Nationalist warriors, some had their heads shaved bald. Within a week we all got rid of our hair.

I tried to remain levelheaded, knowing the Nationalists well, though I too enjoyed their gifts. The truth was that they badly needed men for their army, whereas the Communists had millions of troops and the largest reserve of manpower in the world. That made the two sides treat the POWs differently. I daresay it was the desperate straits the Nationalists were in that forced them to value the prisoners much more. By contrast, the Communists wanted us back mainly to save face.

If only I had known more about the business of the persuasion. Then I might have worked out a plan. Despite longing for my homeland, I was unsure if the Communists would ever absolve me from blame. How could I explain to them my return to this pro-Nationalist camp? I didn't even know whether Commissar Pei and Ming were still alive. If they were dead, it would be impossible to defend myself. On the other hand, if I went to Taiwan, I wouldn't be able to ease my guilty conscience either. How could I let my mother and my fiancée suffer for me while I lived abroad in peace and safety? The harder I tried to think of a way out, the more disappointed I became. My mind was in turmoil, though I had to appear cheerful. I spent more time reading the Bible to curb my apprehension, particularly the Book of Ecclesiastes, which I read repeatedly and which deepened my sense of human futility. These pages calmed me down and taught me that even though I couldn't find a solution now, it didn't mean there wasn't one. I must be patient and learn to resign myself to waiting. There is a time for effort and a time for repose; a time for knowledge and a time for ignorance. At present all I could do was wait with an alert mind.

34. A GOOD COMPANION

That summer I grew attached to Blackie, a dog that roamed our compound. Though people began to think of me as his owner, I could hardly take care of him. A dog doesn't eat grass like a chicken, so I couldn't feed him and he had to look for food on his own. All I could do was fill a chipped crock with water for him. Whenever possible, he'd steal a bite from the kitchen, where some of the cooks would threaten him and even thrash him with a broom.

There were a good number of animals in Camp 13. Our kitchen raised a pig and a dozen chickens. We often heard hens cackle, but had never seen an egg drop in our soup. Apparently the leaders and the cooks ate them. Several inmates each raised a chicken themselves and bartered eggs for things they needed. One man even kept a small nanny goat that wasn't old enough to give milk yet, but he didn't have her for long — the animal got out of the camp one day and didn't return. We guessed she must have been killed or shut away by some civilian. Her owner was devastated and for days waited in vain at the front gate, expecting her to reappear.

Blackie had wandered into our closure the previous winter and stayed. He must have felt safe in the camp, because he wasn't a strong dog; somewhat stunted, he couldn't fight the wild dogs in the marshes. Besides, the Koreans loved dog meat and wouldn't think twice about catching and killing a stray dog. The prisoners called him Blackie on account of his dark coat. He was small in size and almost devoid of fur, scarred in places, but he had a fluffy tail and white eyebrows like a pair of moths. Some men believed he was a Japanese pointer and some said he was a Chinese retriever. I'm not sure what he was, maybe a hybrid. I often patted and stroked Blackie, who enjoyed being touched, and any expression of human affection seemed to give him intense pleasure. Sometimes I would beg the young cook named Nanshan to give him some leftovers — half a sweet potato or a ball of stale barley. Like the inmates, Blackie was undernourished, his ribs showed sharply, and he always seemed hungry, hanging around the mess lines at mealtimes and licking up spots of spilled soup.

As I spent more time with him, he seemed to acknowledge a special bond between us, following me whenever I was in his view. He'd trot beside me with an air of some importance. I was glad to have him around. Before Blackie, I had never really liked any animal, but now my thoughts would turn to him first thing in the morning when I woke up. I wouldn't let him get out of the camp, fearing he might go astray. Whenever I returned from swimming, he would prance at me, whining with such happiness that I would be moved to caress his lop-eared head or squat down to play with him for a while. He would roll on the ground or lie on his back with his paws held back for me to poke his belly, which I would do. Sometimes he nuzzled my face and sniffed at my hand as though eager to get something tasty from me. He made me realize that none of us, the POWs, could ever have his kind of simple pleasure and genuine trust in a man. This realization made me treat him more like a friend, who evoked in me a tenderness that I dared not feel toward anyone around me for fear of embarrassment and betrayal. For this beneficent influence I was grateful. I promised him that I would feed him a lot of meat once we were free.

Most prisoners called Blackie by whistling, at which he would run to them, wagging his tail. If he recognized the man, he'd leap up and place his paws on him, expecting to be stroked. He was such a friendly dog; he seemed to know only the goodness of man.

One night in early August Blackie sneaked through the fence and didn't come back. I searched here and there within the enclosure but couldn't find him. I was afraid some Korean might have kept him or even slaughtered him. Blackie was a grown male now and might have been in rut. To my knowledge there weren't many dogs around the camp. He would have to go a long way to a fishing hamlet beyond a lagoon to find a bitch, and those fishermen wouldn't hesitate to butcher him if they caught him. I waited and waited that night, but he didn't return.

Some men said I had spoiled Blackie, who should have been gelded long ago. I told myself that if he came back, I must take measures to stop him from chasing bitches, or there would be endless trouble.

Early the next morning, my eyes still heavy with sleep, I heard a dog yapping. I jumped out of bed and rushed out. There was Blackie, his scanty fur soaked with dew, prancing around Nanshan, the round-faced cook, who was kicking a shuttlecock like a schoolboy at recess. I whistled and Blackie stopped short, then scampered all the way to me, wagging his tail and whining loudly. He reared up and put his paws on me, licking my hand and belly while his expressive eyes glistened. I noticed a gash on his rump, about two inches long, though the bleeding had stopped. The wound must have been inflicted by a pitchfork. Without delay I took him to the medic, who sterilized the cut with iodine solution and applied some antibiotic ointment to it.

I didn't have the dog neutered, of course. I just couldn't do that, although a fellow who had once been a goat castrator volunteered to do the job. Instead, I got a rope, about thirty feet long, and tied it around Blackie's neck so that I could keep him from running out of the compound. But for the protest of some shed mates who said Blackie had fleas, I would have cut a hole in our door to let him in and stay with me at night. Every night before going to bed, I would tether him to a young poplar. Asleep with his head resting on his front legs, he seemed at home within the confinement. Also, I set a large wooden box on its side against the tree and roofed it with a piece of asphalt felt held down by two rocks. When it was windy or rainy, Blackie would lie curled up in the straw in this makeshift kennel. If I forgot to leash him at night, he would invariably sneak out of the prison. He was a clever dog and always managed to return soon after daybreak.

As we were preparing to leave for the Korean mainland for the final persuasion, I began to worry about him. We were not allowed to bring any animals with us, but if I left him behind he might soon perish, because he'd have to go to the civilians' homes or the airfield to steal food. I wouldn't have minded if a GI had adopted him; the Americans could always feed their pets. Wang Yong told me to abandon the dog. "It's just a dumb animal," he said. "Let it go, all right? We have enough humans to take care of." I knew he'd get rid of Blackie without a second thought.

Desperate, I went to the kitchen and talked to Nanshan, who was in the habit of feeding the dog. I begged him, "Can you take Blackie along when we're headed for the Neutral Zone?"

"I'll try, but what if he barks?"

"I don't know. I just want to keep him as

long as I can. If that happens, I won't blame you."

"Officer Feng, you have a kind heart like the Buddha's. Whatever you say I'll do."

His effusive words amazed me.

Nanshan kept his promise. He got some sleeping pills from the medic and ground them. Before we boarded the ship, he hid Blackie in a field cauldron. He broke a potato in half and smeared both pieces with the sleeping powder and fed them to Blackie. Soon the dog dropped off to sleep. Nanshan covered him with an empty gunnysack, and so Blackie passed the guards undiscovered.

35. IN THE DEMILITARIZED ZONE

On September 10, 1953, we arrived at Pusan, and from there we headed for the Neutral Zone, which was also called the Demilitarized Zone. It was in an immense enclosure outside a small town named Munsanni, just a few miles south of Kaesong. The town had been partly leveled by bombs; a few houses still stood with naked walls, but most of the roofs were gone. When we entered the camp on the sixteenth, the persuasion had been under way for days. The zone was guarded by Indian troops, and the governing body comprised people from other countries as well, such as Poland, Sweden, Czechoslovakia, and Switzerland. There were many representatives from the United Nations, North Korea, and mainland China. We were told that we should expect to stay at least twelve weeks in our new barracks, Compound 21.

Why so long? We were upset and bewildered.

The camp here consisted of about forty

compounds, thirty-three of which held the Chinese POWs. We ate better food now: breakfast was barley porridge boiled in dry milk, and for lunch and dinner we had rice mixed with peas or soybeans, and there were also potatoes and cabbages. Each man now received more cigarettes, one pack every other day.

In the east, toward the Imjin River, stretched an orchard, whose apple and pear trees had all shed their leaves, their branches often bearded by hoarfrost in the morning. In the west rose a hill, treeless but covered with tall grass and teeming with ring-necked pheasants. We often gathered along the barbed-wire fence to watch the birds fly up and away with fluty cackles. From the distance the males' iridescent plumage glittered in the sunlight like tiny explosions and often brought out shouts among us. How we wished we could have gone hunting for them. The soil was dark and rich here, but the fields were deserted, pockmarked by bombs. Still, there must have been some grains, grass seeds, and berries in the wilderness for the birds to eat. The pheasants, unlike human beings, seemed to have multiplied thanks to the war.

Our compound had obviously been inhabited by troops before, because there were bunks instead of plank beds inside the tents. The Indian guards, often armed with lathis, treated us decently on the whole. On the day of our arrival, they even offered us each a cup of coffee and a chocolate. But they guarded the gate so strictly that nobody could get out of the compound without official permission. As a result, all the battalions were isolated from one another. If somebody was sick and had to go to the hospital, which was within the Demilitarized Zone, two or three guards would escort him. On the other hand, the Indian authorities allowed the representatives from China to broadcast to us for three hours on end every day. Some of the persuaders went so far as to threaten us, saying, "Think about your families, who are all on the mainland. You should at least come home for them." Their words intimidated the prisoners so much that many men in our battalion refused to meet with the Communist persuaders. Wang Yong got furious and assigned some men to pound on two upended oil drums with sticks to drown out the broadcasting, but this just produced more din and we still could hear snatches of the speeches. So he ordered his bodyguards to smash the amplifiers at the tips of the tall poles, and they knocked them out with stones. The Indians never had them repaired.

Wang Yong was desperate to communicate with the other compounds after several attempts had failed. One day someone suggested using Blackie to carry messages to Compound 22, which was about one hundred yards to the south. So they got hold of the dog, tied a letter around his neck, and pushed him out through a hole in the fence near the gate. Blackie was a successful messenger, since some prisoners in Compound 22 knew him and he would respond to their whistling. But the guards noticed his missions from the very beginning. I was worried about his safety and begged the secretary not to write any more messages on white paper, which was too eye-catching.

Nanshan had by now replaced me as the owner of Blackie, which I didn't mind, because I might not be able to bring the dog along if I ended up being repatriated. The boy could take better care of him; he could feed him and had already persuaded the other cooks to let Blackie snuggle in a corner of the kitchen. I was pleased that Nanshan loved the dog so.

One night Blackie went out on an errand

and didn't return. I thought he might have gotten randy again, but he couldn't possibly have escaped from the zone, in which, to my knowledge, there wasn't another dog. Both Nanshan and I waited late into the night for him to come back. At about two a.m. I was too exhausted to stay up any longer and went to bed.

Nanshan went to the gate alone the next morning to talk to the Indian guards. He couldn't speak English but pleaded with a lieutenant in Chinese, "Please, please tell me where Blackie is!" The thick-bearded officer kept shaking his head as I approached them. In desperation the boy, assuming they really couldn't make out what he was trying to say, began barking and got down on all fours like a dog. The Indians burst out laughing.

I went up to the officer and asked him if they had seen Blackie. He rolled his gray eyes and told me matter-of-factly, "That dog was a secret courier, so we had him executed."

I told Nanshan, "They killed him."

At those words the boy sprang at the officer, wielding his small fists, but I restrained him in spite of my own tears and dragged him back to our barracks. Together we wept in the kitchen.

When the same bearded lieutenant came in to do the head count that evening, two inmates suddenly lunged at him, each holding a brick. The officer tore away toward the fence while more men pursued him, some brandishing short clubs. They all looked murderous. I was so shocked that I didn't know what to do. I wouldn't have minded if they'd roughed him up some, but killing him might bring disaster on ourselves. Fortunately, before they could corner him, a squad of Indian guards rushed over from the other side of the fence, raised their rifles, and pulled the bolts. So the prisoners let him go.

Blackie's death disrupted our communication with the outside, but except for Nanshan and me, most inmates forgot the dog in a matter of days. Their attempt on the Indian officer's life in fact had little to do with vengeance. Uncertain of their future, most of them were desperate and irascible; they had seized the occasion to vent their emotions.

Wang Yong assigned Dajian and me a job: to talk with the Indian soldiers as often as possible, gather information about the persuasion, and report it to him in the evenings. He issued each of us some extra cigarettes for the job. So every day I tried to approach the guards and chat with them. From them I began to get a better picture of our situation, about which, unfortunately, the more we learned, the more disheartened we became. Two Chinese divisions were less than three miles away in the north. If they attacked, the Imjin River would block our retreat. Furthermore, the Indians who ran the Demilitarized Zone seemed partial to the Communists and might connive with them to send us back to the mainland. We estimated that our chances of reaching Taiwan were at most fifty-fifty. One afternoon, while talking with an Indian officer, I heard something I had never thought of before. The square-chinned man told me that if you were reluctant to go to either mainland China or Taiwan, you could apply for a third country. "Where is that, Chuck?" I asked him, not knowing his last name. His men called him Officer D.

He fluttered his pomfret eyes and said in a nasal accent, "Like India, Brazil, or Argentina."

"Are you sure?"

"Positively." He stressed the third syllable of the word in a chipper voice. "There's already a group of such POWs, you know." He touched his green turban, his hand holding a cigarette I'd given him.

"How big is this group?"

"Seven or eight people."

"What are they going to do in those countries?"

"I don't know. There'll be jobs for them for sure."

"Like what?"

"That'll depend on what skills they have."

This information set my mind spinning for the rest of the day. For better or worse I must not go to Taiwan, because that would amount to declaring I was an enemy of the Communists, who would definitely punish my mother and my fiancée for that. On the other hand, unless I could free myself from the suspicion of treason, I shouldn't return to the mainland either, where a person with my background and my association with the pro-Nationalists might be kept under surveillance all the time, if not re-imprisoned. If I knew for sure that Pei Shan and Chang Ming were back in China, I might take the risk, because they might help clear me. But again, how could I be certain they'd be willing to save a man like me? They had already meant to sacrifice me once, hadn't they? By comparison, a third country would be a better choice, though I had no idea what kind of life I'd lead there. And I wasn't even sure if I could survive in a foreign land.

But wouldn't the Communists hurt my mother and Julan if I went to another country? They might not, because I didn't mean to be their enemy. Perhaps I was naive, but I was driven by the instinct for self-preservation and felt that a third country would be a better destination for a man like me, who had often been an outsider and couldn't fit in any political group among my compatriots. Once I settled down in a foreign land, I would send for my mother and Julan. But would the Communists let them leave and join me? They might or might not. Still, a third country seemed to be the best choice, a risk I was willing to take.

The next question was where I should go. Brazil and Argentina would be difficult because I spoke neither Portuguese nor Spanish. Although English was used in India, it was a country with a large population and a high unemployment rate, where I had heard there was the caste system. If I went there, I would almost certainly live at the bottom of society. Was there another neutral English-speaking country where I might go? This would be the first question

I would ask when I was summoned to listen to the persuasion. I would avoid talking with the persuaders from China and instead speak to the arbitrators directly in English. If there wasn't another country, maybe I would go to Brazil, which was vast and might have more space and more opportunities to make a living. I wouldn't mind subsisting as a drudge for some years; I was still young and should be able to restart my life. On the other hand, I would have to prepare to be a solitary man without a country, condemned to speak a language in which I could never feel at home.

Although I had now made up my mind, I grew more nervous, and a numbing feeling kept rising to my throat, which I had to tamp down continually. That evening I drank a cup of rice wine with the mess officer, trying to calm down before I went to the battalion headquarters to give the daily report. When I relayed to Wang Yong the information I had collected that day, I didn't mention that some neutral countries would also accept POWs. I was afraid he might suspect me. I just informed him that the Communists' persuasion was a total fiasco — as the Indian officer had told me, to date they had persuaded only about eighty men to go home.

The next evening two fellows from another compound who had just gone through the persuasion came to speak to us. We gathered in our largest tent, sitting in front of a table at which the two men were seated. The first speaker was quite handsome, with a thin nose and sparkling eyes. He was tall but slightly hunched. He started:

"Brothers, when my name is called, two Indian guards come up and take me to the fifteenth tent. Lots of people are in there, from different countries. At one glance I can tell who the Reds are. They stand up, smiling and bowing at me like Pekinese. One of them says, 'Dear Comrade, we represent our motherland to welcome you back.'

"I spit on his face and say, 'You can't represent China, you work for Russia. Why should I listen to you?'

"They continue to smile at me after I sit down. Another of them says, 'Comrade Wan Ping-han, your parents are waiting for you to come home. They're heartbroken, crying day and night.'

" 'Screw your grandma!' I yell. 'You Commies beheaded my dad five years ago. My mom wept herself blind and died three months later. Now you have the gumption to tell me they're still alive and miss me!'

" 'Think about this' — the man won't give up — 'you're a good son of China. When I mentioned your parents, I meant the millions of Chinese people of the older generation who expect you to come home.'

"That drives me mad. I jump up, fish some plaster powder out of my pocket and throw it on his face. While he's screaming and rubbing his eyes, I grab the folding chair I was sitting on and hit him with all my might. *Thwack, thwack, thwack* — the Indian guards rush over and drag me away."

Applause broke out. A man shouted, "Fight the Red bandits to death!" We all raised our fists and repeated the slogan.

He yelled again, "Long live Generalissimo Chiang!" We echoed him once more.

Then the other man began to speak. He had a carbuncular face, protruding teeth, a stout nose, and erect ears. He talked in a heavy Hunan accent that brought to mind Mao Zedong's. He told us: "It's a long wait at the rest area outside the tents. When I'm called, they lead me into a tent. The Commies look awful in the company of the men from the other countries. They're like a pack of hungry wolves. Behind them I see through the window more than ten trucks planted with red flags. This sight scares me. Beyond the trucks stands a tall gate with the words *Back into the Arms of Our Motherland* written on the arch. They have obviously planned to ship us back load after load. As I sit down, one of them puts his index finger on the table, leans forward, and says, 'Comrade, you must've suffered a great deal in the enemy's hands. We represent our motherland coming to rescue you. You're a free man now. Please return to China with us.'

"The word 'comrade' sets my heart kicking and reminds me of so much hatred, but I get ahold of myself. 'Actually I didn't suffer that much in the prison camp,' I tell him. 'The Americans have given me food and clothes. It was in your Communist army that I tasted real bitterness. You always treated me like a beast of burden, like gun fodder, and you just used me.'

" 'Comrade, on my word of honor, you will be a free man, free to do anything in our country. You can continue to serve as an officer, or go home to take care of your parents, or live and work in a city. Comrade, think —'

"I lose my temper at last, knowing he's a

big liar. I shout, 'I'm not a comrade of yours. Don't treat me like I'm an idiot. I know you all lie without batting an eye, you damned Russia lovers. I fuck your mothers and grandmothers!' I turn to the Swiss arbitrator and declare in a shout, 'I want to go to Free China.'

"The foreign man nods at me and then talks to the interpreter, who is an overseas Chinese, probably a college student. Then he tells me, 'You can go now.' Before I leave I kick the Commies' table. The thing tips over and sends the paper and pens flying in every direction. I'm so angry I keep stomping the floor and almost go through the door to Red China by mistake. The interpreter catches up with me and says, 'Hey, take the other door.' That saves me from falling into the Commies' snare again."

A loud volley of laughter ensued. Wang Yong got to his feet and said to us, "Soon we'll go to those tents to listen to their persuasion. Be careful and don't let the Reds take you in. Also, remember that the brothers of your group will suffer if you defect. Understood?"

"Yes sir," we shouted.

Bai Dajian raised his hand. Wang asked him, "You want to say something?"

"Yes." Dajian stood up and spoke to the crowd. "According to the two brothers' experiences, it seems that the more you listen to the Reds, the more aggressively they will try to get you. I suggest that we just spit on them, curse them openly, and express our will to go to Taiwan the moment we enter the tent. In other words, we shouldn't give them any opportunity to mislead us." He sat down and stared at me, his shaven skull revealing several bumps. My heart began galloping; I wondered if he had discerned my plan. I nerved myself for his fierce gaze, which at last turned away. I was amazed by his resolve to go to Taiwan. Did this mean he had decided to abandon his charming fiancée?

Wang Yong said to the audience, "That's a good idea. Spit at them like Officer Bai said. Let's get through this damn thing as quickly as we can."

Now it was clear that I would have to face the persuaders before I had access to the arbitrators. This could be daunting, but I might be able to circumvent a part of the persuasion by speaking to the foreigners directly. As long as I was cautious and composed, I should be able to carry out my plan for going to a third country.

Before I went to bed that night, Wang

Yong came into our shed and said to me, "Come along, will you?"

His summons unsettled me, but I followed him out. Together we made for the battalion headquarters. The night was chilly and crisp, and there was a touch of curry in the air from the kitchen of the Indian troops. Two flashlights were flickering beyond the entrance to our compound while the moon cast our shadows at a slant on the pale ground. The inside of the headquarters was well lit and quiet. Toward the center of the room stood a desk, on which sat two plates, one containing fried soybeans sprinkled with a bit of salt and the other, braised pork cubes. Beside the dishes were two mugs and a bottle of saki. At the sight of the food I relaxed some, realizing Wang Yong meant to have a drink with me, though I still had no inkling of his intention. He motioned for me to sit at the table. "I want to have a chat with you tonight, Feng Yan," he said.

"Sure." I didn't know what else to say.

After pouring liquor into both mugs, he rested his elbow on the desk and said, "We've been together so long I feel I know you better now. I like you more than before, truth be told."

"Thank you for all the help, chief."

621

"Drop that title, will you? Just call me Yong or Brother Wang."

"All right, I can do that when we're alone."

"What's your plan after we get to Taiwan?"

"Frankly I have no plan. I hope they'll let me remain in the army, though."

"Of course they will. They'll make the best use of a talent like you, but they'll dump a man like me, illiterate and unskilled in anything."

"Come on, we're the same, we all served in the Red Army and we're all POWs."

"No, no, you're a graduate from the Huangpu Military Academy. That makes you stand out."

"There're a good number of former cadets here. I'm just one of them."

"No, you're special."

"Me? How?"

He swished the saki around in his mug and took a swallow. "You speak excellent English. Don't think I can't tell the difference just because I can't read or write. I can see how beautifully you speak English. Many of the educated fellows here studied English for more than ten years, and still in front of the Americans all they can say is 'hi' or 'thank you' or 'bye-bye.' You're different, you speak with confidence and ease. I can see that even the Americans respect you."

"You think too highly of me. Like you, I'm a prisoner and will face a lot of difficulties in Taiwan."

"Don't lose heart, brother. I'm sure they'll give you an important position. They have to get along with the Americans, don't they? So a man of your caliber will be indispensable to them."

"I hope so."

"Have some more of this meat."

"Sure."

I picked up a chunk of streaky pork and chewed it with relish. Munching the soybeans noisily, he said, "Brother Feng, once you become a big officer, you won't forget me, will you?"

"Of course not." Tears welled up into my eyes. I lifted the mug and took a gulp of the liquor, then told him, "You're a good, simple-hearted man, Brother Wang. I feel secure when I'm with you. I'll remain your friend."

"That means a lot to me." He beamed and his heavy-lidded eyes almost disappeared.

As we were chatting on, he took a photograph out of his wallet and handed it to me. "What do you think of this girl?"

I looked at it and said, "She's pretty." Indeed, she seemed to be a typical Manchurian girl, about eighteen or nineteen, with a round face, round eyes, round cheeks, and round lips.

"You really think so?" he asked.

"Yes."

"Do you want to make friends with her?"

"I still have my fiancée on the mainland."

"That's why I only said make friends with her; I'm not suggesting you become engaged."

I saw his intention and asked, "Who is she?"

"My niece in Taiwan. She's a student in a business school and studies accounting. She knows how to manage money."

"I can't decide now, but can I keep her photo for a while?"

"Absolutely. Here, take it." He was delighted. "Whenever you want to meet her, let me know. Her family in Taipei will be yours if you like her."

I had no intention of befriending the girl, but I wanted to please her uncle. Despite having a soft spot for me, Wang Yong was a loose cannon, who, if vexed, wouldn't think twice about hurting me. So I couldn't afford to level with him.

The next morning while I was reading the Bible, the orderly burst in and told us to assemble in the yard. I knew the time was coming, so I stuffed the book into my jacket pocket and went out. Columns of people were already gathered there. Beyond them were parked eighteen trucks. The drivers were all Americans, which was an encouraging sign to the prisoners. In no time every two squads, about thirty men, lined up behind a vehicle and climbed into the back. When we had all gotten in, the trucks revved and began to wobble out of the muddy yard. Then they sped toward the U.N. quarters just a mile away within the Demilitarized Zone.

It was a fine morning, though the trees still wore a skin of frost. Viewed from a distance, their branches looked smoky. Along the roadside were scattered rotten straw sacks, some of which still contained sand. I didn't expect the U.N. quarters to be so large. It consisted of over forty new tents, two-thirds of which were used for the persuasion. In the front yard were some large, empty, corral-like pens. The moment we jumped down from the trucks we were led into one of these holding pens, in which we formed lines for waiting in groups. Wang Yong put some officers at the front of the lines, so we could have a strong start. Also, the officers were supposed to go first so that we could come back to instruct the others how to confront the Communist persuaders effectively. Wang put me at the head of the second line. This relieved me from having to wait in the nippy north wind for very long, and enabled me to concentrate on my plan.

At nine-thirty about a dozen Indian soldiers came to fetch the first batch of us, and sixty prisoners were marched out of the pen. I was among them. The unarmed guards escorted us toward one of the four rest halls outside the persuasion tents. Ahead of us, the flags of various nations were flapping in the wind, as if a colorful holiday celebration were in progress. I was reviewing my plan as I walked, trying hard to keep calm and focused. A few minutes after we reached the rest hall, more Indians turned up to take half of us to the tents. A tall guard checked my ID tag, then led me to Tent 7. At its entrance he searched me before letting me in.

It was quite warm inside the tent, cozy and bright. The base of the wall was built of plywood, about three feet high; atop the wood was a broad band of Plexiglas, through which sunlight flooded in and above which canvas stretched all the way up to the ceiling. In the middle of the tent sat a large potbellied stove; in it a fire was whirring; it burned oil instead of coal and was much larger than those in our quarters. Unlike the tents I had seen before, this one was really fancy, with even a hardwood floor. In a corner a few men were chatting, and one of them was holding a soda bottle, almost empty. A man who looked like a Pole came over and took a photo of me. This fazed me a little, because the Poles and the Czechs represented the Socialist alliance whereas the Swedes and the Swiss were here for the Free World. I was led to a large chair, facing a long table covered with green velveteen. Evidently the Indians had taken measures to prevent the prisoners from attacking the Chinese persuaders — the chair was screwed to the floor.

I sat down and raised my head. To my astonishment, I saw a pair of familiar eyes. Hao Chaolin! I almost cried out. He was sitting at the middle of the table, accompanied by two other Chinese officers. They all wore spruce woolen uniforms with a piece of red silk on their chests, which carried the golden words "Staff — Persuasion Work." At one end of the table sat two

North Korean officers. To my left were seated five arbitrators from neutral countries, who all had on civvies, while behind me, in a corner, sat three U.N. representatives, one of whom was a Chinese man who must have been an interpreter. I was so astounded to see Chaolin that a surge of vertigo seized me. I reached out for the Indian guard for support.

"What's the matter?" he asked.

"Sorry, I'm dizzy." I regained my composure and gingerly lifted my eyes to meet Chaolin's.

He stood up, mouth ajar, about to run around the table and rush toward me, then he seemed to change his mind and held out his hand instead. We shook hands while he smiled awkwardly, as if he had a sensitive molar. A fresh dark bruise was on his cheek — probably inflicted by an anti-Communist prisoner. We stared at each other without a word. Then another persuader asked me my name, and by force of habit I told him my alias. He said, "Welcome, Comrade Feng Yan." I could tell Chaolin was unsure whether I was their enemy or friend now. It flashed through my mind that since he had seen me, he would definitely report me to his superiors if I refused to return to the mainland. This meant my mother and Julan would suffer on my account, and ours would become a counterrevolutionary family. What should I do? I felt nauseated, short of breath.

"Comrade Yu Yuan," Hao Chaolin said solemnly, intending to remind me of my true identity, his penetrating eyes riveted on my face, "you should come home, where the Party and the people are waiting for you. I'm glad we finally met at —"

"When did I say I wouldn't go back?" I interrupted him. "You know how I got trapped in the camp controlled by the pro-Nationalists, don't you?"

He looked startled; so did the other two persuaders. A slim red-haired man, who must have been a Swiss, looked at me curiously, then at Chaolin. Chaolin realized the meaning of my question and replied, "I understand you were discovered when they checked your fingerprints."

I remained wordless, surprised he knew what had happened. I felt like crying but restrained myself.

He went on, "We won't mistreat a good comrade like you again, I promise. In fact, Commissar Pei is waiting to see you in Kaesong."

"You mean he was released?"

"Yes, yesterday."

"How about Chang Ming?"

"He's there too. They went back as the last batch of 'war criminals.' "

I gazed at him steadily. His eyes convinced me that he was telling the truth. I said, "To be honest, I've never planned to go to Taiwan, but I'm afraid that even my comrades won't forgive me now. I'm completely trapped between the two sides." As I spoke, it grew clear to me that there was no way I could go elsewhere without implicating my mother and my fiancée.

"Yuan, I shall always stand by you. It was the Party that sent you to Pusan, and you won't be blamed for the consequences." He looked tearful, apparently moved by the memory of our prison life.

I was touched too. I said, "Will you testify that it was only under duress that I stayed with the pro-Nationalists?"

"I shall do that, of course."

"No, I mean I landed among them because I was used to take Chang Ming's place."

He lowered his eyes, then lifted them to face me. "You made a great sacrifice, Yuan. Nobody will blame you."

"In that case, I will come home."

I turned to the arbitrator sitting at the end of the table and said in English, "I want to be repatriated."

"You're supposed to have five minutes to make up your mind," he reminded me.

"I have decided to go home," I said.

The young interpreter looked askance at me, perhaps annoyed that I didn't need his help.

"Your request is granted," the arbitrator said. "Please go to the door in the right corner."

"Thank you, sir." I stood up and bowed.

As I was about to turn away, Chaolin rushed over and stretched out his hand, which I shook, his palm clammy. Then he embraced me, his breath sour and hot. Both of us burst into tears and held each other tightly. He murmured, "Yuan, I thought we'd lost you. Thank heaven, you came back alive. This is a miracle!" I said nothing, weeping for a reason different from his. I felt hurt and helpless. Never had I thought I'd return to their ranks this way.

Together we headed for the door that led me to a different and unexpected fate. The whole thing had happened as if I had been in a trance.

36. A DIFFERENT FATE

That same afternoon with eleven other returnees I arrived at Kaesong, which was about ten miles northwest of the Demilitarized Zone. Before reaching there I dropped my Bible into the roadside brambles. When Commissar Pei and Ming saw me, they both hugged me and wept, apparently happy to see me back. I didn't cry this time, though my eyes misted over and my nose went stuffy. They told me that together we would be on our way back to China the next day. The return had happened so unexpectedly that I could hardly absorb its meaning.

The commissar looked at least ten years older than when I'd last seen him, with graying stubble on his chin and a heavy face that seemed more energetic than before. His hair was grizzled now and his hairline was almost an inch higher than it had been three years earlier; it made his forehead appear quite large. The look in his eyes was sad, but still full of confidence, and he walked with a straight back.

I was amazed to see his feet encased in the same pair of rubber sneakers he had worn to cross the Yalu in the spring of 1951, although they were very tattered now, bumpy with stitches and patches (he had always refused to put on American shoes in the prison camp). Despite the affection he showed me, I couldn't but be of two minds about him because he had hurt me deeply. Ming, in contrast, was as convivial as before. He had a slight stoop, though his thick shoulders still looked strong. His catfish mouth smiled a lot as if he couldn't open it without letting out something funny.

A bizarre thing happened that afternoon. Toward four o'clock, an officer came to summon Ming and me to follow him to meet a Korean comrade. He led us into a nearby courtyard. The moment we entered the gate, I saw a middle-aged man in a gray Lenin suit gazing at us. I recognized him. "Mr. Park!" Ming cried, and we hurried up to him. He embraced us, and Ming shed some tears. Mr. Park couldn't speak Chinese, but he talked to us in Korean excitedly. From the look on his face and his gestures I guessed he was wishing us a happy future. He kept patting our shoulders and smiling kindly. He looked the same as the previous year, perhaps even more handsome because of his woolen suit.

Together we attended a reception held in Mr. Park's honor. On a table were some sliced ham, salted eggs, dried duck, kimchee, pickled turnip, and two bottles of Green Bamboo Leaves. When I spoke with Mr. Park through the help of his interpreter, congratulating him on his apparently good health and his achievement as the paramount leader of the Korean POWs, he grimaced. "My future is uncertain," he said, "but I'll be happy to see my family." As a junior officer, I couldn't ask him what he meant exactly. He drank several cups of the Chinese liquor, saying it tasted better than saki, its fragrant aftertaste staying longer in your mouth. After the reception, without delay he departed for Pyongyang. His jeep rolled away, its tailpipe issuing a plume of exhaust and its radio blaring out "The Anthem of the Korean People's Army." (Some years later, to my surprise, I read in a journal that Mr. Park had grown up in Russia and was a citizen of the Soviet Union. He had gone to college in Khabarovsk and was later assigned to supervise a collective farm there. He returned to Korea with the Russian

Red Army to fight the Japanese. During his imprisonment in the top jail on Koje Island, for some reason he confessed to the Americans and told them how he had planned and executed the kidnapping of General Bell. The Americans treated him well afterward, but a year later he wanted to undefect, because he missed his family so much that he wished to see them even at the risk of being incarcerated by the North Korean authorities. That must have been why he grimaced and told me that his future was uncertain. Still, I'm puzzled. Why had he acted like a willful child? This is still a conundrum to me. In any case, I hope that his Soviet citizenship did protect him from being punished severely by the North Korean leaders.)

That evening, after a shave, we went to a cottage to be received by Major General Tong, a lean-faced man with a pointed nose and hawklike eyes. Over jasmine tea and boiled peanuts, the eighteen returned POWs briefly told him our stories. He listened to us attentively, and from time to time asked a question about other comrades. The general encouraged us to study hard to catch up on current affairs in China. He also said there was a recuperation center for the repatriates in Changtu

County, Liaoning Province. We were all going to stay there for some time to recover. He and Commissar Pei had known each other before, so they remained in the house after the rest of us had left.

Ming and I stayed in the same room that night. We chatted for hours on end; there was so much to talk about. He told me that I had been sent to Pusan in his place because the commissar had depended on his service and wouldn't let him go no matter how much he wanted to. I realized he too had been a chess piece on Pei's board, though I had been a more dispensable pawn. He felt sorry for having caused me so much suffering. My grudge against him abated somewhat, although I still believed Pei must also have meant to protect him by dispatching me to Pusan. Our conversation turned to the commissar, who Ming told me had often been depressed in the prison because Pei felt our country had abandoned us. Occasionally Pei craved alcohol so much that he even suggested bartering his felt hat for it with one of the maintenance men, but they had never done that. We also talked about Pei's political career, with which our future might be entwined. I was afraid that he might not be well received by the Party. Ming smiled meaningfully, shaking his head and saying, "You're a smart man, Yuan."

"What do you mean?"

"To tell the truth, for some time Commissar Pei hasn't been in high spirits. He's afraid he'll be condemned and demoted by the Party once he goes back. But so far all signs are good. The higher-ups are very understanding and sympathetic. I'm sure he'll do fine."

I wasn't fully convinced, but his words comforted me some. If Pei's status remained intact, he would be in a position to protect the rest of us. Ming added, "You shouldn't worry too much. You haven't joined the Party yet. If anything bad happens, I'm sure it will affect the Party members first. You'll be the last one to get into trouble."

That made sense and I felt relieved. He went on to tell me that the commissar was now confident that the Party would appreciate our heroic struggle in the prison camps, especially the raising of our flags on the National Day. Gradually the topic shifted to our personal lives. We both wanted to marry as soon as possible, because life had become so precious to us that we didn't want to waste a single day.

At about two in the morning, Commissar Pei returned, his eyes radiating a soft light. He said he had drunk too much tea and couldn't sleep. So we continued to chat. Outside, the autumn wind was rustling the oak trees and blowing more leaves down. Now and then an acorn dropped on the roof, rolling all the way down and falling to the ground with a crisp thud.

"Yuan," Commissar Pei said in a tobacco-roughened voice, "I want to ask you a serious question."

"Sure," I said.

"Would you like to join the Communist Party?"

Taken aback, I hesitated for a moment, then answered, "I want to, but I don't think I'm qualified yet."

"Why not?" Ming put in.

"I went to the Huangpu Military Academy, and for the last few months I got entangled with the Nationalist followers again."

"Don't take that as a burden," the commissar said. "I sent you to the reregistration and the Party is responsible for what happened. As for your past in the Nationalist academy, you have done enough to correct it."

How could I correct my past? His remark amazed me. Ming said, "Don't be so modest, Yuan. You've contributed a lot to our struggle in the prison camps. You're qualified."

"Yes," Pei said, "I can't think of another comrade, except maybe Ming, who has done more than you for our struggle. I don't mean to force you to apply for Party membership. But if you do want to, keep in mind that I'll be happy to be your advocate."

"The same here," Ming added.

"Thank you, I'll remember that," I said.

That ended our long day. A rooster crowed from the village and dawn was breaking, so we all went to bed to catch a few hours' sleep before we set out for China. My heart was again filled with warm feelings. In every way it seemed right for me to go back.

The first snow had covered Changtu Town when we arrived, and the crowns of trees, in which sparrows were twittering hungrily, looked like clouds. The returned POWs were billeted in a large barracks, altogether over six thousand men. The place was called the Repatriates Center. During the first two weeks, some top provincial officials came to visit us. They brought along live pigs and sheep, thousands of solicitous letters from the civilians, and an opera troupe that performed for us twice. One afternoon some girls from a local middle school came to sing to us and presented us with two huge bouquets of fresh flowers. On top of those, a hefty brass medal was conferred on every one of us. The leaders in charge of the center told us that we should rest well and study some to catch up with the country, and that soon we would all go to different jobs. So we felt excited and grateful. The returned officers ranking above regimental commander stayed at a guesthouse in the compound, but they and everyone else had the same kind of board, which was good, much better than what regular servicemen ate. We often had meat and fish; tofu and vegetables were plentiful, though there was more wheaten food than rice, which was scarce in the Northeast. In spite of the nourishing diet, most of us still looked sallow and much older than the staff members running this place who were roughly our age, as though we had all joined their parents' generation. Some fellows already had bald heads and gray beards, and some had lost their teeth.

To my delight, I found my young friend Shanmin here, who hadn't changed much, though he was a bit taller. He told me that Weiming had suffered a stroke and had been hospitalized in Shenyang City. Together we wrote him a letter, but we never heard from that good man.

During the first few weeks we went to study sessions to be briefed about the development of our country, but mostly we relaxed, just to recuperate, and tried to enjoy ourselves. All the men were fond of hot baths, which I rarely took for fear of revealing my tattoo to others in the bathhouse. When I had to bathe myself, I would face a wall while undressing, and would wrap a towel around my waist on my way to a pool. I was not alone in bearing such an embarrassing mark; more than forty men had anti-Communist slogans on their bodies too. I went to the clinic and begged Dr. Liang to remove the tattoo from my belly. He had been helping some other men, cutting the shameful words and signs off their skin. Sometimes he didn't get rid of the whole thing and just removed a word or two to make a dark phrase unintelligible or give it a new meaning. He knew English and would play with the alphabet. In my case, he said the procedure should be easy: he suggested keeping the word FUCK and just erasing all the letters in the word COMMUNISM except the U and the S. I was reluctant at first, but an officer in charge of disciplinary work, who happened to be present, clapped and said this was a wonderful idea, so I agreed. The doctor did a good job and even added three dots behind each word. As a result, the original tattoo was transformed into FUCK . . . U . . . S . . .

We had all written home as soon as we arrived at the Repatriates Center, but not many of us received mail. I was anxious. So was Ming, whose fiancée was in Canton and should have been able to get his letters within three or four days.

From the fifth week on the real study sessions began. By now we had been left in the charge of the Northeastern Military Command; in other words, the leaders in Beijing had washed their hands of us. We were all ordered to confess the crimes we had committed in the enemy's prisons and to contrast ourselves with the hero Huang Jiguang, who had hurled himself on an American machine gun at the embrasure of a bunker after he ran out of grenades. The people running the study sessions announced to us these three principles, which we must follow from now on:

1) The very fact that you became captives is shameful. You could have fought the enemy to your last breath but you did not. Therefore you are cowards.

2) How could cowards carry on the struggle against our enemy? Even if there were some resistance activities in the prisons, they mainly originated from your need for survival. So you have no merit to talk about and must confess your wrongdoings and crimes.

3) You must blame yourselves for your captivity and must not attribute it to any external cause.

The study sessions terrified us. Whoever had served as a leader in the prison camps was now labeled a collaborator, and whoever had told his captors his true name and his unit's serial number was classified as someone who "betrayed state secrets." The fact that you had smoked American cigarettes meant that you had succumbed to the enemy; it was forgivable that you had eaten their food, but your acceptance of the luxury of tobacco was submission. My four merit citations were gone like smoke, not to mention those special ones Pei Shan had issued to the dead men buried on Cheju Island. Many returnees were outraged by this sudden development and often buttonholed Commissar Pei, complaining about the unfair treatment and begging him to protect them and get the citations back for them. In their eyes he was still a demigod who embodied the Communist Party, so they wanted him to confirm their awards, which might have proved their loyalty to our country. He promised to have the citations validated, though by now he must have known that his superiors would never acknowledge them.

The commissar too was under investigation and was having trouble saving his own skin. It was rumored that the Americans at Camp 8 had once drugged him and made him give a reactionary speech, which later had been broadcast on the radio. He himself had been unaware of this. Now he might not be able to clear himself from the charge of collaboration. Furthermore, his superiors believed that at least five thousand people of our former division had been taken prisoner, and that the large number indicated that the division's leaders hadn't organized their men to fight determinedly. Therefore, as one of our top officers, Pei was held responsible for our defeat. To avoid being confronted by his men, he stopped coming out of the guesthouse. But fortunately he stuck to his word in my case, asserting that it was he who had sent me to Pusan to get reregistered in place of Ming, and that I had landed in the pro-Nationalist camp while serving the Party's cause. So I wasn't classified as a traitor, though the leaders wouldn't let me off without many rounds of denunciation.

Besides Shanmin, who insisted I had saved him from the pro-Nationalists' clutches, Ming also stood up for me. When I was ordered to confess what I had done in Camp 13, I said I had spent most of my time learning English. They asked me what I had read; I dared not say the Bible and instead mentioned some newspapers and magazines. Every day I was ordered to recall something new about my helping Father Woodworth teach the hymns and about my serving Wang Yong as his interpreter and henchman. I couldn't remember all the details, so they wouldn't let me go.

Then one afternoon Ming rose to his feet and spoke on my behalf. With a red face and a bulging neck, he said to the officers presiding over the mutual criticism session, "Look, Comrade Yu Yuan did make a mistake in mixing with Priest

Woodworth. But he got stationery from him and passed it on to me. Unlike most graduates from the Huangpu Military Academy who paid only lip service to our Communist cause, Yu Yuan helped us and participated in our struggle constantly. He saved Commissar Pei by speaking to the American commander Smart before our comrades boarded the ships bound for Cheju Island. Nobody among us could do that, could we?" A few men shook their chins. Ming went on, "When he was jailed in the troublemakers' cell, he led two comrades in creating the Pei Code, without which communication between Commissar Pei and the camp would have been impossible. Later he helped his battalion chief get a falsely signed document back so that the enemy officer couldn't use it to clear himself of his crime. Some comrades here saw with their own eyes what kind of role he played in that struggle. Without his negotiating with the American officer, we couldn't possibly have gotten the signature back. Last spring he was ordered to go to Pusan in my place, to get reregistered there. He went without a murmur. We all thought he wouldn't come back because the Americans might dispose of the four officers they had summoned. Many comrades shed tears when seeing him off. Tell me, what else do you need to prove a comrade's loyalty to the Party? The Party told him to die, and he went to die. It was a pure miracle that he returned. Let me tell you this: on our way back from Korea, Commissar Pei and I decided to recommend him for Party membership. There isn't another comrade here who deserves it more —"

"Sit down, Chang Ming!" barked one of the officers in charge of the session. "You don't even know if you yourself will remain in the Party while you think of inducting others. You must be out of your mind. Have you forgotten who you are, just like Pei Shan who gave merit citations right and left? Ridiculous, as if every one of you were a big hero. From now on, you must first regard yourself as a criminal."

That stunned and silenced Ming, whose record in the war had been impeccable. But his speech did help me, and since then I was pressed less often and less forcefully.

Then they began interrogating those who couldn't pass the self-criticism sessions. It was said that there were a large number of American and Nationalist spies among us, and the higher-ups vowed to ferret them out. Every week some men got arrested and sent to a prison in Fushun, a coal-mining city about a hundred miles to the south. This frightened us and made us more obedient. Many of the repatriates tried hard to please the authorities by "exposing" others and criticizing themselves more severely. Some even admitted that they were cowards and had helped the enemy, though they couldn't come up with any convincing evidence for their crimes. A few even claimed that they would have cracked if they'd been imprisoned longer, if the Party hadn't rescued them in time. I was puzzled why they reviled themselves like this, as if they had been real traitors. Probably their guilt was too deep and too convoluted for them to find a more appropriate way to express it. They often wept like wretched little boys.

Finally I heard from my fiancée's elder brother. He wrote in red ink that my mother had passed away a year ago and that if I really cared about his sister, I mustn't bother her anymore, because she couldn't possibly marry "a disgraced captive." He also said: "Don't think ill of Julan. She was good to your mom and tended to her till her last day. I hope you can sympathize with my sister and see the difficulties she is facing." I felt as though time had played a cruel joke on me. If only I had known about my mother's death when I was in Korea; if only I had foreseen that home was no longer the same place. Then at any cost I would have gone to a third country, where I could have lived as a countryless man, and probably as a lonely drudge for the rest of my life. Or I might have gone to Taiwan and restarted my life there. But now it was too late to change anything. I was crushed and took to my bed for a week. I sent Julan two more letters and also the jade barrette half, but I never got a response from her.

Then disaster befell Ming. In one of his letters to his fiancée, he wrote, "I hate the vastness of our country; otherwise we could see each other sooner, without so many mountains and rivers between us." He had always been a careful man, but he blundered fatefully this time, having forgotten that our mail was monitored. That sentence was distorted by those officers waiting to bear down on him. He was turned into a counterrevolutionary who had maliciously wished the map of our country were smaller. I felt terrible for him but couldn't do anything to help.

As I calmed down, it grew clear to me that for a long time we, the POWs, had already been written off as a loss. The reasons our delegates at Panmunjom had frequently mentioned us were that they could use our suffering to embarrass the enemy and that if they hadn't shown some concern for us, more prisoners would have gone to Taiwan, and mainland China would have lost more face. Now that we were back and couldn't possibly join the Nationalists anymore, we were no longer a concern to the Party, which finally handled us in any way it liked.

What surprised me most was that the top officer, Commissar Pei, didn't fare any better than the rest of us. In other words, he and we had all been chessmen on the Party's board, though Pei had created his own board and placed his men on it as if his game had been identical with the Party's. In fact he too had been a mere pawn, not much different from any of us. He too was war trash.

We were not allowed to leave the Repatriates Center until the next summer. With few exceptions we were all discharged dishonorably, which meant we had become the dregs of society. All the Party members among us lost their membership, because before going to Korea they had taken an oath at Party meetings that they would never surrender under any circumstances. Therefore the Party viewed their captivity as a breach of their pledges. Hundreds of men were imprisoned again, labeled as traitors or spies. From now on we were all placed under special control for the rest of our lives. Ming was sent back to his hometown in Szechuan to carry water for a bathhouse to make a living; his fiancée married another man who had been Ming's classmate at Beijing University. Shanmin was returned to his home village to be a peasant. Commissar Pei went to a state-owned farm in Panjin, in western Liaoning, to be a rice grower, though nominally he was a vice manager of the farm. Chaolin, who had joined us later at the Repatriates Center, was assigned to a steel plant where he became a foreman in a workshop. We had all thought he'd be able to keep his former rank because of his service on the persuasion team in the Demilitarized Zone, but that operation had foundered miserably — they'd persuaded only about four hundred men to come back. So, like us, he was disciplined and demoted.

Compared with most of them, I was lucky. Because I was not a Party member and had neither broken any promise nor followed the pro-Nationalists to Taiwan despite being a graduate from the Huangpu Military Academy, I was given a job in a middle school, teaching Chinese, geography, and later English. I liked the job, which I held until I retired six years ago. Since the fall of 1954 I have lived in Changchun, the capital of Jilin Province. I have never returned to Szechuan.

In 1965 Ming came to my home and begged me to find him a job in the city, because he no longer had work to do in his hometown. He wore a black overcoat whose padded cotton stuck out all over its ragged cloth as if he were besprinkled with snowflakes. He walked with bandy legs now, which reminded me of the Harry Truman he had impersonated on Koje Island thirteen years before. It was impossible for me to help him find employment. I was merely a schoolteacher with the weight of a problematic past on my back. How could I possibly get him a job? He stayed four or five days and then left, deeply disappointed. I bought him the return train ticket and gave him thirty yuan, more than half of my monthly salary. That was all I could do for him. Afterward I never heard from him, though I was told that he had become an adopted son of an old woman in his hometown, so that he could have a roof to sleep under at night. In the summer of 1972, when again questioning me about the activities of some former POWs, one of the interrogators told me, "Chang Ming has gone to another planet." Hearing of his death, I almost broke into tears in front of the officials.

At the outset of the Cultural Revolution, one morning about two hundred Red Guards came to my home and took me away to my school for a struggle session. They made me stand on a platform; then a girl stepped over and pulled up my shirt to show the audience the tattoo on my belly. They said I dreamed of the United States all the time. The truth was that the word "fuck" had been expunged from all their English-Chinese dictionaries, so they didn't know its meaning. I told them plainly, pressing my forefinger on the word, "This means 'screw.' If I really worshiped the United States, I wouldn't say 'screw it,' would I?" The audience exploded with laughter. That helped save my neck.

In every aspect I'm very fortunate compared with the other repatriates. After my fiancée broke up with me, I swore I would avoid women and remain a bachelor for the rest of my life. But life continues despite our personal misfortunes, and my frozen heart thawed within two years. I fell in love with a colleague of mine, a chemistry teacher, a woman of remarkable beauty, to whom few men would pay attention because her father had been a rich merchant in Shanghai before the new China. We got married a few months later. We had two children, a boy and a girl; both of them have graduated from college. My son managed to come to the States and get a master's degree in civil engineering from Georgia Tech. I even have two American grandchildren, and I love them dearly and wish I could stay with them longer. To my knowledge, few children of the returnees from the U.N. prison camp went to college. For twenty-seven years, before the final rehabilitation of the repatriates in 1980, their fathers' tainted past made it impossible for them to get a decent education. In contrast, my wife and I taught our son and daughter so well that they excelled in the entrance exams when colleges were reopened after the Cultural Revolution.

One summer evening in 1986, soon after China had begun to open itself to foreigners, by chance I saw Bai Dajian appear on the Northeastern TV. He had come back from Taipei to visit his hometown in Liaoning Province and was received as an honored guest because he hadn't forgotten his birthplace and had donated an elementary school to his home village. He had also promised to build a middle school for the local county. Apparently he was a wealthy man who must have had a successful career after he reached Taiwan. At a glance I recognized him, his left hand having only three fingers. He was robust now, with a full head of graying hair, and could easily pass for forty. He smiled with dimmed eyes, but all the diffidence that had once shadowed him had vanished from his animated face.

Several of the former POWs I knew had also seen the news and often talked about those men who had refused to repatriate. They would sigh and regret, only in private, that they had risked so much to come home so as to pursue and fulfill their illusion of loyalty. It was true that most of those prisoners who went to Taiwan lived a decent life. Some of them attended college and a few rose to senior positions in the army. Having retired recently, some even returned to the mainland to live, where they were well received; some were even appointed local officials. Indeed, China generously embraced them as patriots in spite of their belated love. Even some former POWs who had returned in 1953 wrote to their local governments to express their support for the new policy of welcoming these nonrepatriates home, because it would help bring about the unification of Taiwan and the mainland.

But the reappearance of the nonrepatriates in their hometowns didn't always bring joy. Some of them found that few of their family members were still alive. Some saw that their home villages remained in the grip of dire poverty and ignorance. A few shocked their parents and siblings, who had been informed three decades ago that they had perished in Korea as Revolutionary Martyrs — their families had visited and swept their empty graves every spring ever since.

I wondered how Wang Yong was faring. I still had his niece's photograph in my album.

Bai Dajian's appearance on the TV threw my mind into turmoil for a few days, because I felt I was at least as capable as he, though I understood that a wealthy businessman like him must be a rarity among those POWs who had gone to Taiwan. But soon I recovered my equilibrium. No matter how awful one's life is, there are always others who get it worse. In contrast to Chang Ming, Hao Chaolin, and Pei Shan, I was fortunate, with a happy family and two good children and three grandchildren. There should be no reason for me to indulge in lamenting my personal losses. One must never regret one's fate.

These days I often watch *The Simpsons*, which I like very much. Last week I saw Bart, the mischievous boy, get a tattoo removed from his arm. This gave me the idea of having mine erased. I asked my son about the possibility. He called around in Atlanta and found out that Dr. Stone at Emory Hospital often performed the procedure. He told the doctor that I had an anti-American slogan tattooed on my belly by the Communists. I guess there was no way he could explain my case clearly. My monthly pension is less than $120, so Dr. Stone agreed to consider a discount. He said the procedure would take just a few minutes and the laser would cause little pain. I'm glad I will see him next Thursday.

I never saw Pei Shan after I left the Repatriates Center in 1954, but I was in touch with Chaolin, who died of a massive heart attack four years ago. In 1995 he told me that recently he had gone to Tianjin to see Pei, whose lung cancer had reached an advanced stage and whose sister had gotten him to come to the city for chemotherapy. Painfully, our former commissar blamed himself for having ruined his only son's life. The son, already in his late forties, was still unmarried; when he was in his twenties, no young woman wanted to enter his home, darkened by his father's past, and later he somehow lost interest in women and preferred to remain a bachelor despite his parents' urging him to marry and have children. Pei had another regret: he had forgotten his former bodyguard Tiger's home address; the boy had saved his life forty-four years before, but Pei had only remembered he was from Gansu Province. If only he had been able to do something for Tiger's parents, who must have died long ago. Pei said to Chaolin, "Tiger was a good comrade. I still meet him in my dreams."

Chaolin had also told me that some weeks later he had paid a last visit to Pei Shan, who was now on the point of dying. The final words our former leader gave him were "Please write our story!"

Chaolin had said to me, twisting his withered lips, "Yuan, my mind's no good anymore. What can I write about? There's only loss and grief — the heavy feeling weighs down my heart like a millstone. All the memories are messed up in my head, no way to sort them out." He still had a few teeth, but couldn't help dropping crumbs of a walnut cookie while chewing it over a cup of hot tea. Indeed, he had aged so much that I could tell he didn't have many years left. Shriveled, almost skeletal, he was half a foot shorter than four decades ago.

Now I must conclude this memoir, which is my first attempt at writing and also my last. Almost seventy-four years old, I suffer from gout and glaucoma; I don't have the strength to write anymore. But do not take this to be an "our story." In the depths of my being I have never been one of them. I have just written what I experienced.

AUTHOR'S NOTE

This is a work of fiction and all the main characters are fictional. Most of the events and details, however, are factual. For information on them I am indebted to the following authors and their works:

Bradbury, William, Samuel Meyers, and Albert Biderman. *Mass Behavior in Battle and Captivity: The Communist Soldier in the Korean War*. Chicago: University of Chicago Press, 1968.

Burchett, Wilfred, and Alan Winnington. *Koje Unscreened*. Beijing: Published by the authors, 1953.

Da Ying. "Zhiyuanjun Zhanfu Jishi" (Records of the POWs among the People's Volunteers). *Kun Lun*, no. 1 (1987): 157–238.

Dean, William F. *General Dean's Story*. New York: Viking, 1954.

Dvorchak, Robert. *Battle for Korea*. Conshohocken, Pa.: Combined Books, 1993.

Forty, George. *At War in Korea*. Addlestone, England: Ian Allan, 1982.

Goldstein, Donald, and Harry Maihafer. *The Korean War*. Washington, D.C.: Brassey's, 2000.

Halliday, Jon, and Bruce Cumings. *Korea: The Unknown War*. New York: Viking, 1988.

Hastings, Max. *The Korean War*. New York: Simon and Schuster, 1987.

He, Kongde. *Yige Huajia Yan Zhong de Chaoxian Zhanzheng* (The Korean War in a painter's eyes). Beijing: People's Liberation Army Arts Press, 2000.

Hooker, John. *Korea: The Forgotten War*. North Sydney, Australia: Time-Life Books, 1989.

Knox, Donald. *The Korean War: Pusan to Chosin: An Oral History*. New York: Harcourt Brace, 1985.

Knox, Donald, and Alfred Coppel. *The Korean War: Uncertain Victory: An Oral History*. New York: Harcourt Brace, 1988.

Leckie, Robert. *Conflict: The History of the Korean War*, 1950–53. New York: Putnam, 1962.

Liu, Lang. *Liuxie Dao Mingtian* (Bleeding till tomorrow). Tongluowan, Taiwan: Asia Press.

Spiller, Harry, ed. *American POWs in Korea: Sixteen Personal Accounts*. Jefferson, N.C.: McFarland, 1998.

Tomedi, Rudy. *No Bugles, No Drums: An Oral History of the Korean War.* New York: Wiley, 1994.

A Volunteer Soldier's Day. Beijing: Foreign Languages Press, 1961.

Wang, Jian-guo. *Renhai Da Beiju* (The tragedy of human-wave tactics). Tongluowan, Taiwan: Asia Press.

Wang, Shuzeng. *Zhongguo Renmin Zhiyuanjun Zhengzhan Jishi* (The battle records of the Chinese People's Volunteer Army). Beijing: People's Liberation Army Arts Press, 2000.

Weintraub, Stanley. *War in the Wards: Korea's Unknown Battle in a Prisoner-of-War Hospital Camp.* San Rafael, Cal.: Presidio Press, 1976.

Zhang, Shu Guang. *Mao's Military Romanticism: China and the Korean War, 1950–1953.* Lawrence: University Press of Kansas, 1995.

Zhang, Zhe-shi, ed. *Meijun Jizhongying Qinli Ji* (Personal records in the American prison camps). Beijing: Chinese Archives Press, 1996.

ACKNOWLEDGMENTS

My thanks to LuAnn Walther for her critical and careful attention to the manuscript; to Lane Zachary for her enthusiasm and suggestions; to my son, Wen, for providing information on U.S. weaponry; to my wife, Lisha, who persuaded me to write this book.

A NOTE ABOUT THE AUTHOR

Ha Jin left his native China in 1985 to attend Brandeis University. He is the author of the internationally best-selling novel *Waiting*, which won the PEN/Faulkner Award and the National Book Award; the story collections *The Bridegroom*, which won the Asian American Literary Award, *Under the Red Flag*, which won the Flannery O'Connor Award for Short Fiction, and *Ocean of Words*, which won the PEN/Hemingway Award; the novels *The Crazed* and *In the Pond*; and three books of poetry. He lives in the Boston area and is a professor of English at Boston University.

CORE COLLECTION 2005